BILLIONAIRE COUNTRY

SILVER JAMES

NASHVILLE SECRETS

SHERI WHITEFEATHER

MILLS & BOON

First Published in Great Britain 2019
by Mills & Boon, an imprint of HarperCollinsPublishers,
1 London Bridge Street, London, SE1 9GF

ISBN: 978-0-263-27174-4

0319

MIX
Paper from responsible sources
FSC™ C007454

This book is produced from independently certified FSC™ paper to ensure responsible forest management.

For more information visit: www.harpercollins.co.uk/green

Printed and bound in Spain
by CPI, Barcelona

BILLIONAIRE COUNTRY

SILVER JAMES

To best friends,
families and dreams that come true.
Many thanks to Charles, my editor,
who challenges me every step of the way,
all so my own dream can come true.
And with special thanks to Denise,
with the Metropolitan Nashville Department
of Communications, and the Nashville Police
Department for service above and
beyond when it came to dumb questions.
Thank you for all you do!

One

Tucker Tate was a man who knew where he was going. His life was exactly on track—and precisely where he wanted it. As the chief operating officer of Barron Entertainment, that life was never boring. The sun was shining, and he was tooling down Life's Highway in a vintage T-Bird, top down, wind in his face, radio cranked loud. He was single and free of familial duties, thanks in part to his brother Deacon getting married and adopting a baby, causing his mother to tone down the marriage rhetoric where her other six sons were concerned. Thank goodness! His cousin, and boss, Chase Barron, had also jumped onto the happily married-go-round, turning more of the business side over to Tucker. Which brought him to this glorious spring day.

He'd driven to eastern Tennessee from Nashville to check out a band performing at an amusement park with an eye to offering them a recording contract with Bent Star, the record company owned by Barron Entertainment. He had their demo tape and was leaning toward signing them, though he wanted one of the producers at Bent Star

Records to take a listen. At the moment, he just wanted to enjoy a day of freedom. He'd opted to drive the long way home—heading to Gatlinburg for lunch before meandering through the Smoky Mountains as he headed vaguely north and west.

He didn't spend much time in the country. He appreciated his suite at the Crown Casino in Las Vegas and the company's luxury town house in Nashville's West End district. When he had to be home in Oklahoma, he stayed at the family ranch—mostly for holidays and the few command performances decreed by his mom.

The sun still hung high as Tucker drove toward I-40, taking every back road he could find. He passed a small country church perched on a low rise just off the road. A dirt and gravel drive led up to it and the clapboard building was surrounded by a variety of trucks and cars, some so beat-up he wondered that they still ran while others were tricked out enough to be show cars. As it was Saturday and there appeared to be an abundance of paper flowers and streamers on the vehicles, he figured a wedding was taking place.

It was a good day for a wedding, he decided—so long as it wasn't his neck in the noose. Marriage and kids were the very last thing on his mind. He was enjoying the heck out of his life.

Shifting gears, he took a curve in the road a little faster than was smart. He wasn't expecting the car charging up his six.

Jerking the wheel, Tucker cursed and fought gravity but kept the T-Bird between the lines. He blinked at the car that passed then pulled away from him. Was that a Trans Am? He laughed out loud. It was. It was a freaking *Smokey and the Bandit* Trans Am. Covered in paper flowers and trailing cans. *Good grief.* Then something white and filmy flew up through the Trans Am's open T-tops. He watched, fascinated, as the backwash from the car sent the thing soaring. Tucker slowed and downshifted, paying more attention to the material sailing toward him than the road.

A truck hit its air horn, and for the second time, Tucker jerked his car back into the correct lane—just in time for the white material to snag on his radio antenna. He slowed further, reached over and grabbed the lacy thing. It wasn't until he had it in his hand that he realized it was a wedding veil. Complete with a glittering tiara. Yeah, that gathering had definitely been a wedding, and evidently the newlyweds were in a real hurry to start the honeymoon. He accelerated back to the speed limit and wondered if the groom had the bride in his lap while he was driving, then hoped they wouldn't wreck.

Twenty minutes later, he spotted a cloud of smoke just over the crest of a hill. *Crap.* He hoped his wayward thoughts hadn't jinxed the couple. Tucker slowed down as he hit the hilltop. Halfway down, the Trans Am was pulled off to the side of the road. Oily black smoke poured from the exhaust pipes, but he didn't see any flames. The thing had probably blown its engine. As he edged his car closer, he caught sight of a woman wearing a white dress. She had the frothy skirt hiked up around her thighs as she kicked the car with her white Western boots. She glanced up—briefly—then went back to kicking.

Tucker pulled over and parked in front of the Trans Am. He looked around for the groom, but it appeared the bride was alone. *Curious.* He got out, and as her curses washed over him, he approached with a bit of trepidation. Apparently, the woman was not happy with the entire male gender. Taking his life and manhood in his hands, he stopped out of kicking distance.

* * *

What had she ever done to deserve all this bad karma?

Zoe kicked the Trans Am's door and enjoyed the boot-sized dent she inflicted. Movement flickered in the corner of her eye and she panicked. Once the Smithees figured out she'd run away, she was hosed. She rubbed her side.

"It's all gonna be fine," she murmured. "Momma's gonna fix everything." All she had to do was figure out how. The thought of that family getting their hands on her child sent ice water through her veins. They'd kept her a virtual prisoner until today. Seeing the Trans Am outside the church window and knowing she had a set of keys? She'd climbed out that window and run.

Zoe huffed out a breath when she recognized the classic black T-Bird with its lone male driver rolling her way. She started to raise her hand, but something stopped her from flagging him down. When it came to men, her instincts were on the fritz.

She kicked the car again, her massive ball-gown skirt gathered up in her arms to give her boot easy access to the metal. Dad-blasted piece of junk. Bad enough she'd had to drive it after Redmond's incarceration but the idea that she'd take it to go on her honeymoon with his block-headed brother…

Good grief but Norbert was a moron. And his mother? That woman terrified her. Etta Smithee would be the mother-in-law from hell. The old bag should be run over by a reindeer. Or better yet, a Mack truck! Why the Smithees thought she would willingly marry Norbert just because he was Redmond's brother and Redmond was the father—

Someone cleared his throat and Zoe jumped. She whirled to face the stranger she'd passed on the road. Oh, good lord, why was she being so sorely tested? This man was… gorgeous. He was tall—towering at least a foot over her.

His dark hair was short, cropped almost like a soldier's but had way more style. He looked perfect, unlike the Smithee brothers and cousins. Who would be on her trail all too soon. She refocused her attention on the intruder. He had eyes the color of cornflowers, which were crinkled in amusement. And his mouth. She could kiss that mouth for days and never need to come up for air. In other words, he was trouble in spades as he stood there in those tight blue jeans that hugged him like a jealous lover.

"Having a little car trouble?"

"Ya think?" She snapped at him and didn't know what to do when he grinned. She clutched the layers of material closer to her body, like her wedding dress would protect her from his sexiness.

"I'm a man. We're masters of the understatement." He eyed the beast, his expression dubious. "Need a lift?"

"I'm fine."

"Uh-huh. Sugar, I think you blew the engine. This bird isn't going to fly anytime in the near future." He gave her the once-over and she felt—actually felt—his gaze touch her. She shivered inside. *Guydar. On the fritz*, she reminded herself sternly. She realized how she'd hitched the ball-gown skirt of the wedding dress up around her middle, which bared her legs.

The dude cleared his throat. "So, sugar, want me to call a tow truck for your car?"

"No." Technically, it wasn't her car. Red had left her the keys, told her to drive it. She didn't give a flip if it sat here on the edge of the road from now until the day after the end of the world. A thought hit her. Leaving it might slow down her pursuers. Before she could ponder that further, her would-be rescuer spoke again.

"Look, this is the back of beyond. Let me at least give you a lift to the next town."

"I'm not goin' to the next town. I'm headed to Nashville."

"Fancy that. So am I. I'll take you."

And that was the whole problem. She wanted him to take her. He was still looking her up and down, interest sparking in those too-blue-to-be-safe eyes of his, and dang if she wasn't checking him out in return and hoping for a caveman. *Ugh.* What was wrong with her?

"All the way to Nashville?" That would give her a big head start on the Smithees. Red was in prison down in Alabama. Norbert was his mother's son and the Smithee cousins all followed Etta's orders.

"All the way." He held up his phone, and his brows creased in a cute way that made her want to kiss his forehead. *Whoa, girl*, she chided herself. This whole Handsome Man Syndrome was what had landed her in this mess to begin with. "Huh. No bars. I'll call a wrecker when we hit civilization."

Zoe leaned in through the door and grabbed her duffel bag and guitar case. Everything she owned fit in both. "Fine. Let's go." She marched past him, skirts still bunched around her middle, and got jerked to a stop when he snagged her bag.

"I'll put these in the trunk. The T-Bird doesn't have a back seat."

While the man deposited all her worldly goods into the minuscule trunk, she stomped to the passenger side door and snorted when she saw her veil crumpled there. Bad karma. Definitely. Zoe stuffed the ugly thing onto the dashboard and did her best to maneuver into the seat.

"May I help?"

She startled and banged her shin on the car door. Dang but the man was sneaky. She'd need to remember that fact. "No, I'm good. Thanks kindly."

He stood back, arms folded across a chest that filled out

his crisp button-down shirt as well as his butt did those jeans. He'd rolled the sleeves up to reveal tan forearms sprinkled with dark hair that glinted copper under the sun.

With much huffing and puffing, she squirmed her way into the tight fit. Between the hideous excuse for a wedding dress and everything else, she'd need a forklift to get her out of the darn thing.

She reached for the door to close it, but the guy beat her to it. He stuffed the trailing edges of her dress in around her and managed to shut the car door without catching any part of her skirt. "I'd tell you to buckle up, but that dress is a built-in airbag."

"Ha ha, funny," she groused, pushing part of the tulle and netting down and tucking it around her legs. First gas station they came to, she was ditching this virginal white travesty and getting comfortable. With effort, she fought to stretch the seat belt over the material and got it fastened.

Moments later, he was settled behind the wheel. "I'm Tucker," he said, holding out his hand.

"Zoe." She eyed his hand while weighing the risk of touching him. Her palm all but itched to feel his skin. She gave in to temptation and they shook. His palm was warm and dry. But those were *not* little tingles racing up her arm. *Nope. Definitely not.*

"Should I ask where the groom is?" He gave her a sideways glance as he started the T-Bird. And didn't that sweet engine purr pretty? He pulled out onto the rural highway.

"Nope. Let's just say our nuptials weren't meant to be." She grabbed the veil and tossed it over her head. She watched it through the side mirror and laughed when it draped across the firebird graphic on the hood of the Trans Am.

He cut his eyes her direction for a moment. "Cold feet?"

"Good sense." She flashed what she hoped was a reassuring smile in his direction.

"Okay." He dragged the syllables out.

She smoothed down her dress even more, grimacing at the miles of material. "You wouldn't happen to have some scissors? Or maybe a knife or something sharp?" The man—Tucker—glanced her way again so she explained, fluffing up the copious amount of material in her lap. "I want to cut some of the superfluous crap off this thing."

"No, sorry. Nothing that would work on that dress."

Zoe wanted to explain she hadn't picked out the dress, like this guy would care about her tastes in clothing. Still, she wanted him to think well of her. They rode in silence as miles passed. Fidgeting, she said, "You aren't from around here."

Tucker grinned. "Oklahoma originally. You?"

"Smoky Mountains, mostly, but I'm ready to get out and never look back." That was the truth. She sighed, wishing she'd dug her sunglasses out of her bag, and added under her breath, "One of the biggest mistakes I ever made was goin' to Gatlinburg to sing at that bar."

She glanced at Tucker, who was still watching her from the corner of his eye. She wanted to bite her tongue. Zoe knew exactly the picture she presented, and this guy had money and class stamped all over him.

"So you're a singer?"

Zoe hid her discomfort with a shrug. "Yeah, I am. And some days—" she tossed him her cheekiest grin "—I even get paid for it."

Zoe smooshed down some of the skirt between her thighs and squiggled her legs, still attempting to get comfortable. The silence returned. After several minutes, she glanced over at Tucker. He was casting surreptitious looks her way—only he wasn't checking out her face. Nope. He'd finally noticed her rounded belly.

Tucker cleared his throat, opened his mouth to speak, and evidently thought better of it because his jaw clamped shut. Zoe decided silence wasn't so bad. The man lasted all of five minutes.

"So, it was a shotgun wedding?"

"You could say that. Only it was my head they were holdin' the gun to."

He slammed on the brakes and her hands flew to the dash to brace her body. "What? What's wrong?" She swung her head back and forth looking for whatever emergency caused him to stop.

"Sorry! Sorry," he repeated, swiveling in the driver's seat to face her. "Please tell me that was…a euphemism. Or a joke. Or something."

"I wish I was jokin'." He scowled at her. "Hey, I didn't plan on my life takin' this detour." She shrugged. "I will admit, however, t'bein' young and dumb at the time."

"And now?"

"Older and wiser. Gettin' ready to have a kid and watchin' my life turn into a bad soap opera will do that to a body."

Tucker glanced at her rounded belly. "Yeah? And you figured all this out when? All of…what, eight months ago?"

"About that." Zoe pressed her lips together, wondering how far she could trust this stranger. "My life is a tad crazy, Tucker. I figure the best I can do is grin and bear it. You know, laughter bein' the best medicine and all?"

"Don't you have family to help?"

She curled her lips between her teeth and bit down. Her eyes burned, and she looked away so he wouldn't see. The compassion she saw in his expression was about to undo her. "Don't have any family t'speak of. There's just me."

"I…wow." He looked surprised. "I can't imagine what that would be like. I have a huge family."

A big family? There'd only been Zoe and her dad. "Lucky you."

His smile was warm and fond. "Until they get all up in my business."

Zoe felt a sharp twinge. Grimacing, she pressed her palm against her side.

"You okay?"

"Yeah, it's just those Briggs & Stratton things."

He looked confused, opened his mouth to speak, then pressed his lips together for a moment. He eventually asked, "Don't you mean Braxton Hicks?"

Eyes twinkling, she tilted her head, pretending to think about it, because of that whole laughter-being-the-best-medicine thing. She went for the cheap laugh. "Braxton Hicks. Doesn't he sing at the Grand Ole Opry?"

Two

Tucker hadn't missed the sheen of moisture in her eyes or her attempt at humor. From the white cowgirl boots to the froth of tulle and lace, she looked like a refugee from a hillbilly comedy show, but in her case, the clothing didn't define the woman hiding behind the caricature. In their short time together, he'd seen determination, warmth and an effervescent spirit. He admired the first and as a man, could appreciate the rest. He also sensed she was far more lonely than she wanted anyone to know. Given her circumstances? Totally understandable. He decided to play along. For now. "Ah, no," he said, hiding a grin. "Braxton Hicks are like false labor."

"No, really?" she said dryly, giving an exaggerated roll of her eyes. A moment later, she tilted her head to study him from under creased eyebrows. "How would a man like you know somethin' like that? You married?" He caught her checking out his left hand where it lightly gripped the steering wheel.

Biting back a bark of laughter, Tucker shook his head. Settling down was the last thing on his mind. "Nope. But that big family I mentioned? I have brothers and cousins. Some are married with kids." And his cousin-in-law Jolie, a nurse, had schooled everyone on the stages of pregnancy and birth when his Barron cousin Kade and wife, Pippa, went through the process. His gaze strayed to Zoe's belly again. Her hands were laced over it and he found the gesture…sweet.

Tuck eased off the brake, realizing he'd stopped in the middle of the road. Good thing there wasn't any traffic. "So tell me something." He glanced at her, waiting until she faced him to continue. "Were you serious about it being a shotgun wedding?"

An expression he couldn't immediately decipher flickered across her face. She shifted to stare out her side of the car, and he thought she'd ignore his question. Then he heard her sigh.

"That there would be a very long story. Are you sure you wanna wade around in my can of worms?"

And that there was a good question, he mused. By stopping and picking her up, he'd dived headfirst into her mess, and to be honest, his curiosity was getting the better of him. "It's a long drive to Nashville. We've got time."

"Well, sir, you've asked for it. Question becomes, where should I start?"

"The beginning always works for me."

"True, that. So…about nine months ago, I was singing my way from honky-tonk to roadhouse, and one night, I was fillin' in as a singer for the house band at Shooter Jake's." She looked his way to see if he was following along. "You've heard of it?"

He nodded. Shooter Jake's, in Dalton, Georgia, was one step up from a roadhouse, but the owner had an ear for music and a willingness to give talented newcomers a chance. He wasn't going to admit precisely how familiar he was with the place. It had been Jake himself who put Tuck on the trail of the band he'd just auditioned.

"So anyway, it was a one-night deal. Their lead singer came down with something and couldn't perform. Mr. Jake introduced me to 'em—the band, I mean. Come dark, there I was, front'n center on the stage."

"Okay?" He wondered if maybe one of the band members was responsible for her current condition.

"That night I was singin' my heart out and there was a guy sittin' there at a table. He was downright good-lookin', if you know what I mean?" She cut her eyes toward him and winked. "Not as handsome as you, but dang close. Anyway, he bought me a drink. And then another. And so on, until...well, you get my drift." She paused and waggled her finger in his direction. "Now, I might not be a good girl, but I ain't normally stupid, even if I've drunk way more whiskey than is good for me. We took precautions but..." She sighed. "Sometimes, stuff happens. Come mornin', he went his way while I went mine."

"Uh-huh." Tucker was fascinated, despite his better judgment.

"Well, due to circumstances..." She patted her belly. "That stuff happened. I bought a test to confirm it."

Tucker had the insane urge to touch her belly. "It was obviously positive."

"Yup. So, I went lookin' for the man. I figured he had the right to know, seein' as he was the daddy and all." She glanced over at him. "I mean, wouldn't you want to know?"

He considered the question. "Yes, I would."

"Took me two months to track Redmond down, and by then, it was a little late to be doin' anything about the situation." Her chin rose in a stubborn jut. "Not that I would have, even if that's what he wanted. That solution is fine for some people, but not me." She rubbed her belly with one hand, a gesture both protective and soothing, and one Tucker thought she was unaware of. He found it…endearing.

"So…" Tuck stretched out the word. "You wanted him to marry you?"

"Oh, hell no! I mean really, it's not like love had a thing to do with it." She inhaled deeply and breathed out slowly. "And I wasn't out to trap him. I'm not that kind of woman."

Given that she was running away from her wedding, obviously not. Tucker said as much. "Since you're here with me and not on your honeymoon, I sort of figured that."

Zoe blinked rapidly at him. "I told you my life has turned into a soap opera. Are you sure you want to know all this?"

At his nod, she continued. "I didn't discover until too late that I shoulda just hightailed it outta there. Redmond let on that he was prouder than a bantam rooster about bein' a daddy, but did he take care of me or help with doctor bills? Nope. That sonavagun dragged me all over the South, stallin' every step of the way." She dropped her voice as she mimicked. "Just one more job, baby girl, then I'll give you some money." She rolled her eyes and grimaced. "I plead pregnancy hormones because if I'd been in my right mind, I would have ditched that man way before I did."

"Uh-huh." He didn't hide the dubious tone in his voice.

"Trust me, I'm serious. Anyway, we were down in Tuscaloosa, Alabama." She started to say more but caught herself. "Let's just say things went downhill. He turned out to be a…well, Redmond liked the ladies. A lot. And it got him in a whole heap of trouble."

Tucker didn't like the way her voice sounded. "What kind of trouble?"

"Unbeknownst to me, he took up with another man's wife. And got caught with his britches down. T'make a long and sordid story short, there was a shoot-out. Red walked away. The husband didn't."

She heaved out a sigh and rubbed her side. Tucker waited, silent now. This was quite a tale, but he felt the urge to reach over and take her hand, to tell her that everything would be okay.

"I was ready to take off as soon as he was arrested, but Etta Smithee, his momma, had different ideas. She made me stay in Tuscaloosa for the duration. Sat me down in the front row, right there behind her baby boy every day of that trial. She bought me all these frilly maternity clothes and there I sat, day after day, lookin' and feelin' like a fool. I didn't love that man, and he deserved to be sent to prison for killin' that boy."

"I..." Tucker paused. What could he say?

She favored him with a sidelong but understanding look before continuing. "As soon as the jury read the verdict, I was ready to hit the road. Before I could go, Miz Smithee got all sweet, sayin' it was up to her and the Smithee family to look after me and the baby. Things were fine until she decided to make an honest woman of me. Since I wouldn't marry Red, I'd just have to marry Norbert, his brother." She issued a long-suffering sigh. "Mama Smithee wants all her chicks in a row and all her loose ends tied up. And those loose ends would be me and Baby Bugtussle here."

Tucker tried to wrap his brain around this information, failed and gave up. "Why would she want you married to Norbert?"

"That woman is covered in crazy sauce. She decreed that her first grandbaby should have the Smithee name, and I should just be dancin' with joy to marry Norbert. Like any smart woman, I hitched up my skirts and hightailed it out of town first opportunity I got. I went back to singing and was doin' pretty good despite the extra baggage." She patted her belly, a big smile curling up the corners of her mouth—a mouth Tucker found most intriguing. "I got a job in Gatlinburg. I had no idea the Smithees roosted around there. There I am, strummin' my guitar and singin' a Miranda Lambert song and who walks in the door?"

"Norbert."

"Got it in one, slick." She winked at him, but her smile faded and a haunted look filled her eyes. Tucker tensed, not sure he wanted to hear the rest. "Next thing I know, he's stuffin' me in his old truck and drivin' like a bat outta hell straight to his momma's house. That woman locked me up in a bedroom until she could—" Zoe paused and formed air quotes with her fingers. "Make arrangements."

"Did those arrangements include that...dress?" He wanted to banish the ghosts lingering in her eyes so he tried her trick of making a joke.

"Absolutely." She squirmed a little and sighed. "Speakin' of, got any idea how far it is to the next gas station so I can change clothes? And..." She pressed her side and stiffened a little. "This little sucker just loves stompin' on my bladder. I could use a rest stop." She blew out a breath. "Sooner than later."

Tucker couldn't decide how much of Zoe's tale was fact and how much was fiction. He had to admire what his mom would call gumption. She was all alone and he caught a hint of the distress she tried so hard to hide. She was sweet and funny and he wanted to protect her, as inexplicable as that seemed, considering they'd just met. He resisted reaching for her hand. Again.

In the back of his mind, a thought formed—he should have his brother, Bridger, who worked for their cousin Cash Barron at Barron Security Services, look into the Smithees. Out loud, he said, "I think I can manage to fulfill that request."

Zoe stashed the hated wedding dress in the dumpster behind the truck stop and finally felt like herself. Struggling out of the darn thing, even in the handicapped stall, had been an exercise in futility. Surrendering, she just ripped at it until all the buttons popped, pinging off the metal walls like BBs. The tussle left her dizzy, and she had to sit on the commode and gather herself for a moment before she could pull on yoga pants. Topping them with an oversize T-shirt and slipping her swollen feet into flip-flops was pure indulgence. The hideous dress had been gag inducing. The cheap boots followed the dress into the trash.

Grabbing her duffel, Zoe schlepped back toward the store portion of the truck stop. She had just enough cash to grab something cold to drink and maybe a sandwich. She'd locate Tucker and then they could hit the road again. She reached the back door but hesitated to open it, opting instead to peer through the glass. She froze. Two Smithee cousins stood in the checkout line. Could Etta Smithee be far behind?

She ducked away from the door. Pressing her back against the sun-warmed concrete wall, Zoe breathed through the panic. She couldn't go inside to grab Tucker. *What to do? What to do? Think, think, think.* She needed her guitar. Which was locked in the trunk of Tucker's car. She shifted just enough to peek through the glass door. The cousins were still there but there was no sign of Tucker.

Edging along the wall to the corner of the building, Zoe checked the busy parking lot. Tucker had parked away from everyone else. That was a good thing. The T-Bird couldn't be seen from inside the store. She located a rust-bucket pickup she'd seen parked at the church. The truck was empty. The minute those two saw her, the jig would be up, but if Tucker would come out, they could escape unnoticed. She was running out of time and options. Fast.

Zoe glanced at the big semis idling in the truck lot. Maybe she could hitch a ride. But that meant leaving her guitar behind. And Tucker. Leaving him behind didn't seem like much of a solution. Which was dumb because that man owed her nothing and would probably turn her over to Etta and Norbert just on principle. Too bad he was so pretty. And manly. And made her think of things no woman within a month or so of giving birth should be considering.

But Zoe didn't truly believe Tucker would hand her over to the Smithees. That meant she had only one option. Wait for Tucker. Sneaking over to the T-Bird without looking like she was skulking through the parking lot wasn't all that easy. Worried other Smithees might be around, she ducked down on the driver's side of the classic car. Too bad it was so low-slung. Sexy, yes, but dang hard to hide behind.

"C'mon," she murmured, sending vibes winging toward Tucker—not that she believed in any of that woo-woo stuff. But five minutes later, her headache-inducing concentration worked. Tucker, holding a plastic bag, stepped out of the store and looked toward where he'd parked the T-Bird. Zoe watched his brow knit as he glanced back inside. That was her cue. She popped her head up, put two fingers in her mouth and issued a piercing whistle. His head jerked back toward her and she waved him over, her arm flailing, as she climbed in.

As he walked up to the passenger door—the side of the car nearest the store, she pleaded, "I need the keys." She gripped the steering wheel with white-knuckled strength so Tucker wouldn't see how badly her hands shook. When he didn't respond fast enough, she added, "Get in. Please! We have to move fast."

He stared at her very pregnant belly crammed against the steering wheel and raised a brow. Okay, he might have a point as she tended to waddle when on foot, but she was driving, and they had a need for speed.

"How can you—"

"C'mon, rich boy. We gotta go and go now!"

The doors behind him opened and shouts echoed over the growls of idling diesel engines. Tucker glanced around, saw two men bearing down on them. He tossed the keys to Zoe and she managed to get the right one inserted into the ignition as Tucker vaulted into the passenger seat. Zoe floored the accelerator before he got settled. Thank goodness Tucker had backed into the parking space.

The men lumbered after them but gave up within a few yards, turned and trotted to their truck as Zoe watched through the rearview mirror.

"Pull over," Tucker ordered.

"Not until we lose them." She was adamant.

"Who are those guys?"

"They woulda been my in-laws, if I hadn't run like hell." She pressed back against the seat and fought the car around a tight curve, refusing to slow down. "Well, sort of. They're Norbert's cousins. Won't be long until Etta and him will be on our trail."

Tucker reached over, placing a hand over hers on the steering wheel. "I won't let them hurt you."

Her eyes filled with tears that she blamed on the wind, since she'd forgotten her sunglasses again. And she ignored the twinge in her chest where her heart beat in loud thumps. Tucker was just a nice man helping out a stranded woman in trouble. That's all. Nothing more. But no man had ever said those words to her and meant them. She didn't have to swipe at the tear on her cheek. Tucker did it for her with a gentle fingertip.

"We got this, sweetheart." He rummaged in her duffel and pulled out her sunglasses. Then he reached into his plastic bag. He gave her a wink and a grin. "Wouldn't be a road trip without junk food."

Three

Tucker let Zoe drive as she seemed to have some clue about their location. She didn't pop the clutch when she shifted gears, instinctively braked before hitting the curves, then powered through them by accelerating. The day was sunny, not too warm, and her not-quite-in-laws were way behind them. Besides, by not driving, he could study his runaway bride.

Zoe was pretty, though not in the beauty queen sense. Her eyes, hidden now behind big sunglasses, were a deep chocolate brown. Her chin was too long, her mouth too wide but not full and her nose tipped up on the end. Her long, dark brown hair fell in twisty—and hair-sprayed—curls down over her cleavage. There was just something wrong with him for thinking about her in any sort of sexual way, but he couldn't help himself. She wasn't the sort of woman he normally would be attracted to, yet he was. She exuded a sweet vulnerability that called to him.

Her accent was thick enough—and country enough—he could cut it with a knife. He had a Harvard MBA and remembered all too acutely the disdain he'd received there for his Okie accent. He'd worked hard to smooth out the rough edges. But Zoe? Her language was colorful and brash, and whenever she opened her mouth, the lyrics to a country song spilled out. Maybe that was why she fascinated him. Tucker continued to study her.

She had long, supple fingers—and didn't the idea of them gripping him like she had them wrapped around the steering wheel make him shift in his seat. They ended with short nails covered in chipped red polish. Her arms looked toned and he wondered what her figure was like before the pregnancy. He jerked his thoughts away from jumping down that rabbit hole.

She drove with a carefree abandon *and* a determined focus. She was a free spirit, not ready to settle in one place. Except she'd decided to keep the child of a man she claimed was a one-night stand she didn't wish to marry. Zoe was a paradox and his curiosity might just kill his cat. Good thing he didn't own one.

"You're staring."

"Yup."

"I need to pee again."

"Okay."

She cut her eyes his direction. "I'll be stoppin' at the next place we come to. You can drive after that."

"Gee, thanks," he said dryly. "Considering it's my car." He flashed her a mock glower and added, "Though I'll admit you're not a bad driver."

She made a *pfft* sound before she laughed. And, man, did her laughter arrow straight into his core. "Honey, I learned to drive when I was ten so I could borrow the neighbor's car. My daddy couldn't drive so I'd take us down to the local dive where I could play for my supper and his drinks."

This woman fascinated Tucker. And he worried about

that, just a little. She was raw and…real. She said what she thought with no filters, and no matter how horrified he might be, he still found himself enjoying her company. In the back of his mind, though, resided that little voice of doubt. Was she telling a tall tale, or was this the truth of her life? He understood that not everyone had the '50s sitcom life he and his brothers had grown up with—a strong mother, a doting father, hard work but lots and lots of love, and parents who gave their boys the freedom to fly when they left the nest. All but his baby brother, Dillon. But that was okay. Between him and Deacon, they were keeping him in line.

Pulling his thoughts back to the woman driving his car, Tucker noticed Zoe was squirming in her seat. He surreptitiously searched the map app on his phone. "Can you last five more miles?"

Zoe glared at the speedometer then scowled as they passed a speed limit sign. The little car sped up. A lot. Tucker choked off a laugh. Less than five minutes later, she braked to a sliding stop at the travel mart just off I-40. She got the stick shift in Neutral, heaved out of the seat and waddled inside. Zoe wore such a determined look on her face that men scrambled out of her way. Tucker waited until she was out of sight and then he burst out laughing. Several people walking past the T-Bird stared at him. He didn't care. He'd been totally charmed by his hitchhiker.

By the time Zoe returned, Tucker was sitting in the driver's seat. He started to get out to hold the door, but she waved him off.

"I may be as big as a small barn, but I'm not helpless. The day I can't open my own door, I'll be flat on my back in a coffin."

"Yes, ma'am, if you say so."

"Are you makin' fun of me?"

"No, ma'am. Not me."

She gave him a narrow-eyed scowl. He just managed to keep his face averted so she couldn't see the grin teasing his mouth. Too cute. Even pregnant with swollen ankles and a small bladder, she was too cute. "I'm taking the interstate so we're about two, two and a half hours from Nashville. You gonna need to stop again?"

"Your guess is as good as mine. It depends on Baby Bugtussle." She suddenly sat up straighter and blew out a slow breath. "Swear to the angels above this child is gonna be a placekicker for the University of Tennessee Volunteers."

Tucker glanced past her, watching traffic, before pulling out onto the highway. "Do you know what it is?"

"Etta Smithee is convinced it's a boy."

"You haven't had an ultrasound?"

"I've had three. The little dickens gives the camera its butt. Not one scan has shown this child's privates. If I had a nursery, I'd have to paint it lavender."

"Lavender?"

"Yup. Mix pink and blue. Makes lavender."

"How about green? That seems like a neutral color."

"Nope. Baby Bugtussle has done stepped on my last nerve. Gonna paint everything lavender. Then if it is a boy, he can just explain things to his friends."

"Why not just name him Sue?" Tucker muttered.

Zoe laughed and launched into a few measures of Johnny Cash's "A Boy Named Sue." She offered a raucous rendition of the song. The part of him always on the lookout for new talent picked up something in her voice, but she stopped singing before he got a handle on just what he heard. He realized her voice made him think of moonlight and rumpled sheets, of a man and a woman entwined in the dark. He liked the vision in his head—probably a little too much.

They didn't talk. At highway speed, the wind blew away

their words. Zoe gathered her hair in one hand to keep it from whipping around her face. The silence wasn't uncomfortable, which surprised him. He caught himself watching her almost as much as he kept his eyes on the road. Her voice and laugh burrowed their way into him, as did the hint of uncertainty and sadness he sensed behind her good humor. The way her high cheeks complemented the line of her jaw, the curve of her throat as she arched her head back… She was far too attractive for his own good. He found himself lost in contemplating her face. Until he glanced down to the rounded bulk of her pregnant belly. That was like taking the ice bucket challenge every time.

They hit the outskirts of Nashville just over two hours later. Traffic thickened as they approached the east side. He needed to know where to drop her, so he asked. She took her time answering, and Tucker watched the lighthearted mask she hid behind slip a little. She finally asked to borrow his phone, only she didn't make any calls. Her thumbs flew over the screen as she texted someone. Then she waited, eyes glued to his phone.

When she didn't give him directions or an address, he took the exit for downtown Nashville and headed to the restored fire station that now housed Bent Star. His passenger looked up as the car rolled to a stop at Second Ave.

"Where are we?" Zoe's forehead crinkled as she gazed around.

"I'm headed to my office unless you have someplace else in mind?"

She tucked her chin and shook her head. "No. Not really. I texted a friend of mine, but he hasn't replied yet. I was going to camp out on his couch."

Tucker didn't like the idea of this male friend of hers. Which was ridiculous. Except he liked Zoe and was worried about her being stuck in Nashville all alone. He didn't say anything until he pulled into the parking lot at Bent Star and cut the T-Bird's engine. With both hands on the steering wheel, he slid his eyes her direction but didn't look at her full-on. "Do you have another place to stay, Zoe?" She lifted a shoulder, head still down. "I can take you to a hotel."

"I'm good," she insisted. "Don't put yourself out. I'll just head to my friend's." He watched her shoulders slump in a defensive move. "Can I get my stuff from the trunk?"

"Sure." He slipped out of the car and retrieved her guitar case and duffel. He carried both around to the passenger side and after watching her struggle for a long moment, set down the bag and extended his hand. "Here. For leverage," he added when she scowled at him. Once she was out of the car, she slung the straps of the duffel over her shoulder, handed him his phone and clutched her guitar case.

"Well, thanks for all the help and stuff. Sorry for getting you caught up in all my drama." She offered a wan smile, turned away and started walking.

Tucker glanced down at his phone and noticed a reply text. "Well, crap," he muttered. His mother would disown him if she ever found out he let a down-on-her-luck pregnant girl just walk off into the sunset. "Zoe!"

She kept walking, picking up speed when Tucker yelled her name. If she could get downtown, she might find one of the clubs with an open mic night where she could sing for tips or something. That would get her a room until she could reach the guy she'd hoped to stay with.

Pounding steps echoed behind her, then a warm hand settled on her shoulder, halting her.

"Your friend texted back." He held out his phone so she could read it. "He's out of town, touring with a band." She closed her eyes to hide the tears prickling there. Just once she wished things could go her way. She felt wrung out, and so tired she hurt all over.

"You don't have any other place to go, do you?" Tucker's voice sounded full of compassion. She hated that he might pity her but before she could make up something, he continued. "And I'm betting you don't have much money, either." He tugged the duffel off her shoulder and hefted it over his own. Then he relieved her of the guitar case. "C'mon. I have a couple of things to take care of at the office. Then we'll go eat something and figure out things from there."

"Look, you don't—"

"Yeah, I do. I'm not going to just dump you out on the street, Zoe. I wasn't raised that way."

They walked back to the redbrick Victorian building. Once upon a time, it had been a firehouse. There was no sign to designate what sort of business occupied the space. Tucker hadn't mentioned what he did for a living. Given the expensive boots and the classic car he drove, he had money.

He held the front door for her and ushered her inside. He could do…almost anything. Lawyer. Real estate. Heck, this was Nashville. He could be in the music business. The reception area had a country-western feel with lots of leather furniture and barn wood with a logo shaped like a Texas Ranger's star behind the desk.

Tucker led her down a long hall that opened into another waiting area, still decorated in the same theme, only the artwork consisted of album covers and awards. Agent, she decided. Tucker must be a music agent. Either he window-dressed a good story or he had some major clients, according to the stuff lining the walls.

"Have a seat. I'll be a little while," he said, then disappeared behind a closed door—with her guitar case and bag. She was too tired to object.

She wandered around the space, stretching her legs. The

secretary's desk held only a phone console. She found the restroom and availed herself of it. As she wandered back to the sitting area, she noticed a worn acoustic guitar sitting on a stand. Unable to resist, she picked it up and settled in a large chair that could accommodate two people, if one of them wasn't pregnant.

Zoe curled up, as much as her belly allowed, on the wide padded seat. Using her thumb, she tested the tone of each string, listening intently. Surprised to find it in tune, she strummed a few chords. The old Gibson had an amazing sound. She riffed through a progression of chords, humming softly. Lost in the music, she didn't realize she had an audience.

She sang a Carrie Underwood song, then launched into a rollicking Miranda Lambert tune. She finished up with Kelly Clarkson's heartbreaking ballad, "Piece by Piece." Zoe didn't get to sing ballads often. Working the bars, the folks there wanted up-tempo dance tunes. But her soul found solace in the ballads, the songs like this one, or like Cam's "Burning House." She lay her cheek against the swell of the guitar and just let her hands wander along until they started picking the melody to Striking Matches' "When the Right One Comes Along." She raised her voice to sing, getting through the first stanza of the duet. She took a breath before starting the part where the male voice would harmonize, and almost dropped the guitar when a voice picked up where she'd left off.

Jerking her head up, she gaped at the five men standing there, but it was the singer who held her attention. He'd picked up the song on his own guitar and winked at her as he waited for her to catch up. Her voice found his pitch, and as she began to sing again, he altered his tone to match hers. Outwardly, she remained calm but inside? Inside she was squeeing like a fangirl sitting in the front row of this man's concert. Deacon Freaking Tate. Along with his band, the Sons of Nashville. She managed to get through the song, even adding some harmony from the guitar in her lap.

When they finished, the band applauded, but she was so flustered she couldn't speak. Was this what it felt like to be famous? Fame had been a pipe dream from the time her daddy had put that first pawnshop guitar in her hands.

Deacon walked up to her, a big smile on his face. She'd thought he was sexy on TV but in person he was off the charts. He held out his hand.

"Deacon Tate."

She sucked in a breath and thought, *Of course you are.* Then she introduced herself, placing her hand in his. "Zoe Parker."

"Nice to sing with you, Miss Zoe Parker."

"Trust me, the pleasure's all mine."

"Aren't you married?" a gruff voice barked from behind the band. "And doesn't your wife carry a gun?"

Deacon laughed, the sound as rich and lyrical as his singing voice. "Yes, and yes, Tuck. You didn't tell us you had such a talented lady waiting for you. We'd have finished sooner."

Zoe forgot to breathe as Tucker pushed through the cluster of band members and halted next to Deacon. Only then—with them side by side—did she recognize the similarity. "Are you… I don't…?" she sputtered.

"Zoe Parker, I'd like to introduce my brother, and the chief operating officer of Barron Entertainment, Tucker Tate," Deacon interrupted. He bumped Tucker with his shoulder, amusement lighting up his handsome face. "And there's no need to be jealous, little bro."

Her gaze darted between the two men for about five seconds as her brain roller-skated on a hamster wheel. Tucker Tate? He was like a gazillionaire. And important. Breath caught in her lungs. *No hyperventilating,* she ordered herself. Something twinged low in her back and the pain that had been building there all day exploded as her water broke.

Zoe looked up, horrified and embarrassed. The men stared at her, then at each other. She pressed her hand over her mouth as they erupted into shouted orders and pandemonium as everyone started running around shouting and flailing their arms.

"Call nine-one-one!"

"There's not time!"

"I'll get the car!"

"We need an ambulance!"

Then Tucker and Deacon were beside her, holding her up. "Shh, Zoe. It's okay," Tucker soothed.

She gazed into Tucker's face. He appeared only slightly panicked. "If you say so."

"I do. Just hang on." His arm slipped around her shoulders. "We got this, remember?"

And then the EMTs were there, bundling her onto a stretcher and moving her to the ambulance. They loaded her, and she saw Tucker standing outside, staring at her and looking as lost as she felt.

"C'mon, Dad," one EMT said, waving Tucker aboard. "I have the feeling the baby isn't going to wait for an invitation. You need to be close."

Tucker climbed in and moved to crouch on the bench near Zoe's head. The second EMT headed to the ambulance cab and in moments, they pulled out, lights blazing and sirens blaring.

"I'm Ted," the EMT said.

"Zoe."

"I need to take a peek, Zoe, to see where we are in the process. Okay?"

Tucker looked away as the EMT cut off her pants and

checked. He gulped when the guy said, "Ah, darlin'? You need to stop pushing."

"Stop pushing?" Zoe yelled. "What in bloody blue blazes are you sayin'? This baby wants out!" She waved her left hand in Tucker's direction.

He grabbed it out of sheer instinct. She squeezed hard, grunted, then panted. She clutched his hand so tight, he lost feeling in his fingers. The EMT *tsked* a few times as he draped a thin cotton blanket over Zoe and fussed with getting monitoring equipment on her.

"I don't wanna do this," Zoe wailed.

"Little late for that, angel." Tucker smoothed a tangle of hair off her face and wondered what it would feel like once the hairspray was washed out. Her face was pinched from pain and her eyes were fixed on him. He tried to smile but he wasn't nearly as calm as he tried to project.

A low moan escaped from between lips pressed tightly together and her shoulders came off the stretcher. "Gotta push," she snarled between clenched teeth.

"Just hang on, little momma. We're almost there." Ted lifted the blanket to check her again, his gaze bouncing to the monitoring equipment.

"Aren't you supposed to be doing some breathing or something?" Tucker wanted to distract her. He got a growl and a light punch in the arm for his efforts.

"So not funny, you—" Whatever she meant to say was lost in another, more powerful groan.

"Speed it up!" Ted yelled toward the cab of the ambulance. The ambulance accelerated.

Tucker watched as the EMT muttered something and flipped the blanket up to Zoe's knees and positioned himself between her legs. Moments later, Ted said, "Looks like we're doing this anyway. Time to push, Zoe."

The contraction hit, and Zoe squeezed Tucker's hand

again as she bore down. He slipped an arm under her shoulders and gave her support as she pushed.

It seemed like an hour before she went limp, leaning back into him as the EMT held something pink and squirming. Which then started screaming at earsplitting levels to rival the siren. Tucker barely had time to catch his breath before Ted was placing a naked bundle in Zoe's arms.

Tucker looked down at the tiny, scrunched-up face and felt his heart stop. He brushed a fingertip along the baby's cheek and the child stopped crying. Able to breathe again, he marveled at the tiny thing, all thick dark hair and blue eyes. Part of him was stunned but another part was full of awe, and some emotion he couldn't—nor did he want to—define. But his brain spun through the possibilities despite his best efforts. Protectiveness. A weird tenderness. Tucker figured in that moment that he was a goner. This kid would own him heart and soul if he didn't guard against it.

"Congrats, Mom and Dad. It's a boy."

Four

Tucker didn't have the presence of mind to correct the EMT. Zoe cradled the baby in her arms and stared at her child, teary-eyed, her expression filled with wonder. He glanced at his own expression, distorted as it was in the gleaming metal of the cabinet across from him. He and Zoe both looked like they'd been struck by lightning—dazed, confused and in awe of the tiny person who'd just made his grand entrance into the world.

Sitting here in an ambulance, amid the chaos of a birth, Tucker should have been totally freaked out. Except he wasn't. Maybe it was shock—because what he'd just seen couldn't be unseen—but at the same time, there was a deep sense of peace. *That's* what was turning him into a babbling idiot. Tucker clamped his teeth together to keep the babble in his head.

He concentrated on Zoe. She had no place to stay, no friends, no family. He should take care of her, but at the same time, he was a stranger and one with slightly ulterior motives, after hearing her sing. Tucker was well aware of all the scandals involving powerful men and the women with stars in their eyes those men exploited. He was *not* that guy. Never would be. But he couldn't deny his attraction to her, either.

The ride smoothed out as the frantic rush to the hospital wasn't quite so necessary now that the baby had arrived. The ambulance rolled to a stop, then backed into a slot beneath the covered parking at the entrance to Vanderbilt University Medical Center's emergency room. The back doors opened, and the paramedic's partner appeared, along with a trauma nurse and orderly. Bemused, Tucker watched as Zoe and her baby were unloaded.

"Yo, Dad! Ya comin'?" the paramedic called.

Shaking the cobwebs out of his head, Tuck clamored down and followed the little parade into the emergency department. No one stopped him, not even when he trailed after the gurney into a partitioned cubicle. When Zoe didn't chase him out, he settled onto a short "wheely" stool. A scarily efficient woman in scrubs covered with rainbow unicorns conferred with Zoe, tapping information onto an electronic tablet with a stylus. As she finished the intake, a man and a woman bustled in.

"OB-GYN and pediatrician," Unicorn Lady explained as she stepped out of their way. Tucker rolled back into the corner and pushed off the stool. Time for him to go. Before he could make an escape, questions flew fast and furious from the doctors and Unicorn Lady.

"Due date?"

"Blood pressure?"

"First child?"

"Apgar?"

Zoe ended up with her feet in stirrups, knees spread, while the mumbling OB-GYN ducked under the sheet a nurse had spread over Zoe. The male pediatrician bundled the baby up in a blanket. Tucker got two steps before Zoe grabbed his hand.

"Please?" Her breathy voice tugged at him just as hard as her hand did.

She looked scared and overwhelmed and totally alone. Tucker's protective instincts surged, and he gave her hand a gentle squeeze. "I'm not goin' anywhere, Zoe." The smile she flashed was radiant—and relieved. His breath clogged in his chest as he smiled back.

The pediatrician noticed him. "Congratulations. You have a healthy if slightly impatient son." He held out the blanket bundle and Tucker dropped Zoe's hand as the doctor placed the child in Tucker's arms, then turned to Unicorn Lady to answer her last question. "He'd be a ten but since he's two weeks early, mark him a nine on the Apgar just to be safe. We'll want to watch for jaundice so get a bilirubin count on him."

Tucker didn't breathe as he stared down at the crinkled face of the little boy. The child yawned, jamming a tiny fist in his mouth. A firm hand landed on his shoulder.

"Remember to breathe, Dad."

Yeah, about that. He really needed to explain the situation since Zoe hadn't. Tucker hadn't taken his eyes off the baby, and now realized he'd settled onto the edge of the bed close to Zoe and that her hand rested on his arm next to the baby's head. The words refused to come.

The pediatrician reached for the baby and Tucker discovered he was reluctant to let go. "Now that you've had some daddy bonding time, this little guy needs to try to eat. You had planned on breastfeeding, right, Zoe?"

Another nurse bustled in. "Her room is ready. We'll move her once she's fed the baby."

Tucker was still wrapping his head around the idea of breastfeeding as the doctor took the baby. Unicorn Lady moved in to help Zoe get situated. Before he could gather his wits, he and Zoe were alone in the cubicle and the little one was making happy noises beneath the blanket that covered Zoe's breasts. Slightly embarrassed by this most private event, Tucker turned to leave.

"No!" Zoe rasped out. Her panic was back. "I can't go to a room. I can't stay here." She lowered her eyes, as if ashamed. "I ain't got the money to stay in the hospital. Heck, I can't pay for the ambulance or this ER." She bit her bottom lip as it trembled.

Instinct had him cupping her cheek. There was no way he could walk away and leave her in this mess. She continued talking. "I had money saved for a birthing center and midwife and had one picked out here in Nashville, but Bugtussle here blew that plan. I didn't exactly have time to get settled and make appointments." She glanced down before meeting his gaze again. "I don't like owin' people, have always paid my own way." A tear escaped and rolled down her cheek. "I don't know what to do."

"I do." He brushed a stray hair from her forehead. "I'll guarantee your bill." She opened her mouth to protest but he stopped her with a gentle finger laid over her lips. "Shh. I got this. We'll work out a way for you to pay it off."

She pressed back against the pillow so she could look into his eyes. An expression of resignation tinged with relief suffused her face. "I *will* pay you back."

"Damn straight you will." He said the words with a hint of humor in his voice.

Unicorn Lady returned with the other nurse and two orderlies. "I know you want to stay with the family, Dad, but time to deal with business." She ushered him from the room while the medical personnel bustled Zoe and her baby deeper into the hospital. By the time Tucker had explained the situation and dealt with payment details in the business office, his phone had blown up with messages. The whole gang from Bent Star had gathered in the ER waiting room. He strolled in to find balloons, flowers, teddy bears and bubble gum cigars—both pink and blue.

"It's a boy," he announced. "Seven pounds, ten ounces, and twenty inches long. Baby and mother are both doing fine. They want to keep her at least overnight to make sure things are all working correctly."

The entire group trooped to the maternity wing, leaving all the pink items at the nurses station to be passed out to the families with baby girls in the nursery. Having Deacon and the Sons of Nashville on the floor flustered the staff and caused curious faces to peek out through the doorways of patients' rooms. Since visitors were limited, the guys happily schmoozed with medical personnel and new moms alike.

Zoe, with her sleeping baby in a bassinet, was napping, but one by one, under Tucker's watchful gaze, the band members tiptoed in to admire the little boy and leave their gifts so she'd wake up to a plethora of flowers and balloons. Deacon leaned against the wall outside her room while Tucker shuffled from foot to foot under his brother's scrutiny.

"What?" Tucker knew he sounded defensive but didn't care.

"You wanna tell me what's the deal with this girl?"

"There is no *deal.*"

"Uh-huh."

"Seriously, Deke." Tucker lifted his hand, wanting to rub his temple, then stopped himself. "Look, I found her on the side of the road." *Wearing a wedding dress and kicking the door of a classic Trans Am.* "She was having car trouble and needed a ride to Nashville. That's it. End of story."

"Uh-huh." Deacon's lips twitched. "Don't make me call Mom."

Dropping his head, Tucker gave in to the need to rub his forehead. "She was wearing a wedding dress. I had no idea she was pregnant."

"Whoa. Back up. Wedding dress? This sounds like a story where I need a beer in my hand while I'm listening."

"It's a long one, Deacon. The kid is basically alone and I felt sorry for her, so instead of dumping her at the first truck stop, I brought her to Nashville."

"So what now?"

"I don't know. She texted a friend but he's out of town. She has no place to stay. I do know she doesn't have much money, and no support system. What was I supposed to do?" He pinched the bridge of his nose. "I offered to buy her dinner and to help her figure things out. I…brought her inside. And now this."

"Maybe I *should* call Mom."

Tucker panicked and clenched his fingers in his brother's shirt. "No! Just…no."

"So what are you going to do?"

Releasing Deke with an embarrassed shrug, he stepped back and glanced inside Zoe's room. "There's room at the town house."

"You should call Bridger. He and Cash can check her out."

"Yeah. I should." He curled his lips between his teeth and gave a series of short nods. "I feel sorry for her, Deke."

His brother inspected him for what seemed like a very long time. "What else do you feel for her, Tuck?"

That was the rub, wasn't it? What *did* he feel beyond a hint of pity wrapped up with admiration? There was a tug of sexual attraction—okay, it felt more like a sledgehammer to the back of his head—but that feeling was seasoned with a lot of respect for her as a person. And watching her panic had brought out every protective bone in his body.

He glanced at Deacon. "She doesn't have much, is almost too proud to ask for help. I feel like doing that. Helping her out. So, that's what I'm doing."

"If Quin was here, I'd have her go shopping with you," Deke finally said. "You need to call the Bee Dubyas and get a list of what Zoe needs for the baby."

Calling any of the women married to his Barron cousins ranked right up there with calling his mother. "Why can't I call Quin?"

Deke laughed and three nurses stopped midstride to moon over him. "Because my beautiful wife is as new to motherhood as I am to being a father. The Bees have it down to a science."

Collectively, the Barron Wives were a force of nature. Still, better them than Katherine Tate. His mother would be on the next plane to Nashville. Deke patted him on the shoulder and said the words that meant Tuck owed him big time.

"I'll call Jolie and ask her to make a list of the fundamentals and email it to you."

When Zoe woke up the next morning, she found a fancy diaper bag and clothes—for her and Bugtussle. She hadn't decided on a name yet and she wasn't about to use his birth father's name. The room was full of flowers and balloons and she got misty-eyed. Was this what it felt like to have a family? To have friends? She'd been on her own for a very long time and hadn't stopped in any one place to put down those kinds of roots. Tucker had to be behind this, or maybe the band, because she'd lay odds the hospital didn't have a new baby welcoming committee with this kind of swag.

A female doctor breezed in, followed by a nurse. "Good morning, Zoe. I'm Dr. Sagawa. We met briefly last evening."

Zoe's smile was tentative, but she admired the woman's no-nonsense manner. "I need to take a look to make sure everything is still fine." The nurse took Zoe's vital signs while Dr. Sagawa gave her a checkup. "You're in remarkable shape. I'd release you today but Dr. Lucci wants to keep your baby at least another twenty-four hours. He has some concerns about jaundice."

"Is he okay?" Zoe leaned forward, her elbows braced against the partially raised bed.

Dr. Sagawa shrugged. "Not my department. Dr. Lucci will be in when he finishes rounds." The woman looked up and blinked. Zoe felt like all the blood had drained from her face. "No, no, Zoe. I'm sorry. My bedside manner is… well, technically, the baby isn't my responsibility, but everything is fine. Dr. Lucci always errs on the side of caution." She patted Zoe's shoulder. "An abundance of it," she mumbled, then added in a normal voice, "Since the little guy came early, we just want to make sure he's healthy before we release you."

After a few more minutes, the doctor bustled out, leaving the nurse to fuss over Zoe. Five minutes later, a second nurse arrived, cradling a swaddled baby in her arms. She scanned Zoe's armband, then the baby's to make sure the microchips matched, then she helped get everyone settled for feeding.

After the semi-successful feeding, with Bugtussle napping in her arms, Zoe considered her options. She closed her eyes and scrubbed at her forehead with the heel of one hand. She needed to find a job. And a place to live. And a babysitter so she could work that job—all things she'd planned to do once she escaped and got to Nashville. Tears leaked from her eyes. She brushed them away with an angry swipe. She'd been in tight corners before. She'd fight her way out of this one.

Zoe looked down at the sleeping baby and felt the smile tugging at her lips, despite her tears. Her baby. He was perfect. And she loved him more than life.

Movement and the soft clearing of a throat jerked her attention to the doorway. Despite his care and concern, she hadn't truly expected to see Tucker or anyone else. In her experience, rich folks like them didn't get involved with people like her. Finding Deacon Tate standing there left her speechless. And embarrassed.

"May I come in?"

She nodded mutely.

He stepped closer and leaned forward to see the baby. "Good-lookin' boy," he said with a big smile.

Zoe nodded again, feeling like a bobblehead doll.

Deacon chuckled. He hooked the leg of the visitor chair with a booted foot and pulled it closer to the bed. He sat and offered her another dazzling smile. "Tucker would have been here, but he was called back to Las Vegas on an emergency."

Eyes wide, she swallowed. "Las Vegas?"

"My little brother is mostly based out of Vegas. He's in charge of the Crown Casino and Resort. Heck, Tuck has his fingers in every Barron Entertainment business. Our cousin, Chase Barron, depends on him to keep things running smoothly. But if not for whatever went down in Vegas, I'm pretty sure he'd have been camped out here all night."

Zoe jerked back against the raised bed, blinking rapidly in surprise. "Why would he do that?"

Deke laughed. "He's a Tate, Zoe. It's the way we're wired."

How should she respond to that? While she hadn't expected the Tates to stick around, she'd really hoped Tucker would. She'd pretended not to be disappointed and learning that he would have been there created all sorts of warm feelings in her chest—feelings she shouldn't feel. She hated to admit, especially to herself, that she felt safe when Tucker was there. She opened her mouth but only one word came out, breathy at that. "Okay…"

"In the meantime, we need to talk."

"We do?"

"Yes. Do you have any place to go?" Zoe lowered her eyes, unable to meet Deke's. He followed up with a second question. "Job?"

"No," she mumbled. Then her pride asserted itself. She raised her head and met his gaze dead-on. "I'll figure it out. I always do. I'm not afraid of hard work and I always pay my own way."

His smile was approving as Deke continued, "From the discussion I had with Tuck, I sorta figured that's what you'd say. Two things. First, the company has a condo. You can stay there until you get your feet on the ground." She sucked in air to protest but he cut her off with one of his devastating smiles. "No argument. The place is sitting empty as long as Tucker's in Vegas. You might as well use it. Okay?" He waited until she nodded.

"Good. Now second, there's someone I'd like you to meet." She scowled and he held up his hands, palms out, to delay her response. "He's an old friend of mine. In fact, he helped me get my first gig here in Nashville. I played your video for him."

"My video?" She was completely confused. "What video?"

"The one Kenji recorded on his cell phone yesterday. Of you and me singing." He rolled his eyes. "He might be the best drummer in Nashville but that dude is far too attached to his smartphone apps."

Heat suffused her face and she just managed to resist fanning her cheeks. "Oh?" The word came out strangled.

"Don wants to meet you. He's mostly retired these days, but there's not an agent around who understands the music business better than him." Deke paused, watching. Zoe held her breath. "I can set that up after you're released, assuming you want to be in the music business?"

She remembered to breathe and played the bobblehead again. "Oh, yes!" she exclaimed. "That's the whole reason I came to Nashville."

Five

Tucker rubbed the back of his neck in a vain attempt to ease the low-level headache throbbing behind his eyes. He'd caught a late flight from Nashville to Las Vegas, and though he'd been in first class, he remembered why he preferred the company jet to flying commercial. He walked into his office at 8:00 a.m. freshly showered but with no sleep.

Janet, the administrative assistant who served both him and Chase, rose as he entered. She paused long enough to pour him a cup of coffee, grab the bottle of acetaminophen, then followed him into his office.

"Ever the model of efficiency, Jan." He offered her a sour smile as she handed him two capsules and the coffee mug. He tossed the pills into his mouth and took a big swig.

"You're welcome, boss. Bart is on his way up."

He resisted the urge to grumble. If the security chief for the casino was up and moving this early, that meant he'd gotten even less sleep than Tucker. He'd at least been able to catch an hour's nap on the flight. Tucker tapped his finger on the back of his cell phone, debating whether to call the hospital to check on Zoe and the baby. Ridiculous thought. Why would he want to check up on them? They weren't his responsibility. Not exactly.

Except he felt like they were. He needed to find out if the baby had developed jaundice, if Zoe had slept well. Deke promised to look after them while he was out of town, though his brother had ulterior motives.

Zoe had talent. He'd heard it, had seen Deke and the band react to that impromptu concert at Bent Star. And Deke hadn't freaked out that Zoe was playing his prized Gibson guitar. That said a lot right there. He should call Deke, talk to him about Zoe. Her talent, he amended, when he realized his slacks weren't so slack anymore. Good grief. The woman had just given birth and here he was—

"Sorry to make you fly in like this, Tucker."

Tuck glared up at the man standing in front of his desk. Bart Stevens wore a hand-tailored suit that looked like it had come off the discount rack. He was as big as a football linebacker and one look made a person think cop, soldier or mafia hitman. He'd been the first two and Tucker wasn't entirely certain about the third. Bart accepted a mug from Jan then waited for her to settle in one of the guest chairs before he took the other.

"So," Tucker began. "What's the problem?"

Three hours later, he wanted to rip out his hair but it was too short. The headache had bloomed into a full-blown migraine and there weren't enough pain pills in Las Vegas to touch it. The debrief by his staff didn't take long at all. To quote one of his mother's favorite expressions, things had gone to hell in a handbasket. There were two fires to put out. The first crisis would take some hands-on negotiation. The service workers union was making threats of a work slowdown. Tucker put that one on the back burner. The second involved a major whale.

Whale was a term he wasn't overly fond of, but was the way all the casinos referred to the people who dropped big bucks on the tables. The casinos sweetened the pot with perks like free rooms, drinks and other fringe benefits but sometimes there were problems. In this instance, it seemed one of the cocktail waitresses didn't appreciate a particular whale's wandering hands. Rather than create a scene, she reported the man to the bartender who notified the manager, who then assigned a male waiter. The whale took offense. Security was called. When Tucker approached him, the whale threatened to sue. Tucker suggested he'd get bigger perks at another hotel. The jerk was still muttering insults and invectives as staff settled him into the back of the hotel's limousine and sent him down the street. Tucker turned to his security chief and banned the whale. Nobody harassed his staff like that.

Now it was back to the first crisis. The threatened walkout would take time. Which meant he'd have to stay longer in Vegas. He should have been happy about returning to his normal routine, but every time he closed his eyes, he saw a pair of warm brown eyes, a pert nose and a mouth he really wanted to kiss. It didn't help that when he rode up to his suite, he shared the elevator with a couple and their baby. He caught himself before asking if he could hold the kid. What in the world was wrong with him?

Tucker entered his suite on the penthouse floor. He glanced at his expensive wristwatch and did some quick math. Then he pulled his cell phone out and called Nashville.

Deke ducked out into the hall while a nurse helped Zoe clean up. She heard his phone ring and wondered if maybe it was Tucker. She really needed to stop thinking about him. "Your guydar is broken bad," she muttered to herself.

With some wincing and ouching, Zoe made it to the small bathroom. The nurse untied the strings on the hospital gown and helped her sit on a plastic stool. "I have some shampoo in my duffel bag," Zoe said.

"I'll get it and I'll grab one of the pretty gowns that arrived."

Twenty minutes later, Zoe was clean, and her hair—still wet—was tamed and braided. She had a touch of makeup on and wore a short shell pink nursing nightgown with a matching pink-and-white striped robe. The nurse helped her settle in bed, then opened the door. Deacon waited in the hall, looking amused. As the nurse slipped out, he walked to the bed, cell phone in hand. He punched in numbers, then handed her the phone and walked out.

"Zoe?"

She blinked at the male voice and her heart hammered for a panicked moment. Then she recognized it. Not Redmond. Not Norbert. Tucker. She exhaled in relief. "Howdy, cowboy."

"Are you okay?"

"I'm fine."

"That's…ah…good." He sounded odd, like he didn't quite know what to say and she wondered if he felt as awkward as she did. Then he added, "So…have you talked to Deke?"

"Deke?"

"Yes. About staying at the condo. I'm stuck here in Vegas for a while."

Zoe didn't understand why his staying away longer would make her sad but it did. She didn't realize until that moment that she'd been counting on seeing him. Soon. "Oh."

As if he'd picked up on how small she was feeling, Tucker's voice dropped lower and he said very gently, "I'll be back as soon as I can. Until then, please, will you stay at the condo? Deke and his wife are just next door, and he's offered his nanny's expertise."

The idea of being alone in some strange condo worried her but his last statement gave her the reassurance she needed. There'd be someone nearby to help. All she had to do was say yes. Her pride reared its head, but she smacked it across the nose with a rolled-up newspaper. She had Baby Bugtussle to think about now. She sucked in a deep breath, exhaled to ease her anxiety and said, "Okay."

"Okay?" Tucker sounded surprised…and relieved.

"Yeah, cowboy. Okay."

Zoe awoke the next morning to a nurse checking her vitals. "Is it time to feed Bugtussle again?" she mumbled.

The nurse chuckled as she stuck the thermometer in Zoe's mouth. "Good morning. And no, not quite yet. Looks like you and the baby will get to go home today."

She blinked the grit out of her eyes and noticed the weak sunlight streaming in through the window. Real morning. Not for the first time, she wished for coffee. Yeah, no love there. Not until the baby was on a bottle and food. Dang it. Zoe rubbed her face and hoped breakfast would arrive before she was discharged. This whole eating-for-two thing was playing havoc with her appetite.

A firm tap on the door interrupted her thoughts. "Yeah?" she called.

The door eased open and a pretty African American girl peeked in. "Zoe?"

"That would be me."

"Hi! I'm Keisha Selmon. I work for Deacon and Quin Tate as their nanny. Deke asked me to come by and help out." She nudged the door with her shoulder and stepped in. She had bags and bundles and a fancy baby carrier.

"Once you and the little one are discharged, I'll take you to the condo and help you get settled in. In the meantime, I'll show you how all this paraphernalia works."

Zoe snapped her mouth shut and heard the nurse *tsk*. "Your blood pressure just spiked, young lady," the woman scolded. "Just calm down. This is all good."

Nodding, Zoe tried to tally up how much she would owe everyone. As if Keisha could read her mind, she forged ahead.

"This is all good, Zoe. You need to just relax. Let some nice people do nice things for you. Trust me. Deacon and Quin do stuff like this all the time. And don't even get me started on the Bee Dubyas."

"The what?"

Keisha laughed and fluttered her hand as if waving away any explanation. "You really don't want to know. Suffice it to say that I work for some very nice people who can and will help others. You're in a tight spot so they're helping." She deposited everything on the chair but one bag. "Quin and I guessed on sizes. If the jeans are too big, there's a belt. I hope you have shoes. We didn't want to take a chance guessing the size on those."

An hour later, after the doctors checked Zoe over and gave the baby a clean bill of health, a nurse came in to help her dress. Surprisingly, everything fit, and the baby looked darling in a onesie decorated with embroidered cowboy boots and guitars. She could only guess who chose that outfit.

She settled into the wheelchair the nurse insisted she ride in, then smiled as Keisha handed the baby to her.

"The guys are waiting to box all this stuff up, Zoe, and they'll take it to the condo for you," Keisha said, gesturing at the flowers, balloons and stuffed animals that filled the room. "I suggest that you pick out maybe a couple of plants and a flower arrangement or two, then let the nurses spread the rest around?"

Zoe gave a distracted nod, then said, "Uh…the guys?"

"The guys in the band. They've been talking nonstop about you and the baby. When Tucker called Deacon for volunteers, they fell all over themselves wanting to help." Keisha glanced around as if someone might be eavesdropping before leaning closer. "Tucker is driving Deacon nuts. He can't get away from whatever is happening in Vegas and he calls all the time, wanting updates." She deepened her voice. "Is the condo ready? Did you babyproof it? Is there food?" She straightened and rolled her eyes. "That man, I swear."

When Zoe had finished with the discharge paperwork, a nurse wheeled her and the baby out of the hospital. Keisha waited beside a silver SUV idling under the covered portico at the medical center's door. The base for the carrier was already installed in the back seat. Keisha showed her how it all worked and once the baby was in place, the nanny helped Zoe into the SUV beside the baby. Dillon Tate turned around from the driver's seat.

"You ready, sugar?"

For the first time in ages, Zoe didn't feel weighed down by the world. She flashed a grin at Tucker's youngest brother. "Ready and willin'."

Zoe flicked her attention between the baby and the scenery passing outside the window. The university campus gave way to a mixed-use area of shops, restaurants and residential. The SUV stopped at a stop sign and Dillon hit the left-turn signal. She leaned over the baby seat to stare out the passenger side window at a park with a large, Greek-inspired building in the center. "Is that the Parthenon?" She'd read about it—and everything else about Nashville she could get her hands on.

"That would be it," Dillon agreed. He turned left onto Parthenon Avenue and drove a block. "Here we are. I'll go around the block so you can see the place from the front."

She sucked in a breath a few moments later as he pointed to a group of town houses. The corner unit was a huge, white granite edifice that echoed the Parthenon's Greek influences. There was a smaller, brick unit that looked sort of English on the right.

"The brick condo is where you'll be staying. Believe it or not, the Greek thing on the corner belongs to Deacon." He circled the block then turned down a paved alley. Stopping at an iron gate, he hit a clicker button on the visor and the gate swung open so he could drive through.

After parking in the private garage, Dillon helped her out and then showed her how to release the carrier. He winked and admitted, "I practiced all last night to make sure I could do it right and not jostle Junior here."

She stiffened as her heart did a funny lurch in her chest. Her baby would never be a junior—especially not a junior Tate. That said, he still needed a name. She was mulling over names as Dillon, still holding the carrier, ushered her and Keisha into an elevator. Who had elevators in their houses?

When the doors opened, they stepped out into a hallway. Dillon pointed toward the front of the house. "That's the master suite." Zoe held her breath then released it with a relieved huff when he pointed in the opposite direction. "That's the largest guest room. It has a private bath. C'mon."

He led the way and when he opened the door, all she could do was stand there and stare. If this was a guest room, the master suite must be magnificent. The queen-size bed was covered in a downy coverlet the color of a favorite pair of denim jeans. The head-and footboards were the color of aged barnwood and the walls were polished stucco the color of parchment. Where there'd once most likely been a sitting area, someone had set up a crib, rocking chair and baby accoutrements.

Dillon put the carrier down on the bed and scrubbed at the back of his head. "I have no clue what 90 percent of this stuff is. I hope the store left the instruction booklets."

Turning around in a slow circle, her arms outstretched, Zoe fought the tears burning in her eyes. "Who did all this?"

He flashed her a dimpled grin, looping an arm around Keisha's neck. "Tucker, of course. Well…sort of. He got the list from the Bee Dubyas, called the baby store, and told them to deliver and set everything up."

"Tucker did this?" She stared at Dillon and Keisha.

Dillon stared back. "Well…yeah."

Six

Resisting the urge to throw the computer against the far wall took far more effort than it should have. Tucker read the information scrolling across the monitor with a jaundiced eye. Someone was stirring up the union against several Barron properties. And someone else—or perhaps the same someone—had tried to block building permits necessary for two different Barron projects. He'd sent the info to Chase, along with Chance Barron, the family legal eagle, and to his brother Bridger and Cash Barron at Barron Security for further investigation.

Tucker grabbed the mug at his elbow and took a swig. Sputtering, it was all he could do not to spit cold coffee all over the keyboard. He caught the smirk Janet didn't hide in time. "I hate cold coffee," he groused.

Without a word, his very efficient assistant snagged the mug, emptied it in the sink on the coffee bar across the room, poured him a fresh cup and returned to set it carefully at his elbow before she settled one hip on the corner of his desk.

"Wanna tell me why you're in such a foul mood, boss man?"

"No." Okay, he sounded as pouty as a teenager. He wasn't sulking. Much. He didn't want to be here in Vegas. He wanted to be in Nashville. He glanced up to find Janet staring down at him.

"Gotta be a woman."

He pushed away from the desk, leaned back in his chair and challenged her with a quirked brow. "And how did you come to that conclusion?"

"C'mon, boss. You know this place is a rumor mill. Besides, ENC already has an online spread with pictures of you at the hospital in Nashville."

Tucker dropped his head and closed his eyes. The Entertainment News Channel could be a real pain in his ass—unless he was the one manipulating the stories. He'd have to get Barron Entertainment's PR department to start damage control. Pinching the bridge of his nose, he glanced up. "How bad is it?"

Janet shrugged. "Pictures don't show much. A woman on a gurney holding something in her arms all bundled up. You climbing out of the ambulance looking shell-shocked. Pictures taken in the waiting room of Deacon and the band with flowers and balloons—pink *and* blue. Which was it, by the way?"

"Boy."

"You want to explain who the girl is?"

He started to say "nobody," but that wasn't true. Zoe Parker was somebody. And so was her baby. His chest tightened as he remembered looking down into the baby's eyes that first time. Tucker wasn't one to willingly explore feelings. They were fine for everyone else and he was more than happy to offer advice to his brothers and cousins. But when it came to him personally? Nope. "She's a singer Deacon was auditioning, and she went into premature labor."

"Uh-huh." Janet wore a dubious look that said loud and clear she didn't believe him for a minute. "So why were you in the ambulance with her?"

Why had he been in the ambulance with her? Oh yeah, because he'd been hovering and the EMT mistook him for the father. Yeah, that bit shouldn't get out. Because he wasn't the father. And he didn't have feelings for Zoe. Or her baby. Except…maybe he did.

"I…she didn't want to ride alone. No one expected the baby to come as fast as he did."

Laughing, Janet stood up. "I can see it now. You sittin' there wringing your hands, saying over and over you know nothing about birthing babies."

He would have laughed along except he'd pretty much been thinking that at the time. "Shut up, Janet. Don't you have real work to do or something?"

"Or something." She sashayed to the office door where she paused and glanced back over her shoulder in a dramatic gesture. In a purely fake Southern accent, Janet announced, "After all, tomorrow is another day."

"Shut the door behind you," Tucker growled. Tomorrow *was* another day—another day he didn't want to be here. He needed to be back in Nashville and that was messed up beyond belief.

He swiveled his desk chair so he could gaze out the window. The view wasn't all that great as they were only on the fourth floor, but it beat staring at the walls of his office. What was it about Zoe Parker that drew him like a hungry man to a T-bone steak? She wasn't beautiful. She was cute and quirky. She had Dolly Parton's sense of style. Which was cute and quirky. She was a single mother—a cute and quirky single mother, and when her son had stared up at him with those big, luminous blue eyes, Tucker had fallen hard. He totally understood Deacon now. When a baby had been left on Deke's tour bus with a note claiming he was the father, his big brother had fallen for the angelic baby named Noelle, even though he wasn't her father. Deke married Quin, the Oklahoma Highway Patrol officer assigned to the case, and they'd adopted her.

Business. Tucker needed to keep his thoughts on business. He couldn't get back to Nashville until he cleared his desk here in Vegas. Damn. He was in so much trouble.

Tucker swiveled back to his desk and snatched the phone receiver. With the first call, he requested that the company plane be ready to fly him to Nashville at a moment's notice. The second call went straight to his brother Bridger.

"What's up, Tuck?"

"Did you get my email about the stuff going on with the union and those permits?"

"Sure did. Cash has called a meeting. Can we patch you in via the closed-circuit link?"

"Set it up with Janet. In the meantime, I have something else I want you to check out, little bro."

Zoe didn't breathe for a minute. Asleep. She'd been asleep. Something woke her. Where was she? Heart beating as fast as a hummingbird's, she forced air into her lungs. She sat up and peered through the twilight filling the room. She heard a small hiccupping cry and her breasts were suddenly swollen. The baby was awake, and hungry. They were in Nashville. In the guest room at Tucker's condo. Safe.

Shadows lurked in the corners of the room though streetlights sparkled outside. She caught the faint hum of traffic but no other sounds. Rolling off the bed, she reached into the crib and gathered her baby into her arms. Zoe nuzzled the dark fuzz on his head as she settled onto the comfortable rocking chair and got him situated so he could nurse. She hummed softly as she watched the city lights through the window.

A sense of peace settled around her and her nonsensical hum began to form a melody. She drifted along, everything right in her world. Then the door creaked open and part of a face peered at her. Zoe let out a scream and scrambled to her feet, looking for a weapon.

"Whoa!" a familiar voice said. "Easy, there. It's just me, Zoe."

She collapsed into the rocker, her mouth dry and her heart galloping. "Don't scare a body like that, Tucker!"

"I'm sorry. It's late. I thought you'd be asleep. I just wanted to check on you."

She inhaled, glad the room was dark as she got herself put back together. Still hungry, the baby nuzzled in. She cuddled him, all the while watching the very handsome man standing in the doorway.

"Didn't expect you back." She hadn't but now that he was? Her heart was still beating fast but for an entirely different reason. "But I gotta say I'm glad. Ramblin' around in this big ol' house alone is…" She lost her train of thought as he came into the room and stood staring down at her. She patted her hair, the gesture self-conscious. "I must look a fright."

"No," he said, his voice husky. "You look…" He swallowed and smiled. "You look just fine, Zoe."

They stared at each other for a long moment then he cleared his throat. "I guess I should let you two get back to sleep."

"Yeah, it is sorta late an' all."

Tucker backtracked toward the door but then paused. "Are you hungry?" he blurted out, then hastily added "I picked up some stuff for sandwiches on my way in from the airport. Or I can order takeout. You know, if sandwiches don't appeal."

Her stomach grumbled, and she giggled. "I suppose I might be. A sandwich sounds just fine."

"Do you need any help?" He stepped closer.

Zoe patted the baby's bottom and smiled. "He'll be full in a minute. If you can grab that carryall thing, I'll just get Bugtussle settled when he's done and then we can head down to the kitchen."

Tucker didn't move. He just stood there and stared, as if transfixed by the scene.

"Tucker?"

He startled when she said his name. "Yeah. Carrier. I'm on that."

A few minutes later, Zoe sat on a leather and wrought-iron stool watching Tucker preparing sandwiches on the other side of the high bar separating the dining area from the kitchen. The baby cooed in the carrier and gurgled at her when she reached over to tickle his toes. She gave Tucker directions on building her sandwich.

He paused, squeeze bottle of mustard in his hand, and stared at her. "How are you really? Has Keisha been helping?" He squeezed out some mustard. "I know she's busy with Noelle and all. Maybe I should hire a nurse to come in for a few days."

Zoe studied him. He sounded so…something. He was at once insistent and insecure, an odd combination for this man who had the world at his fingertips. She couldn't resist saying, "Okay."

He continued talking, like he hadn't heard her. "You won't owe me anything. Despite rumors to the contrary, I can be a nice guy. Having a new baby is hard, even when there's not much to clean or look after. And…well…it seems I've sort of adopted you and—" He glanced over to the baby and frowned. "Have you decided on a name yet?" The abrupt change in subject came with a silly googly-eyed face he made at her baby. "Bugtussle Parker is just plain mean."

Zoe burst out laughing, startling both the baby and the man. "Oh, I don't know. I think it has a certain ring to it. Your brother Dillon calls him Junior." She reached over and grabbed the baby's feet, kissing them which made him coo again.

When she glanced up, the expression on Tucker's face rocked her down to her very toes. He looked like he'd been mule kicked. His gaze was full of longing, like he hungered for something he couldn't have. Had her comment about Dillon caused this response? She remembered her own reaction the first time Dillon called her son that. No, Bugtussle would never be a junior, but someday, if the two of them were lucky, he'd be the son of a good man—a man like the one fixing her a sandwich in the middle of the night because he was lonely but wouldn't admit it.

He watched the baby now and there was an inherent sweetness in his look that revealed a side to Tucker Tate she'd never expected to see. Her heart melted more than a little, despite the stern lecture she was mentally giving it. Hooking up with Tucker was wrong on so many levels. They came from different worlds. He lived in luxury and everything she owned fit in an old army duffle and her guitar case. He was a nice guy and she was the single mother of another man's baby.

Was it possible that being wrong just might be right this time? She sneaked a look at him and told herself not to hope.

Seven

Zoe did her very best not to fidget. She'd been staying at Tucker's for over a week. He'd been sweet and supportive, and she figured they were on their way to being friends if not something—nope. She was not gonna go there. She was already nervous enough.

Tucker had left for work when Deacon called to tell her about this meeting. She'd left Bugtussle with Keisha and Noelle and gotten ready.

Deacon had given her the thumbs-up when he picked her up to bring her to the Bent Star offices. She wore faded jeans, a really cool top in a Native American print that slipped off one shoulder and her lucky Ariat boots. She had her guitar, though Deacon had offered her his very sweet Gibson. She was ready. Maybe.

A knock on the door convinced her she wasn't. She sucked in a deep breath when Deacon smiled at her. "You got this, darlin'." Louder, he called, "C'mon in."

Deacon approached the other man and they shook hands. "Thanks for coming, Don. I'd like to introduce you to Miss Zoe Parker."

The agent looked to be in his seventies, with a shock of silver hair and a trimmed mustache. He walked over to Zoe and offered his hand. "Don Easley," he said.

Laughing, Deke added, "Most people know him as Dandy Don Easley."

Zoe's heart skipped a beat. *That* name she recognized. Dandy Don had guided some of the biggest names in country music for almost fifty years.

"I'm very pleased to meet you, Mr. Easley."

"Deke here tells me you can sing a little."

Her gaze darted between them, but she managed a slight tuck of her chin in the affirmative and a mumbled, "A little."

"Since we're in a recording studio, I'd like to hear you in person, as well as maybe lay down a track or two?" He glanced at Deacon and received a nod. "Wanna sing something for me?"

Voice frozen in her throat, Zoe figured her eyes must be the size of half-dollars. Deacon urged her to the stool sitting in front of a microphone and handed her the Martin D35 acoustic guitar she'd scrimped and saved for ages to buy. It was old and battered but still played sweet. She sat, settled the guitar in her lap and riffed a few chords.

"What would you like me to sing?" she asked without looking up.

"Let's do something vintage," Mr. Easley said. "Give me a little Dolly?"

Her fingers automatically found the chords for "Jolene." Her voice didn't have the distinct tonal qualities of Dolly's, but she could do a fair job with the song. She sang the first verse and chorus and when no one stopped her, she transitioned to Reba McEntire's "Fancy." After a couple of verses, Zoe's grin turned wicked as she plucked the opening to Miranda Lambert's "Gunpowder and Lead."

By the time she finished, the sound studio's control room was clogged with people, all listening. The last chord still hung in the air when the applause started. She searched the faces lining the window but didn't find the one she was looking for. She pretended not to be disappointed that Tucker wasn't there.

Zoe was pretty sure her blush ran all the way to the roots of her hair, but she didn't care. Her cheeks hurt from the big smile she wore and the approval on both the face of the country music star and the old man who'd started a whole bunch of careers had her blinking away unshed tears of happiness.

"Dang, darlin'." Mr. Easley sighed happily. "You an' me are gonna do some good things."

Over the course of the next hour, she explained her situation, including the fact she owed Tucker a bunch of money. Don eyed Deke, who hastened to explain. "My brother guaranteed her medical bill."

"And why would he do that?"

Deke grinned and Zoe wondered at the twinkle in his eye. "Because the EMTs mistook him for the daddy and bein' a Tate, he stepped up."

Mr. Easley, who insisted she call him "Don," didn't blink an eye at that. After she explained her daddy had raised her to respect her elders, so it would have to be either Mr. Easley or Mr. Don, she went on to insist, "I gotta do this on my own talent, not because nice folks think I need a handout." Deke and the older man exchanged a look, but she kept on before they could interrupt. "I gotta pay my own way, Mr. Don. Period."

"Fine," Don agreed. "In the meantime, I have a guesthouse. The missus fixed it up when I started draggin' stray singers home. It's not fancy but it's clean. You can live in it until I make sure you earn enough to pay your way." He smiled and held out his hand. “You’ll be makin’ that soon enough, but it’ll do for the time being. We gotta deal?”

She glanced over at Deacon, wondering if she should trust any of them. “Sugar, take this part on a handshake. When Dandy Don offers a real contract, I’ll have my attorney look it over for you. Okay? Don’s not offering representation yet so he’s not taking a percentage.”

“Not yet, but darlin’, I think you’ve got a lot of talent. It won’t be easy totin’ a little one around and startin’ from scratch. I’m mostly retired, but I like to keep my hand in the game from time to time. I can give you a safe place to live if you want to move out of Tucker’s place. I can line up some gigs. None of it will rub any skin off my nose. You got talent. You show me the drive, and we’ll probably do business. Deal?”

Zoe was pretty sure her face was going to break from the huge smile. She stuck out her hand.

“Deal.”

Mr. Don didn’t waste time. After her audition yesterday, he wanted Zoe in the studio first thing this morning. She didn’t like elevators. But hauling the baby and all his paraphernalia up and down numerous flights of stairs in the condo was a struggle. Not to mention there was something far more interesting to leave her breathless besides climbing stairs.

And that something was standing there as the elevator door opened.

She sighed. Inwardly, of course. It wouldn’t do—wouldn’t do *at* all—for him to know how she felt.

Tucker Tate was just plain delicious. He could let his hair grow out but those blue eyes of his? And that little bit of scruff? She’d always been a sucker for a man who sported it. As he stood there towering over her, she felt petite. And pretty, because she was experienced enough to recognize appreciation for a woman in a man's eyes.

"Zoe." His voice was low, husky, and promised all sorts of things she wanted. Things she couldn't have. She squashed down the flicker of hope sparking in her chest. The only luck she had concerning men was bad.

She had to swallow before she said, "Tucker."

"Where you headed?"

"Bent Star. Deacon asked me to come down to the studio."

"I'll give you a ride."

Her mind went straight to a place it had no business being—and it wasn't the rodeo. She breathed out and licked her lips. His eyes lasered in on her mouth, then he leaned down. Oh, glory. Did he mean to kiss her? Her eyes drifted shut in anticipation.

"Got everything you need?" His lips almost touched hers as he spoke. All she had to do was purse hers and they'd be kissing. Then she felt the weight of the baby carrier lifted from her hand.

Zoe opened her eyes. Tucker was standing back, holding the carrier, and dang the man but he was grinning like he knew how hard her heart was pounding. She curled her lip in a little snarl. "I need to get my guitar. It's in the livin' room."

He slipped the diaper bag from her shoulder. "I'll put the kiddo in my car."

When they got to the Bent Star offices, Don Easley was waiting and without a backward glance hustled Zoe away. Tucker disappeared with the baby, still in his carrier. She was waved into the sound booth where Deacon and the band waited. Four grueling hours later, they broke for lunch. She was hoarse and gulped down the large glass of ice water the sound engineer handed her.

"Gotta say, sugar," he said with a grin. "You've got a distinctive voice."

She wasn't sure if that was a good thing or a bad thing. She was still considering the implications when Tucker arrived.

"Your boy's fussing. I changed him so I figure he's hungry and that's something I can't do."

Wait. What? Tucker *changed a dirty diaper?* She was speechless as he ushered her to his office. A woman about her age was walking the floor with the baby on her shoulder. Tucker's secretary, Zoe figured, and she looked so relieved Zoe had to smile.

About twenty minutes later, when she walked out of Tucker's private office with a full and happy baby, the man himself was waiting.

"I'll take you to lunch."

As they hit the front door, she added those to her list of famous last words. They stepped out into a yelling throng of paparazzi.

"Who's the girl, Tucker?"

"Tucker, is that your baby?"

"You gonna marry your baby momma, Tucker?"

The warm fuzzy moment of sizzle and almost kissing they'd shared that morning dissipated in the jumble of cameras. She'd been crazy. Crazy to dream about a singing career. And crazier to dream that something might be simmering between her and the handsome executive who was propelling her back inside the building.

Don Easley stood in the foyer, hands fisted on his hips. "Well, that settles it." He glared at Tucker as if that mob outside was all his fault. "They know where you live cuz Deacon lives right next door. Zoe's movin' into my guesthouse." Tucker opened his mouth like he planned to argue but Don cut him off. "No arguments, boy. Rosemary n'me, we'll take care of her and the little nipper."

"But—" Zoe began, only to be interrupted.

"No arguments. I've been handlin' the paparazzi longer than you—" Don stabbed a finger at Tucker "—or you have been alive."

Tucker's expression turned stubborn, but Don swept his arm out, encompassing the entrance. "You wanna live with all that commotion right outside your door? I know Deacon dang sure doesn't."

Zoe saw the moment Tucker capitulated. Maybe he was tired of having her and the baby underfoot. Maybe he wanted his life back.

"Fine." Tucker bit out the one word.

And that was that. Zoe's heart sank. Yeah, so much for pipe dreams. Especially that almost kiss.

Eight

Zoe pushed a heavy fall of hair over her shoulder as she nervously picked out a tune on the strings of her guitar. She sat in the dark hallway at the back of Calamity's waiting for her turn to sing. Mr. Don hadn't wasted any time in getting her this gig. Granted, it was only an open mic night, but he'd gotten her on the bill so she was guaranteed a spot. He appeared beside her, a big smile on his face.

"No reason to be nervous, sugar. Have you decided what to sing? You've got two numbers."

She tilted her head, thinking hard. "Is it better to do covers instead of my original stuff?"

Mr. Don rubbed his chin. "That's a good question, girl. I think for t'night, yeah. Do one up-tempo number to get 'em stirred up and then follow with a ballad. Got any ideas?"

Zoe let her fingers wander through some chords as she considered her options. The singer currently on the stage was doing his best to cover a Toby Keith song. That was chancy at best because Toby Keith was one of a kind. Whatever she did, she'd have to make sure her distinct talent shone through. She grinned. "I have a couple of ideas. I'll wait to decide once I'm out there and can gauge the audience."

The singer finished to lackluster applause, and he shuffled off the stage. Yup, she would have to bring out the big guns tonight. She wiped her sweaty palms on the short jean skirt she wore and stood up. The pregnancy hadn't affected her legs and the uppers on her favorite pair of boots climbed all the way to her knees. She'd opted for a loose top with some fringe on the bottom and a wide neck that dipped over her right shoulder when she strummed the guitar.

She moved to the edge of the stage, waiting while the announcer did his spiel. Mr. Don patted her shoulder. "Sing your heart out, girl. I'll be in the front row cheerin' you on." With that, he slipped away.

"Calamity's is pleased to welcome a newcomer to our fine stage tonight," the MC announced. There were some groans from the audience. On open mic night, that could mean a singer like the guy preceding her. She'd just have to prove them wrong. "Put your hands together for Zoe Parker."

A few people clapped enthusiastically, and she figured it came from Mr. Don's table. Plastering a big smile on her face, she strode onto the stage and slung her guitar behind her while she adjusted the microphone.

"Hey, y'all," she said, her voice husky. "I'm mighty pleased to be here tonight. We got any rednecks out there?" She lifted her hand to shade her eyes against the glare of the stage lights and surveyed the room. Zoe got a few whistles and yells as she pulled her guitar back into position to play. "We got any redneck women out there?" And before anyone could respond, she launched into Gretchen Wilson's rollicking "Redneck Woman."

By the end of the first stanza, she had the entire room eating out of her hand. When she got to the part in the second chorus asking for redneck girls in the audience to respond, they did with a big, "Hell, yeah!"

Zoe finished the song to screams, whistles, stomping feet and thunderous applause. She found Mr. Don in the audience, with his ear-to-ear grin, and choked as she recognized the other people at his table—Deacon Tate with a pretty woman tucked against his side, the rest of the Sons of Nashville, some with dates, some solo. And there, standing and whistling with his fingers between his lips was Tucker. Her heart lurched.

Her fingers plucked at the strings, almost of their own volition, and the crowd settled down. She knew the song she wanted to sing but Dierks Bentley's "Black" was a little too sexy for the situation because she did not need to be thinking those kinds of thoughts about Mr. Tucker Tate. Her left hand found the correct chords and she played the opening measure for Little Big Town's "Better Man" instead.

She did her best to let her gaze roam across the crowd, stopping and holding the eyes of an audience member as she would normally. Tonight wasn't normal. Tonight, her gaze kept lingering on Tucker. The song didn't fit him. The words spoke of love lost, of families divided, of emotional damage done in the name of that most elusive of emotions. But she couldn't help wondering just what kind of man he was. The words of the song spoke to her—mostly. She'd never been married, and she'd never truly been in love. Mainly because she had lousy luck and no sense of self-preservation when it came to the men she picked.

Tucker Tate was Armani suits and she was Daisy Dukes. He was aged bourbon and she was cheap beer. She almost missed a chord as her thoughts became the words to a song and matched with notes in her head. She needed to get off the stage so she could write the song down before it fluttered away. Pride, she reminded herself. She needed to show some and start living her life. She didn't need a man to take care of her. She never had. Never would. It didn't matter that Tucker was sitting there handsome as all get-out, those deep blue eyes of his watching her every move with a hungry look in them.

The hardest thing she'd ever done was pack up and move but Mr. Don was right. She couldn't live under the same roof with Tucker. Which was a dang shame. For that couple of weeks, she'd forgotten to be lonely.

That man was gonna be trouble and she needed to steer clear. She had a baby to raise—and she loved him with all her heart. Baby Bugtussle would always come first. But to take care of him, she needed a career, not just a job, and in between all that, she had a life to live. A life that didn't have room for a rich man with pretty blue eyes and a mouth that the devil himself would be jealous of. Tucker was a better kind of man, one that women would want to love. She couldn't afford to lose her heart.

Then he smiled at her.

Tucker had groused all the way downtown. He did *not* want to sit surrounded by the noise and crush of Calamity's. It was open mic night. He had things to do—like harassing the PR Department to work harder at quelling the rumors so the paparazzi would leave him and Zoe alone.

When he, Deacon and Quin arrived, the Sons of Nashville were already occupying a table just to the right of the stage. Pitchers of beer and mugs, baskets of pretzels and buckets of peanuts littered the crowded table. A couple of the guys had dates but they'd still managed to scrounge four extra chairs. Tuck eyed his brothers, wondering if they'd set him up with a blind date. Dillon was especially prone to doing so. Kenji filled three mugs with beer and passed them to the newcomers.

Quin's hands went to the neckline of her shirt. She fussed for a second then pulled out a Day-Glo orange hearing protector. She fitted the earplugs on the end of the band into her ears. Smart. He tapped her on the shoulder and pointed.

"Got any more of those?"

She laughed but shook her head. "You guys are on your own. I made the mistake of coming here when Deke decided to play one night. The noise level was insane."

Tucker rolled his eyes as he flashed her a thumbs-up. Deke was prone to do that. Toby Keith had a restaurant in Bricktown—the entertainment district near downtown Oklahoma City. Like Toby and other entertainers, Deke and the Sons had shown up there unannounced and played on more than one occasion. The locals and tourists alike lived for those moments. He wondered, since the whole band was here, if they had something planned for Calamity's.

The first act, a quartet, did decent covers of two Oak Ridge Boys songs. The second, a kid who looked to be about twelve, had trouble with his voice breaking. Ah, the joys of puberty. The third guy tried to imitate Keith and since there was and could be only one Toby, the natives were growing restless. As the announcer took the stage, Tucker looked up when Dandy Don Easley slid into the chair next to him. That could mean just one thing. Tucker sat up, his whole body vibrating.

He'd stayed away from Zoe for the two days since she'd moved into the Easleys' guesthouse, convincing himself that dropping by to check up on her and bring food would alert the paparazzi to her location. They'd been two of the longest days in his life. That first night, he lasted three hours. Then he camped out at Deacon and Quin's, playing with Noelle, and rummaging in their fridge for food. He wouldn't admit the empty condo bugged the hell out of him. Good thing Deacon had bought the town house on the other side for the band. Last night, Quin had sent him next door to hang out with them.

Tucker wouldn't admit he missed Zoe and the baby, but here he was, leaning toward the stage impatient to see the woman he spent far too much time thinking about. The announcer introduced her and his chest got tight. The table erupted with applause and encouraging cheers, but Tuck knew the audience here at Calamity's. They hadn't been too thrilled with the last guy and now here was Zoe, a newcomer to the scene. *He* knew she could sing but these other loudmouths didn't. Would they settle down and give her a chance?

Zoe stepped to the microphone and Tucker forgot everything. When she launched into her first song, he felt it all the way down deep. The place went wild. She strummed that guitar and belted out the lyrics, owning the stage, the audience…and him. He was in so much trouble.

When she rolled over into "Better Man," he surrendered. He might as well carve out his heart and hand it to her on a silver platter because every time her eyes fell on him, she made him want to be the man she wanted, the man she needed. Which was just crazy. Love at first sight didn't happen. Despite what his mom said. She was convinced that each of her boys would meet the right woman and know immediately that she was the one. He glanced over at Quin and Deke. Their chairs sat side by side and his brother had one arm draped over her shoulders. They held hands and as he watched, they looked into each other's eyes, smiled and exchanged a soft kiss.

That was love. Real love. Deep love. The kind of love that a man found once in his life if he was the luckiest son of a gun around. His parents had that kind of love. And his cousins had found it. Deke had it. Tucker was all about business. Since Chase married Savannah, Tucker was all but running Barron Entertainment. He didn't have time for love. But being around Zoe and the baby? *Nope.* He stuffed those thoughts down deep, to be ignored. He would help her out but that was all.

He pulled his gaze away from the couple and focused once more on the stage. Surrounded by lights, Zoe all but glowed up there. Her hair fell in a long, soft wave and her bare shoulder peeked out from behind the silken curtain. He wanted to kiss that shoulder. And her neck. Her mouth. Her nose. He wanted to kiss her in far more intimate places, and he didn't give a flip that she was a new mother. Except he had to. She was vulnerable and too easy to take advantage of. Business. She needed to be business, not pleasure. Good thing he didn't have time to get involved with anyone, much less her.

She played the crowd like a pro, but her eyes returned to him time and again. His heart did weird things in his chest each time her gaze fell on him. The song was almost over, and she looked like she was living every word of the lyrics. He smiled at her. And something in her eyes gave him pause. Tucker needed to slam the brakes on. So what if he'd gotten used to having her—and her baby—around? Big deal. He traveled. A lot. He didn't want an anchor. He glanced around the table. Deacon and the band wanted him to sign her to Bent Star. She had a lot of talent. Another reason to stop his brain—and maybe his heart—from going places neither had any business being. He was a businessman. And he needed to keep things between them professional. So that's what he'd do. Period.

Then the song ended and the place erupted in cheers and whistles, hard applause and stomping boots. Everyone came to their feet. Zoe remained on the stage looking stunned. The announcer joined her, but the crowd didn't settle down, not even when he held up his hands for silence. They wanted more. For a fleeting second, Tucker felt sorry for the entertainer scheduled next. That's when he realized Deacon and the boys were on their feet and moving to the stage. He didn't think it possible for the noise level in the room to increase but it went up a hundred decibels.

Tuck chanced a quick glance at Quin. She sat, smug smile and ear protection firmly in place. She'd known. This wasn't some impromptu gig. Deke had planned it. Quin caught his eye and winked, then patted the chair beside her. He sank onto it, knowing now that the show was far from over. Zoe Parker was the new princess of the Nashville country music scene.

When the impromptu concert ended, Zoe, Deacon and the band disappeared backstage. Tucker ushered Quin, Don and the band's dates through the crowd. Quin and the girls rushed into the packed hallway to connect with their significant others. Tucker stood back, observing. Zoe, surrounded by people, positively glowing. She looked up and her gaze fell on him. Her face lit up like a Christmas tree and suddenly, she was flying toward him. She leaped. He caught her. And then their mouths clashed. Her legs circled his waist and he held her with one hand cupping her butt, the other the back of her head so he could control the kiss.

Time passed—seconds or minutes. Tucker wasn't sure. Then sound returned. Laughter. The buzz of conversation. Reality intruded, hitting him and Zoe at the same time. She unhooked her ankles. He loosened his grip. She slid to stand with both feet on the scuffed floor. Neither spoke and then she was gone, pulled into the group by Don, who was shouting over the hubbub. Tucker took a step back, astonished at what had just happened. That kiss had been… he didn't have the words. But watching Zoe walk away? He had a word for that. *No.*

Tucker stared at her retreating form. He wanted to hear her voice. He wanted to see her even more. Touch her. And that was just…no. Too many complications. He wanted to sign her to a record contract. He wanted to kiss her again. He wanted…

"I'd give a hundred bucks to know what you're thinking," Deacon said as he approached. "You know I can read you like a book, Tucker. You want to go after her."

"Oh yeah? If you're so sure of that, why did you offer me a hundred?"

"Conversation starter. Why don't you ask her out on an actual date?"

He considered the various answers he could offer as justification—all the ones he'd been debating in his own head. "She's vulnerable."

Deke leaned his elbow against the wall beside Tucker's head and stared at him with an amused expression. "How so?"

"Seriously? You really have to ask?" Tucker held up a finger. "For one, she's all alone in Nashville. Two, she wants to be a singer. Three, she's a single mom. Four—"

"You like her and are attracted," Deacon interrupted. "There's nothing wrong with that. And…" He held up a finger. "She's not alone. Don Easley is looking out for her. Two, she *is* a singer, she just needs help with her career. Three, so what? I've seen you look at that baby, Tucker. The kid owns you." His grin was astute as he added, "I know that feeling well. I felt the same way about Noelle."

"Four," Tucker persisted, "she thinks she needs to pay me back and she's made it abundantly clear she wants to make it on her own. Five, business doesn't mix with pleasure. Refer back to number two."

"Mixing business and pleasure worked fine for cousin Clay. And Cash." Deke shrugged. "And technically, for me."

"It's complicated."

Deke burst out laughing. "Of course it is. We're Tates, little bro. If we didn't complicate things, we'd be..." He laughed again. "Well, not Barrons, because our cousins have *complicated* hardwired into their DNA."

"So you're blaming Mom for this?" Tucker tried hard to hide a smirk.

"Not goin' there. You saw how she was with Quin and Noelle. And you know there's a reason we call our irritating little brother Dill Pickle. He's probably called and told her everything. Do us all a favor? Just take her out. Get Zoe out of your system if it's only an attraction. If it's more, you'll know, and we'll all deal with it." Deacon straightened and patted his brother on the shoulder. "Just get a move on, Tuck. At the very least, I'd like her to open a few of our upcoming concerts. If you aren't going to date her, sign her. If you *are* going to date her, still sign her. She needs to understand that her talent and your horniness are not mutually exclusive."

Tucker heard his big brother laughing all the way down the hall as he rejoined the band and Zoe's fans who'd made their way backstage. He'd never been affected like this by a woman. Zoe slipped through all the cracks in the wall he threw up between them. Because she *was* business. She'd be a phenomenal addition to Bent Star's lineup of singers. He'd be a bad businessman if he didn't sign her. But he really, *really* wanted the pleasure of getting to know her better.

For the past three weeks, Zoe had pretended that she hadn't thrown her arms around Tucker Tate and kissed him in the aftermath of her successful debut at Calamity's. She'd pretended even harder that he hadn't kissed her back. Of course, the jerk hadn't called either—not that she was paying attention to whether he did or not, because she wasn't. Nope.

"We don't need a man in our lives, do we, Bugtussle?" The sleepy baby yawned and stared up at her with big eyes. She made big eyes back. "Our lives are full and you know it."

That was true. She had a gig at Calamity's playing a full set two nights a week and was hitting up other clubs for open mic nights. Money wasn't pouring in, but she was making enough to save up for a used car and put money in her Pay Tucker Back Fund. She'd splurged and bought a cell phone, and texted the number to Tucker...because. He'd texted back a quick Thanks. Her jumbled feelings for the dang man hadn't been helped when her doctor pronounced her healed at her six-week appointment.

"What's that mean, exactly?" she'd asked.

She blushed when Dr. Sagawa explained Zoe could "start dating" though not in those exact words. Zoe had insisted that she had absolutely no intention of getting involved with a man. Any man. Period. The doctor simply smiled in the way that doctors did, recognizing BS when she heard it. Of course, the only man who might get her stirred up was Tucker Tate, but he obviously wanted to keep things strictly business.

Despite that kiss. Hang the man. Why didn't he call?

Her cell phone chose that moment to dance across the tabletop, and she snatched it just as it tumbled over the edge. She had it on vibrate because the baby was sleeping. "Hello?" she answered, her voice a husky whisper.

"Zoe?"

"Yeah?"

"It's Tucker. You sound... Is everything okay?"

She knew who it was the moment he said her name. Her heart pounded with excitement. Stupid thing. He was just calling to check up on her. That's all. "The baby's asleep. Trying not to wake him."

"Oh." He sounded…hesitant?

Silence. She waited.

"Are you working tonight?"

Is that why he was calling? "No." Now she sounded hesitant.

"Would you like to go out?"

"Out?"

"Yes. Like…out. To dinner or something."

"Like a…date?" She held her breath.

"Yeah…sort of."

"What does that mean? A sorta date?" She glowered at the phone then realized she could hear Tucker breathing. Hard.

"I'm messing this up. I've been…thinking about you."

Uh-huh. Was he thinking about her like she'd been thinking about him? All tangled sheets, sweaty bodies and wet kisses? She reminded herself to breathe.

"I've been thinking things over. And, well…" He didn't finish his thought. She waited. "I've stayed away because of the paparazzi and I had to take care of some stuff out of town, but… I'd like to get to know you better, Zoe. And I want to…"

Want to what? Kiss her again? Like she wanted to kiss him?

"Dinner. I want to take you to dinner."

She snarled a soft *grrr*. Of course he wouldn't mention jumping her bones. Tucker was a gentleman. "Tonight?"

"Yes."

"I don't have a babysitter," she blurted. Don's wife, Rosemary, watched the baby when Zoe played in the clubs and the rest was momma and Bugtussle time.

"I have one. Deacon and Quin are going out and taking Noelle with them. Keisha agreed to babysit for us."

Breathless, she asked, "What time?"

"Now?"

Zoe glanced at the black-and-white cartoon cat clock tacked to the wall. "Now?" she squeaked. "It's only three o'clock."

"Well, yeah. But I have a surprise for you and…well… can I come pick you up?"

She calculated how much time she'd have to get ready and tried really hard not to read more into Tucker's invitation. After virtually ignoring her for weeks, here he was asking her out. What was the right thing to do? Her head was adamant. *Don't go down this rabbit hole.* Her heart? Her heart answered before she could think too hard. "Sure."

"See you in about twenty minutes."

Her phone went dead. Zoe was tempted to bang her head on the table. She was now officially, certifiably crazy. Twenty minutes? She squawked, leaped up and charged to the bedroom.

True to his word, Tucker arrived twenty-one minutes later. She'd counted them off as she frantically dressed, fussed with her hair and makeup, and got the baby ready. She was stuffing baby things into the fancy diaper bag when Tucker tapped on the door.

A few minutes later, baby and carrier were strapped into the back seat, and they were off. During the ten-minute drive, Zoe wondered if Tucker considered the condo his home because he didn't seem to spend much time there. Feeling bold, she asked, "Is Nashville home for you?"

Tucker glanced over and she caught his wry grin. "Not exactly. Barron Entertainment owns the town house."

"Then where *is* home?" This was supposed to be a date, right? And he'd said they should get to know each other.

He shrugged, keeping his eyes on traffic. "I have an

apartment in the Crown Barron Casino in Las Vegas. I spend most of my time there." He chuckled. "And I still have my room at Mom's, on our ranch near Oklahoma City."

Zoe rolled her eyes and clapped her hands to her chest. "Oh no! A momma's boy."

"Katherine Tate raised seven sons. Trust me, we're *all* momma's boys."

Tucker drove around back, entering through the secured gate to park behind the row of town houses. Keisha was waiting for them. He gestured for Zoe to remain in the car while he dealt with the carrier and diaper bag.

Zoe couldn't stay in the car. She had to get out and give her baby a kiss. "You be good for Keisha, baby boy."

"Little man and I get along just fine. Don't you worry, Zoe. Go have some fun." Keisha's curls danced in the breeze as she laughed. "Have you decided on a name yet?"

Zoe hated to admit that every name she came up with didn't feel—or sound—right. Her brain had wrapped around that whole "Junior" axle and wouldn't let go. She'd mulled over names, discarding most of them. She wondered what Tucker would say if she revealed her thoughts.

The baby cooed up at him and, with a split second of insight, Tucker now totally understood Deacon's reaction to baby Noelle and subsequent feelings for Quin. That wall he'd built between him and Zoe cracked more. He'd never intentionally buttoned up his emotions. He just didn't wear his heart on his sleeve. He wasn't wired that way. Until now, maybe. It was like he'd been living, if not in the dark, then in the shade. This woman and her baby were spreading little rays of sunshine that continuously caught him off guard. There was just something about being with Zoe that warmed him from the inside out.

In answer to Keisha's question, Zoe said, "I was thinkin' about naming him Peter."

Tucker stared at her. "Peter. Peter Parker. Like… Spider-Man?"

"Ohh. That's why the name sounded so familiar."

His jaw dropped, causing Zoe to laugh, and he caught the twinkle in her eyes. "Good one," he admitted, chuckling as well.

"Dillon suggested Rockwell Toppington Parker," Keisha informed them, perfectly straight-faced.

"My brother is—"

Zoe's laughter interrupted him. Giggling, she said, "I could call him Rocky Top for short."

The baby gurgled and kicked his legs. Tucker tightened his hold on the carrier. "Not happenin', little dude," he assured the happy child.

Zoe's expression sobered. "I'm thinking Nashville, because I want to call him Nash for short, but that's kinda stupid. I can't think of any other real name that would work."

"If you want to call him Nash, just name him that. I like it." He flashed her a grin that shaded toward sad, matching the flash of uncertainty he was feeling. "Not that it matters what I think."

Her face softened as she gazed at the baby. "Nash Parker. Plain and simple, like the kind of folks we are." Except she didn't want them to be plain and simple. She had plans. Dreams. She wanted to give her baby the best life she could—one filled with love and happiness and silly fun.

Tucker snorted. "Sugar, there is nothing plain or simple about you in any way, shape or form."

"Nashville Vanderbilt Parker," Zoe blurted out. "And the paperwork's been mailed in. I shoulda kept it simple!"

She looked…not quite panicked. Tucker immediately

moved to soothe her. “That’s quite a moniker. He’ll grow into it.”

Still looking uncertain, Zoe asked, “Are you sure it’s not…too much?”

He smiled broadly and held out a hand. “We’ve never been formally introduced. I’m Tucker Cornelius Tate.”

Nine

Zoe couldn't help rolling down the window and waving madly. Keisha, holding Nash, stood on a balcony waving goodbye. She felt odd leaving Nash with the Tates' nanny while she went off on a date. Work? No worries. But a date? Okay, it was the whole date thing that had her feeling weird.

As if sensing her mood, Tucker reached over and took her hand, giving it a gentle squeeze. "Why Nashville Vanderbilt Parker?"

She hesitated before answering, fearing her reasoning might sound dumb. "Because he was born in Nashville on the way to Vanderbilt hospital and my last name is Parker."

"And you like the name Nash," Tucker added.

Smiling in relief, she agreed. "And because I like the name Nash."

They rode in a silence that felt companionable but Zoe being Zoe, she had to chatter. "So how come we're startin' this shindig in the middle of the afternoon?"

"You deserve a break. You work hard looking after Nash and singing. I think it's time you get to do something just for you."

"Like what?" Not that she was suspicious or anything.

"Like shopping."

"Shopping? I don't have the mon—"

"But I do." They were stopped at a traffic light and he looked at her again. "You've been traveling light for a long time now, Zoe. You're putting down roots here. And you're working hard. You have a lot of talent, and Don Easley is going to showcase that. You have a unique style and that's part of your image, which goes along with your talent. We're going to hit a store I know of. There will be a personal stylist to handle things so we shouldn't be there too long. Then I'm going to take you out to dinner. We'll be home in time for Nash's bedtime feeding. Hopefully, you'll have had some fun, with the bonus of some new clothes for your wardrobe."

She plucked at a small fray in her denim skirt. Decent clothes would be nice, especially now that she *was* working. He was right about her image. Still, it felt funny to let Tucker pay for it. She began her protest. "Tucker, I don't have—"

He preempted her. "Business, Zoe. Consider this an investment in your career."

"But I don't work for you."

"Not yet." He turned his head just enough for the movement to draw her attention to him. "I want to help. No strings attached."

"I already owe you so much, Tucker." She did a quick calculation of the money she'd stuck into the Pay Tucker Back Fund. She'd managed maybe a hundred dollars. "I've always paid my own way, beholden to no one. It's simpler that way."

He dipped his head toward her and she caught sight of his crooked grin—the one that hinted at a dimple. "I know all about pride, angel. Sometimes you just need to let go and let people help you. You ever heard of a warm fuzzy?" She scowled and he laughed, grabbing her hand and squeezing it. "Let's just say that you're my warm fuzzy. I like tak— helping you out."

Zoe caught the quick shift in wording and wondered what he'd started to say. "I'm not used to people doin' things for me," she muttered.

That got a full-on laugh from him. "Coulda fooled me, darlin'! You're so gracious when anyone tries to do something nice."

She huffed out a breath and leaned away, hoping he'd get the hint. But he didn't let go of her hand. She didn't like the fizzy warmth zinging up her arm from his touch. Nope, didn't like it at all. Much. She sighed inwardly, giving in to what she really wanted to do—keep holding hands with him.

Twenty minutes later, Tucker maneuvered the SUV into a street-side parking space and came around to open her door. He helped her out and maintained a hold on her hand as he led her down the street. She stopped in front of the redbrick storefront and gaped. They were standing in front of the Cumberland Gal Boutique. Nashville's biggest music stars shopped here. She didn't move as Tucker opened the door.

"Zoe?"

"Do you know where we are?" she whispered in a reverent voice. Shopping here was the culmination of just about every fantasy she'd ever had.

"Ah, yeah. Since I drove us here."

"Tucker…" she breathed.

"Zoe…" he teased.

"Hey, y'all!" A perky blonde bounced in their direction. "C'mon in. I'm Marla. You must be Zoe." The young woman stuck out her hand and Zoe shook it. "Mr. Tate gave me an idea of what we're lookin' for today. Y'all just settle over there on that couch, and we'll bring some things out for you to see. Once you've picked out some outfits, we'll go try 'em on."

Tucker led Zoe toward the back of the store; she was so busy rubbernecking at everything she bumped into a table. She caught a stack of sweaters before they toppled and flashed a cheeky grin at Tucker.

"This place..." she murmured. The wooden floor was buffed to a soft patina. Concert posters from country music superstars were painted directly on the exposed brick walls. There were antiques and clothes and boots. Shoes and purses. Jewelry. Everything a gal with any fashion sense at all could want.

A second woman arrived, only slightly less bouncy than the first. "May I get y'all somethin' to drink? We have several nice wines, champagne, a variety of soft drinks, flavored coffees and sweet tea."

Zoe started to decline, but Tucker ordered for them both. "Mocha coffee for Ms. Parker, and I'll take my coffee black. Thanks."

She was reminded once again that Tucker missed very little. Maybe she should have been creeped out from all the stuff he remembered about her but she wasn't. Nope. Not her. She was pleased as all get-out that he knew she liked mustard and horseradish but not mayonnaise. That she liked mocha coffee and café au lait. When she could drink sodas again, it'd be Diet Coke. She liked her beef medium rare, her chicken fried, and the only fish worth eating was fried catfish. Tucker remembered all those things about her—everyday things they'd shared while living under the same roof.

Tucker urged her to sit on a love seat and then joined her. Zoe had been conscious of Marla's assessing looks. Embarrassed by her clothes and overall shape, Zoe plucked at a string unraveling from the hem of her shirt. She felt lumpy and dowdy, especially given the fashionable sales staff and customers.

Their drinks were served and a few moments after that, Marla reappeared with two others in tow, all wrangling hangers. For the next twenty minutes, Zoe was treated to a variety of outfits. Whenever she hesitated before rejecting something, Tucker told Marla to set that item aside. If not for this, she would have had only one thing to try on—a pair of jeans with rhinestones on the pockets. Now, as Marla led her back to a large dressing room, she had skirts and tops, dresses, jeans, more tops and all the accessories—boots, belts, necklaces, bracelets.

Zoe was reluctant to undress because of her post-pregnancy body. Marla ignored her hesitation. "Honey, you look pretty freakin' good for only bein' six weeks past a baby, and you don't even have a personal trainer. I picked out things that'll look good on you. Trust me, okay? This is what I do."

And she did it well, Zoe admitted. There were only two outfits she disliked so much she refused to leave the dressing room to show them to Tucker. The first outfit she modeled was a coral trapeze dress made of chiffon. Sleeveless, it floated down to just above her knees. Paired with a chunky necklace and cowboy boots with lacy cutouts, the dress made her feel almost pretty. Marla suggested a belt matching the boots. It had a large silver buckle set with coral and turquoise. Zoe walked out and the expression on Tucker's face made her want to do a celebration dance right there.

Back in the dressing room, Marla laughed. "I'd say this outfit is a keeper."

Zoe noticed things, too. Whenever Tucker's eyes lit up, that outfit went into the buy pile back in the dressing room. When she'd tried on all the clothes, there were two piles and a bunch of pieces already back on hangers. Those were the rejects and the two assistants removed them without comment. That left her with the "must have" pile and the "maybe" pile, which was at least three times bigger than the "must haves."

Marla handed her the coral dress and accessories. "You'll want to wear this for your date tonight. I know where Mr. Tate is taking you to dinner. This is perfect."

She changed into the coral chiffon as the piles, including boxes of boots, a few purses and a basketful of accessories all disappeared—as did her skirt, worn boots and the shirt she'd walked in wearing. When she emerged back into the store proper, Tucker was at the cash register. He turned, smiled and held out his hand. Before she could ask, he said, "The store delivers. We're going to dinner. I'm starved."

So was she, but the look on his face? Yeah, she'd seen that look on men's faces before. Tucker Tate looked like he wanted to eat her with a spoon. And dang if that didn't put a smile on her own face.

Romantic. That was Zoe's first thought as they pulled up in front of the historic mansion. A discreet metal sign with gold letters swung from a metal pole. The redbrick house was surrounded by an intricate wrought-iron fence. Black shutters and trim looked dramatic against the weathered brick. The valet handed her out of the passenger seat before hurrying around to the driver's side. Tucker offered his arm—which turned out to be a good thing. Zoe gawked, and paying no attention to her feet, she tripped over a step.

The Rutherford was one of those landmark restaurants, a place famous for food, service and ambiance. Zoe had added it to her bucket list after seeing it in a story on the Entertainment News Channel. She'd heard reservations were impossible and the cost of dining there equaled a week's pay for a singer like her.

She couldn't stop staring as they passed inside. Antique furniture and chandeliers caught her eye, and while she was staring wide-eyed at the walls and ceiling, she hooked the toe of her boot in the beautiful Persian rug cushioning the rich, wooden floors. Once again, Tucker came to her rescue, holding her upright and covering for her by claiming to be the clumsy one.

"So sorry, darlin'. My big feet are always trippin' me up."

As if. The dang man moved like a dancer. Or a boxer. He was all lithe grace and rhythm, each move calculated and sure. He tucked her up close to his side and she pretended not to notice the zing dancing across her skin when he touched her. She also ignored how well she fit under his arm. They should be poster children for "opposites attract" because they were definitely that. It didn't help the way he made her feel, though—all melty inside and craving his kiss. As they followed the dark-suited hostess deeper into the restaurant, she moved ahead of him but Tucker's hand remained on the small of her back, providing a warm connection.

They sat in a little nook with windows overlooking the back gardens and Zoe imagined what it might have been like when this was a house—with a family, and her as the… what? Matriarch? That word put her too much in mind of Etta Smithee and she shivered. She kept waiting for that shoe to drop, surprised it hadn't already. Leave it to Tucker to notice her reaction.

"Are you cold?" Before she could respond, he had his sport coat off and draped over her shoulders. The material carried both his body heat and his scent—a cologne that reminded her of sea spray and sand and blue skies.

Dinner…happened. All of it a blur. The beef melted on her tongue, and she didn't even fuss at the baby vegetables because some sort of tangy sauce had been drizzled over them. The jacket fell away at some point, but she was still surrounded by all things Tucker so she simply surrendered to the magnetic pull he exuded. Emotions she'd stuffed deep inside rose to the surface, and Zoe had to press her lips together to keep from blurting out her feelings. She wanted him. She wanted to be with him. Skin to skin. Heart to heart. A poet would write about their souls soaring into the heavens, joined by a love so eternal that one would not exist without the other.

She burst out laughing. She was such a romantic fool. Tucker wasn't her soul mate. He was just a guy who was mostly nice to a girl down on her luck. He didn't feel her feelings, didn't look at her like she was his only hope of breathing. Except sometimes he did, when no one was looking, when shadows danced over his face. There'd been times when she'd glance up, sometimes when she was holding Nash in her arms, and she'd catch him watching them both, his expression a mix of hunger, longing, tenderness and sorrow—like she and the baby were something he wanted but was convinced he'd never have.

Without thinking, she reached out and touched his cheek. "What are we doin', Tucker?"

"I don't have a flipping clue, angel, but I'm willing to find out. Are you?"

The truth was there on his face. He wanted her in his bed. He didn't have to say it out loud. She wasn't some naive girl blinded by the stars in her eyes. She'd told herself over and over that hooking up with another man was a bad idea, but she couldn't help herself. Didn't want to, in fact, when it came to this man.

Zoe surrendered to her own yearning. "Yeah," she murmured. "I do believe I am."

Ten

Tucker asked the waiter to box up their dessert and passed over his credit card before the bill was brought. His head was full of ideas—all the things he wanted to do to this luscious woman once he got her into bed. He might not wait that long. He could…stop right there. Business and pleasure shouldn't mix. He inhaled in hopes of reining in his thoughts. And decided he didn't care. They both wanted to explore whatever was simmering between them. When she turned to look at him, he smiled. The smile she offered in return went straight to his heart. Yeah, he was in trouble and he planned to enjoy every moment of it.

The waiter returned and Tuck signed the receipt after adding a large tip. As he moved to pull Zoe's chair back from the table, the top of her head collided with his chin, cracking his teeth together. She flushed, color climbing up her chest to her cheeks. The server had the good sense to duck his head and retreat before laughing. Tuck had to agree. The situation was pretty funny.

"Are you okay?" Zoe asked, rubbing her scalp.

Tucker worked his jaw before saying, "I'm fine. You?"

"Daddy always said I had the hardest head of anyone he knew. Guess he was right." She passed his jacket over and Tuck shrugged into it as Zoe grabbed the gold-foil bag with their boxed desserts. Taking her free hand, he led her toward the front entrance.

The valet saw them coming and darted off to retrieve the SUV. Tucker drew her hand to his mouth and dropped a light kiss on her knuckles. That's when the night exploded with camera flashes and questions.

"Are you and Zoe an item, Tucker?"

"How long have you been together?"

"Is her baby yours?"

Zoe gasped at the horde of reporters. Tucker pulled her behind him and glared. The Rutherford was now officially on his shit list. He and other Nashville celebrities dined here because the place had been discreet, but not anymore.

After Zoe moved to Don's, the media had forgotten about them. This horde had caught him flat-footed.

People blocked the street, and the valet was caught in the crowd. Tucker retreated, urging Zoe back into the restaurant with his body. The hostess had the door open, and she slammed it shut as soon as they were inside.

The manager bustled up, red-faced, wringing his hands and apologizing profusely. He escorted them through the restaurant, into the kitchen and toward the back door. A few moments later, the SUV appeared, backing into the delivery area.

Once in the vehicle, Tucker worked to contain his anger. He wanted to call Bridger and demand security for Zoe. He heard a snuffling sound coming from the passenger seat and tightened his hands on the steering wheel. If those idiots had made Zoe cry…

She pressed one hand to her mouth and her eyes glistened with tears. Tucker leaned closer, trying to decipher the sounds she was making.

"Oh, lord," she huffed out. "I don't think I'm ready for this."

Tucker made sure the area around the condo was clear before he pulled in and parked in the garage. He figured after the incident with the paparazzi, he should gather up the baby and take them to Don's guesthouse. Except he didn't want to do that. He wanted her to stay with him tonight. Wanted both Zoe and Nash under his roof where he knew they were safe. Yeah, he absolutely needed to call Bridger about security.

Keisha met them as the elevator opened onto the living room and gave her "nanny debriefing," as she called it. "Nash had an easy night, and is currently sleeping soundly. He enjoyed his bath, and should be in a dry diaper, though he's had a bottle." Her eyes twinkled as she added, "I also set up a baby monitor." Before either of them could react, she slipped away, leaving Tucker alone with Zoe.

He couldn't take his eyes off her. As she bent over the borrowed crib, he shed his jacket and draped it over the back of a barstool at the kitchen bar. He couldn't help but peek over her shoulder at the sleeping child. Being this close to Zoe, breathing in her soft cologne made him almost reckless. He cleared his throat as she straightened and turned to look at him. "Do you want to go home?"

She shook her head. "No. Not unless you're ready to get rid of me and Bugtussle here."

Never, he wanted to shout but wisely kept the thought to himself. Tonight was about…what? Seduction? A quick lay? He wanted her, yes. But he wanted her to want him just as much. If they made—no, *when* they made love, it would be a step into the future, one he could never take back.

"I'd like you to stay." When she nodded in assent, he moved away from her, asking, "Would you like something to drink?"

Her shoulder brushed his chest as she faced him, her smile almost shy. "I'm good."

And she was. So very, very good. His hands went to her waist and he leaned down. She very slowly stretched up on her toes, and their lips met. Tuck circled her waist with one arm, supporting her, and pulled her against his body. He deepened the kiss as she opened to him. Her normally nimble fingers sent bolts of pleasure through him as she fumbled with his buttons. "I'll do that," he said, grabbing her hands.

She stepped back as he flicked his shirt open. Zoe watched and licked her lips, giving him all sorts of ideas. He whipped his shirt off and reached, drawing her back. Then he remembered the baby. With only one part of his brain working on logic, he located the monitor and saw it was on. "Upstairs," he murmured as he scooped her into his arms.

Tucker got them into the elevator, got them up a floor, and into the master bedroom. He put her back on her feet and pulled her to him again. Her breasts were full, and even covered by the filmy material of her dress and whatever bra she wore underneath, they felt wonderful pressing against his chest.

He gazed down, his fingers brushing over her bare shoulder. "May I?" he asked, his voice husky.

"Help yourself." Her voice came out raspy, filled with secret promises.

He traced a fingertip along the scooped neckline of her dress while his other hand eased down below her waist to caress her rear. "I've wanted to touch you like this for weeks."

He stroked her breast and forgot about all the reasons he shouldn't do this. He forgot about everything except her—and the idea of seeing her naked. He'd dreamed about the feel of her silky skin, the brush of her hair against his skin. Cupping her face, he kissed her. As the hot, sweet taste of her filled his mouth, she melted in his arms. He became lost in the texture of her, her scent, her taste. But like a horny teen, he kept waiting to get caught, or for Zoe to change her mind.

For one brief instant, sanity attempted to reassert itself. This might be a mistake. Seducing her now, like this, edged very close to something off-limits. But temptation won out over good sense.

He tugged the dress away from her shoulder, set his lips on bare skin. Her breath caught and with that quick inhalation, her breasts teased his chest. When her head fell back, he kissed his way toward the throbbing pulse in her throat.

"If you plan to say no, now's the time," he murmured, and bared her other shoulder. "Otherwise, I've got all sorts of plans for you."

"What kind of plans?" She was all but purring now and he buried his nose in the soft skin at the base of her neck.

"Wicked plans. Sexy plans." He fumbled in his pocket and pulled out a condom. "Plans that include this."

Panting, she leaned back just far enough to put a modicum of distance between their bodies. "You got a smoke detector in here?"

Tucker stared at her, nonplussed. "Why?"

A naughty gleam flashed in her eyes. "Because if we keep goin' the way we're goin', we might wanna disable it so the fire department doesn't come to put out the fire we're gonna light."

Laughing, he gave her a smacking kiss with a lot of

tongue. This time, he was the one who broke the kiss. "I have a fire extinguisher."

"Good, 'cause you might just have to use it on me."

Still grinning, he laid his lips against hers, the hand at the small of her back dipping to her sweetly rounded butt to pull her closer. Her eyes lit up, and she rocked her hips the moment she encountered his erection.

"I could go seriously crazy over you." Zoe's breathy words teased his mouth.

He kissed and nibbled her lips. When he came up for air, he asked, "Does this have a zipper? The dress, I mean."

"Nope. It's a peel-off."

"Hot damn, my personal favorite." He worked slowly, drawing out the process, the silky material bunching in his hands as he rubbed them up the length of her body. He kept his mouth on hers until they were both trembling. Finally, he drew back and whisked the dress over her head. Then he just looked at her.

She wore a plain white bra with a hint of lace. It was both virginal and the sexiest damn thing he'd ever seen. He wanted to be that bra, cupping her breasts. Her boy-short panties matched, clinging to her full hips and showing him just where to grip her. Zoe's hands, hanging at her sides, fluttered like nervous birds, and she wouldn't meet his gaze.

"I'm trying to think of something memorable to say, but it's really hard when all the blood's drained out of my head."

That got him a nervous laugh, but she said, "Give it a shot."

"Wow."

Her hands fluttered over her belly and her eyes had a pinched look that begged for honesty. "Yeah?"

Tucker pulled her close and kissed her forehead. "Yeah, angel. You're beautiful."

She pushed against his chest and he loosened his embrace. “No I’m not.” She was back to not looking at him.

On impulse, he dropped to his knees, his hands on her sides. He rubbed his thumbs over her skin. Yeah, there were some stretch marks and her belly had this little pooch thing, but seriously? He found it sort of adorable. He’d dated sleek showgirls, fashion models, and there’d been a few actresses, but none of them was as real and sexy as Zoe. Not to him. There was just something about her. He pulled her toward his face and began to kiss his way from one hip bone to the other. If she widened her legs a little, he could taste her. He liked that idea. A lot.

He hooked his fingers in her panties and tugged them down. She was still wearing her cowboy boots and damn if that wasn’t a turn-on, as well. She placed her palm on his head to steady her balance as she lifted first one booted foot, then the other to get her panties off.

“Spread wider, angel,” he ordered. She did, and he used his fingers to tease her. She ran her nails across his close-cropped hair as if looking for something to hang on to. He decided she should lie down for this next part.

Standing, he maneuvered her to the bed and pressed her down. She fell back, all but boneless. He knelt and pulled her legs over his shoulders, dipped his head and tasted her. He nipped and kissed, licked and sucked. She was panting and arching against him one moment, and the next, she shattered, and he felt her climax all the way through him. Zoe blinked open her eyes and watched him down the length of her body.

“I like the way you’re looking at me,” Tucker said.

She flushed, once again a full-body reaction, and he loved it. “Gotta admit, cowboy, I’m kinda enjoying the way you’re lookin’ back.”

He stood and toed off his boots. Moments later, he

kicked his feet free of his pants. He liked the way her eyes widened as she caught a glimpse of his erection.

"Is all that just for me?" she teased.

"Absolutely." He stilled as soft burbles sounded from the monitor on the bed. No other noises came. First thing in the morning, he'd turn the guest room into a nursery because he was not nearly done with this woman. Not by a long shot. Tucker kissed her as he rearranged her on the bed, located the condom he'd dropped on the floor and suited up. Zoe's eyes tracked his every movement.

"Like what you see?" He waggled his brows at her.

"Oh yeah," she breathed. "You're even…better than I ever imagined."

"You imagined us like this?"

"Darn straight. I'm a red-blooded country girl. Of course I imagined us doin' the deed."

Tucker laughed. He couldn't help it. He lowered his body until their hips rested together, his erection nestled against her wet heat. Then he buried his face in her hair and breathed deeply. The wavy strands spilled across the couch, like ink on parchment. The scent of ginger and peaches surrounded him, dazzling his senses. Would he ever take another breath and not remember what she smelled like?

Zoe whimpered as she shifted her hips, and then he was sliding into her warm depths. He forgot to breathe for a moment. He pushed up on his elbows, taking most of his weight off her. Her round, firm breasts were large enough to still press against his chest. He withdrew slowly and she tensed, trying to hold him in. He surged into her, then they were in perfect sync.

He faltered when she asked, "What do you see when you look at me like that?"

His sex-fogged brain tried to process the question. How was he looking at her?

"You have this sort of faraway look in your eyes, but you're staring at me like you can't quite figure me out."

Tucker's mouth quirked again. "That's because I can't. Being here with you, like this? It feels so fantastic that I don't want to stop. And trying to think and talk when something feels this good—when *you* feel this good? Angel, that's just plain mean."

She rolled her eyes and laughed, her breath hitching in the middle as he sank all the way into her. "Okay, no more talking. I promise."

And they didn't, because he made sure to kiss her and kept kissing her until they were both panting so hard he had to stop so they could breathe. Hot waves of pleasure rolled through him. He hadn't been kidding when he told her that making love to her felt fantastic.

Zoe kept her eyes open, watching him. She'd never done that. Before, she'd always hoped the guy knew enough to help her get off, had closed her eyes so she didn't have to see the faces he made as he grunted above her. Tucker wasn't like that. She'd already had a big orgasm and a bunch of little ones courtesy of Tucker. The way he filled her, the way he kissed her, the way he *looked* at her. Like he couldn't believe she was there, like she was special—special to him. She wanted Tucker like she'd never wanted any other man. And she was terrified that she'd screw things up. That he'd love her and leave her like every other man, including her father, had done.

She locked her hands around his neck, rocking with his rolling rhythm, feeling tingles in her fingers and toes. This thing between them, it was happening too fast, and not fast enough. Was it real? "I don't care."

Zoe realized she'd said that out loud when Tucker paused and stared down at her, his expression puzzled. "Angel?"

She couldn't remember when he'd first called her that.

Somewhere back along the way, but she noticed he never called anyone else angel. Darlin's and sugars and sweethearts aplenty but she was his only angel. She wanted to always feel this way, to have the zings of electricity zapping her skin each time he touched her, the slow build of anticipation as he brought her to the very edge before she plunged over. To have him look at her the way he was now, his eyes soft and so blue they reminded her of the summer sky right before dawn.

She realized in that moment that she could be reckless, could grab the pleasure and the passion Tucker offered, and that he not only would give it all to her, but he'd be there to catch her when she fell. And she would. Had. Fallen hard. She didn't know what love was, not for sure, but looking up at him, she wanted to find out.

"Do things to me," she pleaded. "Do all those wicked things you promised." *Make* love *to me,* she added silently.

Tucker did. His strong hands fondled and caressed, teased and pleasured her. His mouth devoured hers, and when she could catch her breath, he trailed nips and kisses across her skin. Her heart galloped. Her skin was tight and itchy, like it was going to burst if she didn't come soon. She was so hot she could be running a fever. And still he pumped into her, finding just the right spot inside her, finding just the right spot outside her. He got her right *there,* and she was shaking so hard she thought she might buck him off.

She watched his face, studied the planes and hollows, raised her cheek to rasp along the bristle of his five o'clock shadow. She met his gaze, because he was watching her, too. Those blue eyes of his grew darker and he tensed. He buried his face in her hair, groaning softly as he emptied into her. And then it was glorious for her, too. She didn't shatter. She imploded.

Zoe shook from the aftershocks, chilled and fevered both, as she lay trapped beneath Tucker's body. Was he breathing? Was she? He sucked in a ragged breath and she wanted to laugh, only to discover she didn't have enough air in her lungs. She sucked in a breath, pleased as everything that she'd been the one to do this to him.

"You okay?" he rasped.

"No," she admitted, and felt him stiffen. As he started to roll away, she squeezed her arms around him. "I'm not okay. I'm fantastic." He relaxed. "What about you?"

"Angel, if you make me come that hard every time we make love, I may not survive."

She could live with that.

Eleven

Zoe woke up and lay still, listening. Traffic was a faint hum outside the window. She panicked for a minute when she didn't hear Nash breathing. Then she caught the soft, puffing breaths from the monitor. And she remembered. She wasn't in the guesthouse. She was at Tucker's.

She'd been up with Nash every three hours and her eyes felt puffy, like she'd just spent three days sleeping on the beach. Blinking several times, she brought the alarm clock into focus. Nine o'clock. Wow. Nash had slept for over four hours. She stretched until at least half the bones in her body popped, then she punched up the pillows behind her shoulders and stilled, listening once more.

She heard no sounds but those on the monitor. As luxurious as this place was, the rooms were probably soundproofed. At least she hoped so. Nash had a set of lungs on him, and he'd used them several times through the wee hours of the morning. The first time, she worried Tucker would get mad. He didn't. He was the one who got up, changed Nash, then handed her baby over so she could feed him. He'd disappeared only to return once Nash was full. Tucker explained he'd moved the porta-crib up to the guest room down the hall. He then scooped up the baby and left to put Nash down in his crib. She'd fallen back to sleep almost immediately.

She vaguely remembered Tucker getting up, kissing her goodbye with a murmured, "Have a meeting. Sleep in. I'll be back in time for lunch." As if her stomach was hard-wired to her thoughts, it picked that moment to grumble. She wondered how much longer Nash would sleep. Did she have time to grab a shower? Deciding to take a chance, she moved the monitor into the bathroom. She'd hear if he woke up. She could shower, brush her teeth and try to feel—and look—more human.

Thirty minutes later, she found her underwear carefully folded on a chair, her dress draped over the back. Zoe didn't remember picking stuff up last night. Nope, she was too busy enjoying the multiple orgasms. Tucker must have done so before leaving. Was it possible he really was as nice as he seemed?

"Don't look a gift horse in the mouth," she muttered as she slipped on a robe she'd found in the bathroom. She'd dress after taking care of her now very awake child.

Nash was in a happy mood and she cooed at him on the way down in the elevator. The door slid open and she let out a startled scream. Which, of course, startled Nash, who used those magnificent lungs of his to full capacity.

Two women turned to face her and she recognized them immediately. Keisha dashed toward her, apologies falling out of her mouth.

"I told you we should have called first," she scolded Quin, who held a cooing bundle of pink froth. "I'm so sorry, Zoe. Quin and I didn't mean to scare you. Here, let me help."

Before Zoe could resist, Keisha had the carrier and was headed back toward the breakfast bar. "You just sit yourself down. I'll make you some breakfast. I'd offer coffee but you're still breastfeeding. Don't want to introduce this little guy to caffeine quite yet." She tickled the now cooing baby's cheek. "You'd never get him to nap if you do."

Heart still pounding from shock, Zoe eased over to the breakfast bar and stepped up onto an empty stool. Quin laughed and waved a hand. "Don't mind Keisha taking over. Deacon hired her as a nanny but won't let her nanny. She'll use any excuse to snatch children away from their unwary parents so she can cuddle them."

Keisha was whisking eggs and milk in a bowl while waiting for a pat of butter to melt in a small frying pan. "Your husband hired me because I'm writing my doctoral dissertation on the emotional impact of adoption on early childhood development."

Quin rolled her eyes and Zoe found herself smiling. "That, too. Poor Noelle. I hope Deke will have all his emotional baggage sorted by the time we think about having another one of our own." Sliding off her stool with the little girl snugged securely on her hip, Quin sauntered to the fridge and pulled out a bottle of water and a bottle of orange juice. She set them in front of Zoe, then sniffed the air appreciatively. "You didn't mention bacon."

Her mouth watering, Zoe opened the OJ and gulped it down. Her stomach set up a continuous growl, causing her cheeks to redden. Keisha grinned as she dished up scrambled eggs and a plate of fried bacon. "Enjoy."

Quin added, "I trust our baby expert here, even if she tends to go overboard and get all bossy. Keisha has all the degrees in early childhood development. Plus, she likes to cook and insists on doing the grocery shopping."

"Good thing, or this family would starve to death."

"Hey, I can cook."

Keisha slowly turned her head and all but stared down her nose at Quin. "Oh, really?"

"I can make oatmeal." Quin looked defensive. "And tuna salad."

"As long as you don't have to boil the eggs," Keisha teased.

"Hey! That wasn't my fault. Deke distracted me."

Leaning conspiratorially toward Zoe, Keisha stage-whispered, "She left the eggs boiling on the stove and they boiled dry. You ever smelled burnt hard-boiled eggs? I threw the pan away. There was no salvaging it."

Quin tossed a dish towel at the other woman. Keisha caught it with one hand, and Noelle giggled. Zoe was almost jealous of this easy camaraderie. She finished her eggs and chewed on the last piece of bacon. Still hungry, she hesitated to ask for more. When both women leveled their gazes on her, she swallowed down the last bite and braced herself.

"So," Keisha began.

Quin finished, "We haven't had much time to visit. What's your story?"

Aware of how Deacon and Quin met and married from coverage on ENC, Zoe wasn't dumb. She'd had more than her share of interactions with law enforcement. She recognized the other woman's tone of voice. Quin might be sitting there jostling the one-year-old in her lap looking all concerned, but she was all cop at the moment. She concentrated on the bottle of water, taking long, slow swigs to buy time. What had Tucker already told his people? The whole story was a bad soap opera, and a little part of her wanted Deacon Tate's wife to like her—wanted Tucker's sister-in-law to like her. Did she have to tell the whole story, or could she just touch on the most pertinent parts and skate over the rest?

She cleared her throat. “Simple story. I had car trouble and Tucker played white knight. Since we were both headed to Nashville, he gave me a ride.”

Quin cut her eyes to Nash. “And the baby’s father?”

“Not in the picture.” Zoe snapped her mouth shut. She hadn’t meant to sound so waspish. At the same time, though she might want these women to like her, they were getting a little too pushy about her past. “Not that it’s any of your business.”

The smile on Quin’s face didn’t touch her eyes. “Anything to do with my brothers-in-law is my business. At least you aren’t claiming Tucker is the father.”

Zoe blinked as her mouth dropped open. “Are you kiddin’ me?” She snapped her mouth shut and considered Quin’s implication that she might be some gold digger or worse. “Wow. I suppose there are some people nasty enough to do somethin’ so low. But that ain’t me. Tucker’n me have only known each other a couple of months. He’s just a really nice guy with a big heart.”

That statement was met with an incredulous look. “We are talking about Tucker Tate, right? The shark of the entertainment world?”

“Well… I don’t know about sharks. I do know he drove by, took pity on me and then Nash decided to make an early entrance. Tucker just sorta got caught up in the situation. I appreciate the stuff y’all did for me and Nash after I got out of the hospital. It was really nice an’ all, but no offense? This is startin’ to get personal. You should go ask Tucker, you wanna know anything else.”

“You spent the night. In Tucker’s room.” Quin was persistent.

“Yes, ma’am, I did. But I don’t see how that’s any of your business. This is Tucker’s house, not yours.”

"Tucker doesn't bring strange women here to spend the night."

This was way more information than Zoe wanted to know—even though she was secretly pleased that Tucker didn't bring just anybody home. But Quin, who had always seemed friendly, still had her cop face on and that made Zoe extremely uncomfortable.

"Thanks for breakfast. I'm sure y'all have way more important things to be doin'." She stood up and looked pointedly toward the front door.

"I'll just clean—"

She cut Keisha off. "You're so sweet, but I can wash the dishes. Thanks kindly for droppin' by."

Quin stood and hitched Noelle on her shoulder, gesturing with a jerk of her head to Keisha. "Guess that's our cue to leave." They headed toward the front door where Quin paused. "A word of advice, Zoe. Tucker is family. I don't like it when anyone messes with mine."

The solid wooden door closed behind the two women with a soft snick that was as much a message as if Quin had slammed it shut. Zoe glanced down at Nash, who was cooing and trying to pull off his socks. "What's she got to be all bent out of shape over? She's the one who came here nosin' around like a bloodhound on the hunt."

Tucker looked up as his office door opened. Deacon walked in, a paper bag in his hand. He kicked the door shut behind him. Deke deposited the bag on Tucker's desk, then went to the sideboard to grab the coffee carafe. He poured himself a cup then refilled Tucker's.

"Dude, seriously? Your wife didn't fix you breakfast?"

His brother rooted around in the bag, pulled out a sugary doughnut and plopped into the guest chair. "Quin doesn't cook. Keisha did, but it was all healthy and stuff. Besides, it's time for a midmorning snack." Deacon leaned forward and edged the bag toward Tucker. "There's a bear claw in there."

Tuck snatched the bag and looked inside. He'd just taken his first bite when Deacon said, "So…?"

Tuck chewed and swallowed. "So what?"

Deacon let out an exasperated huff. "So…you had a houseguest last night."

"Seriously? You were spying on me?"

"Not true. I had the game on. And I heard noises."

"Uh-huh."

"And you're my brother."

He snickered but didn't reply, sipping his coffee between bites. He settled back. Tuck knew his brother so he waited, in silence. Deke lasted until the end of his doughnut.

"Why are you doing this, little brother?"

"What am I doing, big brother?"

"Don't play dumb. You probably have the most brains of all of us, but if I have to spell it out, I will. What's up with you and Zoe?"

Tucker considered Deacon's question. "I don't know." He held up a hand to stay any protest. "I don't, Deke. It's…new."

"She has talent."

"I know."

Deacon leveled a look at him. "What happens if y'all break up?"

"What do you mean?"

"I mean, she has talent. A lot of it. Talent I want to help along. If the two of you get together and then you break up with her—"

"Whoa right there," Tuck interrupted. "Why are you automatically assuming I'd be the one to break it off?"

His brother stared at him until he wanted to squirm. Deke finally said, "Seriously?"

Okay, Deacon had a point. Tucker didn't stick with a woman very long, but truthfully, he usually dated only when he needed a plus-one, or if someone really caught his eye. He didn't do relationships. Ever. Until now. He should be rattled by the thought of something long-term with Zoe. Why wasn't he? And that did freak him out. He defaulted to his usual excuse. "Business is business, Deke. I want her to succeed, too."

"Okay, fine. Just don't mess it up. Now tell me how this whole thing started."

So that's just what he did, sparing no detail. And realized he was in even deeper trouble than he thought.

Twelve

Zoe folded the dish towel next to the sink. All signs of her presence upstairs, her visitors and breakfast had been erased. She glanced at her phone to check the time. She could wait until Tucker came home and tell him about the visit from his sister-in-law. She still smarted over Quin's insinuation that she was trying to trap Tucker or something. Or she could call a cab and go back to the Easleys' because she felt funny staying at Tucker's house now. That was probably her best bet.

She gathered up the diaper bag and Nash in the carrier and stepped out the front door. She sat down on the front step to wait. When the cab arrived, she dialed Deacon's number while walking to the street. Keisha answered.

"I'm leaving, and I don't have a key or anything. Thanks for the loan of the porta-crib and for babysitting. Could you ask Mrs. Tate to lock up and set the alarm?" She clicked off before the nanny could respond.

The cab pulled away as Keisha and Quin appeared. Zoe didn't look back. She got lucky with the cabdriver. He wasn't the nosy type, which was good because she had tears in her eyes. Stupid hormones. She had just enough cash on her to pay the fare with a little extra for a tip. He pulled up at the end of the Easleys' driveway and was gone before she'd taken a few steps after getting out.

For the second time that morning, Zoe let out a startled squeak as a woman, dressed like a professional in a suit with killer heels, stepped out of the bushes.

"Zoe Parker, I presume?"

Zoe eyed her suspiciously. "This is private property."

The woman waved her hand in an airy gesture. "Dandy Don knows I'm here."

Studying her, Zoe considered what to do. She seemed awfully darned familiar with Don. And she looked vaguely familiar. The woman fluttered inch-long eyelashes over blue eyes and brushed a strand of her platinum hair away from her face.

"I'm Parker Grace," the woman announced as if Zoe would automatically recognize the name.

Zoe tightened her grip on Nash's carrier in case she needed to hotfoot it to Mr. Don's house.

"Yeah, and?"

The woman's smile turned predatory, with a hint of cat eating the canary for spice. Zoe hated her. "I'm a reporter with Entertainment News Channel."

"Uh-huh." Zoe turned up the drive and started walking. Mr. Don had warned her about handling the media—as in he'd take care of everything and she wasn't to talk to them without him there. And he was nowhere to be found. "Well, Miz Grace, that's real nice an' all but you aren't on my schedule today."

The woman *tsked* at her, but Zoe kept walking. "I believe you'll want to talk to me. Especially since you spent the night with Tucker Tate."

Zoe's step faltered but she caught herself and kept going. How the heck did this reporter know that?

"I'm sure you're aware that the Tates and the Barrons are two of the richest families in the country."

"So?" Zoe hoped her shrug and "whatever" expression would give the woman a clue. She hadn't realized how long this driveway was and since the reporter continued to dog her, Zoe wondered how she would get inside the guesthouse without a hassle. She glanced up the drive but didn't see either Mr. Don's or Miz Rosemary's cars.

"You really should agree to an interview, Zoe. I know all about these people from personal experience." The woman grabbed for her arm.

Was this Parker Grace person threatening her? Zoe wished Mr. Don was here. Heck, she'd even settle for Tucker. All she knew was that she was tired, Nash was fussing and needed to be fed, and this woman had invaded her space. She hooked the carrier over her elbow, fished her phone out of the diaper bag and dialed 911, swiping the speaker button as the call rang through.

A recorded voice answered, "Nine one one, what is the exact location of your emergency?"

"Yes, hi. This is Zoe Parker. I'm stayin' with the Easleys on Valley Brook just off Woodmont. They aren't here and this woman confronted me an' my baby in the driveway."

Parker fisted her hands on her hips, her face looking so hard Zoe was afraid it might crack when she spoke. "Fine. I'm leaving. But don't say I didn't warn you, Zoe."

Zoe grabbed Nash's carrier and scuttled up the driveway, keeping an eye on the reporter. If she'd been alone, she might have duked it out with the woman right there, but she couldn't do things like that anymore. Because of Nash. The woman sauntered away, a taunting smile on her face. "Don't get your hopes up, little girl. Men like Tucker Tate eat starry-eyed wannabes like you for breakfast." She flicked a card that landed in the baby carrier. "Call me when you grow up and want to talk."

"Hello?" a live 911 operator said into the sudden silence. "Are you there?"

Zoe stared at the phone a long moment before replying. "I'm sorry. Yeah, I'm here."

"What's happening? I have a patrol car headed your way, but I need the exact address."

"Thank you, but you can probably tell them they can go on about their regular business. The woman who confronted me is gone now."

"Are you sure you're safe?"

"Yessum. Turns out she was just one of those gossip reporter people. She mistook me for someone else. S'all good. I'm sorry to have troubled you."

"Zoe," the operator's voice was full of compassion. "If someone is still there and you feel you can't talk—"

"No, ma'am. She left." Zoe glanced at the card. She didn't want any trouble, especially not after her little confrontation with Tucker's sister-in-law, but she didn't like Parker Grace either. "She said her name was Parker Grace and claimed to be a reporter with ENC."

The dispatcher sucked in a breath. "I've heard of her. Are you sure you'll be okay?"

Nash chose that moment to wail. He was probably wet and hungry. "Yes, ma'am. Thank you kindly. I need to look after my baby now." She soothed Nash as she walked. First, all those photographers at the restaurant last night, and now this Parker Grace lady—Zoe snorted. *Lady* might be a stretch. Having a reporter trespass on the Easleys' property made her nervous. She should call Tucker, tell him about the incident, but she worried. Would Tucker get mad at her?

Think she'd done it on purpose, lookin' for publicity? Since nothing had happened, maybe she'd just keep it to herself.

Tucker clicked off the call and immediately redialed. The phone on the other end rang and rang. Just like it had the first time. Zoe always answered. Had something happened to her? To Nash? Or maybe she'd taken off for parts unknown?

Bent Star's administrative assistant, a no-nonsense woman with a tendency to mother, stood as he passed her desk. "Tucker? What's wrong?"

"Nothing. Everything. I don't know, Patty. Zoe isn't answering the phone." He trotted down the hall, the woman dogging his steps.

"Are you calling her cell phone?"

"Yes."

"Where is she? Is she still at the Easleys'?"

He glanced back at her, and huffed out a breath, confessing, "I left her asleep at the town house."

"Call the house phone. Maybe she's down in the kitchen or something, left her cell upstairs." Patty favored him with her "wise mother" look. "I've never seen you quite so frazzled." She left off the implied *over a woman.*

"You'll feel better if you go check on her. Take her to lunch. Your schedule is clear. Spend the afternoon with her. And if you need a babysitter, call me." She gave him a gentle shove and a knowing smile.

Deciding to take Patty's advice, Tucker reached the front door of Bent Star's offices, only to be hailed by his brother.

"Yo, Tuck. You headed home? Can I catch a ride?"

Tucker kept walking. "Yes, and why?"

"Spending time with one of my favorite brothers isn't reason enough?"

Tuck snorted and kept walking. So did Deke. Tucker

drove the company SUV since he had the keys. It was a short trip and Tucker made mental bets on how long it would take for Deke to open up. He hadn't anticipated the answer to be immediately.

"So… I couldn't help overhearing that you can't get in touch with Zoe."

"Uh-huh. Do you know something about that?"

"Quin called me a little bit ago."

Tucker cut his eyes to his passenger, as he braked and the SUV rolled to a stop at a light. "And?"

"Well… She and Keisha went over to see Zoe this morning."

Now he turned his head to stare at Deke. "I'm not going to like this, am I?"

Deke scrunched up his face, trying to look both apologetic and brotherly. "Probably not. Quin didn't come right out and say that she'd interrogated Zoe but given her rant over the girl's reaction to—" he made air quotes "—'a few friendly questions about her background,' I don't think it went well."

Tucker growled but returned his eyes to the road when the car behind them honked because the light had turned green. "What did your wife do, Deacon?"

A long sigh answered the question. "She sort of called in a favor and ran a background check."

Furious, Tucker hit his blinker and whipped the big SUV over to the side of the street. Throwing the transmission into Park, he turned on his brother. "Dammit, Deacon—"

Deke held his hands up, palms facing Tucker as he cringed back against the passenger door. "I know. I had strong words with her. And I'm probably looking at a fight when I get home. She was totally out of line, but—"

"But what, Deke? You think I didn't have Bridge check? Nash's father is serving a life sentence for murder. Zoe's father died in a county jail, most likely of cirrhosis of the liver. She's dirt-poor, a single mother and wants to sing for a living. What the hell can you or that snoopy wife of yours tell me that I don't already know and haven't already thought?" He snarled and banged his hands on the steering wheel, surprised at both his anger and the hollow feeling growing in his gut. What if Zoe had packed up Nash and left? They could be anywhere. Except… She didn't have much money. "I ought to make you get out and walk home."

Muttering imprecations under his breath, Tucker slammed the transmission into Drive and managed to merge back into the midday traffic.

He growled again when Deke continued. "Zoe and the baby left in a cab. About thirty minutes after Quin and Keisha went home. She called Keisha to tell them to lock up the town house since she didn't have a key." As much as Tucker wanted to ditch Deacon, he didn't have time and maybe having his brother grovel on behalf of his wife would help smooth things over with Zoe. He changed their course, heading for the Easleys' estate. He remained silent for the rest of the drive. So did Deke. When Tucker finally pulled up the driveway and parked, he was calm enough to speak without cussing.

"You tell Quin to stay out of my business, Deke. And she's not to go near Zoe again. Tell her to pass on that message to the Bee Dubyas. I don't want any interference from them. We clear on this?"

His brother huffed out another long-suffering sigh. "They care, bud. We all do."

"Yeah? What about Zoe? Do you care about what happens to her? To her baby?"

Deacon's quiet reply didn't come until Tucker opened the door and was halfway out of the SUV. "Not as much as we care about you."

Thirteen

Zoe moved the porta-crib out to the gazebo next to the pool. Nash was down for his nap so Zoe ate the lunch she'd heated in the microwave—tomato soup along with two pieces of cheese slapped between slices of bread. Not exactly a grilled cheese sandwich but it was gooey. She did her best to ignore the hollow spot inside her that no amount of food would ever fill up. She'd let her pride—and her insecurity—get away from her. Of course Deacon's wife would want to know about her. The woman had been a highway patrol trooper—she still was for all Zoe knew. And they had a baby girl. Like that reporter said, the family was rich. Zoe could have been just what Quin said. She could have been a thief. Or worse.

She wasn't. Still, the fact they didn't trust her hurt on a level so primal she couldn't wrap her head around the sick, empty feeling it caused. She pushed the bowl and plate aside, her appetite gone. Nash was still napping so she unpacked her guitar, pulled out her notebook and settled in to play. She often played and sang to him while he slept.

Though her fingers plucked the guitar strings, her brain

didn't focus on music. She'd been an idiot to think there might be something between her and Tucker. They were worlds apart, the gulf so wide that one night of mind-blowing sex wouldn't bridge it.

One thing Zoe had always been was honest with herself. She was country roads and Tucker was straight-up city lights. No matter how hard she imagined it, Tucker would remain a dream she couldn't quite reach. Not at this point in her life. Maybe when she got famous—if she got famous. She'd make a life for Nash, one way or another—a better one where he would grow up to be whatever he wanted to be.

She stared out across the wooded backyard, eyes unfocused. She'd discovered that the gazebo was a good location for songwriting—the breeze blowing gently, dappled sunlight, birds chirping, the occasional squirrel darting playfully across the lawn. And it was just her and Nash. This was a cozy place. Peaceful.

Zoe played a riff on the guitar, trying out different chord progressions until she found a tune she liked. Playing it over and over until she had it memorized, she stopped to make notations in her book. Then she played the tune again, humming along. Her thoughts returned to Tucker, to the daydreams she'd had of lazy mornings as he lingered over coffee before leaving to go conquer the world, to late nights curled up in his bed after coming home from her current singing gig before making sweet love.

Tucker was handsome enough to be a matinee idol. She smiled at the old-fashioned term. There'd been an old lady who lived next door to her and her daddy at some point. She dyed her hair blue and swore that she'd been kissed by Clark Gable when she was a giddy girl of eighteen. At the time, Zoe had no idea who Clark Gable was. She'd crept into the local library and looked him up. That was the summer she discovered she could check out movies if she had a library card. She dragged her dad down there to sign for her and then she found a cheap VHS player at the pawnshop. She swept the floors and cleaned the bathrooms for two months in trade for it. That was her introduction to Clark Gable, Humphrey Bogart, John Wayne. She'd wanted to be as strong as Lauren Bacall, as intelligent and witty as Katherine Hepburn and as beautiful as Grace Kelly when she grew up.

She hummed the first line and then sang, "You can't be the hero." A few more chords and the chorus came to her almost whole. Then she put everything together. "You can't be the hero, not in my story. You aren't the kind of man who would ever share the glory. You won't ever love me. We just can't be."

Zoe leaned over to write down the words and to change one of the chords, then she played and sang the chorus again. No more words came so she just stared at the garden. Storm clouds gathered overhead and within moments, the sun's light was muted, washed in somber grays. She knew how the sun felt. And it sucked.

She closed her eyes, wrapping the feeling around her, then jotted down the words as they came to her.

I'm not lookin' for true love,
'Cause I'll just find a broken heart.
But when I look at you,
I want to give you everything.

She strummed the chords, found the key and sang them. Then she added the chorus. She didn't fight the melancholy. This was her reality. Tucker Tate was so far above her. Someday, maybe. If her dreams came true, then yeah. She might be able to walk up to him as an equal. And just like that, the second verse came to her. Zoe captured the words then sang them.

You can't be the one for me,
No matter how hard I wish it.
But when you look at me,
I want to give you everything.

Deke grabbed his arm as they approached the guesthouse, effectively stopping him in his tracks. Tucker gave him a hard look and then he heard the music floating on the breeze. Deke held his finger to his lips, cautioning Tuck to be quiet. His brother obviously wanted to listen without Zoe knowing they were there.

He was smart enough to know he wasn't as good a judge of talent as Deke and Chase were. His forte was the business side of things, but there was just something about Zoe that pricked his senses. Her voice resonated like a young Dolly Parton's, only deeper, huskier. When Zoe sang a love song, a man felt it deep inside, and it put thoughts of rumpled sheets and sweaty sex in his brain. His upper lip curled into an unconscious snarl. He'd need to check with Deke and Dillon about what thoughts Zoe put into their heads. He wasn't sure he liked the idea of a bunch of fans thinking what he was whenever Zoe got up onstage.

He caught whispers of her guitar and remained still. Yes, he fully intended on eavesdropping because he was as intrigued as Deke. They stood just out of sight.

"You can't be the hero," she sang, voice low and sweet. "Not in my story. You aren't the kind of man who would ever share the glory. You won't ever love me. We just can't be." Her voice grew husky, then cracked on the word *can't* and Tucker's heart cracked a little, too. There was so much loneliness in the words. And hurt. Was she singing about

Redmond Smithee? He wanted to beat the hell out of him. The man had been a cretin to throw away this wonderful woman and her child.

It took conscious effort on his part to unclench his hands. Part of him wanted to burst around the corner, sweep Zoe into his arms and kiss her until she wasn't lonely anymore. The rational part leaned against the guesthouse wall and considered the situation. Tucker wasn't a protector. That was Hunter and Bridger. He wasn't the strong, silent type. That was Cooper. Deacon and Dillon were the sensitive types—while still keeping their man cards. Boone? He had brains and mad organizational skills. Hunt called him a dog robber, a term from his oldest brother's military days describing someone who expedited things. Need something or want something done? Ask Boone. He could find anything, and he made things happen. Him? Tucker wrinkled his forehead. He understood numbers. Business. Profit and loss. He didn't do feelings—not really. He wasn't cold. He loved his mother, brothers, cousins and their wives—most of the time.

That said, he'd never been in love. Heck, he'd never gone steady—not in high school, not in college. Tucker had never loved a woman he wasn't related to and from his current perspective? That just sucked, especially given the woman sitting in the gazebo. He'd wanted to wake up next to her that morning, share coffee with her, breakfast. But he'd had a meeting at the office—one that couldn't be canceled. So he'd gone, albeit reluctantly. And then Quin stuck her nose in, and now things were awkward at best, more likely totally screwed up.

The irrational part of his brain insisting he go gather Zoe into his lap and hold her was squashed by the logical part that decreed he sneak away, then return making a lot of noise to announce his arrival. *Then* he would sweep her into his lap and hold her. He almost snorted out a laugh at that thought.

Deke flashed him a look and jerked him back toward the driveway, and they walked far enough away she wouldn't overhear their conversation.

"Why didn't you tell me she was a songwriter?" Deke hissed at him.

Favoring his brother with a confused look, Tucker said, "I had no clue."

"Well, I'm tellin' you, we need to lock her into a contract, bro, and it needs to be done before you do something stupid to mess up your relationship."

"We don't have a relationship." Of course, after last night, he should probably reconsider that denial. He stabbed a finger toward Deke. "And wasn't your wife the one who scared Zoe off this morning?"

Deacon had the good grace to look sheepish. "I said I'd talk to Quin." Tucker held up a warning finger. "And the Bee Dubyas," Deke finished with a disgruntled huff. "Get with Don and get her signed, Tuck. You sit her down with Dillon? I can name five female singers who would catfight over recording that song. Heck, *I'd* record it, but it's not written for a man." Deacon hooked his thumbs in his pockets and stared at Tucker. "You know, our opening act is taking a break."

Tucker had been staring at the pool. "Wait. What? Sugar Tree? What's up with them?"

"Something to do with family. It's college venues until we hit Talladega in two weeks. We planned to play solo. But, dude, I'm walking up to that gazebo and asking Zoe to come on the road to open for us. You'd best work a deal with Dandy Don." Deke turned to retrace his steps, but Tucker snagged his arm, holding him in place.

"She can't go on tour. What about the baby?"

Deke shrugged. "Quin's taking some vacation time. She, Noelle and Keisha are coming with me. Keisha can look after both kids."

"How's that going to work since Zoe and Quin aren't exactly best friends at the moment?" Tucker did *not* like the idea of Zoe and Nash out on the road somewhere. Away from him. He put his brain on hold. Why should it matter? Just business, right?

"Good point. We'll lease a tour bus for her. She and Nash will stay in it and Keisha will watch him when Zoe's performing."

Tucker folded his arms over his chest and scowled. "Sounds like you have this all planned out."

Rolling his eyes, Deacon wasn't intimidated in the slightest. "Look at it this way. It'll give you a chance to take her shopping again. She'll need outfits to perform in."

"And who's paying for them? She's already plotting how to pay me back for what I spent on her yesterday." Still, Tucker grinned, remembering when he'd taken his cousin Chase Barron's new bride shopping in Las Vegas. A Choctaw cowgirl, Savannah had been the Western version of Eliza Doolittle, and Tucker had played Professor Henry Higgins, without the romantic bits. He'd reinvented the rodeo rider so she could hold her own against Chase's demanding family.

"Work a deal with Dandy Don. Tell her it's an advance on her earnings. We leave in two days. You need to get a contract drawn up and get on this, bud."

Numbers, Tucker reminded himself. The bottom line. That's what he was good at. And it was time to show Zoe Parker just what she could be. With that in mind and making logistical plans, he followed Deke to the gazebo.

Deke called out as soon as they turned the corner. "Yo, Zoe! You got company, girl."

She scrambled to hide a notebook under her guitar in its battered case, then she stood. Tucker took in the off-the-shoulder drape of her oversize T-shirt and the tight jeans molding their denim to her lush curves. The memory of everything they'd done the previous night rushed to the front of his brain.

She was too busy scowling at Deacon to notice him, though. "I'm not sure I want your company at the moment," she finally said.

Fourteen

Zoe almost laughed—almost. Watching both men grovel was a sight to behold. The thing was, she believed they were sincere. Deacon looked and sounded contrite and apologetic for his wife's insinuations. Tucker? Tucker was downright angry on Zoe's behalf. When Nash woke up crying, it was Tucker who moved to pick him up. She wasn't quite sure how to process that. Both men moved toward the baby, but Tucker was quicker. Of the two, she'd figured Deacon had more experience, since he was a daddy and all. Then again, he did have a nanny. All Zoe's preconceived notions were being blown out of the water.

"He's wet," Deacon announced, utterly positive.

"I'll change him," Tucker said. "You explain to Zoe what you have in mind and tell her to call Dandy Don."

Call Mr. Don? Zoe sank onto the cushioned patio chair and eyed Deacon suspiciously. "What's goin' on?"

Deacon dropped into the chair across from her and stretched out his long legs. Zoe pushed her chair back and propped her feet in the chair between them, her boots sticking out like stop signs.

"Are you aware that Sugar Tree has been opening for me on this tour?"

She nodded. Sugar Tree was an up-and-coming female duo and they'd hit the jackpot when they got the Red, White and Cool tour gig.

"They've had to take a hiatus for a few weeks. I'd like you to fill in for them."

She blinked. Tilted her head. Blinked again, then scrunched her face up in concentration as she processed what he'd just said. Then thoughts tumbled through her brain like dominoes in one of those YouTube videos. How could she tour with Nash? Who would look after him? Was she ready for that kind of gig? Would she be expected to stay with the band on their bus? Her brain circled the drain. What would she do with Nash?

Deacon reached over and patted her boots to get her attention. "Breathe, Zoe. It's okay. You'll need to call Dandy Don, but here's what I'm thinking. We'll lease an RV, provide a driver. Quin and Noelle are coming with me so that means Keisha, too. She can look after Nash when you're performing. It's a few weeks, but good exposure for you and money in your pocket. What do you think?"

She didn't hide her scowl. "Question is, what does your wife think?"

Deacon winced but it was Tucker, still holding Nash, who spoke. "I'll go with you to run interference in case there's a problem. What do you say?"

Zoe answered before she thought things all the way through. "Yes!"

Tucker climbed down from the corporate jet at the Morgantown Municipal Airport, his angry strides quickly eating up the distance from the plane to the terminal. He'd been called to Barron Tower in Oklahoma City for a huge strategy meeting. Someone was screwing with Barron Enterprises, which meant they were messing with the family. It turned out the troubles in Vegas were just the beginning. He hadn't planned to be gone from the tour for four days. He was so mad at his brother—and himself, truth be told.

The call had come at 4:00 a.m. that morning. Zoe. Sounding lost and scared. The driver hired for her bus was drunk and weaving all over the road.

Grim-faced, Tucker brushed past people in the terminal and headed outside. A taxi awaited him. He climbed in and clenched his jaw shut to keep from yelling at the driver to go faster.

Idiot, he berated himself. Who had vetted the driver for Zoe? He'd damn sure find out and then heads would roll. He'd stayed on the phone with her while he called his lame excuse for a brother from a different phone and rousted his butt out of bed. And he'd talked to her until the buses stopped, and she and Nash transferred to Deke's personal bus. The driver was arrested by highway patrol.

And then he'd called for the corporate jet. Now he was only a few minutes away from her. And he needed to calm the hell down. Before he took a swing at his brother. Because it wasn't Deacon's fault. And he couldn't be angry at the Barrons for keeping him away. The family was under siege and he had a responsibility to do his part. But Zoe had been alone. With a drunk driving her and the baby. Something could have happened. He could have lost them. And he didn't like that thought one bit.

The cab rolled to a smooth stop at the cluster of sleek RVs. He stuffed a couple of twenties through the plastic barrier and got out. The door on the newest RV, commissioned by Deacon when he married Quin and they adopted Noelle, popped open. He was expecting to see Deke. He got his sister-in-law instead.

"Don't start, Tucker," she preempted. "You won't be saying anything we haven't already."

He scrunched his brows and glowered at her, surprised. "Deke promised to look after her."

"It's not Deke's responsibility."

"You're really gonna go there?" He was still annoyed with her for the way she'd treated Zoe back in Nashville. "Where is she?"

Quin shrugged. "Once we got here, she went back to her bus. We asked her to stay."

Tuck backed up a step. "We? Like she'd stay with someone who accused her of…what, Quin? Being poor? Of working her tail off? Of having dreams *above her station*?" That last bit was so coated in sarcasm he could taste it on his tongue. "She's never been given a thing in her life. All she has is her pride, her talent and sheer stubbornness." He shook his head. "You of all people, Quin, should have some degree of sympathy for her. Tell Deke we'll talk later. Alone."

He pivoted and headed toward Zoe's RV. When Quin called after him, he simply held up a hand, gesturing to leave him alone. As he reached the RV's door, it swung open. One of the roadies stuck his head out, nodded and climbed down with a quiet, "Zoe and the kid are fine."

Tucker wouldn't take the guy's word for it. He had to assure himself that Zoe and Nash were okay. He slipped inside and heard Nash gurgling happily but no response from Zoe.

When he arrived at the bedroom area, Nash held up his arms and cooed. Zoe looked ragged, dark circles under her eyes so large her eyelashes couldn't disguise them. He scooped up the baby, located the diaper bag and took the kid into the living area. He put Nash in a fresh diaper, then found a baby bottle in the little fridge and settled in.

The next thing Tucker knew, he must have dozed off on the couch, with Nash on his chest. Zoe's soft laughter woke him.

"Thanks for lettin' me sleep in," she murmured.

"You had a rough night." He carefully maneuvered until he was sitting upright, the baby now cradled on his shoulder.

Zoe bustled around the kitchen area fixing coffee, which got her a raised eyebrow from him. "I called his pediatrician before I left Nashville. He said switchin' Bugtussle to formula full-time at this point isn't a big deal. So I did. Easier on both of us, I think."

When the coffee maker stopped dripping, she poured Tucker a cup—black. She mixed creamer and sugar into hers and joined him on the couch. "Wasn't expectin' you to drop everything and come."

"I'm just sorry I wasn't here. I'll be around now."

She blinked rapidly, and was that a glint of moisture in her eyes? "But you're..."

"I'm what, angel?"

"A busy man. You've got all those companies to see to, and...and..."

"Shh. It's not like I have to be in an office every day." He should be but he couldn't get Zoe out of his head and being apart from her—and Nash—made him all kinds of crazy.

He leaned over and kissed her, whispering against her lips. "I'm never too busy for this."

Zoe stood in the middle of the large stage filling one end of the West Virginia University Coliseum. She'd just finished singing "Take Me Home, Country Roads" and the place had erupted. She always sang unaccompanied until the last song of her set. In Tuscaloosa, at the University of Alabama, she'd owned the crowd the moment she played the opening notes of Lynyrd Skynyrd's "Sweet Home Alabama." In Lexington, it was "My Old Kentucky Home." And each time, halfway through the last song, the Sons of Nashville joined in, behind her in the dark. Then Deacon would walk out and join her, to new applause, whistles and shouts.

"Zoe Parker," Deke announced when the song was over, and her name echoed through the huge space, rising above the frantic noise. Then Deke was in the spotlight and she was scrambling offstage, to be met by a grinning Tucker.

Resisting the urge to run into his arms, she slung her guitar behind her and fisted one hand on her hip. "And just what do you think you're lookin' at, mister?"

"You, angel. I'm looking at you."

She waggled a finger. "Don't start that romance stuff with me."

Tucker stepped to her, grabbed the finger and brought it to his mouth. "You don't like romance? Cool. We can get straight to things then."

Cocking her head to study him, she considered his expression. There was heat in his eyes as they roamed over her body. Heat and hunger. This man wanted her. A whole lot. "Nuh-uh. I'm hungry."

"Fancy that. Me, too."

She waved her hands at him like she was shooing chickens and backed up a couple of steps. She needed space and air because the way he was looking at her? She was about to combust. "Not that kind of hungry," she managed to say, though her voice came out husky and needy. "Food. Real food. Greenroom food."

"We'll get it to go."

He snagged her hand and pulled her through a gloomy corridor toward the room that had been set up for the stars to relax in. She filled a plate with bread, cold cuts and cheese, fruit and cookies. Tucker followed, filling a plate with the exact things she put on her own. She tossed him a narrow-eyed look.

"I figure you'll want to eat the leftovers tomorrow while we're traveling."

How did he know? She eyed the bottles of water, sodas and energy drinks. Her hands were full, and her guitar was still slung over her back. Tucker snatched the plate from her hands. "Whatever you think needs to get done, do it now. Then tell me what drinks you want. I'll put them in my pockets."

"Are you reading my mind?"

"No. I just know how that mind works."

Five minutes later, they were crossing the crowded parking lot to the area where the tour buses had been cordoned off with sawhorses and road barriers. Inside her RV, he indicated she should eat while he put everything else in the fridge. He glanced at the watch on his wrist. "We have two hours. Eat fast."

She laughed. "But you just said we have two hours."

He growled low in his throat and stalked to her. "We have two hours. I don't intend to stand here and watch you eat the entire time. I have far sexier things in mind." He eased the shirt off her shoulders and stared at her bared skin. Zoe fought the shiver his gaze elicited but it won. When he skimmed his lips over her neck and shoulder, she moaned.

"Eat fast, angel."

A ball of lust curled in her belly and she forgot she was hungry. For food. Her hunger for Tucker? It exploded. She lifted her chin and tilted her head to give him more room. "You need to stop that."

"Not a chance. Eat faster."

She gulped and despite the tiny rumble her stomach

emitted, she was sure she couldn't take a bite, much less chew and swallow.

"You have five minutes. Then I'm stripping you down and eating what I'm hungry for." His voice came out in a purr as he rubbed his lips over her skin.

"I'm not hungry now."

He said nothing, but his hand moved to cup her breast. His thumb and finger found her nipple and played with it through the material of her shirt and bra.

"Tucker?" Goodness. Was she sounding breathless again?

"Mmm?"

"Did you hear me?"

His gaze lifted to hers, and she tumbled into blue eyes the color of a hot summer sky. Nerves fluttered in her stomach. No way would she be able to eat now. "We better put this in the fridge."

"*Mmm.*" He licked up the side of her neck.

"I'm not kidding, Tucker."

"Neither am I." He grabbed the plate and shoved it in the fridge, then swiveled and leaned forward so he could grip her hips. He slid her toward him, and once her legs cleared the table, he hitched her up. Her legs wrapped around his waist in self-preservation. "Are you ready for this?"

Was there any way to be ready for the intensity of this man? He backed unerringly down the length of the RV, turned when his knees hit the bed and crawled onto it with her still clutching him.

Swamped by the heat of him, by the scent of his expensive aftershave that reminded her of sand and sea and wind, she clamped around him. If she didn't hold on, she might rocket off into the night. He was kissing her now, taking her mouth, owning it. Now his mouth was on her breast. When had he taken off her shirt? "Hold on," she murmured. "Hold on tight."

"You do that, angel," Tucker whispered into her ear.

His hands and mouth were everywhere. So many sensations bombarded her, she could barely catch her breath. Her skin was hot, tight, like she might burst out of it if he kept touching her. Then she was naked, but that didn't help. She wanted something. Something…more. His fingers teased between her legs. *Yes. Yes, there.* She squirmed but he held her still with an arm across her hips. And then he was inside her and the pressure built and built and built. Quivering, shaking, unable to breathe, she came with a scream that he caught with a kiss.

Tucker's hands were rough yet tender as he petted and smoothed and eased her down from her orgasm. She was staggered by the intensity of it. Then she realized he was still dressed. She glanced down. He'd done that to her with just his mouth and fingers? Torn between anger and amazement, she tugged at his shirt. She wanted flesh. His. Her lips on his skin. Her hands on him. Her mouth. She fumbled with his belt.

"Here, angel, let me."

No, no, no. She had to do this. "No. Me." She pushed against his right side with her thigh, rolled him to his back and straddled him. She had to hurry. She wanted him—*all* of him—inside her. She needed to touch him, taste him. She inhaled, his scent filling her senses again, only now there was a fragrant musk along with the sea and sand. She got his belt undone, his zipper down, but his jeans stuck. Frustrated, she jerked and pulled.

"Easy, baby, easy," Tucker soothed. "We've got time. Hang on. Just hang on a minute." He lifted her off him, much to her consternation, but only long enough to kick off his boots, slither out of his jeans and briefs, and dig out a condom. Then she was flat on her back, legs wide, as he settled between them. "You can ride me later, sweet girl," he murmured into her hair.

She shuddered beneath him, rolling her hips against his hard length. She reached out and closed her hand over him, lined him up and accepted all of him inside her. She wanted him buried so deep that they would be joined together always. She knew that it was wrong. That he wasn't the man who could love her. It wasn't possible, but she'd already torn through the boundary of good sense. She couldn't go back now, no matter how badly her heart would shatter when the end came. And it would. It always did. But she had the here and now with him. It would have to be enough.

Pleasure saturated every cell of her body as he plunged into her, driving over and over as she arched her hips to meet his thrusts. She watched his clear, blue eyes blur with his arousal and desire. She felt his muscles tense as he throbbed inside her and then he was coming and coming hard, a moan escaping from deep in his throat. And he was hers. For this moment—even if this was the only time she would have with him, for this moment, he was hers.

She swallowed the sudden surge of saliva in her mouth and watched Tucker watch her throat work. His eyes shaded into sapphire territory. Good lord, but she was in so much trouble when it came to this man. She craved him like a dying man craved salvation. Oh yeah, this man was her salvation and her damnation all at the same time. She couldn't have Tucker Tate, not in the long run, because he *was* Tucker Tate, richest of the rich tycoons, and she was Zoe Parker, a free spirit with a beat-up Gibson guitar and a brand-new baby. She was most definitely *not* the type of woman a man like Tucker would hook up with—not for the long haul. But she wanted him, for as long as she could have him. She only hoped that when the time came, she and Nash would be okay.

Zoe startled when Tucker stroked her cheek with the back of his knuckle. “Hey, angel. What put that sad look on your face?”

And then the tears, as sure as rain in April, started dribbling down her cheeks. Strong arms gathered her close and a warm hand rubbed her back. “I am such a mess,” she blubbered, trying to push away so she could hide her embarrassment.

“Shh, Zoe. I’m not going anywhere and neither are you. Now tell me what’s wrong.”

He continued murmuring comforting things to her, most of which she tuned out, content just to be held. She couldn’t remember the last time a man held her like this, the last time she felt safe and protected. Not even when her daddy was alive.

She didn’t answer him, afraid she’d spill everything—all her hopes, her dreams, her feelings for him—if she opened her mouth. She evened out her breathing, closed her eyes, pretended to sleep, waiting for him to do the same.

“Men like you don’t fall in love with girls like me,” she finally said.

“Sometimes we do,” Tucker murmured into her hair.

Fifteen

"Tucker!"

When the convoy stopped for lunch at a huge travel center, Tucker waited outside by Zoe's RV, talking to the replacement driver. Zoe went into the rest stop to buy snacks.

Now she was flying across the travel stop's apron, Nash on one hip, flapping a tabloid in her other hand. A clerk chased after her.

Tucker met her halfway and held his hand up to the clerk as he tried to make sense of Zoe's babbling. She finally thrust the paper at him, and he snatched it before it blew away.

"She didn't pay for that!" The clerk advanced on them.

"Just hold on. I'll pay for it."

"Tucker!" Zoe persisted, shifting Nash to her other hip. "You have to read that…that trash. It's…none of it's true!"

The clerk's eyebrows rose, her gaze bouncing between Tucker and Zoe. "Oh em gee!" The girl squealed. "Will y'all sign a copy for me?"

Several people stopped to gawk. Tucker herded the

women back inside the convenience store and found a spot where he could read the headlines. "Billionaire's Baby Mama Lives in Secret Love Nest. Barron Entertainment's second in command, Tucker Tate, hides his lover and their child on a private estate in Nashville." He pinched his nose and kept reading. It got worse. He backtracked to check the byline. Parker Grace. Of course. Had to be her. After the stunts the reporter pulled on his cousin, Senator Clay Barron, and Clay's wife Georgie, the woman was fired. He'd heard she was freelancing for whoever would buy a story.

His phone buzzed in his pocket. Pulling it out, he saw *Mom* flashing on the screen. He hit Ignore. Thirty seconds later, the screen flashed *Bridger*. He hit Ignore. For the next few minutes, his phone periodically pinged with calls from Chance Barron, his cousin and the family attorney, and Chance's brother Cash, who was Bridger's boss at Barron Security Services. He waited. It was just a matter of time before Chase, his own boss, called. And bingo. There it was.

"What are we gonna do?" Zoe spat out, keeping her voice low.

Tucker rubbed the back of his neck. "We're going to pay for whatever you're buying, including this rag. I'm going to make some calls." He lifted a shoulder in a shrug looking far more nonchalant than he felt. "This isn't a big deal, angel. My family deals with this stuff all the time." They did, but this mess hit too close to home for comfort and it all seemed too orchestrated. Was someone after Zoe? Or him? He most definitely had a conference call in his future.

"But that's a whole pack of lies," she insisted.

"Need I remind you that this is a tabloid? The people who matter don't believe this stuff." Yeah, of course they didn't. The headlines had nothing to do with his phone blowing up. Nope. Not at all. "C'mon, darlin'. We need to get on the road."

And he needed to get to the bottom of things. Zoe didn't deserve this kind of attention. He stifled his anger as he considered the idea that this was his fault. Maybe he shouldn't have gotten so personally involved. Doubt shadowed his thoughts as he got to work.

Zoe wanted to find a deep, dark cave to crawl into. The tabloids were still at it, paparazzi constantly hounded her and Tucker and they'd had to hire extra security. What hurt, though, were the insinuations that she was on this tour not because of her talent, but because she was with Tucker. She tried not to let it affect her, but it did. She'd been so wound up last night, she'd picked a fight with Tucker. He'd slept on the couch.

He kept assuring her that the PR folks and his cousin's law firm were on top of things but it dang sure didn't feel that way. Zoe was terrified the whole mess would affect her singing, and her chance at a career.

Tucker had grown distant since all the stories hit. Somebody had managed to dig up Nash's birth certificate, and she was sure glad she'd left off the father's name, though that just fueled more rumors.

She had this one last concert to perform—at the University of Tennessee in Knoxville. Once it was done, she could go back to Mr. Don's guesthouse and lick her wounds. Just her and Nash. If she had to move out of Nashville and work little clubs and stuff, so be it. She wasn't sure she was cut out for all this craziness.

Normally, once her sound check was completed, she'd walk back to her RV. Security wanted her to wait until the Sons of Nashville were done so they could all go back together, which she did. Now, she walked between Tucker and Deacon, with the band and security surrounding them. The men scowled at the reporters.

Tucker gave her hand a squeeze. "We'll get through this and then we'll head back to Nashville tonight right after the concert. Okay?"

She nodded, unable to answer as a swarm of reporters descended. A reporter shouted, "Zoe, Zoe! I have it on good authority that your baby's father is doing life in prison—that he killed a man for you, and you ran off, leaving him to face arrest and the trial alone."

Oh, that got her dander up, but before she could respond, there was a commotion at the back of the pack. She recognized Parker Grace, and when Etta and Norbert Smithee appeared beside the reporter, Zoe stopped breathing. *Oh, hell no!*

"That woman framed my baby boy so she could take off with my grandbaby," Etta yelled. "I got the papers right here, all signed and legal, that Redmond wants me to raise his son, not that witch."

Pandemonium erupted. Tucker rushed her toward the RVs, burly bodyguards clearing the way. She needed to grab Nash and run away. No way in hell would she let that woman touch her baby. She stumbled but Tucker grabbed her up and held her in a princess carry as he jogged toward the circle of motor coaches, trucks, trailers and the Volunteermobile, the classic Winnebago normally parked in the Easleys' driveway.

Don and Rosemary had driven it to Knoxville in a fit of nostalgia. Their kids had all attended UT and every fall Saturday there was a home football game, the Easleys were there tailgating in the Volunteermobile.

The whole group crowded into Deacon's coach, leaving the guards outside to protect them. Zoe immediately snatched Nash from the play crib and cuddled him close, tears streaming down her cheeks.

"They're not gonna get you, baby boy. You hear me? Momma won't let those nasty people have you," she vowed into his sweet-smelling baby hair.

Deacon explained the situation while Tucker, his back to the group, made phone calls. Quin stood off to one side, watching Zoe, assessing her, as if Quin didn't quite trust her or this turn of events. *This isn't my fault!* Zoe wanted to scream. She didn't. She clamped her mouth shut and held on to Nash for all she was worth. She had to make a plan.

Zoe paced the length of the corridor that led to the stage. She did not want to be here, and her insides were so knotted up, breathing was painful. How was she going to sing? But how could she not? If she flaked out, her career would be as good as dead. If she ducked and ran, the paparazzi and the Smithees would still hound her, no matter where she went. Her daddy might not have been the best father in the world, but he'd taught her to keep her chin high, to stand up for herself and to not back down—not from anyone.

She was beginning to have a career. She had a bank account with money in it—money to take care of Nash. It all depended on her walking out on that stage, singing her heart out and fulfilling her contract. So that's just what she was gonna do. She had to get through tonight and then figure out all the rest. Like Tucker. If he didn't walk away from her after this. *No.* She couldn't think about him. She had songs to sing.

The stage manager whistled at her and she walked toward him, her gait determined. She was gonna rock the house—well, football stadium. She would raise her voice to the sky and give it all she had. And then she'd figure out what to do.

The stage manager walked her to her spot on the blacked-out stage and when the spotlight hit her, she was ready. She opened up with Miranda Lambert's "Gunpowder and Lead," a song that fit her mood perfectly. She'd show the Smithees—and everyone else—just what she was made of. She followed Miranda with "Redneck Woman," another anthem to strong women everywhere. The stadium was rocking. She slowed the tempo down with "Fancy," a song about a woman rising from dirt poor to rich man's wife. That only happened in songs and the movies, right?

When she finally got to the last song, she let the lights come down, waiting for the crowd to quiet just a bit—and for the Sons of Nashville to get into place behind her on the darkened stage. It felt like the whole place was holding its breath. Her fingers danced over the strings of her guitar as she slowly plucked the opening notes to "Rocky Top," the unofficial fight song of the University of Tennessee. Then, a cappella, she sang the first two lines of the chorus. Right on time, Xander, the Sons of Nashville's banjo picker, kicked in, upping the tempo. The audience erupted. Lights blazed on the stage and Deacon came out to join her as everyone sang.

The crowd was on their feet screaming by the time they were done. The audience's energy wrapped around her. Dang it. She *wanted* this. She deserved this and those damn Smithees wanted to take it all away. Her eyes burned with unshed tears when she took her bows and slipped offstage as Deacon and the Sons launched into their opening song, "Red Dirt Cowgirl."

Tucker wasn't waiting for her as she exited. Her chest tightened. Something was wrong. She headed for the greenroom at a trot but passed by the door when she heard angry voices farther on. She peeked around a corner to find Tucker, two of the Barron bodyguards and several stadium security guards facing down the Smithees, a weaselly little man in a ratty suit, and a big guy with stringy hair, fingerless leather gloves and a bad attitude.

"You're the one who doesn't understand," Ratty Suit whined. "My associate and I are here to ensure that justice is done. We have papers to serve and a pickup order for Baby Boy Smithee."

This. Was. Bad. Zoe panicked. Retreating to the greenroom, she slipped inside. She found Keisha, Quin and both kids. Zoe put away her guitar with studied calm even though her brain was whirring like margaritas in a blender. That's when Don Easley walked into the room and came over to her.

"I'm gonna get you and Nash outta here, darlin'. Get 'im packed up."

Zoe didn't stop to think. She slung the diaper bag over her shoulder, scooped up Nash in his carrier and her guitar, and headed for the door as Don said, "I'm takin' Zoe out the back way while everybody's otherwise occupied." They were gone before Quin could respond.

Don led her to an exit far away from the confrontation. He pressed a keyring into her hand. "Take the Volunteermobile. Nobody will look for you in that. Got your phone?" She nodded. "I'll let you know when it's safe to come back."

Come back? Would that ever be possible? What would Tucker do when he discovered her gone? She figured he'd be relieved to be rid of her but her secret heart hoped he'd miss her. And could get over being mad, because this would pretty much send him over the edge.

"Coast is clear." Don shoved a wad of money into her pocket and pushed her out the door. As much as she wanted to run, she walked sedately to avoid attention. Sticking to the shadows, she made it to the Volunteermobile with no one noticing. She fumbled the keys trying to unlock the door, dropped them. Crouching to pick them up, she heard voices and froze.

Tucker stared at the so-called attorney representing the Smithees. He'd brought a process server cum bounty hunter but no official law enforcement, much to his relief. He figured not even Quin would go up against real law enforcement. Of course, he didn't believe for one second that any judge had signed an order transferring Nash's custody to these people. Baby Boy Smithee? Seriously? With no father listed on the birth certificate, a real judge would demand DNA proof.

"As I've told you, I am Ms. Parker's representative. If you have official court papers to serve, you can serve me."

"But we want Redmond's baby," Etta Smithee said.

"Do you have proof he's the father?"

The attorney waved a sheaf of papers at him. "It's all right here. Sworn testimony."

Tucker snatched the papers and leafed through them. They carried only the seal and signature of a notary public. No judge of any jurisdiction. The attorney continued to whine. "Redmond woulda married the girl if that unfortunate incident hadn't happened. We're workin' on his appeal, and he should be gettin' out anytime now. He wants his momma to raise his boy till he's freed."

"Tucker!"

He turned at that sharp call. Quin stood in the hallway leading to the greenroom and the look on her face sent cold chills racing down his spine. He walked to her without a word. At her urgent whisper, he pivoted to stare out the glass doors leading to the parking lot. He was just in time to see the lights on an orange Winnebago flare to life. He went from standing still to a dead run, hitting the exit doors so hard they both banged back against the windows beside them.

Sprinting full-out, he reached the parking lot exit with seconds to spare. He planted his body in the middle of the drive, hands fisted on his hips. Tires squealed, but the RV kept coming, closer and closer. He caught a glimpse of Zoe's horrified face as a horn blared "Rocky Top."

Sixteen

"I could have killed you!" Zoe shook so hard the driver's seat rattled.

"But you didn't." Tucker stood beside her and tried to get his heart rate under control. Noise filtered in from outside, and he looked out the window. "Move over, I'm driving."

Zoe followed the direction of his gaze. A horde of reporters and photographers surged toward them in a menacing wave. Leading the pack was the Smithees, their ambulance-chasing lawyer and the thuggish process server. She squeaked and surrendered her seat.

"Buckle up," Tucker directed as he slid in behind her. He put the Winnebago in gear and pulled out onto the street just as the thug banged on the back of the RV. They left him in a cloud of diesel smoke.

"That was close." Pulling onto Neyland Drive, Tucker plotted the best way out of town.

"Where are we going?" Zoe's eyes were fixed on the side mirror.

"No clue. You were the one running away. Where were

you going, Zoe? What were you going to do when you got there?"

She buried her face in her hands, and a few minutes later, Tucker caught her muffled, "I don't know."

He didn't get a lot of satisfaction from that answer. Tuck debated whether to ask the question on the tip of his tongue. The logical businessman knew it would be a mistake, but the man? The man wanted to know. In a quiet tone, he voiced his fear. "Were you running away from me?"

Zoe took too long to answer, and her silence was deafening. Tucker did not like the way it made him feel—angry, tense and…hurt. Her reticence made him question his feelings. Maybe he needed time to get his head on straight. He'd get her and Nash safely away, then Dandy Don and Deacon could look after them. Bent Star and the music business? Not his forte, obviously. It was time for him to get back to his real work. Except the thought of leaving Zoe and Nash left a hollow spot deep inside.

Nash fussed and without speaking, Zoe heaved out of the passenger seat and walked to the back of the RV. Tucker's phone played the theme from *Cops*. Quin. He swiped the phone and put it to his ear. "Yeah?"

"Seriously, Tucker? That girl—"

"Woman, Quin. She's a woman. And a mother. And she's in trouble. I don't want or need a lecture."

Silence stretched for almost a full minute. "Fine." He could almost hear Quin's teeth grinding. "You left the legal papers behind. I scanned and emailed them to Chance. Katherine says you need to go home."

"To Las Vegas?" Except that wasn't really home.

"No, dummy. *Home.* Oklahoma. The ranch. She's mobilizing the troops."

Now it was Tucker's turn for silence while he mulled it over. Katherine Tate was a force of nature. And despite his reluctance to get the Bee Dubyas involved, he had no such compunctions about their husbands or his brothers. When he approached the intersection with US 129, he turned north. "Okay," he agreed. "As soon as I hit I-40, we're heading west." He glanced at his phone to get the time. "We should be there around noon. Will you…"

"Yes. I'll call your mother." He pictured Quin rolling her eyes.

Zoe called from behind him. "Where are we going?"

"We're making a run for the border."

Zoe slept through the four-car wreck, the construction zones where they came to a complete halt and woke up just after dawn when Tucker pulled off at a travel center. In clipped words, he filled her in on the delays while maneuvering the Volunteermobile to a gas pump. He was filling the tank when she stepped out, Nash in a baby chest pack. She adjusted the UT baseball cap she'd swiped from the Volunteermobile's closet. "I'm going inside. Want food?"

He glanced up. Tucker looked…tired. Of course he was tired. He'd been driving all night. She'd had a nap at least. He shook his head, saying nothing. Yeah, he was still upset with her.

The first thing that caught her attention as she pushed through the entrance was the rack of tabloid papers lining the checkout area. Ducking her head, she headed to the ladies' room. When she came out, a few people stared.

She pushed past them, her hand pressing Nash's face to her chest, her own face down and veiled by her hair and the cap bill. Hungry, Zoe had planned to grab some hot breakfast to go from the buffet. Too late for that now. Awareness rolled through the crowd of people in the convenience store like rain moving across a field. She slipped through the exit. Would this circus never end?

Tucker joined her in the RV a few minutes later, holding two to-go boxes and a tall coffee cup. She popped one open to find scrambled eggs, bacon and sausage patties. The second held biscuits and gravy. "Hungry?"

Tucker shook his head. "Nope. That's all for you. Eat up." He left her sitting at the dinette. Shoving bites of biscuits covered in cream gravy into her mouth, she watched him while he got them back on the road. He was always feeding her. Taking care of her. She wondered if he realized what he was doing.

She ate, then gave Nash a bottle. Once he was asleep, she settled into the passenger seat beside Tucker. He drove with his right hand, left elbow resting on the window ledge. The silence wasn't exactly comfortable. She huffed out a breath, which stirred her bangs. "I'm so sorry about all this."

"Not your fault, Zoe. We'll be home in a couple of hours."

Zoe. Her name. Not an endearment. Yeah, she'd really put her foot in it. She needed to fix things. "Going there will make a difference?"

He wheezed out a laugh. "I *have* mentioned my family, right?" She nodded but didn't say anything. "One cousin is a US senator. One is a fancy-smancy attorney no one wants to mess with. One owns a huge security company. My brothers all work for the Barrons in one form or another. The Barrons are a big deal in Oklahoma, and that stuff rolls downhill on us Tates."

Zoe mulled that over. "Good lord. How many of you are there?"

"Six Barrons, seven Tates."

She blinked. "Um…sibling rivalry much?"

Tucker laughed. The sound made her tummy do cartwheels. So often, Tucker looked serious and acted so single-minded but when he laughed? He was the sexiest man she'd ever seen. Yup, she had it bad, and she needed to get things settled because she didn't know where this whole deal was going.

"Thank you," she said.

He glanced over. "For what?"

"For being here for Nash and me."

He shrugged, returning his attention to the road. She settled back against the seat. She liked Tucker. A lot. Too much. He made her want things she couldn't have and she was pretty sure he didn't want to give. Except he was so sweet to her and Nash.

They rode in silence until Tucker pulled off I-40 and into the Cherokee Travel Plaza. He stopped at the pumps, stretched and yawned. "We're about three hours away. We can take a break here."

The miles of silence left her with plenty of time to think and she'd finally figured out what was broken. Maybe. Nervous, she gazed at him. "Tucker?"

He stopped and turned to look at her. "I'm sorry."

"Not your—"

"It *is* my fault but that's not what I'm apologizing for. I…" She had to inhale to settle her stomach. "I panicked. I was just…running. So, yeah. In a way, I guess I was running away from you. If it means anything, I'm glad you caught me."

His smile came slow but didn't quite reach his eyes. "Are you sure?"

"Positive." She ached to touch him but kept her hands in her lap.

"I'm going to grab coffee with an extra shot of espresso. You want a mocha?"

Nodding, she said, "Tucker, are we—"

He cut her off. "It's all good."

She hoped it was.

* * *

Three people stood on the front porch—two men who looked a lot like Tucker flanking a woman. They all wore jeans and boots. Zoe eyed the formidable woman with trepidation. No wonder a touch of awe entered their voices whenever Tucker, Deacon or Dillon spoke of their mother. Dark hair, attractive and very much in charge. Zoe clutched Nash a little tighter.

"Mom, this is Zoe." Tucker said it like Mrs. Tate would know exactly who she was. He handed the empty baby carrier to the nearest man saying, "Zoe, this is Cooper." Then he urged her toward the front entrance without giving her a chance to gape, because there was a *lot* to gape at. The house was huge.

"About time y'all got here. Bring that baby inside." The woman swept her with a cool, appraising gaze, then her eyes flicked to the Volunteermobile, and her lips might have twitched just a little. The movement was so quick, Zoe couldn't be positive. "Come in, come in."

Like ducklings, the brothers followed their mother into the house. Zoe slipped through the door behind Tucker and followed the herd into an airy kitchen and family room.

"You're staying the night." Mrs. Tate said the words to Tucker but she was staring at Zoe. "I have your room ready, Tucker."

Tucker leaned down only a little bit to kiss his mother on the cheek. "Thanks, Mom."

"And we're having fried chicken and all the fixings for lunch," Mrs. Tate said, giving Zoe another long look. A thought hit her. What would happen if Katherine Tate tangled with Etta Smithee? A scene of the two women wrestling in a WWE ring popped into her head and Zoe burst out laughing.

"Zoe can stay, too."

Yippee, Zoe thought, a touch apprehensive.

"But she sleeps in the guest room."

Well, that was a no-brainer. Zoe shifted Nash to her other hip. His mother watched.

"Zoe, stay. The rest of you, out of here."

The woman shooed her sons out of the kitchen like they were chickens. Not one lingered.

"Sit, girl," Mrs. Tate ordered.

What was she, a dog? Sit. Stay. But who was she to argue? Zoe hitched her hip on a tall stool at the kitchen island. "I'll be happy to help cook, ma'am."

"You can help by telling me what's going on between you and my son."

She gulped. That was a good question—one she'd like the answer to herself. "Not quite sure what you mean, Miz Tate."

"Call me Katherine. And don't play dumb, Zoe. You aren't. You know exactly what I mean. You and my son are sleeping together, and don't think for a minute that he won't try to sneak into your room tonight."

Zoe blushed and fussed with Nash's clothing for a moment to regain her equilibrium. Katherine kept right on talking.

"My sons are grown men, Zoe, and they aren't saints. Their father and I prepared them for the real world as best we could and raised them to be responsible, caring men. Now that Deacon has settled down—given he was the wildest in the bunch—I have hopes for the rest of them. I want to know about you."

Shoulders square, chin jutting, Zoe faced down the older woman. "Since your daughter-in-law ran a background check on me, I figure you pretty much know everything there is to know."

"My son Bridger checked long before Quin even thought

of it." She poured a glass of sweet tea and slid it over the countertop to Zoe. "Don't get your panties in a twist. That's the way this family works. Always has. We like to know who we're dealing with. You notice that you are still part of Tucker's life, yes?"

Zoe closed her mouth with a snap and focused on her glass of tea. "What's that mean?"

"It means that I trust my sons. And it means that Tucker cares about you. There is no way he'd be caught dead driving a Tennessee-orange Winnebago with the UT emblem plastered on the back otherwise. That boy's a graduate of the University of Oklahoma and his blood runs crimson and cream."

Zoe snickered, and took a drink to help disguise her amusement. "Yeah. He's had to toot the horn a time or two. I thought he was gonna go apoplectic or something."

Katherine knitted her brow. "Don't tell me it plays 'Rocky Top.'" Zoe nodded and Mrs. Tate burst out laughing. She was about to take a sip of her drink when a new man walked in. He had to be another Tate brother. He was older, with crinkles at the corners of his eyes and a watchful air about him.

"Hunter, this is Zoe Parker. And Nash." Katherine sidled over and plucked Nash out of her lap before Zoe could react. "Here," the woman said, passing the baby to him. "You need practice. Now get out of here until lunchtime." She fluttered her hands at him, moving him along.

"Hey!" Zoe protested.

He scowled but did as his mother asked, though he glanced over his shoulder. "Nice to meet you, Zoe. Don't worry, I'll take Nash to Tucker."

Katherine poured her own glass of tea and settled on a stool across from Zoe. She took several sips, then sighed and said, "You've got my son worried, Zoe."

"Which one?"

The look Tucker's mother leveled on her would have turned a steel magnolia into a puddle of goo. "Do not play dumb with me, young lady."

Zoe blinked and leaned away from the intensity in Katherine's stare. "What would Tucker be worried about?"

"You. And your baby. Tucker has feelings for you. Deep ones. I want to know if you return them. If not, tell him now and put him out of his misery."

She hung her head. Zoe did have feelings but admitting them? It left her too vulnerable. "I'll talk to him."

Seventeen

Tucker watched Zoe and his mother from his hiding place like they were players in a tennis match. He'd thought to hang back to hear their discussion but then Hunter walked down the hall where he was eavesdropping. His big brother handed the kid off and pushed him on down the hallway.

"Mom catches you, there'll be trouble. Besides, we need to talk."

That didn't bode well. Neither did Cooper and Bridger standing in the game room like gate sentries. With their feet spread and arms crossed over their chests, they radiated determination. "You're the last one of us I'd pick to be in this mess," Bridger said. Hunter and Cooper agreed.

"I know what I'm doing." Tucker glowered at his brothers.

"We don't think you do." This from Cooper.

The *intervention* went downhill from there. Oddly, Hunter never said a word and Tucker wondered whose side his big brother was on. Nash finally saved him with a dirty diaper. His mom called them in for lunch as he finished changing the baby.

Zoe picked at her food. His brothers kept up a running commentary of their lives. Tucker shoveled food into his mouth. His mom was a great cook, and homemade fried chicken with mashed potatoes, gravy, biscuits and fresh green beans was his favorite meal. And with his mouth full of food, he didn't have room to stick his foot in there.

After nibbling on a drumstick and stirring gravy around in the mashed potatoes on her plate, Zoe slipped out of her chair and carried her plate into the kitchen. Tucker watched his mother watch Zoe. Then her gaze focused on him with laser-sharp accuracy. Of course, his three brothers also turned their gazes on him.

"Don't y'all work for a living?" he muttered.

"It's Sunday," Bridger reminded him.

"Hence, fried chicken for lunch?" Cooper hinted, like they hadn't had fried chicken for Sunday lunch their entire lives.

Tucker glared at Hunter, waiting for his oldest brother to weigh in, but Bridger spoke up instead. "Speaking of lunch, guess who I ran into the other day?" he said to Hunter, who looked bored and took another bite. "Tanya McDaniels."

Hunter choked as the rest of them froze, all eyes on Bridger. "Seems she's moved back to Oklahoma City."

Gulping the iced tea in his glass, Hunter seemed to have his breathing back under control, though his temper wasn't. "In case you've forgotten, Bridger, that's not a name I want repeated. We clear on that?" Hunter pushed back from the table, his chair scraping on the wooden floor. He cleared his plate and followed Zoe to the kitchen.

Silence reigned for several long moments, then Katherine rose and walked out of the room. Cooper hit Bridger in the biceps. Hard. "Way to go, numbnuts."

"I thought he needed to know." Bridger shrugged. "That whole deal with Tanya was screwed up, even to me, and

I was just a kid. We all know she messed him over while he was deployed with the Marines." He muttered a few strong words under his breath, none of them flattering. "Just sayin'."

Tucker scraped the last bit of gravy off his plate with his biscuit, stuffed it into his mouth and stood. He smacked the back of Bridger's head with his palm, gathered his plate and headed to the kitchen before his brother could retaliate. He glanced out the French doors and saw his mother and Hunter sitting on the back porch talking. Nash was secured in his carrier on the kitchen island, playing grabby-toes and giggling. Zoe was washing dishes.

"You don't have to do that, angel."

"Yeah I do." Though quiet, Zoe's voice was filled with conviction. "Gotta pay my own way, and with the Smithees—"

"C'mere." Tucker cut her off and pulled her into his arms. He kissed the top of her head, speaking into her hair. "Let me explain something about my family. We stick together. When one of us is in trouble, we all come running to help. That includes our cousins, the Barrons. It'll be all right, Zoe. I promise."

Zoe stiffened. "Don't make promises you can't keep. The Smithees have that awful lawyer workin' for 'em. They're gonna make a big ol' stink and I've dragged your family right into the middle of it."

"My family wants—"

Nash wailed, cutting him off. Zoe ducked around Tucker, snagged the carrier and swung it off the island. She then grabbed a bottle from the refrigerator. "I gotta feed Bugtussle."

Tucker wanted to follow her to explain that *he'd* involved his family and why, but the appearance of his cousin, Chance, a drumstick in one hand and a folder in the other, had him reversing directions. “The study,” he directed. By the time they arrived in the cozy den-like space his father once used as an office, Chance had finished the chicken. Tucker settled a hip on one corner of the desk while Chance stood in front.

“I emailed Zoe’s recording contract to Don Easley,” Chance said without preamble. “Now, I just have one question for you, Tuck.” Tucker raised both brows in a look of inquiry, waiting for him to continue. “I’ve talked to Redmond Smithee. How much money are you willing to pay him to sign away his parental rights?” He stopped Tucker from answering with another question. “Why are you doing this, cuz?”

Good question. He dropped his chin and rubbed the back of his neck. “Already had the familial intervention, *cuz.*”

“No intervention, Tucker. I just want you to think things through. So, back to my original questions. How much and why?”

How much was easy. Why? He wasn’t impetuous. He didn’t just *do* crazy stuff like pick up a runaway bride stranded on the side of the road. He didn’t help babies get born. He didn’t fall for sweet-voiced country girls. Except he’d done all those things. He’d probably been falling in love with Zoe since the moment he stuffed that awful wedding dress around her in his T-Bird.

“I’ve got another question, Tuck. Have you talked to Zoe about this? About terminating the father’s parental rights?”

That question he could easily answer. He squarely met Chance’s gaze. “No, but she didn’t list Smithee on the birth certificate. A DNA test would prove he’s the father so I want that preempted. She wants those people out of her life, and out of her son’s.” Tucker breathed. “As for your other questions, first, how much? However much it takes.” He’d pay a million dollars to get the Smithees out of Zoe's and Nash's lives. Hell, he'd pay ten million.

"As for the why?" He looked down at the toes of his boots before answering. "Because I'm fairly certain I'm falling in love."

"That's all I needed to know." Chance spread out the papers from the file on the desk. "I need a cashier's check for one hundred thousand dollars. I'll fly to Alabama tomorrow with the check, get Smithee to sign the papers and then I'll put those funds in a trust account for him and his family. Now sign here, here and here."

As Tucker signed, he said quietly, "How big a deal would adoption papers be?"

"A bit premature, don't you think?" Chance looked concerned. "Given the circumstances?"

Tucker lifted one shoulder in a studied shrug. "Yeah, maybe. But you know me. I'm a planner. Just in case, I want them ready. For when the time comes."

Chance favored him with a searching look, as he gathered the papers. "If that's what you want, bud." It sounded like a question.

The two of them headed for the back door. Katherine was puttering around in the kitchen, Zoe nowhere in sight. Chance paused to kiss his aunt on the cheek and then, with her admonition to toss the drumstick in the trash on his way out, he laughed and did. Tucker breathed easy for the first time in a while. Getting the Smithees out of Zoe's life was worth every penny.

"That's a lot of money," his mother said in a soft voice—one he knew far too well. She was not happy.

"It's my money, Mom. And you shouldn't have been eavesdropping."

"This is my house, and you're my son. I'll do whatever

it takes to protect both. What do you really know about this girl, Tucker?"

"I know everything I need to."

"Is she worth a hundred thousand dollars?" Katherine held up her hand. "Think about it before you answer me. Examine your motives, son. Chase is married now. And Deacon, who stumbled into a ready-made family. You always did try to imitate both of them."

He bristled. "That's not what I'm doing, Mom."

"It's okay to care about this girl and her baby, but do you really need to get so involved? She might be talented—and according to Deacon and Dillon, she is. But how long would it take her to pay you back?"

"I don't want her to pay me back."

"I don't understand you, Tucker."

"I don't exactly understand you at the moment, Mom. I thought you liked Zoe."

"I do. But she's not the woman for you." His mother wiped her hands on a dish towel hung on the horseshoe nailed to the cabinet over the sink. "She has a child, Tucker. A child who isn't yours. You're an executive with a Fortune 100 company. She's…she wants to be an entertainer. How will that work? She won't be home to take care of her child or you. Or do you plan to trail around after her like a well-trained dog?"

"That's enough, Mom. We're done here."

"We're not even close. Who gives up their dream, Tucker? Have you thought about that? Your life is in Las Vegas or wherever else Barron Entertainment needs you. That apartment at the Crown Casino is as close to a home as you have when you aren't here. In the room you grew up in. You stay in condos owned by the company when you travel. You need a real home. A real wife. Suppose it does work out between the two of you. Will you stay in Vegas while she lives in Nashville? Do you live separate lives with a nanny looking after her baby? Or do you give up everything you've worked for just so she can do what she wants?"

He growled under his breath, unwilling to admit he hadn't thought things through completely, which was so unlike him. He was the logical one, the one who made plans and followed them. Or he had been until he met Zoe. Ever since he'd picked her up on the side of the road, he'd been running on emotional adrenaline. Maybe he did need to step back and assess the situation. Except he didn't have to. He knew how he felt.

Zoe and Nash…he loved them.

Tucker, jostling Nash against his shoulder, watched Zoe slap icing on a blue cake. The thing looked like half a ball. The icing was white and there was a package of coconut flakes on the counter. Maybe it was supposed to look like a snowball.

"Ah, darlin'?"

"What?" She glanced up and he saw a dab of icing on her cheek. He had to refrain from licking it off.

"What are you doing?"

"What does it look like I'm doing? I baked a cake and now I'm icing it."

"Fair enough. *Why* did you bake a cake?"

"Because…well… I needed something to do. I've been here three days." She tore the bag of coconut open with her teeth and began throwing handfuls at the cake. She finally stopped, then backed away until her butt was braced against the stainless steel Sub-Zero refrigerator. Shoving her hands into her pockets, which caused her shoulders to curve forward in a dejected slump, she huffed out a breath. "You just don't get it."

Something in her voice kept him silent when he would

have offered up a quip or worse, some meaningless platitude. Tucker waited. He seemed to be doing a lot of that lately.

"I want to be a singer, Tucker," she said, almost in a whisper. He had to strain to understand her words.

"You *are* a singer, Zoe. What does this have to do with baking a cake?"

In a stronger voice, though one thick with tears, she added, "Nothin'. I just… It's…it was somethin' nice to do for your family."

His instincts told him to gather her into his arms. When he walked toward her, she held up her hands to halt him. "My whole life, all I've ever wanted to be is a singer. I want the albums and the studio time and performing in an arena in front of thousands of fans. I wanna win Entertainer of the Year from the Country Music Association."

He didn't catch the smile forming on his mouth in time. Her lips thinned but not in anger. Too late, Tucker realized her bottom lip was trembling.

"Your family feels sorry for me. I know people take one look at me and think I'm a joke. Just some no-account hillbilly girl with stars in her eyes." Her gaze flicked to the baby in his arms. "One too dumb not to get pregnant by a stranger and then not smart enough to take care of it if her career is that all-fired important."

He tried to interrupt her. "That's not true, Zoe."

"I might be from the back of beyond, but so was Miss Dolly. So were a lot of country stars before they came to Nashville and made a name for themselves. I can sing. I'm not afraid to work hard, and I'll do whatever it takes to make my dream come true and take care of my baby boy." Her head *thunked* against the metal fridge. "Well…not exactly *whatever*. I'll get there on my talent, not my back."

That got his attention—not that she didn't have it before. "Zoe—"

"No. Hear me out. I don't wanna believe that you think I'm doin' the deed with you to get a contract with Bent Star, but I gotta wonder." Her gaze was steady as she looked at him. "I got dreams. Big ones. Important ones. Important to me, anyway. I always have. And nobody is gonna stop me."

"I'm not trying to stop you, Zoe. In fact—" He was about to tell her that Dandy Don had her contract from Bent Star, that he wanted to sign her and not because he'd mixed business with pleasure but because he believed in her, but he didn't get the chance.

Because just then, Bridger walked in, a tabloid rolled up in one hand and a business card in the other. He paused, staring at Zoe, his face inscrutable. Tucker straightened as Bridge tossed the items onto the island.

"Bridge?" Tucker stared at his brother, concerned.

"Found this stuff in Nash's diaper bag when I changed him earlier."

Tucker recognized the tabloid—and its secret love nest headline. He picked up the card and he clenched his teeth when he read the name. "Parker Grace?"

Tucker tore his eyes from his brother and focused on Zoe. "What is this? Have you had contact with this woman?" Zoe's voice rang in his head. *I'll do whatever it takes to make my dream come true.* Had he been so wrong about Zoe? Had she been working with the one reporter his whole family hated?

To say the mood in the room was tense was an understatement. "She ambushed me at Dandy Don's. I told her to leave. You can check. I called nine-one-one to report it." Zoe's gaze darted between the two men, as she worried they didn't believe her. Her heart broke a little and then her temper flared. "Why in the deep, dark recesses of hell would I want my name splashed all over the tabloids?"

"Publicity," Bridger said.

"Seriously? Y'all are crazy. Bein' tabloid trash sucks. Y'all don't know what it's like havin' people stare at you like you're cow manure stuck on the bottom of their boots."

"Zoe. We've never... *I've* never—"

She marched up to Tucker, plucked Nash from his arms and cuddled the baby close. She stared at the men—there was no compassion in Bridger's eyes and only confusion in Tucker's. Hot tears pricked the back of her eyelids. She would not cry. She would not show them how much this hurt. She should have expected something like this to happen. Bad stuff always did and she'd been a damn fool for ever thinking that she and Tucker might have something real and lasting. She was just a girl from the wrong side of the tracks who could sing a little and he was Tucker Tate, Mr. Billionaire Country, or he would be if there was a beauty contest like that.

She had to reach deep for some dignity and deeper still to find the stubbornness that saw her through every bad thing that happened in her life. She didn't need Tucker Tate. Didn't want him. Much. But she'd just learned something, and sometimes the lessons of the heart were the hardest and most painful. If he didn't trust her, he'd never care about her.

"Zoe."

Tucker reached for her but she dodged him. "I'm done here."

Zoe stomped out of the kitchen, flying on adrenaline. She couldn't stay in the same room with Tucker. Heck, she couldn't stay in the same house with him. She'd pack up her and Nash's stuff and go stay in the RV.

While she gathered their belongings, she came up with

a plan. Digging out her cell, she called Dandy Don. She swallowed hard, forcing her voice to stay firm but failing as she said, “Hi, Mr. Don.”

“Are you okay, darlin’?” His voice, while full of fatherly concern, sounded far away.

“Yeah. I’m fine.” She could lie now because she would be fine. Eventually. “I wanted to let you know I’m headin’ back to Nashville to return your Volunteermobile. I’ll be there tomorrow.”

“Is Tucker—”

“No.” She cut him off. “He ain’t. I’m drivin’ back alone.” It wasn’t like Tucker and his family wanted her there.

“I’m not sure that’s a good—”

“We’ll be fine, Mr. Don, Nash and me.” And they would be because she was taking back her life.

Eighteen

Tucker stared into his coffee cup, the reflection staring back at him looking morose. The call from Don Easley that morning had been a double whammy—Zoe was driving back to Nashville and Midnight Records had offered her a contract. Dandy Don refused to discuss the terms, which made Tuck suspicious, given how liberal Bent Star's contract was.

As Bridger and his mother entered the kitchen, he snarled. "She's gone." He ignored the look they exchanged.

"We know," Bridger said, pouring his own cup. "I called in a favor from a federal agent who owed me one. He did some checking. It was those Smithee people stirring up the press. And we all know Parker Grace has a grudge against us." He pulled a stool up next to Tucker and clapped his shoulder. "I'm sorry. I was wrong about Zoe."

"Me, too," Quin added as she and Deke walked in, followed by the rest of his family.

"It doesn't matter." How could he have been so totally… stupid? There was a reason he didn't do relationships. And now he'd pretty much ruined whatever chance he had with Zoe—personally *or* professionally. Deke had been right to warn him. He felt hollow inside.

"I'm disappointed in you, Tucker."

That brought his head up, and he was too stunned to avoid scowling at his mother. "Excuse me? You're the one who insisted she'd never be a real wife, that she wasn't good enough for me."

"And you're the one who was supposed to fight for her if you loved her."

Tucker opened and closed his mouth several times, unable to form coherent words. Reverse psychology? *That* was his mother's plan? Deke shooed everyone out, a gesture Tucker appreciated. He didn't need—or want—his brothers to see his misery. Their mother remained in the doorway, lips pursed, eyes fixed on him. He'd messed up. Bad. And while Katherine Tate loved her sons, she never hesitated to call them on the carpet when they were wrong. Tucker buried his face in his hands, unable to meet the censure in his mother's gaze any longer.

He glanced up, hoping to be alone, but Deke had remained, though his mother was gone. Silence stretched between him and his older brother. Tucker waited for Deke to break it. Deke didn't.

"Go ahead," Tucker finally said. "I know you're dying to tell me what an idiot I am."

"Naw. It'd be too much like kicking a puppy."

Tucker raised his head, stared at his brother. "I didn't get it."

"Dude, you're a guy. Most of us don't until some smart woman nails us with a clue-by-four." Deke hitched a hip on a stool and folded his arms across his chest. "The question becomes, what are you going to do about it?"

"She has an offer from Midnight Records. If she signs

with—" Tucker bit his tongue when his brother reached over and cuffed the back of his head. "Owww."

"This isn't about Zoe signing with another label. This is about your feelings for her, and hers for you."

"Yeah, but…" Tucker huffed out a breath and scrubbed at his hair. Feelings. He didn't want to talk about *feelings* with his brother.

"You need to talk to her."

"I tried calling. She wouldn't pick up."

"Then go after her."

"She has a head start."

Deke rolled his eyes. "How are we even related? Tuck, who do you work for?"

"Barron Entertainment."

"And what is your title?"

"Chief Operations Officer."

"And what's sitting in a hangar at Wiley Post Airport?"

Tuck stared at Deke and scrunched his forehead, thinking hard. He brought up his hands and lifted his shoulders in a gesture that said, *What?*

Deke sighed dramatically then said each word slowly. "The corporate jets, including the one we all flew in on last night."

He leaned forward until his forehead bounced a little on the granite counter. "Brain-dead. I'm totally brain-dead." He'd been so wrapped up in misery that his calm, collected and highly organized mind simply shorted out.

But now hope loosened the knot in his chest. He could be in Nashville before Zoe got there. He could meet her before she did something they'd both regret. He could fix this. All he had to do was grovel. He could learn to do that in the two hours it would take to fly there. And he would. Grovel. Until he got her back.

"You also need to make a grand gesture."

"A what?"

"A grand gesture. To show her how much she means to you."

"Like what?"

"Like Chance telling Uncle Cyrus to take a flying leap and helping Cassie with that cattle drive."

That had been a grand gesture. Their Uncle Cyrus had been a tyrant trying to ruin Cassie's life. To meet a payment on a bank loan, and with no other way to get her herd to market, Cassie pulled off—with Chance's help—a modern-day cattle drive.

Deke's smile softened. "Like Quin standing in front of the stage on New Year's Eve holding up a sign asking me for a second chance." Tucker stared at Deke, his mind blank. "Seriously? I really am starting to doubt we're related. Do you remember how furious I was over losing Noelle?" Tucker nodded. "I know I told you how she apologized in front of the whole crowd."

"So?"

"So? You're hopeless. Go pack. I'll call the hangar. Maybe you'll think of something before you get to Nashville."

Zoe paced the backstage area of the Grand Ole Opry. Two days after returning to Nashville, Mr. Don called to say she was appearing at the Opry on Saturday night. It was almost time. She'd rehearsed two songs with the Opry's backup musicians: Gretchen Wilson's "Redneck Woman" and Striking Matches' "When the Right One Comes Along." Mr. Don was convinced they'd showcase her voice perfectly, even though the second song was a duet. The last time she'd sung it had been at Bent Star. Given her situation with Tucker, the lyrics ripped her heart open. Her stomach knotted, and she wanted to throw up but there wasn't time. The announcer was introducing her.

"You got this, darlin'," Mr. Don said, giving her a pat on the shoulder. "Now get out there and show 'em what you got."

She plastered on a big smile she didn't feel and strode into the spotlight like she'd been born for this moment. The show always went on.

The crowd loved the first song, clapping and shouting along with her. When she launched into the second song, a hush fell over the audience and when the chorus arrived, she sensed their anticipation. Surprised almost speechless, she just managed not to drop a note when Deacon appeared beside her to sing the duet. This shouldn't be happening since she'd left Tucker—and Bent Star.

As the last sad notes echoed in the auditorium, the crowd went wild. She took her bows and accepted a kiss on the cheek from Deacon. She turned to leave the stage, but Deke snagged her arm and hauled her back to the microphone.

"As y'all know, Zoe's been opening for the Sons of Nashville the past couple of weeks," Deke said into the mic. "Not only is she a fantastic performer, she's a heckuva songwriter, too." The crowd whistled. "Zoe doesn't know what I'm about to say and I'm hopin' she won't be mad."

Confused, Zoe stared at Deacon and mouthed, "What are you talking about?"

He winked at her and continued. "Tonight, I'm pleased that the Sons and I get to back her up on the debut of her new song, 'We Can't Be.' Ladies and gentlemen, Zoe Parker!"

Zoe stopped breathing. Her first instinct was to run off the stage but before her panic won, Deke leaned close and whispered in her ear. "You got this, darlin', just like we practiced all those times in all those greenrooms. Yeah?"

The lights lowered, and the Sons played the opening bridge before Zoe was ready. They played it a second time before she gathered enough wits to join in on her guitar. Third time through was the charm and she opened her mouth to sing. "I'm not lookin' for true love, 'cause I'll just find a broken heart. But when I look at you, I want to give you everything."

The band joined in with backup vocals on the chorus. "You can't be the hero, not in my story. You aren't the kind of man who would ever share the glory. You won't ever love me. We just can't be."

The second verse was just her and her guitar. "You can't be the one for me, no matter how hard I wish it. But when you look at me, I want to give you everything." Her plaintive voice filled every corner of the Grand Ole Opry. The band sang the chorus while she remained silent.

When she belted out the third verse and final chorus, the music rose to a crescendo. "You're standin' there watchin' me through eyes that are full of lies. But when you turn to leave, I want to give you everything. I still want to give you everything, but you won't ever be the hero, not in my story. You aren't the kind of man who would ever share the glory. You won't ever love me, we just can't be. We can't be."

Tucker waited in the wings, a huge bouquet of roses and fancy flowers he couldn't name. He also had a small velvet box tucked in the pocket of his jacket. He was as ready as he'd ever be. He was also so nervous he couldn't stand still. Shifting from foot to foot, he breathed deep through the tangle of nerves tying him into knots. This was his moment to fix everything. This would work. It had to. And he owed Deacon and Dillon big-time. His brothers had really come through for him—and for Zoe. Deke worked his magic and contacts with the Opry, and Dillon had been the one to help Zoe refine the song while they toured.

He could see part of the audience but mostly, he focused

on Zoe. Hearing her sing, listening to the crowd's reaction, seeing the surprise on her face when Deke joined her, then the Sons performing *her* song… Once she came off the stage he'd show her how much he loved her.

The words Zoe sang hit him. Hard. He realized he'd never heard this song all the way through. "You're standing there watchin' me through eyes that are full of lies." Did she think he'd lied to her? Was he too late? Surely not. Surely, she would let him explain. Let him tell her how he felt. About her. About Nash. But the words hit home, as sharp as an ice pick jamming into his heart.

The song ended, and she got a standing ovation—just like she deserved. For the first time in his life, he was panicked at the thought of talking to a woman. No, not *a* woman. *This* woman. The woman who owned his heart, the woman he wanted to spend the rest of his life with. She came off the stage surrounded by Deke and the band, and then Dandy Don was there, steering her toward a group of men. People swarmed the backstage area as they set up for the next entertainer, and he lost sight of Zoe for a moment. He finally spotted her in the hallway leading to the dressing rooms. He walked up as Easley introduced the men.

"Zoe, I'd like you to meet Chuck Goodman, Dan Decker, Bill Albright and Joe Henderson from Midnight Records."

Zoe's smile lit up every dingy backstage corner until she caught sight of him. Her expression blanked before she turned away. The men crowded around her, touching and complimenting, and Tucker's vision narrowed to red-and-green flashes of anger and jealousy.

The Midnight Records deal should have been dead. No way Don would let Zoe sign with them. Or would he? Tucker pushed forward again, his hand raised to catch her attention. Then he heard words that sliced through his heart like a razor.

"Your performance tonight was a test you passed with flying colors. Let's talk about your recording contract."

"Thank y'all so much for doing this!" The excitement in Zoe's voice was another slash. "Let's go to my dressing room and talk."

He just stood there as they walked away. Zoe ignored him. When a stagehand jostled him, Tucker gathered up what little dignity he had left, turned and headed for the exit. An industrial-sized trashcan flanked the door.

"Tucker! Hey, Tucker! Wait up!"

He glanced over his shoulder to see Deacon dodging around people trying to catch up with him. Staring pointedly at his brother, Tucker lifted the lid of the trashcan and dumped the bouquet, along with the card he'd written, inside.

So much for grand gestures and falling in love.

Nineteen

Zoe stared at the contract. All she had to do was sign her name and every dream she'd ever hoped for would come true. A recording contract. An album. Her own tour. Well, eventually. They promised she'd be a headliner before a year was out. After all, they were the ones who'd arranged for her to appear at the Opry, according to Bill Albright, Midnight Records' promotions manager. They'd hinted that Deke and the Sons agreed to perform with her because Midnight was looking to acquire Bent Star. She should be excited about their interest. Yeah. *Should be* was the operative phrase.

"You don't have to sign it tonight," Dandy Don said, quietly shutting the door behind him.

She glanced up and saw the huge bouquet of roses and other blooms he was holding. "Aw, Mr. Don, you didn't need to—"

"I didn't," he quickly interjected.

Zoe was confused. "Then who did?"

"An admirer. If you're ready, I'll drive you home."

She gathered up the contract and stuffed it into her guitar case. Grabbing her belongings, she followed him out of the dressing room.

"Don't forget your flowers, Zoe," Don reminded. The parking lot was mostly empty but lights shone everywhere. *I'm country roads and he's straight-up city lights.* Someday, she'd write that song when thoughts of Tucker didn't hurt so much.

By the time they'd pulled up at the guesthouse, Zoe had made her decision. She turned to Don. "Do I sign it and give it to you?"

"Sign what, darlin'?"

"The contract."

"Which one?"

Startled, she blinked at him. "What do you mean which one?"

"There's another offer on the table."

"You didn't tell me that!"

He reached over and patted her shoulder. "I didn't mean for you to decide tonight, sugar. The boys from Midnight were insistent about seeing you and presenting their contract. Their biggest backer is gettin' pushy. We'll talk tomorrow. You've had a big night. Go get some sleep."

Zoe grabbed her things, including the bouquet, from the back seat and headed inside. Rosemary Easley, who'd been babysitting, met her at the door, gave her a hug, then joined her husband. Zoe stood at the threshold, watching until they were out of sight. Finding a plastic pitcher under the sink, she filled it with water and stuffed the flowers into it. They smelled sweet. An admirer, Mr. Don had said. Maybe Deke and the boys in the band.

Two contracts. Singing at the Opry. Her thoughts kept zinging around her brain like a pinball on steroids, but she crawled into bed and tried to sleep.

Nash was up early, as usual. Zoe wondered how people worked nights and dealt with kids on a daytime schedule. She dragged herself into the kitchen, warmed a bottle and fixed coffee. Good thing she could yawn and feed Nash at the same time. Her eyes kept straying to the flowers. Who'd sent them to her? If not the Sons, maybe it was the men from Midnight.

Two cups of coffee later, she noticed a card tucked into the ribbons and greenery. Curious, she pulled it out. Three words caught her attention.

Deacon walked through the front door of the town house without knocking. Tucker glowered at his brother. "Go away, Deke."

"What happened? I saw you dump the flowers."

"Nothing. Obviously."

Tucker wasn't in the mood for brotherly concern.

"Are you sulking?" Deke asked, dropping into one of the guest chairs.

"No." He wasn't. Sulking didn't even come close to what he was feeling.

"Look, Tuck. Zoe will get over her snit and—"

"Snit? Did you hear that song, Deacon? I mean you *were* singing the damn thing with her."

Deacon held his hands out in a soothing gesture. "Easy, little brother. It's just a song."

"About me." Tucker challenged Deke with a look. "You know it is." His brother shrugged but didn't dispute his assertion. Tucker buried his face in his hands and mumbled, "I royally screwed up everything."

"Wow. Pity party much?"

Raising his head, he glowered at Deke. He was entitled because…well, because. "And so much for your grand gestures. She thinks Midnight Records got her the Opry gig."

"Why would she think that?"

"How the hell should I know, but she thanked them for it last night right before she ushered them into her dressing room to talk about their contract."

"Was Don there?"

"Yeah."

Deke rubbed his chin between thumb and forefinger, thinking. "He would have set her straight. And discussed the contract Bent Star offered." He leaned forward. "What I don't get is why you didn't barge in there, run them off and make your case."

Tucker's scowl turned into disbelief. "I ask again, did you hear the words to her song?"

"Seriously, dude. You need to get over yourself. She was writing that song before you two broke up." Deke held up his hands to stay Tucker's retort. "I repeat. It's *just* a song, written by a talented songwriter. She's writing a song for me and you aren't anywhere in the lyrics."

"So what's your point?" Tucker was still grumpy.

"Do you love the girl?"

"Of course I do."

"Is she worth fighting for?"

Tucker's answer was a dirty look with a side helping of derision.

"Then I rest my case. Why aren't you tracking her down and telling her how you feel?" Deacon studied him. Tucker ignored his brother.

"You're going to let Midnight Records steal your star *and* the love of your life? Since when did failure become an option for you, little bro?"

Traffic was backed up for blocks. Between a series of accidents and construction, the two lanes going his direction were at a complete standstill. After hearing that Zoe had an appointment there this afternoon, he was headed downtown to Midnight Records' office located in a high-rise building. Steel and glass. Cold. Impersonal. Just like Midnight Records. They wouldn't know what to do with a talented singer like Zoe. They'd use her up and toss her aside once they got their pound of flesh. Why would Don counsel her to sign with them? If he got there in time, he'd convince Zoe to...what? Sign with Bent Star? Marry him? Yes, that's exactly what he'd do.

With the window down on the SUV, he heard horns blare. Above them all came a sound that made him laugh—a horn that played "Rocky Top." He caught a glimpse of Don Easley's RV turning the corner. He followed it. He still had time, could still fix the fragile thing growing between them that he'd broken.

Failure is not an option. The words beat out a rhythm in his brain. He kept his eyes on the prize—the Volunteermobile. The vehicle was dead ahead. *Failure is not an option.* He chanted it over and over in his head. He looked around and realized he was headed back toward the town house. He caught up to the RV as it stopped in front of his house. He threw the transmission into Park and leaped out. Banging on the RV's door, he waited for it to open. When it did, Zoe stood there, staring down at him.

She crossed her arms over her chest in a protective gesture. "Tucker—"

He interrupted her. "Don't sign with Midnight Records."

"Why?"

"Because I love you."

Her face softened. "Yeah?" she whispered.

"I wanna be the hero in your story, Zoe."

"You do?"

"Always, angel. Will you let me?" He cupped her face, brushing away a tear with his thumb. "I never meant to hurt you, Zoe. And I do believe in you. Don has a contract for you from Bent Star." Zoe tried to speak, but Tucker continued talking over the top of her protests. "And *I* set up the gig last night at the Opry, with Deke and the band to back you up to show you that I get it. And I love you and Nash. And—"

She pressed fingers against his mouth, hushing him. "I know," she said.

The crushing tension in his chest eased. "You do?"

"Yeah. That's why I'm here. To tell you. I'm sorry, Tucker."

"Sorry? For what?"

"For not listening. For not giving you a chance. For runnin' away. Don told me about the contract. And I read the note on the flowers."

"Flowers?"

"Yeah. But why didn't you deliver 'em in person?"

His brain felt like a dog chasing its tail. "I…ah…see…" He huffed out a breath. "I heard you talking to those jerks from Midnight Records. So I…well, when you ignored me, I dumped the flowers in the trash and left."

Her look of confusion returned. "Then how did Don get them?"

Yeah, how *did* Dandy Don get the bouquet? Deke's smug expression earlier now made sense. And so did Don's call. "Someone played Cupid." He dropped down on one knee. "What about it, Zoe Parker? Will you let me be the hero in your story?"

"Absolutely!"

He was on his feet instantly, wrapping her in his arms and lifting her. "Where's Nash?" he mumbled against her lips as he kissed her.

"With Rosemary."

"Good." And it was a good thing he was so good at

multitasking. His mouth was very busy kissing her as he scooped her into his arms and all but ran to his front door and bumped it open. Zoe snagged the door as he carried her inside and slammed it shut behind them. “Lock it,” he growled.

She laughed, the sound breathless, which fanned what had been his slow, steady arousal into something resembling a bonfire. Upstairs in the master suite, he set her down on the bed and dropped to his knees. He snatched the velvet box from the nightstand, opened it and pulled out the diamond engagement ring. “I want to marry you. If you’ll let me, I want to be a father to Nash. I love you both more than I’ve ever loved anyone or anything. Please marry me, Zoe.”

“Yes,” she breathed.

He slipped the ring on her finger and gathered her close, kissing and stroking her with an intensity he’d never felt before meeting her.

She gulped and stuttered, “W-what are you doing, Tucker?”

“I’m making love to Bent Star’s newest singing sensation and the woman soon to be my wife.”

She melted in his arms and the kiss deepened as her mouth sucked greedily at his. The taste of her, the very essence of her seeped into him, filling up an emptiness he’d never acknowledged. Desperate for her, he wasn’t very careful as he tore at her clothes, then his own. Her skin flushed rosy as he skimmed his hands across her, cupping her breasts and testing the warmth between her thighs. Zoe’s breath hitched as she moaned, a husky sound of approval. Her hips arched in a demanding invitation. He managed to put on the condom—barely—and slid inside. He’d come home at last. They moved together, and she trembled beneath him. He tried to stay gentle, but the need for her overcame everything as he plunged in and out. She met each of his thrusts until both of them were panting.

Zoe clenched around him, going stiff when her release burst around him. He followed her over the edge, seeing stars dancing across his vision. He lay over her, weighing her down, knowing he needed to shift off her so they both could breathe. Then he heard voices coming through the open window.

"I'm tellin' you, big brother, the bumper sticker says if this RV is rockin', don't bother knockin'."

Dillon. And from the sound of the laughter in response, Deke. He was going to kill his brothers. Kill them dead and tell his mother they died in their sleep. Zoe shook under him as he stared at her. Her eyes were squeezed shut, and he worried that she was upset and about to cry. Then laughter burst out of her.

"Good thing we came inside, huh?" she managed to say around her giggles.

He laughed too, but the option of killing his brothers remained on the table.

"I love you, angel."

She raised her head and kissed him. "You still want to be my hero?"

"Absolutely," he vowed.

Epilogue

The gazebo in the backyard of Katherine's home was bedecked with flowers touched by the last golden rays of the setting sun. The clouds decorating the western sky blazed with brilliant colors, a picture postcard background as Judge Nelligan, Tucker and Chase waited for the bride. Family and friends sat on rows of white wooden chairs. Deacon, Dillon and the Sons of Nashville sat off to one side, providing the music. Keisha came down the aisle between the chairs, carrying Nash, who was trying to eat the flowers of the boutonniere pinned to the lapel of his miniature tuxedo.

Zoe appeared on Don Easley's arm, and Tucker remembered to breathe when Chase elbowed him in the back. His bride was…beautiful. Her wedding dress was the exact opposite of the one she'd worn the first time he saw her. Made of heavy lace, it clung to her curves, but the skirt was just full enough to make walking down the aisle and stepping into the gazebo easy. She wore boots with stitching to match the lace of her dress, a white Stetson with lace, flowers and a veil. His mother's pearls, the same strand Quin had worn when she married Deacon, circled Zoe's neck. And her smile lit up the countryside. Tucker was captivated.

The judge offered their vows and they dutifully recited them. Tucker added a diamond-covered band to the engagement ring on Zoe's finger. She placed a platinum band on his. Before Judge Nelligan pronounced them husband and wife, the Sons began to play. After a soft piano opening played by Dillon, Deke sang. "This is the day, when I give you my heart. Knowing we're together, knowing we'll never part. All I can see is you standing there, seeing in your eyes the love that we share. And then it comes over me. This is the way it should be. Now and forever, my life is with you."

"My newest song," Zoe whispered, her eyes misty. "For you."

"You may kiss your bride," the judge announced. Tucker did. Thoroughly. He took her into his arms, bent her back over his arm and kissed her deeply. Righting Zoe, he reached for Nash. He held his son easily in one arm with his wife gathered under his other. Tucker Tate was a man who knew where he was going. His life was exactly on track—and he was precisely where he wanted to be.

* * * * *

NASHVILLE SECRETS

SHERI WHITEFEATHER

One

Mary McKenzie sat on a bench in the downtown Nashville park, with a view of the river, waiting for Brandon Talbot to appear. He walked his dog here every Sunday, just after daybreak. She hadn't met him yet, but she knew all sorts of things about him.

Brandon was a classically handsome, highly successful attorney, oozing with sophistication. He was also the man she was supposed to seduce. Not to the point of sleeping with him. Heaven help her, she would never do that. But it would be a seduction just the same.

Maybe she would get lucky and Brandon wouldn't show up. Or maybe he would have one of his glamorous lovers with him. That would certainly get her off the hook.

She glanced up and saw him in the distance, just him and his canine companion, a Siberian husky with a silvery coat. Should she abort this insane mission and go home?

No, she thought. If she quit now, she would be excusing the pain his lying, cheating, country superstar dad had caused her mom, as well as what Brandon himself had done.

Mary returned to the book she was pretending to read. Typically, she liked to read. It was one of her favorite pastimes. But for the past few Sundays, she'd been using it as her cover while she spied on him. A lone girl with her nose buried in a book, a persona that actually fit her quite well.

She waited, trying to time her approach so it seemed natural. Finally, she closed the book and put it in her bag. She stood, as if she was preparing to leave the park.

As she headed in Brandon's direction, she wished that she didn't find him so attractive. The last thing she needed was a crush on the enemy.

She adjusted her cardigan over her blouse. The early-morning air was a bit chilly. The month of June could be funny that way.

She kept going, getting nearer to Brandon. He was wearing a gray pullover, sweatpants and pricey sneakers. By now, she could see the logo on his shoes.

Once they were close enough to make polite eye contact, she lifted her gaze, and he nodded a silent greeting. If Mary didn't know better, she would mistake him for a good guy. His demeanor was friendly. She tried to seem friendly, too.

Seizing the opportunity to speak to him, she said, "I've seen you here before, and I've been meaning to tell you how beautiful your dog is." She'd been practicing that line for weeks, readying herself for this moment.

Brandon smiled, so composed, so freaking gorgeous. He stood tall, with lean muscles, jet-black hair and piercing blue eyes. Mary's heart was pounding so hard, she feared it would pop out of her chest and roll straight into the river.

"Thanks," he replied. "His name is Cline."

She already knew the dog's name. She'd seen tons of pictures of him on Brandon's Instagram. "I'd love to have a husky. But I share an apartment with my sister. It's a cute little place, but there's barely room for the two of us, let alone a big dog." Mary decided her best course of action was to mix lies with the truth, and their cozy apartment was the truth. "Is it okay if I pet him?"

Brandon nodded. "Sure."

She knelt to stroke the husky's thick fur. He stood patiently, highly trained and wonderfully behaved. "Look at those eyes. They're so blue." Like his master's, she thought. But she wasn't about to say that. She rose to her feet, coming face-to-face with Brandon again. "Cline is an unusual name."

"It's for Patsy. She's my favorite singer." He smiled again. He had straight white teeth and a jawline to die for. "So I figured Cline was the way to go."

She forced a smile. She had a gap between her two front teeth. Some people thought it was trendy, considering the models who'd become famous for flaunting theirs. But Mary wasn't model material. At five-three, with natural red hair and a light dusting of freckles, she was only mildly pretty. Her sister disagreed. She insisted that Mary was the ultimate girl next door, created for secret male fantasy. Of course, Alice had a vivid imagination. In fact, it was Alice who'd concocted this seduction plan. Mary never would've hatched it by herself. She wasn't a femme fatale. She wasn't even sure how she was going to get Brandon interested in her.

Before she got lost in anxiety, she returned to their discussion. "I like some of Patsy Cline's songs. My grandmother used to listen to her." Her mother used to play those old records, too. Mama loved Patsy's music. But she was being cautious not to bring Mama into this.

Brandon knitted his eyebrows. Suddenly he was looking at her in a troubled way. Then he asked, "Do you know who I am?"

Good God. Mary struggled to maintain her composure, but all she could muster was a dumbfounded blink. Why was he being suspicious of her? Was it his lawyer's instincts, his ability to sniff out liars? Even Cline was cocking his head, taking a cue from his master.

Determined to hang tough, she found the phony will to say, "I'm sorry. But am I supposed to know who you are?" She quickly added, "Are you a politician or something?"

A light breeze stirred his hair. He wore it combed straight back, expertly cut and groomed. "Is that what I look like to you?"

"Sort of. But it was just a guess." She was still worried about why he suspected her of knowing his identity. Nonetheless, she spoke casually. "So are you going to tell me who you are?"

He shrugged. "I come from a famous family."

"You're not related to the Kennedys, are you?" She stayed on the political vein, trying not to veer too far from what was supposed to be her first impression of him. "A nephew? A cousin?"

"No, it's nothing like that. I'm Brandon Talbot. I'm an entertainment lawyer, and my brother and father are country musicians. Tommy and Kirby Talbot."

"Oh, wow." She acted surprised. "You're related to Tommy Talbot?" It was easier directing the conversation toward him. Tommy wasn't part of the ordeal with her mom. "He's superfamous, especially in this town."

"And my father is considered a legend." He laughed a little. "Sometimes he'll even be the first to say it."

Dang, she thought. He was making jokes about his dad's ego, and her mind was drifting back to the past, to that fateful summer, eight long years ago, when Mama had taken a trip to Nashville hoping to become a published songwriter.

Lo and behold, the almighty Kirby had noticed her peddling her songs around town. And while he was charming her into bed, he promised to buy them. After their short-lived affair ended, he ghosted her. Mama returned to Oklahoma feeling like a tramp and a failure. Only she hadn't given up. She'd continued to reach out to Kirby, trying to get him to make good on his promise. He'd treated her like a crazed fan instead, even filing a restraining order against her, which was where Brandon came into it. He was the attorney who'd drafted the order, making Mama out to be a stalker.

Nothing was ever the same again, and no matter how hard Mary had tried to hold her family together, it didn't work. Mama spiraled into a horrible depression, and Alice became a moody child who eventually grew into a rebellious teenager. Mostly, though, what Alice wanted was to get back at Kirby, and Mary vowed that someday she would help her do it. So after Mama died this year, they'd put their plan into action.

Initially they considered suing Kirby, but since they didn't have any proof that he had promised to buy their mother's songs, it didn't seem like a viable option. But taking it to the court of public opinion did. They decided that they could sell their story to a celebrity gossip site and expose Kirby for the bastard that he was.

They changed their minds when Kirby's brand-new biography hit the stands. Once they read the book, they discovered that it was filled with scandalous tales, far juicer than anything they could tell the press.

Alice concocted a new plan that involved Brandon. From what she uncovered, some of his friends on social media commented that he needed to find "a nice girl" and settle down. Mary assumed the remarks were made in jest. But Alice believed it was an avenue worth pursuing. If Brandon was becoming intrigued with everyday girls instead of the socialites who were typically draped on his arm, Mary could win him over. Then, once he was hooked, she could dump him, the way his dad had done to their mom. Afterward, they could contact Kirby and tell him who they were and why they'd duped Brandon, teaching both father and son a lesson.

And now here Mary was, looking into Brandon's vast blue eyes and trying not to drown in them.

She blinked and said, "Doesn't your dad have a biography that was just released?" She tried to sound uncertain. But damn if her heart wasn't pounding again. "I seem to recall hearing something about it. Or am I mixing him up with another country star?"

"No, you definitely heard right." He patted Cline's head when the dog turned to look at a boat that went by. "It's making all kinds of buzz. The bestseller lists, too."

She downplayed her interest in it. "I get most of my books from the library. Or the classics, anyway. I like to read those in hardcover." She shifted her bag for effect, letting him know there was timeless literature inside. "Otherwise, I use an ereader." She hesitated before she asked, "Did you think I was a fan, trying to talk to you because of your family?"

He nodded. "That happens to me a lot. And it's gotten worse since Dad's book came out. But mostly it's Matt who's been bearing the brunt of it. He's our half brother in Texas. He was Dad's secret kid when we were growing up."

She'd read about how horribly Kirby had treated Matt. Kirby hadn't been a particularly good parent to Brandon or Tommy, either. He'd been drunk or stoned for most of their lives. Supposedly he was clean and sober now. But according to the book, even when Kirby was at his worst, Brandon had a favorable relationship with him—unlike his brothers, who'd butted heads with their dad. These days they were working on being one big happy family. She couldn't imagine what that was like. Mama had lost her zest for living long before she'd died.

"Who are you?" Brandon asked.

Mary started. "I'm sorry. What?"

"Your name, what you do for a living."

"Oh, right." She needed to stop being so jumpy around him. "I'm Mary McKenzie." She didn't have to worry about her last name ringing a bell with him. It was different from her mother's. "I work at Sugar Sal's. It's a specialty bakery."

"I've heard of that place, but I've never been there. I do have a sweet tooth, though. It's one of my vices."

She didn't want to think about what his other vices might be. "I've only worked there for three months. I worked at a bakery in Oklahoma City, too."

"Is that where you're from?"

"Yes." She wasn't going to trip herself up by pretending to be from somewhere else. Lots of people were from Oklahoma City, not just the woman he and his father had trashed. "I'm just settling into Nashville."

He smiled his perfect smile. "Well, welcome to Music City. What brought you here?"

If he only knew, she thought. But she had a ready-made answer. She and Alice had concocted a story ahead of time. "My sister met a guy online. He's from Tennessee, and they started a long-distance relationship. She moved here to be near him, but it didn't work out. Alice is only nineteen, and she's already had a slew of boyfriends." That part was true. Alice thrived on male attention.

"That explains why your sister came here, but what about you?"

"I needed a change of scenery." She wished he wasn't staring so intently at her. His eyes were unnerving. The dog was staring at her, too. To keep her words flowing, she prattled on. "I'm a pastry assistant, but I've been taking continuing education courses to become a certified pastry chef. I'm almost done, so now I'm trying to help Alice figure out what she should do."

"Where do her interests lie?"

"She hasn't made up her mind, but she's leaning toward something in fashion. Design, maybe. She'll be starting community college in the fall. She can be a bit flighty, so I hope she sticks with it." Mary wasn't going to lie about her sister's personality. If Brandon ever met her, he would see it for himself. "Sometimes I worry about how much time she spends online and her penchant for partying. I convinced her to delete her accounts when we moved here. I wanted her to have a clean slate, but that didn't last very long. She opened new ones and started partying with new people here." In actuality, Alice had deleted her old pages to erase her former presence online and make her and Mary's past less traceable. But Alice's social life was still wilder than it should be.

Brandon nodded as if he understood. Then he said,

"I know what it's like to worry about a sibling. Tommy used to be flighty, too. Mostly it was his daredevil ways that scared me."

"It's tough to say what will happen with Alice. Maybe she'll become a successful designer someday. She's actually pretty talented in that regard. She just needs to learn to apply herself."

"I'm familiar with the fashion industry. My mother used to be a model. She runs a beauty products empire now. Her name is Melinda Miller."

"She's your mom?" Mary feigned ignorance, pretending not to know who Kirby's ex-wife was. "I've seen her infomercials on TV. Gosh, you really are from a famous family." She made a joke. "Not quite the Kennedys, but…"

He laughed at her silly attempt at humor.

A second later, they both went silent. In the next awkward moment, she searched for something to say.

She finally murmured, "I hope it doesn't seem weird that I told you so much about my sister, about how troubled she is and her boyfriends and whatnot. I'm not usually so open with strangers."

"Me, neither. We've certainly covered a lot of ground." He sent her a teasing wink. "But I think I'd rather hear about your boyfriends."

Mary's cheeks turned hot. He was flirting, and she was standing there like an imbecile. Should she tell him that she was single? Well, of course she should. The whole point was to get together with him if she could.

She went for the truth, letting it sputter off her tongue. "My love life isn't very exciting. I'm twenty-five, and as far as actual boyfriends go, there's only been one significant relationship. And even he didn't matter as much as he should have."

Brandon moved closer to her. "You're still young. You've got plenty of time to meet someone who matters. Now, me? I'll be thirty-seven this year."

"I'll bet you've had lots of girlfriends." She already knew that he did. His online profiles were filled with beautiful women.

He shrugged. "I've had my fair share, but not like Tommy. Women used to throw themselves at him. He's married now, with a baby on the way. It's the happiest he's ever been."

"That's good." She'd read about Tommy and his wife, Sophie, in the book. Matt's relationship with his fiancée, Libby, was showcased, too. Libby was also the author of the book, the biographer Kirby had hired to tell his story. "I guess entertainment lawyers don't have groupies, then?"

"No, I can't say that we do." He moved closer still. "But it's an intriguing idea."

Mary's throat went tight. With the "intrigued" way he was looking at her, you'd think he was picturing her as his sweet little groupie. She could actually feel the air growing thick between them. And now her mixed-up mind was running rampant, and she was imagining what kind of lover he would be.

A powerful one, she thought, who would make her sigh and melt and moan—right at his feet.

Panic set in. "I should let you go." She was overwhelmed by the hunger, the heat, the dizzying urge to share his bed. "You came here to walk Cline, and I'm taking up all of your time." Before she blew it completely, she added, "Maybe I'll run into you next Sunday." She was supposed to be setting a honey trap, not darting off like a scared rabbit.

"Sure. I'd like that." He spoke softly, fluidly, as

smooth as the Tennessee whiskey he probably drank. "I'd like it very much."

"Me, too." Her heart pounded unmercifully inside her chest. She'd just caught a whiff of his summer-fresh cologne. Or maybe it was the scent of a finely milled soap lingering on his skin.

"I'll be here, same place, same time." He rattled his dog's leash. "Same husky."

"Okay." She cursed her pounding heart. She'd captured his interest, doing what she'd set out to do. But for now, she needed to escape with her emotions intact. "Bye, Brandon."

"Goodbye, Mary."

She walked away, doing her best to stay calm. But even as she departed she sensed that he'd spun around to watch her, as aroused by her as she was by him.

As soon as Mary entered their apartment, her sister rushed to greet her. "What happened? Did you talk to him?"

"Yes." And she was still trying to get a handle on the lust-tinged way he made her feel. She removed her sweater and draped it over a dining chair. "I was so nervous I don't know how I got through it."

"You have to tell me everything." Alice grabbed her hand and dragged her toward the sofa.

They sat side by side. Thank goodness the sliding glass door to their itty-bitty patio was open. Mary needed the air.

"So?" Alice pressed.

"Can I have a minute? I need to catch my breath."

"But I've been waiting here for hours."

"All I'm asking for is a minute."

"Whatever." Alice rolled her heavily lined eyes.

She went through phases, and currently she was on a cowpunk kick, where she'd patterned her style after a vintage trend derived from cowboy and punk rock influences. At the moment, she wore a skintight Western ensemble and gothic jewelry. Her bleached platinum hair was short and spiked. But no matter how outlandish she looked, her beauty remained evident. Mama had been gorgeous, too. Mary had always been plain by comparison. Yet she was the one who'd just had an encounter with Kirby's devastatingly handsome son.

"Time's up," Alice said. She pointed to the clock on the cable TV box. "It's been at least a minute."

If Mary wasn't so frazzled, she would have laughed. Her sister was one of the most impatient people she knew.

She started with saying, "He seemed to like me." Just thinking about him was making her breathe harder and faster. "He's even more striking up close. It was different than checking out his pictures or spying on him from a distance. Looking into his eyes was just so… real, I guess."

"So he's hotter than you anticipated? And he seemed to like you?" Alice waggled her brows suggestively. "You shouldn't have any trouble getting him into bed."

"I'm not…" Mary frowned, steeped in her own forbidden desires. "I already told you that even if he took an interest in me, sex was off the table. I couldn't possibly—"

"You're such a prude." Alice shook her head. "But you'll just have to hold his attention in other ways." She leaned forward. "So tell me the rest of it."

Mary expounded on the beginning of their conversation, before she'd started fantasizing about being his lover.

Alice listened and said, "I'll bet you were really scared when he asked you if you knew who he was."

"I was petrified." So afraid he'd figured her out.

"It sounds like you handled it just fine. I knew you'd be a natural at presenting yourself as a nice girl."

"It didn't make me feel very nice." For now, she just felt confused. "What if we have him pegged wrong? What if he isn't responsible for what happened? He might not have even known that his dad was lying about our mom. If he filed the restraining order because he believed that Mama was a stalker, then he was just doing his job."

Alice gaped at her. "You can't be serious."

She hated to think of Brandon as a bad person now that she'd met him. Or maybe she just hated to think of herself being attracted to someone so cold and calculating. "I'm just covering all of the bases."

"Come on, Mar. Don't make him out to be innocent in all of this. Attorneys are known for being shrewd."

"I just want to be sure, that's all."

"I don't have any doubts, and I guarantee when it's over, you'll be convinced that he's as ruthless as his dad."

"You're probably right." But now that the wheels were in motion, she needed to figure him out, to know for certain. "At least I'll be seeing him next week."

"You should bring him some pastries. You can bake something special just for him." Alice waggled her eyebrows again. "A little sugar to tempt his palate."

"He did say that he had a sweet tooth. But I'll have to think about what to make." She had no idea what his preferences would be. "I should bake some doggy biscuits for Cline, too."

"Oh, that's perfect. It's exactly what a nice girl would do. Bring extra treats for that blue-eyed beast of his."

Mary jumped to the husky's defense. "Cline isn't a beast. He seemed really gentle."

"Maybe so, but that doesn't make his master a good guy." Alice frowned, her distain for Brandon obvious. "If he falls for you, I wonder if he'll post pictures of you on his Instagram. Or maybe selfies of you and him and the dog."

Mary didn't want to think that far ahead. Yet she couldn't help but recall how intensely both Brandon and Cline had stared at her. "In person their eyes are almost the same color."

Alice squinted. "It's too bad you're not going to seduce him all the way. Sex would make the revenge that much sweeter."

"Not for me." She feared that sleeping with him would be dangerous to her soul. Not just because of the way he made her feel, but because of her charade, too. "That would be carrying it too far."

"Okay, so you've got your morals. But it's not as if you're a virgin or anything."

"That's not the point." Her sex life wasn't the issue. Or her lack thereof, she thought. She'd slept with only one guy: the boyfriend who'd barely mattered. "Brandon isn't my type, anyway."

"I didn't know you had a type."

"Well, if I did, it wouldn't be with a lawyer who might dominate me."

Her sister looked stunned. "Oh, my God. Did he say something kinky to you?"

"What? No. I didn't mean it like that." She tried to explain, without admitting how deeply he aroused her. "He just seems as if he'd be as powerful in the bedroom as he is in the courtroom, or wherever he does his best work."

"That's quite an observation." Alice leaned back on their floral-printed sofa—the one they'd bought during her boho phase—and lifted her booted feet onto the coffee table. "And seriously, who are you trying to kid? You totally want to shag him."

"Can we change the subject, please?" Mary couldn't bear to sit here and listen to this.

"Well, I'm all for it. As long as you make him suffer once it's over."

What part of changing the subject didn't her sister understand? "I don't want to keep talking about this."

Alice readjusted her position, lowering her feet to the floor. "You brought up the domination stuff, not me."

"And you're making a bigger deal out of it than it is."

"All right, but no matter how attracted to him you are, just remember that we're doing this for Mama. So whatever you do, don't fall for him for real."

"I would never do that." Mary knew better than to develop feelings for a man she didn't even know if she could trust.

Two

On Friday night, Brandon rode in the back of a limo with his date by his side, wondering how many black-tie events he'd attended over the course of his life. Hundreds? Thousands? At the moment, it seemed like millions.

He was bored already, and they hadn't even arrived at the hotel. He served on the committee that was hosting the party. He cared deeply about his charity work, but how many luxurious dinners and big, sweeping dances could he stand?

The real problem, he decided, was that he couldn't get the redhead he'd met at the park out of his mind. Mary McKenzie. So wholesome, so cute, so all-American and average. He doubted that she'd ever worn a glittering gown or been to a fancy ball.

"Are you all right?" Doreen asked. She was one of his occasional lovers—a long, leggy brunette and twice-divorced heiress who relied on a carb-free diet to maintain her figure and Botox to keep her frown lines at bay. Tonight she was wearing a set of spidery lashes. Brandon had gotten used to seeing her in them, but he'd never quite grasped the point. He couldn't imagine gluing something onto his eyelids.

"I'm fine," he said.

"You seem distracted to me."

"I'm just sitting here." And thinking about seeing Mary again—a fresh-faced twenty-five-year-old who worked at a bakery. She was so damned different from his norm. He frowned at Doreen. "Do you ever get tired of the same ol'?"

She gave him a pointed look. "See, I knew something was going on with you."

"Maybe I'm just going through a midlife crisis and wanting things I shouldn't have." That might account for him obsessing about a woman he barely knew.

She turned on the light above their heads. "Did you meet someone who's got your boxers in a bunch?"

He flinched as if he'd been kicked. "What?"

She raised her delicately arched eyebrows. "You did, didn't you?"

His stomach clenched. He'd just gotten called out by a savvy socialite. "You don't know what you're talking about."

"Oh, believe me, I do. A woman knows when a man has another female on his mind."

"There's no one." He wasn't about to admit that he couldn't wait to return to the park on Sunday and reunite with a stranger who made his skin hot. He couldn't remember the last time anyone made him feel that way. He'd been on autopilot for so long, he hadn't noticed until now.

Doreen sighed. "It doesn't matter to me if you want someone else. Because I do, too."

He turned suspicious. Was she making up stories to

try to con the truth out of him? "If you're mooning over another man, then why are you here with me?"

She removed a gilded compact from her clutch. "You and I made these plans a long time ago. And since we haven't been together for months, I figured we were just here as friends."

That was a fair assumption, he supposed. It wasn't just her that he hadn't been with in a while. He hadn't slept with anyone in what seemed like forever. And he didn't want to, either, until Mary had come along.

Doreen opened the mirror and checked her appearance. "The man I'm hoping to nab is going to be at this party, so I thought—"

"You'd use me to get his attention?" If Brandon gave a crap, he would be mad. But he didn't care if she was after another guy. It didn't matter. "Who is he?"

"David Norton."

"The retail billionaire?" He should have known she would aim high. "Wasn't he just named as one of the richest people in the States? He came in at number twelve, as I recall."

She made a duck face, posing as if the compact was a camera. "He was number nine, actually, but who's counting?"

"You are, obviously."

She closed the mirror and tucked it back into her clutch. "I don't need his money. I have plenty of my own."

That was true. Between her inheritance and her ex-husbands, she was set for life. "Yeah, okay, but isn't he a little old for you?" David Norton was a good person, a charitable man, but he was also pushing seventy. Doreen was all of forty.

"He appreciates women my age. And in our social circle, that's saying a lot. Do you know how many twentysomethings have stolen my lovers away from me? I'll bet the gal who caught your eye is a sweet young thing."

Maybe too sweet, he thought. Tigresses like Doreen were more his style.

She snared his gaze. "Is your new love interest going to be at this soiree?"

"She isn't—" He stopped and cursed. He'd just more or less admitted that there was another woman on his mind.

"She isn't what?" Doreen pressured him to come clean.

He went ahead and said it. "She isn't part of this crowd."

"Oh, my." Placing a dramatic hand against the jeweled bodice of her gown, she gave a ladylike gasp. "You're stepping outside of your regal realm? That spells trouble to me."

He hated it when she mocked him. Sometimes she even called him the King of Nashville High Society. "Knock it off."

"I'm serious, Brandon. Those types of hookups don't work."

"I never said I was getting together with her." Sure, he wanted to, but the only thing they'd agreed on was another run-in at the park. Nonetheless, Mary had seemed leery of him. He could tell that he'd made her nervous. "I don't want to talk about her, anyway." He preferred to keep his distorted hunger to himself. "Let's just get this night over with so you can land a date with David."

Doreen's pouty pink lips tilted into a smile. "You're going to help me with that?"

"Sure. Why not?" He turned off the overhead light

that she'd left on. For now, the only thing he wanted was for Sunday morning to roll around so he could see Mary again.

Mary parked her car on a side street and walked to the park, wishing she didn't have to figure Brandon out. It would be easier if she was convinced, the way Alice was, that he was a bad person. But for now, she wasn't sure of anything.

She adjusted the insulated tote bag on her arm. She'd baked a variety of pastries. She'd also brought a thermos of medium roast coffee, and cups and plates and everything else they would need. She was good at packing picnics. Or whatever this makeshift breakfast was going to be.

As she cut across the grass, she searched for Brandon. When she spotted him, her heart jumped to her throat. She continued toward him. By now, he'd seen her, as well, and was heading in her direction with the dog by his side. It was warmer this morning than it had been last week. In keeping with the weather, he was wearing khaki shorts and a pale green T-shirt. But no matter how casually he was dressed, he looked as if he'd just stepped out of the pages of a men's fashion magazine. He'd obviously gotten his sense of style from his mother. His father always looked like an outlaw, draped in shades of black.

As they got closer, Brandon smiled at her with a quick flash of those perfect white teeth. A shadowy chill ran through her, as if she was about to be bitten by a tall, tanned, play-in-the-daylight vampire. A man with no soul? Or just a man with too much sex appeal? Either way, she sucked it up—no pun intended—and returned his smile.

"Hey, Mary," he said, as they stood face-to-face.

"Hi." She adjusted the bag on her arm. "I didn't bring a book today. I brought goodies for you and Cline instead."

Brandon seemed surprised. Apparently the possibility of her baking for him hadn't crossed his mind.

"What kind of goodies?" he asked.

"For you, I made raspberry-and-ginger muffins, chocolate-and-cinnamon scones and crisp apple fritters. For Cline, I whipped up a batch of peanut butter, bacon and pumpkin treats."

"That's so sweet of you." He moistened his lips. "Can we try them now?"

"Definitely." She hesitated. "I brought coffee, too, just in case." He'd mentioned on social media that he was a coffee drinker, but she was pretending to be unsure. She was also trying not to fixate on his mouth.

He gestured to a nearby picnic bench. "Shall we?"

She nodded and warned herself to get a grip. Fixating on his mouth wasn't part of today's game plan.

They sat across from each other, and she was grateful for the tabletop between them. Although Brandon dropped Cline's leash, the loyal husky didn't leave his master's side.

Mary set everything up, making it look as pretty as possible. Presentation was part of her job. She poured the coffee and gave him his. "Cream or sugar?"

"Two creams." He held up two fingers.

She handed him the little packets, along with a stir stick. "I do sugar." She sweetened her coffee while he lightened his. "These are Cline's, obviously." She slid a Baggie of the bone-shaped biscuits across the table. "If you want to give him one."

"You can do the honors." He moved them back over

to her. "Just call him around to your side and ask him to 'sit up.' That will get him begging for you."

She followed Brandon's instructions, and in no time, Cline was sitting up with his nose twitching. She dropped a biscuit, and he caught it. The husky reclined next to her to gobble it up. She returned her attention to his master. "I think I just made a friend for life."

"Can't say as I blame him." Brandon looked at her as if she was as tempting as the pastries she'd brought. "Which of these should I try first?"

"That's up to you." As a flame ignited in her belly, she sipped her coffee and wondered if she should have brought iced water instead. At least she could have cooled herself off with it.

He reached for a chocolate-and-cinnamon scone. It was gooiest of the three, with its thick, creamy icing. She watched as he took a big masculine bite.

He swallowed and said, "Damn, this is good."

"Thank you. I'm glad you like it." She noticed that there was graffiti on his side of the table: an old-fashioned heart with initials inside it. There were dirty words scratched onto the surface, too. Nothing was ever as innocent as it seemed, not even Mary. If Brandon knew what she up to, he would be throwing the pastries back in her face.

"Are you going to join me?" he asked.

Anxious to clear her thoughts, she put a raspberry muffin on a paper plate. "I'll have this. But you can take home whatever we don't eat." She'd packed enough for seconds and thirds.

"I'd be happy to." He drank his coffee. "When I was a kid, I had a nanny named Fleur, and she used to sneak me extra cookies. She said it was because I was always so well-behaved and she thought I should be rewarded for it."

"Did she help raise you?" Mary couldn't have imagined someone aside from her mother kissing her forehead, or giving her cookies or tucking her in at night.

He shook his head. "She wasn't around for very long. I had lots of nannies. But she's the most memorable to me. I was about seven or eight then. I think she left to go back to the Netherlands. I had the craziest crush on her." He smiled. "My first crush and it was all because of those cookies."

She tried to picture him as a child. But all she saw was the polished man sitting across from her. "Were they chocolate chip?"

"I don't remember, but they probably were." He toasted her with his next bite. The scone he was eating had chocolate chips in it. "So who was yours?"

She picked at her muffin, breaking off crusty little pieces. "My what?"

"First crush."

"Oh, right." She had an unwelcome crush on him. That was for darn sure. She could barely focus on her answer. But she searched her memories and said, "In middle school. An older boy named Kasey. But he never liked me back."

Brandon stared across the table at her. "He would probably like you now."

Her pulse dipped and dived. "I got over him a long time ago."

His stare got deeper, more intense. "I kept thinking about you all week. I couldn't get you off my mind."

She tried to keep things light, to fight the sexual feelings he incited. "About me being a new Nashville resident?"

"About everything, I guess. I'd really like to take you out, Mary."

Oh wow. He'd just asked her on a real live date. Things were moving faster than she expected. But she couldn't turn him down, not if she wanted to get to know him better.

"Where would we go?" she managed to ask.

He smiled. "Someplace nice."

For the *nice* girl she was supposed to be? The thought made her breath rush out. "I'm not used to fancy places."

"It doesn't have to be fancy. We can do cozy." He paused and added, "With a good-night kiss."

She panicked. "What if I decide that we shouldn't kiss on the first date?"

"Then I'll be forced to wait until the next time I see you." He finished his scone, swallowing the last glazed bite. "But I hope that doesn't happen. What man in his right mind wouldn't want to kiss you?"

He wasn't just any man, she thought. He was the attorney who'd filed a restraining order against her mother. "You're making my head spin."

He frowned. "Why do I make you so uncomfortable? What am I doing wrong?"

"Nothing." He'd already done it years ago. "I just haven't been on a date in a while."

"That's okay. I'll bring you up to speed. Do you like Chinese food? I can get us a private booth at the Crystal Buddha."

"That sounds good." She toyed with her napkin. "I've never been there, but I've heard rave reviews about it."

"How about Thursday night?"

"That's fine. I'll give you my number and you can text me when you make the reservation. Maybe you should give me your number now, too."

After they completed the exchange, he glanced past her and said, “I guess we’re boring my dog.”

She followed his line of sight. Cline was sprawled out on the grass, fast asleep. “Maybe he needs his own date.”

“I think he’s content just the way he is.”

She nodded. The husky didn’t seem to have a care in the world. In the next quiet instant, she asked, “Would you be okay with me buying your dad’s biography? I’m getting curious to read it.”

He angled his head. “Really? Why?”

“To learn more about your family and how you fit in with them.” And because she could discuss the book with him and get his reactions. “It might make for an interesting conversation when we go out.”

“Sure, we can talk about it over dinner. It would probably be better if you knew my background, anyway, with how public it is. But you’d better read fast because it’s four hundred pages.”

“I’ll do my best.” She couldn’t tell him that she’d already read it several times.

“Too bad there isn’t a book about your family and how you fit in with them. I’m going to have to learn about you the normal way.”

Mary merely nodded. Normal didn’t exist in this farce of a situation. But she had to protect herself. Her and Alice and Mama. “I’m just a regular person from a regular family.”

“We’re going to make a strange pair. You and me.”

“The strangest,” she agreed, praying that she could handle their date—and the kiss that loomed between them.

After work, when Brandon came home from the office to his downtown loft, Tommy made an impromptu visit. Brandon also owned an estate near their dad's house, but this was his main residence.

Tommy entered the loft like the country superstar he was, decked out in fancy Western wear, with his light brown hair loosely tousled. He had hazel eyes and features similar to their father. Brandon resembled their mom, except that his hair was black and hers was blond. Their parents had gotten divorced ages ago, but Mom had forgiven Dad for his indiscretions, and they'd become friends again.

"What's going on?" Brandon asked.

"I had a meeting in the area and thought I'd stop by."

"Was it with the producers of the show?" His brother had signed a megadeal to appear on *Music Mentors*, a popular reality show on a major network.

"Yep. We'll be filming soon." Tommy moved farther into the loft. "As long as I'm here, I was wondering if you'd want to have dinner with Sophie and me?" He patted his stomach. "Chef has been trying to fatten me up. You know, so my pregnant wife doesn't feel bad."

As far as Brandon could tell, the father-to-be hadn't gained an ounce. But the last time he'd seen Sophie, she was beautifully round. "I appreciate the offer, but I'm going out this evening." Brandon strode to the bar to pour his brother a glass of sparkling berry-flavored water. Tommy never drank alcohol. Growing up with an alcoholic father had turned him off to it. Brandon drank in moderation, a cocktail here and there, a glass of wine with a meal. He didn't have an addictive personality. But their old man sure did.

He handed Tommy the water.

"Thanks." His brother took a swig. "Where are you going tonight?"

"I have a date." Brandon thought about Mary's natural red hair. Or he assumed it was natural. To him, it didn't look dyed. So far, he'd seen it only in a braid. He hoped that she wore it loose tonight. If she let him kiss her, he was going to do his damnedest to run his fingers through it. "She isn't my usual type, though."

Tommy looked at him curiously. "So what type is she?"

"She's a pastry chef assistant, but she's working toward getting her certification. She's originally from Oklahoma, shares an apartment with her younger sister and likes to read at the park. She seems sweet—you know, unassuming. I never even noticed her until she approached me about my dog."

"Really?" Tommy widened his eyes. "My aristocratic brother is going out with a commoner? Boy, would I love to be a fly on the wall to see that."

Brandon blew out a breath. "Why is everyone making such a fuss about me getting interested in someone from outside my social circle?"

"What do you mean, everyone? Who else knows about her?"

"I mentioned her to Doreen. She could tell that I'd met someone. But I encouraged her to go after David Norton, anyway." When Tommy gave him a blank look, he added, "The retail billionaire who just opened the new cancer research center here."

"Oh, yeah. That guy. I can see Doreen with him. But you with someone who approached you at the park?" his brother teased. "Now that's epic."

"I don't know. Maybe it is." Brandon glanced around his loft, wondering what Mary would think of his place. He collected modern and contemporary art, and he'd just acquired a trio of abstract nudes he'd hung in his bedroom. They were erotic in nature, and he'd never bought anything like that before. But after he'd met Mary, he'd felt compelled to have them. The way he felt compelled to have her, too?

"So what's the difference this time?" Tommy asked.

Still lost in thought, Brandon frowned. "What?"

"Why are you interested in someone like this?"

He thought about the paintings again. "It might just be sexual."

Tommy finished his water and put the empty glass down. "You're having fantasies about a good girl."

"Yeah, and it makes me feel like a shark." A predator circling for blood. "Hell, I shouldn't even be telling you this."

His brother didn't seem concerned. "At least you're opening up your horizons."

And lusting after a woman who'd had only one boyfriend to speak of? Maybe he shouldn't try to kiss her tonight. Maybe he shouldn't even plan on seeing her again after this. "She hardly knew anything about our family when I first met her. But she asked me if I wouldn't mind if she read Dad's book. I told her it would be okay, so she's supposed to finish reading it before our date."

Tommy scoffed. "Did you warn her about what a jerk our father can be?"

"He's not a jerk anymore." Their dad was trying to make amends for his wrongdoings, for all the times he'd lied to their mother, or ignored him and Tommy or left Matt out in the cold.

His brother squinted. "It's amazing how you never fought with him, not once."

Because Brandon was the son who'd behaved, the one who never caused any trouble. The peacekeeper, as the family liked to point out. Tommy had been trouble on wheels. And Matt? His only crime was being born on the wrong side of the blanket. Dad had hurt a lot of people, but he was different now.

"I'm going to take off," Tommy said. "Have fun on your date, and bring your new lady friend around sometime if you two become an item. I'd love to meet her."

"It's just one night. One dinner." After that, he didn't know what he was doing. "I'm not even picking her up at her apartment. She wants to meet me at the restaurant."

"She sounds independent."

More like cautious, Brandon thought. He changed the subject, letting Tommy get out the door. "Give Sophie a hug from me."

"Will do."

He watched his brother leave. Tommy had married his dearest childhood friend. Initially he was only supposed to be her baby's sperm donor. But during the course of their arrangement, they'd fallen in love.

Brandon had never come remotely close to being in love. Nor did he see it happening to him. Of course, that's what Tommy used to say, too. They'd grown up in a mixed-up situation, where love and marriage never made much sense. Yet in spite of that, both his brothers were creating warm and stable families of their own. So maybe Brandon was wrong about his future, and the possibility existed for him, too.

He shook away the thought and went into his bathroom to take a shower and get ready to see Mary. This was definitely not the time to think about love. Or sex, he reminded himself. He needed to get through this date with a suppressed libido and a clear head.

Three

One. Two. Three.

Mary stood at the bathroom sink, counting her breaths. She remembered Mama doing that whenever she was getting ready for a big event.

Four. Five. Six.

She frowned into the mirror. Mama's old method wasn't working. Mary was still apprehensive about her date with Brandon.

Her sister came into the room, and her reflection appeared behind Mary's, like a hitchhiking ghost. It even gave her a chill. When Alice was little, she used to bug Mary to read ghost stories to her.

"You look really pretty," Alice said.

Mary washed her mind of ghosts. "I do?"

Her sister nodded. "Your hair looks like Mama's."

"I scrunched it with some mousse." But she hadn't done it to emulate their mother. "Her hair was a darker shade of red than mine."

"It still reminds me of those old pictures of her, the ones from before."

Before Kirby Talbot had ruined her, Mary thought. She understood exactly what her sister meant.

Alice sighed. "It's not fair."

"I know." Mama had died of heart failure at just fifty-two years old. "She got a raw deal, first with losing our dad, then with Kirby taking advantage of her."

Alice's expression was tight. "I don't understand why our parents never got married."

"Because Dad didn't want to."

"Yeah, but it was like they were married, anyway. They lived together and had two kids. So what's the difference?"

"I can't speak for Dad or why he didn't think it was necessary. I only have scattered memories of him. And you don't remember him at all." Joel McKenzie was a long-distance truck driver who'd spent months at a time away from home. Then almost a year after Alice was born, he was in an accident that took his life. "He was good to Mama, though. She said that he was, even if he didn't want to get married."

"I think things would have been okay if he'd lived."

Mary nodded. "Mama never would have gone to Nashville or slept with Kirby if Dad had been around." She never would have been with Kirby if he'd been married at the time, either. She just wasn't that kind of person.

Alice sighed. "I miss her."

"Me, too." There wasn't a day that went by that Mary didn't long for their mom. They'd lost her six lonely months ago.

They both fell silent, a huge cloud of sorrow hanging between them. Then Alice said, "I don't know what I would have done if you hadn't been there to help pick up the pieces when Mama got so depressed. You were the one who used to pack my lunches and help me with my homework. Mama could barely get herself back and forth to work every day."

"It was a tough time for all of us." Mary considered the emotional state she and her sister were in now: the anger, the grief, the pain, the emotional cocktail that had become far too familiar. "And we're still affected by it."

"Yes, but at least we're doing something about it."

"With me dating Brandon?" Her anxiety returned. "Is my makeup okay?" She'd used dark brown mascara and an apricot lipstick called Summer Mischief. Somehow the name seemed fitting.

"Maybe just a little more blush." Alice rummaged through the cosmetics on the counter. "I'll do it for you." She swiped the brush across Mary's cheeks, adding a touch more color. "Perfect."

"Will you help me decide what to wear?" Mary was still in her robe. "I laid a couple of things out on my bed, but I'm not sure which way to go."

"No problem. Let's check it out."

They proceeded to Mary's bedroom. Alice evaluated each outfit, then gave the collection a critical eye. "I have something that I think will work better. Hold on."

She darted off and came back carrying a swingy little peach-colored cocktail dress with a lace bodice. "I bought this when I was into pastels, but I never wore it. I think it'll look smashing on you."

They were the same size, but their styles were rarely interchangeable. "Are you sure the front of it won't be too daring? I'm not used to things like that. Besides, I'm supposed be a proper girl. I can't show up for my first date all sexy and such." She was having enough trouble with the urges Brandon brought out in her.

"It's just a bit of lace. There's nothing daring about that. And it's totally lined, so no one is going to see anything but the fabric underneath. Just try it, okay?"

"All right." Mary slipped on the dress and stood in front of her mirrored closet doors to get the full effect. "Oh, wow. This is nice."

"Told ya." Alice went into Mary's closet for a pair of nude pumps. "You can wear these with it."

"What purse do you think I should carry?" She might as well let her sister choose the whole ensemble.

"Let's see." Alice rummaged through the closet and uncovered a black evening bag with a gold chain strap. "This will do. You should add some hoop earrings, too. I have a pair that will sparkle through your hair."

Soon Mary was ready, with every accessory in place.

A second later, Alice said, "You're going to knock him dead."

Mary didn't reply. She just needed to get in her car and go, before she lost her nerve.

From the moment Mary entered the restaurant, Brandon couldn't take his eyes off her. And now, as they sat across from each other in a scarlet booth with a gold velvet curtain dividing them from the rest of the patrons, he was still staring at her. He thought she looked fresh and radiant, an unpretentious woman striking a complicated chord inside him.

Was his attraction to her primarily sexual? Was that what was driving him? Or was it something more? In the past, he always knew what he wanted from a woman. But with Mary, he was conflicted.

The orchid-and-candle centerpiece cast a soft glow,

making the table seem like a gentle barrier, even if the wood was polished to a slick, hard shine.

While they drank hot tea and sampled appetizers, he waited to see if she was going to mention his father's book. So far, she hadn't brought it up. But they were still in the preliminary stages of their date. The small talk, he thought. The stuff he would prefer to get past.

He decided to broach the subject himself. He finished the pot sticker he'd been eating and said, "I'm dying to know if you read *Kirbyville*." That was the title of the biography, as well as the nickname for the luxurious compound where his dad still lived and where Brandon and Tommy had been raised.

"Yes, I read it. I devoured it, in fact." She hesitated, as if she was summoning her thoughts. "I'm fascinated that the author is Matt's fiancée. That they met while she was researching the book. I liked that she included a bit about her relationship with Matt in it and how they became a couple. It was nice that Tommy's relationship with Sophie was highlighted, too." She paused once again. "But the parts about you were the most interesting."

He studied her in the pale light. "Because I'm depicted as the levelheaded one? The glue that holds my family together?"

She reached for her tea, the jasmine brew steaming in its cup. "Is that what you are, Brandon?"

"It's who I've always been, I suppose." But at the moment, he didn't feel very levelheaded. Would she let him kiss her tonight? Would he be able to tangle his hands in her hair? She'd worn it long and loose, just as he'd hoped she would.

"There were portions of the book that I found unsettling," she said. "But I…"

He gauged her hesitation. "If you're concerned about bringing up sensitive subjects, don't be. Everything in Dad's biography is fair game. He's the one who put it out there, and as far as I'm concerned, you can say whatever you think."

"It's about your parents and their relationship." She scrunched up her freckled nose. "In the sections where your mom was interviewed, she said that she would have preferred a monogamous husband. But she allowed your dad to have mistresses because she knew he would have cheated anyway. I don't see where that benefited her."

"I know." He admitted how it affected him. "That was always hard for us kids to comprehend, too. I think it's what made Tommy into a playboy when he got older, and why it took him so long to realize that he loved Sophie. We didn't have conventional guidelines to follow. I'm still not sure if I'll ever settle down. Marriage has always scared me. But maybe I'll get over that someday." For now, he was just trying to come to terms with his attraction to Mary.

After another brief pause, she said, "The other part about your parents' relationship that troubled me was that the only thing your mom ever asked your dad not to do, he still did."

"Having a baby with someone else? Then being a crummy father to that kid, besides?" Brandon couldn't deny how selfishly his father had behaved in that regard. Matt had been born to Kirby's longest-lasting mistress—a woman in Texas who'd more or less raised Matt alone.

"I don't know if I could have forgiven your father if I was Matt."

"You seem like a forgiving person to me." He couldn't imagine her holding a grudge.

She glanced away, and there was an awkward lull between them. A second later, she returned her gaze to his and said, "In the book, I was rooting for your mom when she divorced your dad. She seems like a good person."

"She is. But deep down, I think my father is, too. He's genuinely sorry for all the pain he caused."

"That's what he kept saying in the book, but it's still a lot of hurt. Not just to your mom and Matt and his mom, but to you and Tommy, too."

"Actually, it wasn't as bad for me. He wasn't an ideal parent, that's for sure. But he didn't back me into an emotional corner the way he did with Tommy."

She frowned. "Why would he, as loyal as you've always been to him?"

Brandon frowned, too. "You don't approve of the way I support him?"

"I didn't mean…" She seemed flustered, as if she feared she'd said too much.

"It's okay." He let her off the hook. He'd told her to be honest with her feelings. "Maybe you can meet my dad sometime and see what you think of him in person."

Her teacup rattled when she picked it up. "Maybe we should just stick to the here and now."

Yeah, he thought, maybe they should. This was only their first date and already he was thinking of introducing her to his dad? "I guess that would be a little soon, especially after you just read his book. Tommy is interested in meeting you, though."

She blinked at him. "You told your brother about me?"

"I mentioned that I was going out with someone new." He couldn't tell her the rest of what he'd said about her. About how it might only be sexual. About how mixed up he was about her. If he had his way, he would take her back to his place tonight and strip her beautifully bare.

"Is Tommy interested in every new person you date?"

"No. But I told him how different you are from the women I usually go out with."

"Different how?"

"I described you as sweet and unassuming." He pictured her in his bed, wrapped in a sheet with her hair strewn across his pillow. He had all sorts of wayward images of her rattling around in his mind. "I hope you don't mind being described that way."

She studied him over the rim of her cup. "You can describe me however you want. But the way you look at me makes me feel wilder than I am."

Her admission went straight to his zipper. "Maybe you've just been tempering that side of yourself before now."

"But I've never noticed feeling this way before." She lowered her voice. "I think it's coming from you."

Brandon could've batted this subject around all night, but the waiter arrived with their entrées, putting an end to it.

After their server left, they settled into their meals. They'd both ordered spicy dishes.

Neither of them spoke. They'd gone from an intimate conversation to nothing at all. He couldn't stop staring at her and wondering about the wild feelings she'd mentioned. But he didn't think it would be polite to bring it up again, not while they were struggling for something to say.

He gestured to her paper-wrapped chopsticks and asked, "Don't you like using those?" He noticed that she'd opted for a fork.

She quickly replied, “I’ve never gotten the hang of chopsticks.”

“I can teach you. But it would be easier if I sat next to you.” It was a good excuse to move over to her side of the booth, to sit beside her, to breathe her in. “Do you want to give it a try?”

“Okay. But if I drop some food on my lap, don’t laugh at me.”

“Don’t worry.” He got up from his seat. “I’d never do that.” He scooted next to her, and they turned to face each other. In the next oddly romantic moment, he moved a strand of her hair away from her face. Then, feeling the need to explain, he said, “I was just trying to keep it from getting in the way.”

“Maybe I should do it.” She tucked both sides of her hair behind her ears. With an audible breath, she opened her chopsticks and broke them apart. Then she asked, “What’s the right way to hold these?”

“Just do it lightly. If you grip them too hard, that’s when you might drop your food or send something flying.” He demonstrated with his chopsticks, placing them where they were supposed to go. He explained that the bottom chopstick remained stationary, while the index and middle finger did the lifting with the second one. “See?” He raised a piece of chicken from her plate and put it back down. “Now you try it.”

She kept fumbling and losing her grip. He suspected that her nerves were coming into play, with him sitting so close to her. The sexual energy between them was palpable, as thick and spicy as the sauce on their food.

She said, “Your meal is going to get cold if you stay here and try to help me eat mine.”

He leaned a little closer. “But you’ve almost got it.”

"I do?" She locked gazes with him instead of glancing down at her food.

He stared at her, too. "Just try it one more time."

She gave it another go, lifting a piece of diced bell pepper to her mouth. He watched her. She tried for another bite and missed her mark.

She shook her head. "At this rate, we'll be here all night."

That would be one way of spending the night with her, he supposed. "Just keep practicing when you can."

"I will. And thank you for trying to teach me." She swapped the chopsticks for her fork. "But I think I'd better go back to this."

"No problem." He returned to his seat. The lesson was fun while it lasted.

"Where were we?" she asked.

He resumed eating. "What do you mean?"

"In my review of your father's biography."

"Maybe we should cover that another time." He wanted to learn more about her. "Why don't you tell me what the future holds for you?" He'd already admitted that he wasn't sure if he was ever going to settle down. "Do you plan on getting married someday?"

"I don't know." She heaved a sigh. "I'm probably as uncertain about it as you are."

"Really?" He expected a more conventional answer from her. "Why?"

"It just seems counterproductive to be waiting around for happily-ever-after."

Happily-ever-after aside, he still wanted to kiss her. That desire hadn't gone away. No matter how conflicted he was about her, he kept coming back to that damnable kiss. "Are your parents divorced, too? Is that why you're not any more marriage-minded than I am?" It seemed like a possibility to him, but he was still eager to see what her reasoning was.

She stirred the rest of the kung pao chicken on her plate. "My parents passed away, and I'd prefer not to talk about them. My grandmother is gone, too. Alice is my only family."

"I'm so sorry." He met her fractured gaze. Her eyes were big and brown and sad. He could see her vulnerability from where he sat. "I had no idea it was just you and your sister." His family was quite literally an open book. But hers wasn't, and he needed to respect that. But the less he knew, the less she shared, the more of a mystery she became.

A mystery he didn't have a clue how to solve.

After Mary and Brandon finished their entrées, they ordered fried ice cream for dessert. While they waited for it to be served, she wished this were just a normal date where she didn't have to keep so much of herself hidden.

But still, what about the things she had told him? Like the wild way he made her feel? She shouldn't have said that, even if it was true. Everything about him sent her into a tailspin. When he'd sat next to her to help with the chopsticks, she'd barely been able to breathe. And now they were trapped in another of those strangely silent moments.

Their desserts finally arrived, giving them both something to do.

He picked up his spoon and broke into the crispy shell that surrounded the ice cream. "Have you ever made this?"

"No, but I always wanted to experiment with different recipes. In Asian cuisine, it's common to fry the ice cream in a tempura batter. But it can be made with cornflakes, nuts and cookie crumbles, too." She tasted the dollop on her spoon and let it melt in her mouth. Hers was covered in caramel sauce. He'd gotten his doused in chocolate.

"Dessert is always my favorite part of a meal. I snacked on all of the leftover pastries you sent home with me. I had to hit the gym a little harder this week, though."

She imagined him glistening with hard-earned sweat. "Why do the things that are so bad for us have to be so good?"

"That does seem to be the case. But indulging in the forbidden can be fun."

Or dangerous, she thought. If she indulged with him, heaven only knew what might happen. She still hadn't decided if she should let him kiss her tonight.

"Do you want to trade?" he asked.

"I'm sorry. What?"

"You can taste my ice cream, and I'll taste yours."

It was a common suggestion, she thought. People routinely shared desserts, but with him it struck her as sensual.

He slid his bowl toward her. "Here you go. Have some."

She followed his lead and nudged her bowl in his direction. She wished that he wasn't Kirby Talbot's son. If he was just a regular guy, she could let herself enjoy his company without guilt or fear.

They dipped into each other's ice cream at the same time. They even swallowed in unison.

"What do you think of mine?" he asked.

"It's just as good as mine." Sweet and crunchy and filled with flavor.

"Do you want to switch back or have another bite?"

"I'll take one more." Mary sucked down another spoonful of his ice cream and nearly moaned from the pleasure. The way he was watching her was making her feel sexual again.

After they returned to their own bowls, he asked, "Did you study art? Is it a requirement for becoming a pastry chef?"

She tried to act normal, to respond as if her body hadn't been betraying her. "No, it's not required. But pastry chefs need to be naturally creative and make their work look as appealing as it tastes." She added, "I took a few drawing classes in high school. I was always pretty good at it."

"I can't draw or paint worth a damn. But I'm a collector. I love going to museums and galleries and acquiring new pieces."

"I appreciate how art makes me feel. The emotion it can evoke. I hardly ever go to galleries or museums, though." That just wasn't part of her world.

"Maybe you can go with me."

Was he asking her out again already? He was definitely the most aggressive man she'd ever dated, but her experiences were limited. "So you can teach me how to be a connoisseur?"

"Sure, why not? My favorite is contemporary. But I collect modern, too."

"I always thought they were the same thing." Which proved how little she knew. "My high school art classes didn't cover that."

"Modern begins in the ninetieth century and ends around the 1970s. Contemporary is anything after that period and up to now, where it's forever changing." He leaned into the table. "I have collections in both of my houses."

"Both?"

"I have a city loft and an estate in the country. I don't spend as much time there. Sometimes I'm not even sure why I bought it, other than its proximity to Kirbyville."

The luxurious compound where he'd been raised, she thought, where his father still resided. She'd seen pictures of Kirbyville in the book. Mama hadn't been there, as Kirby had never brought her to his home. Their affair had taken place at a hotel, where Mama had been hidden away from Kirby's private life. But Brandon wasn't trying to keep Mary hidden. He'd already invited her to meet his family. For now, she just couldn't fathom it.

Continuing their conversation, she asked, "Why don't you spend more time at your country estate? And what was wrong with you buying it?"

"I just feel weird, sometimes, rattling around there alone. I have caretakers who run things, but it just seems like a waste of space for one person. I keep telling myself that I should offer it up for charity events, but I never do."

Mary used to help out at a soup kitchen back home, but that wasn't the same as what he was talking about. She wouldn't know his types of charities if they jumped out of a dozen cupcakes and bit her on the nose. "You could sell it."

"True. But then I'd have to relocate all of the art I have stored there."

"You do like your art."

"Yeah, I do. I even bought some paintings that you inspired."

She angled her head. "Do they have pastries in them? Are they hanging in your kitchen?"

He sat back in his seat. He'd already finished his ice cream. "They're in my bedroom at my loft."

Mary nearly fumbled with her spoon. It didn't take a genius to figure out that she'd motivated him to buy something sexy. She could see it in his eyes, hear it in his voice. His bedroom was an obvious giveaway, too. She tried for a joke. "And here I thought they were depictions of éclairs or cream puffs."

He smiled a little. "No, I can't say that they are."

"Silly me." She tried to shrug off her discomfort. "But I think it's time to wrap things up. I have to be at the bakery at 4:00 a.m. tomorrow."

"Do you always work that early?"

"Yes. But I'm basically a morning person, so it's okay." She prattled on, attempting to get the paintings off her mind. "Plus I have weekends off. At least it's a fairly normal schedule."

"I'm a morning person, too. That's why I roll out of bed on Sundays and take Cline for those bright-eyed-and-bushy-tailed walks." He motioned to their waiter, letting him know they were ready for their bill. "But I'll let you go so you can get some sleep." He paused, his gaze riveted to hers. "Of course, I'm going to have to insist on escorting you to your car. I don't want to lose you that easily."

Because he was still hoping to kiss her, she thought. As passionately as he could.

Four

Mary and Brandon stood beside her car, an old Toyota that she'd scrimped and saved to buy. Brandon's fancy new BMW was parked a few spaces away. If she hadn't been feeling the class difference between them before, she was certainly feeling it now. Of course, it was crazy to say that she hadn't been feeling it before. Wealth and power illuminated him like the sun. Or *the son*, she thought, of one of Nashville's most successful superstars. Thank God he didn't look like Kirby. If he favored his father, she didn't think she could tolerate being this close to him. She certainly wouldn't want him the way she did. A want. A need. A disaster waiting to happen.

She backed herself against the driver's door of her car. But that was a bad move. That only allowed him to step even closer, pinning her in place and using his body as the anchor.

He looked sharp and fashionable in clothes, but she suspected that he would look even better naked.

Really? She was thinking about that now? Yes, damn it, she was. And she suspected that if she pulled his shirt out from where it was tucked into his pants and tore the buttons open, she would find rock-hard abs underneath.

She hadn't seen any shirtless pictures of him. He didn't post that kind. No beachfront vacation shots, nothing that bared him to the public. But she was filling in the blanks.

He said, "When I was a teenager, I used to take my dates to this pretty spot in the country to make out." He reached out to skim his knuckles across her cheek. "I've never made out in a parking lot with streetlights glaring overhead."

His touch, just that one simple touch, made her shiver. "We aren't making out. We're just standing here."

"We aren't teenagers, either." He ran his thumb across her mouth, even rolling it across the inside of her bottom lip and making his thumb wet.

Foreplay to a kiss, she thought. If she hadn't been braced against the car, she might've lost her footing.

"Are you going to let me kiss you?" he asked. "Are you going to let this happen?"

She should've told him, "No." But she whispered a soft and throaty, "Yes."

He did it. He captured her lips, dragging her under his spell and stealing the last of her sanity.

His tongue made contact with hers, and she moaned into his mouth. He cupped her chin, and she made another pleasured sound. Lust burned her skin, scorching her, heating her from the inside out. She wrapped her arms around him, pulling him tighter, wanting to scorch him, too.

Was he as aroused as she was? Was he hard and hungry, his muscles bunching, his body tingling?

They rubbed and kissed, two people who barely knew each other, going PDA outside a popular restaurant.

He came to his senses first and eased away from her. Now that it was over, ambient sounds merged into focus and abraded her ears. Other patrons were walking to their cars and talking.

"Mary, Mary, quite contrary…" Brandon's voice was rough. "I don't think I ever thought about that rhyme until now."

Her mother used to recite it to her, but hearing him say it was a whole other matter. "I don't think I'm going to be able to sleep tonight."

"That's not good. I'm already keeping you from your bed."

Her bed was going to be a dicey place from now on. "My room gets hot sometimes. The air-conditioning vent in there never seems to work right, and the maintenance department at our building isn't so great about fixing things."

"So that's what's going to keep you up? A humid summer night in Tennessee?"

He was making the weather seem more humid than it was. But the world seemed hotter and stickier with Brandon Talbot in it. "Summers in Oklahoma can be this way, too."

"What do you sleep in to stay cool?" he asked, making her throat go dry.

This was beginning to sound like phone sex, but they were talking eye to eye, face-to-face. "Just whatever feels right." Her panties and bra, an old T-shirt, a lightweight nightgown. But tonight, she was tempted to sleep naked, to thrash and moan and fantasize about him. "I better go now."

"All right, but when are we going see each other again?"

In her dreams, she thought. Or maybe it would be in her nightmares. She was getting hooked on a man who'd helped hurt her mother. Even if he hadn't done it purposely, he was still connected to Mama's pain.

"When, Mary?" he asked again.

"I don't know." Her confusion was growing by leaps and bounds. "Let's figure it out later."

"Okay." He leaned in to kiss her again. But this time, it was gentlemanly, a protective peck on the cheek. "Will you text me to let me know you got home safe?"

She nodded, then turned to open her car door. She climbed behind the wheel and locked herself inside, afraid that she would never feel safe again.

The following week, Mary spent Saturday afternoon with Brandon. She'd had nine days to recover from his kiss. But she wasn't doing a very good job of bouncing back. He was all she thought about.

Once again, she took her own car and met him at the designated location: a gallery that specialized in naïve art. Mary didn't even know that genre existed, but she soon learned that it referred to works created by artists who lacked formal training. Most of it seemed to have a childlike perspective, concentrating on animals, people and plants, rather than inanimate objects. She noticed lots of bold colors, too.

As they wandered the brightly lit gallery, Brandon said, "I'm looking for a piece to give Tommy and Sophie for the nursery. The due date is getting closer, and I want to send something over before the baby arrives."

He stopped in front of a painting that depicted trees that resembled lollipops. "They're having a girl, and they're going to name her Zoe. They're using Sloane as her middle name because that was Sophie's mom's name, and they want to honor her. Sophie's mom died soon after Sophie was born. Her dad is gone, too. He passed away a few years back."

"Oh, I'm so sorry for her losses." Mary gazed at the lollipop-tree picture, which also had a rainbow shooting across the sky and a river with fish jumping out of the water. "I understand how she feels. But it's just so hard to…" She let her words drift. She could feel him watching her.

A second later, he said, "I understand that talking about your parents is difficult. But if you ever need anyone to confide in, I'm a good listener."

"Thank you." He was the last person she could confide in about her parents. Needing to redirect his attention, she gestured to the painting. "Are you considering this one for Zoe's nursery?"

He shook his head. "I don't think it's girlie enough. They decorated in pink, with bows and frills and whatnot. So I'd like to find something along that vein."

"Do they have a theme? Like butterflies or flowers or anything?"

"They put silver stars on the ceiling. I think that has something to do with how they'd stargazed in Texas when they were visiting Matt and Libby. But it's not a theme, per se. Mostly the room is just pink and pretty." He paused and added, "I don't have any experience with babies, but I'm excited about being an uncle. It's been fun getting to know Libby's son, too. Chance is a charming kid."

Mary nodded. Seven-year-old Chance had been mentioned in the book, in particular that he'd been named after one of Kirby's most famous songs. Libby was widowed, and she and her late husband were fans of Kirby's long before she'd ever been hired to be his biographer.

Brandon continued by saying, "There's a lot going on with my brothers this summer. Not just with Tommy and Sophie's daughter coming into the world, but also with Matt and Libby. Their wedding is in August."

There was nothing going on with her or Alice, aside from them trying to give Mama the vindication she deserved. Mary envied Brandon the happy journeys his family was embarking upon.

"Thanks for coming here with me," he said. "It's going to help to have a woman's touch in picking something out."

"You could have hired someone to choose something. Or told the gallery what you were looking for." He had all sorts of people at his disposal. Even the gallery owner knew him by name. "You don't really need me."

"I think I do." He reached for her hand.

She threaded her fingers through his, tighter than she should have. The more time she spent with him, the more her attraction to him escalated. She already felt as if she was being seduced by him, maybe even in the same way his father had seduced her mother.

How long would it be before she tumbled into bed with him? Before he did wicked things to her? Mary suspected that Mama had resisted Kirby at first, too.

But she kept telling herself that she wasn't going to sleep with Brandon. That she didn't want to carry her revenge that far.

Needing a diversion, she let go of his hand and walked over to a picture called *Magic*.

Brandon followed her and looked at it, too. Then he said, "That's too grown-up for a baby's room."

"I know. I was just admiring it." A crimson-haired fairy was blowing dandelions into the wind. She definitely had an adult quality, as if she might be a siren of sorts. Naïve art could obviously showcase mature subjects, too. "I think it's alluring."

"I can buy it for you."

She started. "What?"

"I said that I can buy that painting for you. Do you want it, Mary? Do you want to take it home and put it in your bedroom?"

"You don't have to buy me anything." She wasn't comfortable accepting gifts from him.

"But it's obvious how drawn you are to it. And the fairy is a redhead, like you."

"That isn't why she appeals to me." Then again, maybe it was. But she didn't want to say that.

He moved closer, nuzzling his cheek against her hair. "It would be nice to know that she's watching over you at night, creating enchantment while you sleep."

He was intensifying the moment, making the fairy an instrument of desire between them. "Will you tell me about the paintings you have in your room?" she asked, curious to know what pictures she'd inspired.

He all but whispered his response. "They're erotic, but they're romantic, too. Nothing like I've ever bought before."

She spoke just as softly, not wanting anyone to overhear them. "It's strange, knowing you got them because of me."

"I couldn't seem to help it."

And she couldn't help feeling aroused by the idea. But nonetheless, she shouldn't be having this conversation with him. They'd come here to find something for Zoe's nursery, not talk about erotic art.

They continued to browse. A short time later, Mary came across a painting with a pink-and-purple carousel, an animated piece with joyous energy.

"This is adorable," she said. "It even has ribbons and bows on the frame."

"That is pretty cool." Brandon smiled like the expectant uncle he was. "Totally perfect for a nursery. I knew you'd be my good luck charm today."

She stayed in the background while he purchased the painting, and after he made the transaction, he said, "They're going to ship it to Tommy's house." They walked outside and he added, "I wish you would've let me buy the fairy for you."

"Buying me gifts isn't necessary." She wasn't comfortable being put in that position. None of this was comfortable.

"Okay, but this is getting crazy, with you taking your own car every time we go out. You have to start trusting me, Mary."

The way her mother had trusted his father? The comparison set her on edge. "It's only our second date."

"And we need to make the most of it. Let's go to my loft. We can fix some lunch and eat on the roof." He moved closer. "Cline would love to see you."

She inhaled the enticing scent of his skin. "Are you using your dog as bait to get me to go home with you?"

"Yes, I am." He took her into his arms and hugged her, warm and tight, using that as bait, too.

Brandon had never chased anyone the way he was chasing Mary. He'd never had to. The women he dated fit naturally into the world he'd carved out for himself, but Mary seemed reluctant to be part of it. So he'd wanted to buy her a gift? So what? His other lovers would have accepted it without hesitation. Of course, Mary wasn't his lover. But that shouldn't matter. It was just a painting.

He looked in his rearview mirror. She was following him in her car. At least he'd gotten her to come to his loft. He was eager to spend the rest of the afternoon with her.

She was an enigma and so was her family. A wild sister and deceased parents she didn't want to talk about. Brandon wasn't a morbidly curious person. But he did wonder how she'd lost her parents. Was it an accident? Had they died recently? Or had they been gone a long time?

Maybe once he met her sister, he would get a better feel for who Mary was. Except that she hadn't offered to introduce him to Alice. Was she keeping him away from her apartment because she wasn't ready for him to get acquainted with Alice? Or was he reading more into this than there was?

He'd already taken the liberty of checking out Alice's Instagram, and she was just as Mary had described her: a party girl with a flair for fashion. As far as he could tell, Mary didn't do any social media. But he intended to ask her about it.

At least he knew that Mary was close to her sister, with how often she talked about her. Brandon had always been tight with his family. Once he decided to become an attorney, he'd specialized in entertainment law so he could represent his parents and Tommy. He had other clients, but his family was his priority.

Even when he'd first heard about his half brother, when he'd learned his dad had a secret kid out there,

Brandon was interested in Matt. Blood was blood, as far as he was concerned.

He rechecked his mirror, making sure Mary was still behind him. He couldn't begin to guess what kind of childhood she'd had, but he suspected that she'd had a hand in raising her sister. Or she was at least trying to provide some sort of guidance now.

He turned onto a side street and entered a small underground parking structure, using a code to open the gate. Once he parked, he motioned to Mary, telling her to take the space next to him.

They exited their vehicles, and she asked, "Where is everyone else? All of the other cars?"

"Everyone else parks on the other side, from a different entrance. This is my private lot." He guided her toward an elevator. "That's mine, too. It requires a key to open it."

"You have your own parking lot and your own elevator?"

"I own the building. I lease space to other tenants, but I like having this part of it to myself. The entire top floor and the roof are mine, too. Overall, it's a great location, and it's close to my office." He unlocked the elevator. "Sometimes convenience matters." To make life easier, he thought. But at the moment, it didn't seem easy.

They stepped inside, and he pushed the button. She stood near the wall and smoothed the front of her loose-fitting blouse.

Brandon ran his gaze over her, aroused by her modesty. He'd never made love in an elevator, and he was fairly certain that she'd never done it, either. Funny thing, too. His friends kept telling him that he should start seeing nice girls. But nice girls weren't supposed to trigger these types of fantasies.

The ride was painfully quiet. He was still fixated on elevator sex.

Once the door opened onto his floor, he led her down the hall. With how the loft was designed, his front door was at the very end, and now it seemed like a long and grueling walk. "In the future, I can give you the code to the gate and a key to the elevator so you can come up here on your own."

She furrowed her brow. "How many codes and keys have you given out?"

"Honestly? None."

"Then how do people visit you?"

"I leave their names at the security desk, and the guard in the lobby notifies me when they arrive. For my regular visitors, their names are always on the list. But Security still lets me know when they're here."

She stopped walking, the sconce lighting in the hallway illuminating her face. "But you'd let me bypass your security?"

"Yes." With how strong his fantasies were about her, he was willing to make an exception. "I can give you a key to the loft itself, and then you can just come over whenever you want to see me." To offer herself to him, he thought. To become his lover. "Maybe even in the middle of the night when I least expect you."

She fussed with the front of her blouse again, plucking at imaginary lint. She seemed to need to keep her hands busy. "I can't imagine doing that."

"Maybe in time you will." He could tell she was as attracted to him as he was to her. But he didn't know if she would follow through. That remained to be seen. "For today, we're just having lunch." He paused. "And maybe a kiss, too."

She glanced up at him. "Are you sure we should…?"

"Yeah, I'm sure." He leaned in and slanted his mouth over hers.

She reacted with immediate passion, and he appreciated how quick she was to enjoy it. As their tongues sparred, she made sexy little sounds. He cupped her rear, pulling her closer. The security camera in the hallway was probably capturing their every move. But he didn't care. He might even watch the tape later. He had access to it from his computer.

Damn, he thought. He could have eaten her alive.

But as exciting as it was, he ended it before he got carried away. The only hunger they were going to sate this afternoon would be for food.

Although Mary was still reeling from Brandon's kiss, she was captivated by his loft, too. His home was beautiful, with banks of floor-to-ceiling windows. He'd decorated with black and gray furniture, creating a strong and masculine vibe. His art collection was magnificent. But for whatever reason, he left his bedroom off the tour, along with the artwork she'd inspired. Maybe before this visit was over, she would ask him to show her those paintings. But for now, she couldn't find the strength to do it, not after he'd invited her to come to him in the middle of the night. She needed time to wrap her head around that.

She walked over to one of the windows in the living room, and Cline followed her. She'd already seen the dog's room earlier. He had his own luxurious space that included a king-size bed and a TV that was programmed to an animal channel.

"This is a spectacular view," she said to Brandon. "I'll bet it's really pretty at night, twinkling with city lights."

He joined her and the dog at the window. "You can come by any night and find out."

She chastised him. "You need to stop saying things like that to me."

"Sorry. It's just the effect you have on me. I'm not usually this badly behaved." He motioned to the husky. "Cline looks like he's trying to protect you from me."

"Maybe he is." The dog kept moving closer to her.

"Cline has definitely taken a shine to you. I think he might even like you better than he likes Rob." He checked her out. "But you're prettier than Rob."

She struggled to ignore Brandon's flirtation. "I have no idea who you're talking about."

"Rob is my dog sitter. He watches Cline when I go out of town. He walks him while I'm at work, too. Sometimes Cline goes on play dates with Rob's Lab."

"Oh, that's nice." She was glad that Cline had a friend. She patted the pooch's head. Then she asked Brandon, "Do you have a housekeeper who does scheduled cleanings?" She already knew that he didn't have a live-in. His guest rooms were unoccupied. But his loft was also spotless.

"Yes, I do," he responded casually. "Her name is Pearl."

She contemplated his life and the people in it. "And how do Pearl and Rob enter your loft?"

"They each have a key to the front door." He softened his voice. "But it's not the same as me giving you one."

She fought a sexy shiver. "Because they still check in with the guard when they arrive?"

"Yes, but also because they were screened before I hired them. As high-profile as my family is, I have to be careful who I let in here."

"That's understandable." She forced a smile, made a

joke. "I guess I'm lucky you let me in. But your interest in me is something altogether different."

"That's for sure." He hesitated before he said, "I hope this doesn't sound creepy, but I looked up your sister's Instagram. I was curious about her."

"It's fine." She'd actually expected him to do that at some point. But she also knew there wasn't anything in it that she hadn't already divulged about Alice. "Everyone looks each other up these days."

"Why don't you do social media? I wanted to follow you on some of the sites I use, but I couldn't find you. You're not using another name, are you?"

"No." She downplayed her reasoning. "I deleted my accounts when Alice and I moved to Nashville. I did it when I convinced her to shut hers down. Only she started up again, and I didn't. I was never very active anyway. It just isn't my thing." Thankfully, that was true. She wasn't a social media hound.

"I do a lot of it. Not as much as Tommy and my dad, but I'm still out there."

"I know. I looked at your pages. You weren't the only one poking around online." She figured it sounded like the normal behavior now that they were dating. She couldn't admit that she'd done it before they'd met. "You have lots of pictures of Cline. He's your online star."

"He definitely is. But he's really into you right now."

She nodded. The dog was still standing protectively beside her. "Has he ever done this with any of your other female guests?"

"No. He appreciates Pearl, though. But she washes his bedding and fluffs his pillows. Just for the record, Pearl isn't just my housekeeper. She's also married to my chef. He makes meals for me and leaves them in the fridge."

"Are they an older couple?" She was curious about the husband-and-wife team.

"They're in their midfifties. They're great together, like one entity. But that's how it should be with people who are meant for each other, I guess. Tommy and Sophie seem like that now, too. My parents never made sense. They're better as friends than they were as spouses."

She wished that she could tell him more about her parents, how they were never married and how much she missed her mom. But he was the last man in the world she could tell her secrets to. She was already getting closer to him than she could bear.

"Do you like me, Mary?"

She nearly flinched. "Why are you asking me that?" Had he just read her mind?

"I can tell that you're attracted to me. But that's not the same as liking me."

She shifted her gaze back to the cityscape. She was too antsy to keep looking at him. "Yes, I like you. Maybe even a bit too much."

"There's no such thing as liking someone too much. And just so you know, I like you, too." He took her hand and held it. "Come to the kitchen, and we'll make lunch."

"What are we making?"

"I figured we could throw some sandwiches together. I have some leftover potato salad Chef made. I always have fresh fruit on hand, too. There's a nice big bowl of strawberries already cleaned and sliced."

"I could go for that." She attempted to relax, to not think too deeply about how much she liked him. He was wrong that you couldn't care for someone too much. In her case, she shouldn't be getting attached to him at all.

They worked naturally together in the kitchen, moving like well-oiled machines. The sandwiches they'd decided to "throw together" were grilled cheese.

"You're a pretty good cook," she said.

"This is barely cooking." He flipped the sandwiches on the grill of his professional-quality stove. "I could never make the stuff Chef makes for me." He glanced over at her. "But I sure as hell like watching you."

Mary's heart skipped a beat. She was making fresh whipping cream for the strawberries. "This is right up my alley."

"You should have seen me with the treats you baked for me. I kept them in my room and ate them when I was in bed, like a kid, getting crumbs all over the covers."

There was nothing kid-like about Brandon, she thought. But his description of himself made her laugh, anyway.

He came over to her. "I like it when you do that."

"Do what?"

"Laugh."

"It struck me as funny." She attempted to shoo him away. "But now you need to go back to your side of the kitchen."

"Not until I have a little taste—" he stuck a spoon into the whipping cream "—of this."

She rolled her eyes. "Now you're just being a pest."

"I know." He had a sinful expression on his face as he swallowed the cream, looking hotter than a man had a right to be.

When he put down the spoon, she wondered if he was going to kiss her, the way he'd done in the hallway.

But he returned to the sandwiches, leaving her suddenly longing for more.

Five

The roof had been designed for entertaining, with a built-in barbecue, a fire pit, a bar, whatever Brandon needed. There was a fenced area for Cline, too. Mary was impressed, but everything about Brandon's life was impressive. She couldn't imagine being so successful. But Mama used to dream about it. If it hadn't mattered so much to her, she wouldn't have gone to Nashville, hoping to sell her songs.

Mary studied Brandon in the sunlight. They sat at a patio table that was anchored to the rooftop. He'd already eaten his sandwich and was working his way through the potato salad, eager, it seemed, to get to the strawberries. She was alternating bites, eating bits of everything at once.

"How much time do you spend up here?" she asked.

He lifted his head. "As much time as I can."

"It certainly is private."

"I grew up in a fishbowl, so I like my privacy at

home. Tommy and my dad have bodyguards. But I don't need that kind of security. It's one of the perks of *not* being famous."

He wasn't a celebrity. But he seemed like one to her, with his chiseled features and natural sophistication. Someone could easily play him in a movie.

"How do you screen your employees?" she asked.

She assumed he did more than just check out their social media presence. Of course, a lot could be uncovered online, which was why she and Alice had been so careful.

He replied, "I use a service for security screenings. My biggest nightmare would be hiring someone who's only interested in working for me so they can get close to my family."

She defended the masses. "Everyone out there isn't a crazed fan, Brandon."

"I didn't say they were. Dad and Tommy have some amazing fans, people who love and respect them. But some of their admirers have gone too far. They've both had their fair share of stalkers."

Mary's heart froze in her chest. She shouldn't have steered their conversation in this direction, not at the risk of him getting suspicious of her. He'd already been cautious, on the day they'd first met.

"I'm sorry," he said. "I'm making everything sound so dangerous. Really, it's not that bad."

No, she thought. It was worse. Her mother was one of the "supposed" stalkers he was talking about.

"Should we change the subject?" he asked.

"Yes, please." She couldn't stand another second of it.

"All right. How about this? Tell me something about yourself, something that you haven't told me before."

"I don't know what to say." She was still feeling like the worst kind of liar, keeping her identity from him.

"Just say whatever pops into your head."

She searched the recesses of her mind for something honest and true. "I used to sing in the church choir. I'm not very good. But it was something both Alice and I did." Their mother had encouraged it. Music had meant everything to Mama. She was an accomplished singer and an even better songwriter.

"Well, you've got me beat. I don't sing or play an instrument or do any of that. I never showed an aptitude for it." He sipped a bottled iced tea. "I grew up around creative people, but I went the corporate route instead."

"You're an entertainment lawyer who collects art. I'd say that you fit in with creative people just fine."

"Yeah, I guess I do." He leaned farther forward in his chair. "Why haven't you asked to see the paintings in my room?"

Her nerves jumped to attention. She turned the question around on him. "Why didn't you offer to show me?"

"Because I was waiting for you to ask. Or hoping you would, anyway."

"I was building up the courage." She noticed that he was going after his strawberries and cream now. "Will you show me when we're done eating?"

He nodded and smiled. "I'd be glad to."

She glanced down at her plate. Was she asking for trouble by going into his bedroom? By seeing where he slept? By getting a firsthand view of the paintings he'd bought because of her? Yes, she thought, she was. But she was going to do it, anyway.

After lunch, they returned to the loft. As soon as they entered his bedroom, Mary got warm all over, heat shooting through her veins. The paintings, three of them, were above his bed.

She moved closer, curious to see every detail. They were abstract nudes, done in oil, big and bold and bursting with color.

Each of them depicted a man and woman together, in various positions of foreplay. Their faces were obscured. In that sense, they could have been anyone. The woman had long straight hair, falling past her shoulders, mostly in shades of red and highlighted with blue and purple. She was lean and fluid, and her lover was rife with strength and power.

Mary couldn't stop staring at them. In the third painting the man was on his knees, preparing to make the woman come.

"So now you know what you inspired," Brandon said.

She turned to meet his gaze. "They're beautiful. But they scare me, too." Her heart pounded at every pulse point of her body. "To know that's how you think of me."

"I've done a lot of things in my life and been with a lot of women, but no one has ever made me feel this way."

She admitted how he affected her. "From the day I met you, I was worried that if I slept with you, you would dominate me. That you'd be dangerous to my soul."

"Maybe I am. But maybe you're dangerous to me, too."

She definitely was, she thought. "But us being together is wrong. We don't belong in each other's worlds." There was too much at stake, too much history he didn't know about.

"When we were in the elevator, I was fantasizing

about making love to you there. All these years I've had a private elevator and I've never ravished anyone in it."

Just the fact that he'd used the word *ravished* made her imagination run wild. "Sex is all it could ever be. And then it would have to end. It would have to be over."

He frowned. "You're talking about ending it before it's even begun."

She walked over to a metal armoire on the other side of the room, trying to put distance between them. "I shouldn't be talking about it happening at all. I can't sleep with you. I can't do this."

His breath rushed out. "I'm not asking you to be with me right this second."

"I can't keep dating you." Everything about it was a mistake.

"Don't cut and run, Mary. Give it a chance."

"But I'm so confused." She wanted to come to his loft in the middle of night and make love with him. But she wanted to disappear, too, and never see him again. At this point, she was even more conflicted over taking her revenge out on him. It just didn't feel right anymore. But maybe it never really did. Either way, she'd gotten herself tangled up in an emotional mess. "I don't know what to do."

He opened a nightstand drawer. "My extra keys are in here, to the elevator and to the loft." He approached her and dropped them into her hand. "In case you decide to use them."

She didn't reply. She couldn't think beyond the lust. She could still see the paintings from where she stood.

He said, "The code to the gate is Mona Lisa, spelled out in numbers." When she blinked at him, he shrugged. "I'm fascinated by her smile." He roughly added, "I like yours, too."

She wasn't smiling now. She was clutching the keys so tightly in her palm that she feared the edges would cut her. "I have to go."

"I hope you come back. I really hope you do."

Mary couldn't make any promises. She darted out of his room and grabbed her purse from the living room where she'd left it.

He followed her to the front door, and she said goodbye and turned to leave. But whether she was coming back again, she couldn't say. For now, she just needed to escape.

A week had passed since Brandon saw Mary, since she'd disappeared from his loft. He waited for her every night, hoping to see her, but she never showed up.

He hadn't called or texted. He didn't want to pressure her. But he ached every minute of the day. He had it bad. He'd never wanted anyone so much. He was drowning in his own desire.

"What the hell is wrong with you?" his dad asked.

Brandon glanced up. His father was in a mood. But so was he. "Nothing is wrong." He wasn't going to admit that he had a woman on his mind.

He and Dad were seated in the main parlor at Kirbyville. As always, Dad was dressed in black, with his graying beard neatly trimmed. Brandon couldn't remember a time when Kirby looked like anything except an outlaw. But that was his persona. Tommy's, too, for that matter, even if Tommy had a more youthful sense of style.

Dad scowled. "I asked you to come by because I have something to discuss with you, and you look like you're spacing out."

"I'm just sipping my brandy." Brandon swirled the

amber liquid in his snifter. His recovering-alcoholic father was sipping ginger ale. "So what's going on? What do you want to talk about?"

"Your mother, for one."

Brandon cocked his head. During the divorce, his parents had fought like rabid cats and flea-bitten dogs, but that was when Brandon and Tommy were teenagers. A lot of time had passed since then. Both his mom and dad were thrilled about becoming grandparents. They couldn't wait for Zoe to be born.

Dad moved to the edge of his seat. "Your mom has a new boyfriend. Some dude who works in finance."

Brandon wasn't alarmed. His mother dated now and then. But it was never anything serious. After what she'd been through with Kirby, she was careful not to get too wrapped up in anyone. "Is that a problem for you?"

"No. But I was thinking that maybe it's time for me to start dating, too."

"Does that mesh with your sobriety? Have you talked to your counselor about this?"

"Yes, and he said as long as it's healthy dating, it'll be all right."

"That makes sense." Except the crazy thing was, Brandon wasn't even sure if healthy dating factored into how he was feeling, not with how hungry he was for Mary.

Dad guzzled his ginger ale. "I'm a little nervous about getting back out there."

Brandon was nervous, too, but for a different reason. He was worried that he might never see Mary again. "Maybe you should give it more time. You've got a lot going on, with becoming a grandparent."

"I can still be a grandpa and have a girlfriend. It gets lonely not having anyone to share my life with."

"Have you discussed this with Tommy?"

"Yes, and he wasn't as supportive as I'd hoped he'd be." Dad got up and moved about the parlor. "He isn't convinced that I've changed, not where women are concerned, anyway."

"I think you have." Or it certainly seemed that way, particularly with how much this appeared to matter to him. "But it's still a big step, and you still need to be sure you're ready."

Dad sighed. "Does that mean I have your blessing?"

"You don't need my blessing to go out there and date. That's something you need to tackle on your own. But I'll be around anytime you need to a shoulder to lean on."

"Thank you for understanding. I wish Tommy was more like you. Matt could take a few pointers from you, too."

If Brandon wasn't so mixed-up about Mary, he might've laughed. "I'm just not as hotheaded as my brothers." Yet at the moment, their lives were far more centered than his.

Kirby grinned. "You've always been my favorite."

Brandon shook his head. "You shouldn't say things like that, Pop."

"I was just kidding." His dad chuckled. An instant later, he turned serious and said, "I love all my boys. You're all special to me. But I always feel better when I bring my problems to you."

"Glad I could help." Brandon wasn't going to bring his problems to anyone. He was just going to wait to see what happened with Mary.

Mary sat in her room, surfing the net on her phone for something to do. It was ten fifteen, and on a Friday night, no less. Most people her age would be out on the town. Or curled up with a significant other or doing something besides fretting alone in bed. She couldn't stop thinking about Brandon, and watching stupid YouTube videos wasn't helping.

She got up and went into the kitchen to get a glass of sweet tea from the pitcher she and Alice kept in the fridge. Her sister wasn't home. She'd gone out with friends. Already Alice had a peer group in Nashville. A bunch of wildings, no doubt, that she'd met on a social app, but at least she was off having a good time.

Mary liked her new coworkers, but she didn't have enough in common with them to hang out outside the job.

She missed her friends in Oklahoma City. She hadn't told any of them the truth of why she'd come to Nashville, though. None of them even knew about her mom's affair with Kirby Talbot or that he'd filed a restraining order against her. Mama was too ashamed to admit that Kirby had duped her, so she'd done her darnedest to keep it a secret, and so had Mary and Alice.

And now, of course, there was Brandon, and Mary's dilemma with him. Should she go to his loft tonight, return his keys and tell him that it was over for good? No more dates? No more kisses? No more talk of sex?

If she ended it now, everyone could go on with their lives without Brandon ever knowing the truth. The initial plan was to get Brandon hooked on her, then dump him in a cold and calculating way, revealing her deception to him and his father. But if Mary stopped seeing Brandon without telling him or Kirby who she was, then at least she wouldn't be deliberating hurting him or rubbing his face in it. She just wanted the revenge to go away. Alice wouldn't like it, but it wasn't up to her.

Mary had the right to break free, to stop seeing Brandon, to stop dating him and playing this terrible game.

Yes, she thought. She was going to end this madness once and for all. But she wasn't going to show up unannounced. This wasn't a booty call. She wasn't going to use the keys he'd given her and slip into his bedroom. No matter how thrilling sleeping with him sounded, Mary wasn't a fool. She knew an affair with him would result in disaster.

She finished her tea and returned to her room for her phone. He might not even be home. If that was the case, then she would just have to wait to hear back from him.

For now, she sent a text. Are you at the loft? Is it okay if I stop by? Need to talk.

He responded immediately with Now? Tonight?

Her heart flew to her throat. Yes, she texted back. But just to talk. She wanted to make sure he'd gotten that part.

Sure. Come over. I'm here.

She had no idea how he was feeling. You could never tell with texts unless someone used emoticons, and even then sometimes people posted smiley faces when they weren't smiling for real.

Winding down the conversation, she typed, I'll see you in a while. Need to get ready.

Okay. See you, too.

She tossed her phone back on the bed and headed for the shower.

Once she was standing beneath the spray of water, naked as the day she was born, she closed her eyes.

And tried not to think about Brandon.

But he swirled through her mind like a mist. She opened her eyes and pumped a glob of bath gel into her hands. Still thinking about him, she lathered her body.

If she touched herself, would the ache go away?

No, she thought. Pressing her fingers between her legs wasn't going to help her cause. She needed to do this cold turkey. Determined to stay strong, she finished her shower, taking extra care in washing and conditioning her hair.

After she toweled off, she blow-dried her hair and styled it in its usual French braid. She slipped on a plain white bra and matching panties. Not that her underwear mattered. She was the only one who was going to see them. But she was trying to keep her appearance as low-key as possible, even for herself. She chose a simple cotton dress with sunflowers on it, a pair of yellow sneakers and a pale pink cardigan that matched her lip gloss. She barely had any eye makeup on. The less sexy she looked, the less likely she was to feel sexy.

Or so she hoped.

A short time later, when she arrived at the big iron gate at Brandon's building, she fumbled with the code. She had to keep looking at the dial pad on her phone to punch in the corresponding numbers for Mona Lisa. She should have written them down before she got here.

Finally, the gate opened, admitting her into Brandon's private parking area. Although it was well lit, it still seemed eerie and isolated.

She made a beeline for the elevator and used the key. After she stepped inside, she wished that Brandon hadn't told her about his elevator sex fantasy. She bit down on her bottom lip to keep from getting turned on.

So much for not feeling sexy.

She cursed her lack of self-control, nearly running out of the elevator when the door rolled open.

Still struggling with her composure, she walked

down the hallway to Brandon's front door. She knocked, the way any proper guest should do.

He answered her summons with his eyes seeming darker than usual, like a midnight sky instead of their typical daytime blue. She entered his home, and they stared at each other.

He whispered her name, and she lost her resolve. Like a woman possessed, she moved closer and leaned into him.

Just one kiss, she thought, as their lips connected. One sweet, sensual kiss before she ended it for good.

Six

Mary didn't stop at one kiss. She pressed harder against Brandon, eager to devour him. He reacted just as eagerly, just as desperately. He backed her against the door, and she dropped her purse onto the floor with a resounding thud and used both arms to cling to him.

He tasted as thick and rich as her favorite devil's food cake, soaked in rum. She was already getting drunk on him. Slick, wet, openmouthed kisses. Could it get any hotter?

She wanted to make frenzied love with him, to have full-on, tear-each-other-apart, animalistic sex.

Right here. Right now.

Mindless, feverish…

Sex, sex, sex…

Was she crazy having those kinds of thoughts?

They came up for air, and she could barely see straight. Nothing was right in her head.

He dropped to his knees, and she fought the fuzziness in her brain. He looked damned fine, kneeling before her, making her heart spin. Trying to process her emotions, she said, "I came here to give your keys back, to never see you again."

"We can talk about that later." He reached under her dress and peeled her panties down her legs.

Mary thought about the artwork in his room. She knew exactly where Brandon's mouth was going to go. "Should I take my dress all the way off?"

"No." He skimmed his hands along her inner thighs. "You can just hold it up for me."

Oh, my. If she wasn't so aroused, she would have blushed. "Can I watch?"

"Absolutely. But you still have to lift your dress for me."

She gathered the hem and raised it an inch at a time. She'd never done anything so brazen before. But she wanted to feel his mouth on her.

"You look pretty tonight," he said. "Sweet and wholesome."

"I was just trying to look like my usual self." Plain, she thought. Simple. But there was nothing simple about the way Brandon was making her feel. She bunched her dress around her hips, exposing herself to him.

He parted her with his thumbs, and she tightened her hold on the fabric in her hands. The bright yellow sunflowers…

He went for it, using his tongue in the most delicious of ways. Mary mewled like a kitten. Or maybe she was rumbling like a mountain lion.

She wanted to tug on Brandon's hair, but she couldn't. Being deprived of touching him made the ache between her legs more pronounced. She lifted her dress even higher.

"That's right," he said. "Show me more."

He increased the heat, the pleasure, the forbidden sensations. He was being relentless, making swirling motions with his tongue. He used his fingers, too. Mary watched him as if her life depended on his very existence. And maybe it did. Maybe she hadn't been alive, *really alive*, until tonight.

She climaxed, feeling hot and frenzied.

When she was done, she feared she might topple over. She was still clutching her dress around her hips.

He stood and smiled. "Now you can take it all the way off."

She removed her dress, along with her sweater, and he reached around to unhook her bra.

Once she was bare, he said, "We need to take this into the bedroom. That's where the protection is."

He scooped her up like a naked bride about to be carried over the threshold. Fascinated with the way he made her feel, she put her hand against his cheek. His skin was warm, his jaw cleanly shaved.

He shouldered his way into his room, where the paintings glimmered in the soft light.

He placed her on the bed and began tugging at his clothes. It was then that she realized he was wearing a novelty T-shirt that said Trust Me, I'm a Lawyer across the front of it.

Could he be trusted? God, she hoped so.

But for now, she just wanted to put her hands all over him.

Brandon sucked in his breath. Mary's touch felt sweet, but wicked, too. So damned good, he thought. She stroked him, making him harder than he already was.

He didn't want to think about the fact that she'd been

prepared to return his keys and stop seeing him. All that mattered was that she'd changed her mind.

"I love how you came for me," he said. "How you looked at me when I was putting my mouth on you."

"I love how it felt." She ran her thumb across the tip of him, making a pearly bead of semen appear. "I knew that you'd dominate me if we ever slept together."

"Oh, yeah?" He rolled over on top of her, pressing his nakedness against hers. "How so?"

"Just that you'd overpower my senses." She writhed beneath him, creating sexy friction.

"Maybe I should dominate you in other ways, too." He grabbed her wrists and cuffed them with his hands, holding her arms above her head. "I've never been into handcuffs or blindfolds or anything like that, but with you anything seems possible." He wanted to explore the woman she was, to unfold her mystery, to draw her into the deepest, darkest recesses of whatever the hell it was that was happening between them. "We can be romantic together or we can be depraved." He paused for effect. "Or we can be both."

She went still. "I'm in trouble."

"Because you're letting me do bad things to you?"

She nodded. "I shouldn't even be here with you."

"It's too late. We already imprinted on each other." Like animals trapped in a mating ritual, he thought. He released her wrists, freeing her from his captivity. "But I'm not holding you hostage. You're here of your own free will."

"Naked and desperate for you? What kind of free will is that?" She snaked her arms around him, and they rolled over in the bed.

He kissed her, tasting the warmth of her lips and

making her sigh. When he raised his head and looked into her eyes, she was staring back at him.

"Are you ready to take me inside?" he asked. He was so aroused, so damned eager, he felt as if he might burst.

"Yes. I'm ready."

He grabbed a condom from the nightstand drawer, and she watched him put it on. She had a naughty knack for watching everything he did. He'd never met anyone who excited him more. She'd become his sexual ideal. A nice girl. A good girl.

He thrust into her, and she keened out a moan and dug her nails into his back. He didn't care if she clawed the crap out of him. He welcomed anything from her. Anything sexual, he thought, anything that made his body run hot.

She matched his rhythm, stroke for lust-driven stroke. They kissed and growled and behaved like the feral beings they'd become. He flipped her over and did her doggy-style. She gripped the posts on the headboard and pushed back against his aggressive thrusts.

Later, he would be romantic with her. Later he would hold her. For now, he just needed to get the fury out of his blood.

He tugged on the end of her braid. Then he went full bore and undid it, making a mess out of her pretty red hair. He glanced up at the paintings above the bed. He wanted to fill his room with artwork just like it, with images that made him think of Mary.

They changed positions again, and Brandon got back on top. He cupped her breasts, intrigued by her nipples. They were ripe and hard, but the color was soft, like the pink dahlias that grew in the garden on his country estate.

He lowered his head to suck on one of her nipples, and she tunneled her fingers through his hair.

They didn't stay that way for long. Soon they were shifting and moaning. She wrapped her legs around him, and he moved in and out, enthralled with having her as his lover.

She was close to coming. He felt her resolve. He used his fingers to intensify the stimulation, giving them both a quick fix.

Brandon was just as close. As pressure built in his loins, his vision began to blur. His image of Mary was hazy now.

He took her mouth, kissing her roughly and deep. She came then and there, bucking beneath him. He pulled his mouth away from hers. He couldn't concentrate on kissing anymore. Brandon was caught in a kaleidoscope of sex, of carnal desire, of making love with someone who left him clamoring for more. He tossed back his head, his orgasm shattering between them.

Struggling to catch her breath, Mary roamed her hands over Brandon's back. She couldn't feel the claw marks she'd left on his skin, but she suspected they were there.

"I thought you weren't going to hold me captive," she said. He was big and heavy, his heart beating next to hers.

He lifted his head, piercing her with his gaze. "I'm just enjoying the moment."

She wished that he wasn't staring at her. He always made her nervous when he did that. But when didn't he make her nervous? "The moment is over."

He moved onto his side and held her, ever so gently. "The sex is over, but the afterglow is just beginning."

She panicked, counting off the mistakes in her mind. She shouldn't have slept with him and she shouldn't have lost herself so deeply in it, either. "I'm not glowing. Am I?"

"You definitely are. I've never seen a more beautifully tousled woman."

She glanced away, feeling shy and self-conscious. And guilty, so darned guilty. She didn't have the right to be glowing in his arms.

Finally, he sat up and said, "I have to get rid of the condom. But don't go anywhere. Stay right here."

Did he think she was going to dash into the living room, gather her clothes, get dressed and leave before he came back from the bathroom? "I will."

"Promise?"

"Yes." Running off like a coward wasn't going to help.

While he was gone, she fussed with the sheet. The least she could do was cover up. He was probably right about how tousled she was. She doubted that he was accurate about her being beautiful, though. But she wasn't going to argue with him. It was nice being admired.

Frighteningly nice, she thought.

She glanced up and saw Brandon returning from the bathroom. He was still naked, still perfect in every way.

He had an amused expression. "Check you out, with the covers pulled up to your neck. It's a little late for modesty, don't you think?"

She lied. "I was cold from the air-conditioning."

"Do want me to adjust the thermostat?"

"No, it's okay. You can just come back to bed with me." She wanted to cuddle with him. But she couldn't ignore her fears, either.

He got under the sheet, but he pulled the fabric lower and looser, so they weren't sandwiched in it. "Why do I get the feeling that you're going to say something I'm not going to like?"

"Because I am." She shifted onto her side, facing him so they could converse. "As wonderful as this is, it's not going to last."

"Why do we have to talk about it being over? Why can't we just see how it unfolds?"

"Because we're not right for each other. We come from different backgrounds. We don't have anything in common." She rattled off the same old excuses, everything except the truth. She couldn't bring herself to say that.

"I think we're getting along just fine."

"We've only had a few dates, and we've never been anywhere where our worlds collide. If you took me into your social circle, you'd see what a mess it would be."

"I disagree. Do you know how many of my friends have been telling me I should find a nice girl like you?"

Heaven help her, she thought, and him, too. "What if I'm the wrong kind of nice? What if what we're doing is riskier than it seems?"

"Why? Because you inspire me to buy naughty paintings and talk about kinky sex? I'll admit that my attraction to you is pretty damn primal. But I want to spend time with you in other ways, too, and get to know you better."

"I want to know you better, too." Only she was wrong to want a real relationship with him. She'd come here to end it, not get closer to him. "But I still don't see how it's going to work."

"Let's just try it, okay? Even if it turns out to be the mess you're convinced it'll be, at least we gave it a shot."

She nuzzled against him, his body strong and solid next to hers. "You make it sound so easy."

"Everything doesn't have to be difficult. Besides, I'm the peacekeeper, remember? That's what I do."

The peacekeeper who'd filed a restraining order against her mother. "Can lawyers be trusted, Brandon?"

He smoothed her tangled hair. "What?"

"The T-shirt you were wearing earlier said that I should trust you."

"I wasn't wearing that as a message for you. It's just a novelty shirt that Tommy gave me. I have tons of them with funny sayings on them."

"So I should trust you?"

He kept smoothing her hair. "Have I done something to you, something that makes you question my integrity?"

"No." He hadn't done anything to her, but there were still the wrongdoings against her mom. "If you damaged someone unknowingly, would you regret it?"

"Of course." He frowned at her. "Wouldn't you?"

"Yes." She moved a little closer, absorbing his warmth, his strength. Her decency had been on the line since she'd met him, but his seemed intact. There was nothing untrustworthy about him, not as far as she could tell. "I'm sorry if I've been saying weird things. I do that sometimes." She didn't know how else to explain her ramblings, but at least he wasn't frowning anymore.

A few silent seconds later, he asked, "Will you spend the weekend with me?"

The change of topic made her blink. "I didn't bring anything with me. I can't wear the same clothes every day. I'd need my toiletries, too."

"I can take you to your apartment tonight, and you can throw an overnight bag together."

"I can run home myself."

He squinted. "As long as you don't ditch me."

"I won't." She intended to come back.

They'd already made love, with tender feelings between them. It wouldn't solve anything to disappear.

For her, the romantic damage had already been done.

By the time Mary returned to her apartment, Alice was home and dressed for bed. The dark makeup was gone and her normally spiked hair was flat, making her look younger than her nineteen years. Even her pajamas were kid-like, with cartoon characters on them.

Mary had hoped to leave her sister a note or send her a text, but now she had to deal with it in person.

After Alice followed Mary into her room, she told her that she was spending the weekend with Brandon. "I went to his house to end it. But then I got caught up in my attraction to him. That's probably no surprise to you. You've been saying all along that I wanted to sleep with him." She took a hurried breath and continued. "Regardless of how long my affair with him lasts, I'm not going to tell him who I am. He's never going to know that we set out to dupe him." No more revenge. For Mary, this was becoming real.

Alice clenched her jaw, disgust flashing in her eyes. "So you're just going to be his adoring little lover and never say anything when it's over? What's the stupid point of that?"

Mary sat on the edge of the bed, which was covered by her old chenille bedspread. "I don't want to hurt him. I don't want him to hate me later, either. It's just better for everyone involved to keep the truth hidden."

"Seriously? You're protecting him, after what he did to Mama?"

"I don't think he did it on purpose. In fact, I'm certain now that he didn't. He's a good person. I'm sure of it."

"And what if you're wrong and he's as conniving as his dad? You're just going to let him and Kirby get away with destroying our family?"

"I told you from the start that I had doubts about Brandon being like Kirby."

"You're so naive."

"I'm just going with my gut."

Alice heaved a noisy sigh. "And now you're falling for Brandon. Even though you said you never would."

"I can't help it." Mary winced, her guilt growing. Feeling much too anxious, she picked at a loose thread on the bedspread. "It all just happened so fast."

"Well, you know what? I can still get my revenge. I can spill the beans and tell him who you are."

Mary turned livid. She'd been nothing but loyal to her sister, caring for her their entire lives. And this was how she was being repaid? "I can't believe you're threatening me."

Alice scoffed like a school-yard bully. "And I can't believe you're choosing him over me and Mama."

"Okay. I get it. You're upset that I care about him. But, please, don't tell him. It'll rip my heart out if you go behind my back and do that."

"Really? Well, he might be the one who ends up ripping your heart out, not me. I know you think he's a good guy, but he's still Kirby's devoted son. No matter how kind he seems, he still has it in his genetics to hurt you."

Mary didn't want to think about anyone hurting anyone. "Just give me your word that you won't betray me and tell him who I am."

"Fine. Whatever."

Alice stormed out of the room, leaving Mary alone to pack. But that was okay. Because for now, all she wanted was to return to Brandon.

Seven

Brandon skimmed a hand down Mary's spine, and she sighed at his touch. They were back in his bed, warm and naked.

"I'm glad you didn't ditch me," he said.

"I told you that I wouldn't." But she wasn't going to tell him about the argument she'd had with Alice. Mary had so many secrets, so many things weighing her down. Her life had always been complicated. She'd spent her youth with a depressed mother and a rebellious sister.

She nuzzled closer to Brandon. Cuddling with him felt good.

"Being around you makes me hungry." He took a pretend bite out of her shoulder. "You smell like cookie dough."

"It's my body spray. I used it right before I came back here." She'd also packed it in her overnight bag. "It's vanilla and cinnamon."

"You must smell like that when you're working, too, except from the real thing."

"Yes, I definitely do." She played with his hair, intrigued by the shiny blackness. For now, pieces of it were falling onto his forehead instead of staying slicked back the way it normally was. She knew he was fascinated by her hair, too, particularly given the way he'd undid her braid earlier.

"Are you tired?" he asked.

She shook her head. She was too exhilarated to be sleepy. She glanced at the clock and saw how late it was. "Are you?"

"Not in the least."

"I'll bet you're not even normally home on Friday nights."

"Not usually, no. There was a gathering I was supposed to attend this evening, but I didn't go. I was hoping that you'd call or come over, and you did."

Curious about the social engagement he'd skipped, she asked, "What kind of gathering was it?"

"A party at a friend's house. He's the architect who designed this building. He and his wife invite me to all of their get-togethers. I have a lot of married friends. I guess it comes with the thirtysomething territory."

She sent him a silly look. "You mean the almost-forty territory?"

He laughed, rolled his eyes. "Easy for you to say, Ms. Twenty-Five and Hardly Been Kissed."

"I never said I'd hardly been kissed. I just said that I only had one boyfriend and that he didn't matter as much as he should have. But I'm never going to describe you as someone who didn't matter." He mattered far too much. "You'll be the one who gave me amazing sex."

He grinned. "Now that works for my ego." As his

grin faded, he asked, “Who was the other guy? Will you tell me something about him?”

She considered what to say and how much to share. Then she realized she didn’t have anything to hide, at least not where her former boyfriend was concerned. “His name was Jim, and he was the assistant manager at the bakery where I worked in Oklahoma.”

“So what was it about him that didn’t matter as much as it should have?”

“I just didn’t feel as strongly for him as I should have. He was nice and easy to be around. But something was missing between us.”

“Where is he now?”

“He still works at the same bakery. He’s not an overly ambitious guy. The last I heard, he was dating someone new.”

“And now you are, too.” He spoke softly. “You and me and the amazing sex.”

She thought about the different positions he’d had her in, bending and shaping her to his will. She thought about the romantic way he’d held her afterward, too. “I’m glad you asked me to spend the weekend with you.”

“Me, too. Do you want to see my other house tomorrow? We can bring Cline and let him run around. There’s lots of acreage for him to play on.”

“I’d love to see it.” She wanted to make the most of her time with him.

“We can stay there tomorrow instead of coming back here. This might sound odd, but I’ve never spent the night with anyone at that house. Of course, I rarely stay there myself. The master suite has a huge four-poster bed. My decorator picked it out.” He adopted a dastardly expression. “I could totally tie you up in it.”

She kicked him under the covers. She assumed he was kidding. Or hoped he was. "That's not funny."

"Then why are you laughing?"

"I'm not." She was smiling like an idiot who didn't know any better. "It's just weird that I inspire bad things in you."

"I think we should do something bad right now."

Her pulse zoomed straight to the V between her legs. "Like what?"

He sat up and reached for his clothes. "Go out for ice cream. There's a fast-food joint nearby that makes the best milkshakes."

Mary leaned on her side to watch him to put his Trust me, I'm a Lawyer T-shirt back on. "That was sneaky."

He zipped his jeans, smiling all the while. "So sue me."

Her mind whirred back to when she and Alice had hoped to sue his father. But this wasn't a good time to think about that.

She hastily said, "I do like milkshakes. Strawberry is my favorite."

"Then get dressed, and let's go."

She obliged him, and they left the loft.

They stepped into the elevator and the door closed, but he didn't push the button that would take them to the bottom floor. He pressed her against the wall instead, kissing her senseless.

While they kissed, while everything inside Brandon went rough and hot, he roamed his hands all over Mary, eager to make his elevator fantasy come true.

When he tore his mouth away from hers, he said, "You can leave your dress on. But you need to take off your panties."

She removed her undies and tucked them into his pants' pocket. "Does this mean we're not going out for ice cream?"

He laughed at her fake innocence. She was turning him on but good. Her panties were burning a hole in his pocket. He just might keep them as a trophy from their affair. "We can still get the milkshakes when we're done."

She bit down on her bottom lip. "Done with what?"

"As if you don't know." In his other pocket he had a condom. He'd stashed it there while she'd been getting dressed. He undid his jeans. He was already hard. He handed her the packet. "Do you want to do the honors?"

She fumbled with the package. "I've never actually been the one to..."

Now her innocence seemed real. Or her inexperience or whatever. Brandon was too damned aroused to wait it out. "No worries. I'll do it." He took it from her.

He donned the protection, yanked up her dress and thrust into her. She gasped and pulled him closer.

They went mad, frenzied and wild, groping through their clothes and kissing. Because he was so much taller, he had to bend his knees and lift her into a position that gave him deeper access.

She moaned, so hot, so vocal.

He liked that she was wearing the same dress from before. He liked how sweet and wholesome it looked on her. Even while they were having lust-driven sex, she still seemed sweet.

Her cookie dough scent was driving him crazy, too.

She clung to him, and he stroked her with his fingers, making her wetter.

"Come with me." He needed a release so damned badly, but he wanted her to have one, too.

She dug her nails into his shoulders, pressing them into his shirt. She'd scratched his skin earlier, and he'd loved every feral second of it.

"Come with me," he said again, nearly growling the words into her ear.

She dug her nails deeper and harder. "I am. I will."

Damn straight, he thought. He felt a shiver rising up in her body and taking over.

Her orgasm triggered his, giving him the release he'd been waiting for, sensation slamming into sensation, pressure building into pressure.

Cripes, it was good.

When it was over, he put his forehead against hers, and they both sucked air into their lungs.

"Where have you been all of my life?" he asked, teasing her with a clichéd line.

She retrieved her panties from his pocket. "When you were twenty, I was eleven, maybe twelve. So for most of your life, I was a kid. And when you were a kid, I wasn't even born yet."

"Listen to you, being so literal." So much for him keeping her underwear. She was already putting her panties back on. He glanced down at himself. He had the condom to deal with. But it was what it was. He removed the rubber and tied it off.

"Elevator safety," she said.

He raised his eyebrows. "Are you making a safe sex joke?"

"After what we just did? Can you blame me?"

"No, I can't say that I do." He pushed the button, and the elevator descended.

Once they were in the parking structure, he tossed the condom into a nearby trash can.

They got into his car, and he asked, "Will you come

to Texas with me in August, to Matt and Libby's wedding?" He knew it was a random question, but now that they were lovers, he didn't want to attend the festivities alone.

She buckled her seat belt. "You want to bring me to something like that, with all of your family there?" She sounded panicked.

"My family isn't going to rip you apart. We're not a pack of wolves."

She didn't look as if she believed him.

Damn, he thought. She was a tough case. He sighed and said, "Just think about it, okay?"

She stared out the windshield. "It's just a lot for me to take in right now."

He fired up the engine and pulled out of the parking lot. "We agreed to give this a shot, Mary. To continue dating and seeing each other."

"I know. But I didn't think that it would include your brother's wedding."

He didn't see what the big deal was. He'd brought a date to Tommy's wedding, too. "I just want us to dance, to sip champagne, to have a little fun."

"I know," she said again, without turning to look at him. "But it's still so new and overwhelming, being with someone like you."

He was overwhelmed being with her, too. And as elusive as she was, he would probably have hell to pay, trying to keep their affair afloat.

He pulled into the drive-through at the burger joint and placed their orders, then they sat in the car as they drank their shakes: chocolate for him and strawberry for her.

"How long were you with Jim?" he asked. Typically,

he didn't care about a woman's romantic past. But with Mary, everything seemed to matter.

She shifted in her seat. "We were together for six months."

"Were you always threatening to break it off with him?"

"No. But I was just used to him, I guess."

"So when are you going to get used to me?" He leaned in her direction, bumping her shoulder and forcing her to feel his flustered affection.

She turned all the way toward him. "I'm sorry if I'm being difficult. But it's hard not to think about how high society you are. Or how famous your family is. That's tough for an average girl like me."

"You're far from average." She was the most complicated woman he'd ever known.

She reached up to touch his face. Her hand was cold from holding her milkshake. "I never expected to get this close to you. It's an emotional process for me."

For him, too, but in a different way than it was for her. He was anxious to bring her into his life, and she was keeping him on the fringes of hers.

She removed her hand from his cheek. "Sitting here with you almost makes it seem as if we tumbled back in time."

"Like teenagers from the 1950s on their way home from a sock hop?"

She nodded. "Where did you go to high school?"

"It was a prep school, not too far from here. I was our class president and the valedictorian. Tommy attended public school. He wasn't interested in a private education. It was too uppity for him. Or that's what he said, anyway. But I think he just wanted to go to the same school as Sophie."

"My high school was in a rough part of town, so we didn't have any rich kids there." She leaned back against her seat. "But you probably already deduced that I grew up poor."

"Yes." But as to how poor, he didn't have a clue. "I can't even begin to know what that was like for you." He had wealthy parents who gave him whatever he wanted, whenever he wanted it. Of course, mostly all he and Tommy ever wanted was for their bleary-eyed dad to get clean and sober.

"We struggled to make ends meet. But some of the kids I grew up with were worse off than us."

"When did your parents die, Mary? I know you don't like to talk about it, but—"

"Please, let's not ruin this night by going there." She glanced at him, a pained expression on her face. "I want to have happy memories of being here with you."

"I'm sorry." He shouldn't have pushed those boundaries. It was only their first weekend together. "I can be aggressive sometimes."

"It must be the lawyer in you."

"Yeah." But it was his interest in her, too, and how strongly she affected him. "How about if we listen to some music?"

"That sounds nice."

"You can go through my playlist and choose."

"Thanks." She scanned his device and picked some old country tunes.

They sat quietly, enjoying the music and their milkshakes. After a short while, he asked, "Have you ever heard Tommy's song, 'The Urban Name Game,' where he pokes fun at some of the definitions in the urban dictionary?"

"No, I don't think I have."

"It's not one of his bigger hits. But he thinks the over-the-top meanings people make up for their names on that site are funny, so that's what inspired him to write it. We can play his song later if you want to hear it. He was going to use my name in it, but I told him I would kick his ass if he did."

"What are some of the definitions of your name that caught his attention?"

"That Brandon is an awesome guy, smart and funny and ridiculously charming. That just knowing someone named Brandon is considered lucky, and it might even help you win the lottery. You can't go wrong with Brandon. Even when he is being a jerk, people are quick to forgive him."

She sent him a wry look. "So you're an awesome jerk with the power to bring luck?"

He laughed at the foolishness of it. "I wonder what some of yours are." He grabbed his phone and got on the site. "Ah, here we are." He scanned the first few entries and raised his eyebrows. "Apparently Mary is a kind and caring girl who will warm your heart. She's also highly committed and will be loyal to only you. Once you get together with Mary, you'll want to keep her forever."

She acted smug. "That sounds about right."

"Oh, sure, the perfect woman." Just for the hell of it, he kissed her, slipping his tongue into her mouth and making everything but the taste of her go away.

When they separated, she said, "I like it when you do that."

"I like it, too." He studied her in the shadowy light. "Do you know the true origin of your name?"

She nodded. "In Hebrew it means 'wish for child.' But it also means 'sea of bitterness' and 'rebellion.' I always figured that the Virgin Mary was the reason for the 'wish-for-child' thing. I don't know about the rest of it." She set her drink down. "What does Brandon mean for real?"

Nothing as interesting as Mary, he thought. "A hill covered with broom."

She cracked a smile. "The kind you sweep with?"

"No, smarty." He tried to seem indignant, but he thought it was funny, too. "A flowering shrub."

"I knew what you meant." She gave a soft sigh. "It's actually a pretty visual, if you think about it."

"You're the pretty visual." He kissed her one more time, before he took her back to his loft and back to his bed.

Mary spent the following day with Brandon at his country estate. The redbrick, two-story home sat on four acres and had six bedrooms, seven baths, a swimming pool and a gazebo.

The whole place was light and airy with dome-shaped windows and rounded archways. The floors were wood and the fireplaces trimmed in marble. Everywhere that Mary looked, on tables, shelves and walls, were stunning pieces of art. But Brandon had already told her that he used the house to store and display the bulk of his collection.

After he completed the tour and escorted her outside to sit by the pool, one of the caretakers, an older woman with a friendly smile, brought them lemonade.

Once she was gone, Brandon said to Mary, "You can see how much Cline enjoys being here."

"Definitely." The dog was playing in the yard, racing around in the grass. "It's funny that you take him for walks in the park every Sunday when you could just bring him here."

"I like going to the park. It makes me feel free, to go out in public and just be with my dog. When I was a kid, I used to wonder what it would be like to come from a regular family. My childhood was like a circus, with all of the fans hanging around at the gate at Kirbyville. The paparazzi were a huge factor, too."

She reached for her glass, which was artfully garnished with fresh mint and lemon wedges. "Do you think Matt's wedding will be a circus?" There was a part of her that wanted to go, to be there with Brandon. But how was she supposed to face his father, knowing what he'd done to her mother?

He replied, "It'll be a private ceremony on Matt's recreational ranch, with plenty of security in case the media tries to crash it. So I don't think it'll be a problem." He caught her gaze. "Are you reconsidering taking the trip with me?"

"I don't know." She was already feeling like a stranger in a strange land, so how could she subject herself to his entire family? Still, traveling with Brandon sounded romantic.

"If you decide to come, it'll be four days. The first two will be wedding stuff, and the last two we'll be on our own. We'd be staying in one of the guest cabins on the ranch. There are lots of things to do—hiking, fishing, horseback riding." He added, "I'm not a cowboy like Matt and Tommy, but I grew up around horses."

"So you like to ride?"

"Definitely. I do Western and English. I played a little polo in college."

That didn't surprise her. He was a Harvard man, and it seemed like something he would do. "I've only been riding a few times, and that was when I was younger."

Mama used to take her and Alice to a rental stable, but it wasn't a luxury they could regularly afford.

"Did you enjoy it?" he asked.

"Yes, very much." But she couldn't tell him about her mother's love of horses and how much it meant to Mama to give her daughters those experiences. Mary even had some old photos of her and Alice astride the rental ponies. But that was before the Kirby fiasco, before Mama got so depressed.

She cleared her mind and glanced around. "Is this property zoned for horses?"

"Yes, but I don't see the point of getting any, not unless I stayed here more often. I can ride at Tommy's whenever I want to."

"Are you and Tommy going to be in Matt's wedding?"

He nodded. "He asked us to be his groomsmen."

Mary went quiet. If she'd met Brandon under different circumstances, if his father hadn't hurt her mother, if Brandon hadn't filed the restraining order, this affair would be so much easier. But as it was, it shouldn't be happening at all.

"You've got that look," he said.

She glanced up. "What look?"

"As if you're considering ending it with me again."

"I'm not." But she should be, she thought. "Really, I'm not." She wasn't ready to let him go. She made a grand gesture, trying to focus on something else. "This really is a wonderful house. It's too bad you don't get more use out of it."

"Why don't we go for a swim?" He smiled. "Cline loves to swim, too, if you don't mind sharing the pool with a big, smelly dog."

She laughed. "He isn't smelly."

"He will be when he gets wet. But that'll just give us an excuse to shower together." He smiled again, sexier this time. "Without the dog."

"Okay," she said, scooting her chair closer to his. "I'm game." She'd seen the shower in the master bath, and it was a huge glass enclosure with a variety of water jets. She could only imagine how glorious it was going to feel. Brandon was fast becoming the lover of her dreams. Dreams she didn't even know she had. "I didn't bring a swimsuit, though. It hadn't occurred to me that I might need one."

"There are tons of brand-new suits in the pool house. I'm sure there'll be some in your size." He shrugged. "My caretakers provide them, just in case I have guests."

"Thank you for inviting me here." As mixed up as everything was, he had a way of making her feel better.

This beautiful man that she was deceiving.

Eight

Swimming with the dog was fun, and the shower with Brandon was heavenly, just as Mary had assumed it would be.

The main fixture poured water over them like a waterfall. The rest of the jets kept steady streams shooting at them from different directions. Luxury at its finest, she thought, with a tall, tanned, blue-eyed attorney. Before he'd come into her life, she couldn't have imagined a scenario like this if she'd tried.

He washed her hair with his shampoo and conditioner, and she inhaled the crisp fragrance. She liked him using his products on her. She liked everything about this weekend with him. Everything except the lies she was keeping. She hoped their affair ended mutually, during a time when both of them were ready to let go, and her secret could fade into oblivion.

Brandon finished washing her hair and spun her

around to kiss her. She latched on to him as if there was no tomorrow, hating herself for what she was doing to him. The more time she spent with him, the more convinced she was that he was a kind and caring person. That he hadn't hurt her mother deliberately. That it had been all Kirby's doing. But Brandon loved his father, just as she'd loved her mother. Nothing good could ever come of this.

He deepened the kiss, and her mind went blank. She reached between his legs and stroked him, making him big and hard. She ran her thumb over the tip, moving in little circles, and he shuddered.

Wanting to give him the same kind of pleasure he'd already given her, she ended the kiss and dropped to her knees.

He looked down at her, and their gazes met and held. He shut off the side jets to keep her from getting drenched, but the waterfall fixture was still running, creating a sensual ambience.

She took him in her mouth, and he played with the wet strands of her hair. She imagined how she must look to him, this nice girl that she supposedly was, taking him all the way to the back of her throat.

She enhanced his experience with flicks of her tongue, and he rocked his hips. The hands in her hair tightened. She felt powerful, knowing that he was having trouble containing himself. But she felt dominated by him, too.

It was a feeling she liked. A feeling that aroused her.

He growled her name, and it echoed through the spray of water. She increased the rhythm, using her hands and her mouth.

Right before he came, he tried to pull away. But she tugged him closer, letting him know that she wanted him to spill into her. So that's what he did, in the midst of rising steam and splashing water, with his stomach muscles jumping and his breathing short and shaky.

Afterward, he staggered, and she eased back. But she didn't get up off her knees. She touched herself, running her hands over her breasts and working her way down, pressing her fingers between her thighs. Mary needed to come, too.

Brandon didn't intervene. By now, he'd recovered from his orgasm. He remained at his full height and watched her. Clearly, he was enjoying the show.

She closed her eyes and let the sensation of performing for him sweep her away.

Finally, when she was sated, she climbed to her feet and turned off the waterfall. Their sexy shower was over.

They left the enclosure and dried off with towels and heat lamps.

Brandon said, "That was incredible." He put his jeans on. They'd both brought clothes into the bathroom. "But how am I supposed to ever be with anyone else after that?"

She got dressed, too. "I'd rather not think about you being with someone else."

"Good. Because I'm hanging on to you as long as I can."

"You're turning me into someone new." Someone far more daring than she'd ever expected to be. She moved closer to him. "I should be blushing."

"Sometimes you blush. I like both sides of you, the good girl and the bad. It's tough to make up my mind which one excites me more."

She nuzzled against him. "I think I'm becoming

more bad than good." But for now her heart was pounding, relentlessly, right next to his.

On Sunday morning, Mary and Brandon took Cline to the park. As they strolled beside the river, she envisioned spending every weekend together. But she knew that wasn't possible.

Brandon stopped to let Cline sniff a tree. "I have to go out of town next week for work. I have an important client in Vegas, so I go there fairly often."

"I thought your parents and Tommy were your most important clients." She knew that he specialized in entertainment law because he wanted to represent his family.

The family he protected, she thought. She'd tried to protect hers, too, but she'd failed where Brandon had succeeded. Her family was a mess, and his was a success.

He replied, "Mom and Dad and Tommy will always come first. But I'm still loyal to my other clients."

As well he should be, she thought. He'd built his practice on some of the biggest names in the music industry. But without his family, he wouldn't have made those connections. He'd grown up around celebrities.

He resumed walking, and she fell into step with him. If only she wasn't developing such strong feelings for him. If only he wasn't burrowing inside her.

"My dad wants to start dating again," he said.

She started. "What? With who?"

"With whoever he is attracted to, I guess. We didn't talk about how he plans to meet someone new. Mostly he just wanted to run it past me. He hasn't been with anyone since he's been clean and sober, and he's getting lonely for companionship. He spoke to Tommy about it, but my brother isn't too keen on the idea."

Her heart thumped. "And you are?"

"It's not my decision to make. But I told Dad that I'd support him. Tommy isn't convinced that our old man has changed, at least not where females are concerned. But I think Dad is respectful of women now."

She tried to curb her distain, but some of it came out anyway. "What if Tommy is right?"

He frowned at her. "You don't approve of my father, do you?"

She glanced away. "I don't even know him."

"But it's obvious that you don't like the way he was portrayed in his book. You made that clear on our first date."

"I just don't like the way he treated his wife and children." And she especially couldn't bear the way he'd treated her mom. After his betrayal, Mama was afraid that all of Nashville would find out that she'd been accused of harassing one of the biggest country stars on the planet. Her dream of making it in that industry had been completely crushed.

"Are you reluctant to attend Matt's wedding because you're uncomfortable about meeting my dad?" Brandon asked.

At this point she couldn't find it within herself to lie. "Yes, he's a big part of it."

"I know that his past isn't very reassuring, but he's taking responsibility for it now. If you met him, I think you'd like him. Sophie gets along great with him and so does Libby. He even walked Sophie down the aisle when she and Tommy got married. No matter how often Dad and Tommy fight, they still have a bond that can't be denied."

Mary missed the bond she'd once had with her mother. She and Alice still had Mama's songbook tucked away in a safe deposit box. For them, it was her most important belonging.

He said, "I'm sorry if I keep pushing you toward my family. I just really want you to go to the wedding with me."

"It's still a month away." By now June was gone, and they were in the midst of July. "Maybe I'll be able to handle it by then."

"I hope so." Behind him, the river was dappled with sunlight, specks of gold dancing on the water.

The setting was too pretty for her to be stressing about Kirby, she thought. But Brandon's father was never far from her mind. "Will you call me when you get back from Las Vegas?"

He looked longingly into her eyes. "Definitely. I can't wait to see you again."

She fought the sudden fuzziness in her brain. Would they ever get enough of each other? Would this feeling ever end?

"I can't wait to see you again, either." To touch him, to feel his naked body against hers. But it was more than just the sex. She felt safe and warm when she was with Brandon, which made no sense.

Mary was confused, as usual. Even Cline was cocking his silvery head at her, as if he was trying to figure her out. Then again, the dog always seemed to sense her emotions.

And no one made Mary more emotional than Brandon.

Mary bustled around her apartment, plumping pillows on the sofa and making sure everything looked as nice as it possibly could. Brandon had just gotten back from his trip and was on his way over, directly from the airport.

This was a big step for her, letting him see her home. It just felt more personal than her going to his houses. But he'd asked if he could stop by, saying that he had some important news he wanted to share.

"Maybe I should hang out for a while," Alice said.

"No." Mary shook her head. "You said you had things to do today." Alice was supposed to be gone before he arrived.

"But I want to meet him." Her sister plopped down on the sofa, scattering the plumped pillows.

"Not now." She couldn't deal with introducing Alice to Brandon, and especially not today. "You know how nervous I am already."

"Maybe you're just afraid that I'll blow the whistle on you."

"You promised that you wouldn't." But was she concerned about being able to trust Alice? Yes, heaven help her, she was. "Please, just go run your errands."

"I'll leave if you agree to invite Brandon over for dinner this weekend. We can cook for him together. We can make it a cozy little get-together."

It sounded like a disaster to Mary, the worst idea in history. "And if I refuse to invite him?"

Alice put her feet on the coffee table. She even clicked her boot heels together. "Then I might be forced to break my promise and tell him the truth."

Mary glared at her. She was being blackmailed by her baby sister. Still, what choice did she have but to give in? Alice had the advantage. "Fine. I'll arrange for you to meet him. But you have to keep my secret. You have to swear on Mama's grave."

Her sister scoffed. "Now there's a low blow. Mama doesn't even have a grave."

Their mother had been cremated, with her ashes scattered in the Oklahoma wind. They hadn't been able to afford a funeral or a traditional burial. But Mama would have preferred being part of the elements, anyway. Mary didn't regret the choice they'd made. "Just swear it."

"All right. I swear. But it seems weird that you're so adamant about lying to him. If you never tell him who you are, he won't understand what went wrong. If you care about him, then don't you at least owe him that much?"

Mary squinted at her sister. "What are you doing? Trying to use some sort of reverse psychology on me?"

"I'm just stating the facts."

"What facts? That you want him to know that we plotted against him? That you want to see him get hurt?" She didn't trust Alice's motives, not one iota. "He'll be better off never knowing who I am."

"If you say so." Alice stood, grabbed her long-fringed purse and stomped over to the front door. "But don't forget to invite him to dinner and tell him how much I'm looking forward to meeting him." She batted her lashes before she left, making an even bigger mockery of their conversation. When she was a kid she used to make ugly faces when she was being a brat. Now she was being all pretty about it.

Once she was gone, Mary righted the pillows on the sofa. She hoped Brandon's news wasn't about the wedding. She'd already been losing far too much sleep over that.

About twenty minutes later, Brandon arrived. He was gorgeous as ever, in a gray pullover and black slacks.

Mary showed him around the apartment, and he lingered in her bedroom.

"So this is where you sleep," he said, stating the obvious.

She nodded. The old chenille spread had been passed down from her grandmother. Mama had used it when she was young, too. Everything was done in pastels, including her furniture.

She watched him walk over to her dresser. He didn't have far to go. The room was small and crowded. He lifted a cupcake-shaped candle from her dresser and studied it. "This is cute. It suits you." He turned to look at her bed. She had three stuffed animals, two bears and a bunny, on it. "Are these from when you were a kid?" he asked.

"Yes." The manner in which he was scrutinizing everything was making her uncomfortable. Suddenly she feared that he knew who she was. That he'd found out somehow and was mocking her with his "cute" comments. Was it possible that Alice had gone behind her back and told him? She could have gotten his number from Mary's phone.

No, that didn't make sense. Why would Alice have threatened to reveal Mary's identity if she'd already done it? And why would she have insisted on inviting Brandon to dinner?

"What are their names?" he asked.

She blinked. "What?"

He gestured. "The stuffed animals."

Oh, right. Her old toys. "The bunny is Beanie and the bears are Daisy and Dilly."

He moved toward the bed and sat on the edge of it. He even picked up Beanie and stroked its frayed ears.

"What's going on?" she asked, needing to know

what his agenda was. "What did you want to talk to me about?"

His face lit up. "I came here to tell you about Zoe."

She relaxed, grateful that his news seemed positive. "What about her?"

He bounced Beanie on his lap. "She arrived two days ago, while I was still in Vegas, but they just brought her home today. Sophie had her in a private birthing center, so they were able to keep it out of the press. Tommy plans to make a formal announcement and release some pictures. But he wants the family to meet her first. I haven't seen her yet. But I intend to make her acquaintance, just as soon as I leave here."

"That's nice, Brandon." She could see how excited he was.

"I was wondering if you'd come with me."

Oh, no. "What about your dad?" This sounded worse than the wedding. Or just as bad. "I need more time to meet him." Or she needed to not meet him at all, she thought.

"Dad won't be there. My parents were already at Tommy's place this morning, helping Sophie and the baby get settled in. They were at the clinic when she was born, too, so they've had lots of time with her. Matt and Libby and Chance are flying in tomorrow. Tommy is trying to keep everyone's visits separate so Sophie won't get too worn out."

"So it'll just be you and me?"

"Yep. Just us."

"I don't have anything to bring." There was always something to fret about, it seemed. "You already gave them a beautiful piece of art."

"I always give people art."

"And normally I bake for people."

"So you can bake for them another time. Tommy and Sophie will understand that this was a rushed visit. Just come with me," he implored her.

"Okay, I will." She wanted to support Brandon. And since Kirby wouldn't be around, she didn't have to panic about running into him. "Speaking of family, my sister wants you to come over for dinner this weekend. She's interested in meeting you."

"Really?" He put Beanie down. "Oh, that's cool. I'd like to meet her, too."

"She might not be that friendly. I think she's jealous that I'm seeing you." Mary figured it wouldn't hurt to warn him that Alice might behave strangely.

"Do you think it would help if I brought her a gift?"

"After you just told me not to worry about bringing something to Tommy and Sophie?"

"That's not the same thing. You just said that Alice is jealous that you're dating me."

"I know. But it isn't necessary to bring her a present." Short of millions of dollars, she doubted that he would be able to buy Alice's affection. And even then, her sister would probably still hate him. Mary went over and sat beside him on the bed. "I think it's better to just let Alice be her difficult self."

"I'm just glad that she wants to meet me. And I'm especially happy that you're going with me today."

"I like babies." But she wasn't thrilled with how much she needed Brandon. She struggled with that every day.

He leaned in to kiss her, and she wished for the umpteenth time that his father had never ruined her mother.

When Brandon broke the kiss, he said, "I can come to dinner on Saturday. Does that day work for you, or would Sunday be better?"

"Saturday is fine. I'm sure that will be fine with Alice, too, since it was her idea."

"I've been keeping my schedule clear for you. There was a ball I could've attended this weekend, but I declined the invitation. I don't want to go alone, and I didn't think you would've agreed to go with me." He paused, sighed. "I'd love to sweep you off to a fancy ball and introduce you to my friends. But I'm already concerned about scaring you away. I'm trying to have this affair on your terms."

"I appreciate that you're putting my feelings first." Except for the part where he wanted her to accept his father—the very thing that scared her most.

Tommy and Sophie lived in one of the biggest, grandest custom-built mansions in Nashville. Once Mary and Brandon passed through the security gate, she worried about what she'd gotten herself into. Brandon fit naturally into the opulent setting, but Mary felt like a little church mouse. She dusted off the fabric of her plain white skirt, wishing that she were prettier and more sophisticated and everything else that Brandon's other lovers were.

He glanced over at her. "Are you okay?"

"I was just thinking about what you said earlier about wishing you could take me to one of your fancy balls and introduce me to your friends. You're right that it would scare me."

He parked in the big circular driveway and reached across the console for her hand. "Maybe in time, my lifestyle won't seem so daunting to you."

"I don't even know how to dance."

"You mean waltz or country dance?"

"Waltz. I can two-step." She'd been reared on down-home music. Her mother used to dance her and Alice all over their ratty little apartment. Mama had even worked at a record store when she was younger—the type that barely existed anymore. Later, she'd worked at an insurance company, doing boring office stuff.

Brandon interrupted her thoughts. "Waltzing isn't that much different than two-stepping. I can teach you."

"It looks different on TV."

"On those dance competition shows? That doesn't count. We wouldn't be competing for a prize. It would just be two people swaying in each other's arms. You and I are good together that way."

Her cheeks went warm. He was obviously talking about sex. "We better go inside and see the baby." They certainly couldn't stay here, with him saying sensually charged things to her.

They exited the car, and she forced herself to breathe, as deeply and calmly as she could.

A woman with salt-and-pepper hair answered the door. Mary soon learned that her name was Dottie and that she managed the household staff and kept the estate running.

Dottie gave Brandon a big warm hug. She was kind and friendly to Mary, too, making the moment easier.

"Just wait until you see Zoe," Dottie said to Brandon. "You're going to fall in love with your niece."

He grinned. "I don't doubt that I will."

"Oh, and the painting you bought for Zoe is just the most adorable thing."

"Thanks. Mary helped me pick it out."

"Well, you have an eye for art, my dear." Dottie patted her hand. "For men, too," she mock whispered.

Mary couldn't think of an appropriate response, but she didn't have to. Brandon quickly said, "Hey. I heard that."

The older lady laughed. "You were meant to."

He laughed, too. "When are you going to leave Tommy and work for me?"

"Never," she replied, just as jokingly. "That brother of yours couldn't get along without me. But seriously, he and Sophie and the baby..." She sighed, quite dreamily. "They're perfect together." She nudged Brandon and Mary toward a luxurious staircase with polished wood banisters. "Go on up and see them. They're waiting for you."

Mary noticed a clear glass elevator in a secluded section of the massive entryway. She was glad they weren't using that. She didn't want to think about elevators right now. It would only remind her of what she and Brandon had done in the one at his loft.

The nursery was on the second floor. It overflowed with the ribbons, lace and bows that Mary expected to see. Even the crib was a lavish sight to behold, designed for a princess.

And Tommy and his family? They were perfect together, just as Dottie had said they were.

Tommy looked exactly like he did in his music videos: tall and decidedly Western, with stylishly messy light brown hair and a crooked smile. Sophie was a petite brunette, beaming with motherhood. She sat in an overstuffed rocker on the other side of the room, with the baby in her arms.

"You must be Mary," Tommy said, before Brandon got a chance to introduce her. "It's nice to meet you. That's my wife, Sophie, over there, and our brand-new daughter."

Mary smiled at him and nodded to Sophie, who gave her a gentle nod in return.

"What a special time this is for you," she said to Tommy.

"It's amazing." He turned toward Brandon and they hugged, clapping each other on the back. Then Tommy asked his brother, "Do you want to hold Zoe?"

"God, yes." A grin stretched across Brandon's face. "I've been waiting to get my hands on that kid."

Tommy gestured for Mary to join them. They headed for Sophie and the baby, and the new mother transferred her child into Brandon's arms, showing him what to do.

"She's beautiful." He held the infant carefully, protecting her neck and head. "Just like I knew she would be."

Zoe was a darling baby, Mary thought, with her thick cap of dark hair, hazel eyes and rosy cheeks. She had a cute little expression on her face, as if she was trying to focus on how handsome her uncle was.

Mary was focusing on the same thing. He looked incredible with the pink bundle in his arms. She glanced over at Sophie and said, "She looks like you."

"That's what Tommy says. That she's a mirror image of me. But she has his eyes. His change colors sometimes, going from brown to green, then back again. Hers will probably do that, too, depending on her moods."

"I can only imagine how happy you are." Suddenly marriage and babies and nesting with the man you loved sounded like something Mary wanted to try someday. But even as the thought crossed her mind, she went into panic mode. Love and marriage and babies should be the last thing swimming around in her head, especially while she was having an affair with Brandon.

Nine

Brandon and Tommy stood on the balcony attached to the nursery and gazed at the gardens below. They'd stepped outside for a few minutes, giving themselves the opportunity to be alone and marvel over the new life in their family.

"I think that's the first time I ever held a newborn," Brandon said, and glanced over his shoulder at the glass door behind him. Zoe was inside with the women. After he'd held her, he'd given her back to Sophie.

"I know. It's amazing, isn't it? How tiny she is, with all of those little fingers and toes?" Tommy smiled. "It's even more incredible than I thought it would be. Every time I look at her, I could burst."

"The love a parent has for a child is supposed to be the strongest bond on earth." Brandon was glad that Tommy was getting to experience it. "It's funny, too, because you're the last person any of us expected to have kids."

"And now I want a houseful." His brother furrowed his brow. "I know Mom loved us the way I love Zoe, but do you think Dad felt this way when we were born?"

Brandon wasn't surprised to hear Tommy question their father's feelings for them, not with how uncertain he'd always been about their dad. "He was messed up during that period of his life, but, yeah, I think he loved us the way he was supposed to."

"He didn't love Matt that way."

"Maybe he did and he was just too afraid to admit it. You know how guilty he was about breaking his promise to Mom and having a kid with someone else."

Tommy's expression softened. "Dad is a wonderful grandpa, I'll give him that much. He's over the moon about Zoe. I practically had to kick him and Mom out of here today. They'd both move into Zoe's nursery if they could."

"But you and Sophie will be doing that instead." They'd created a newly designed master suite adjoined to the nursery. They'd added luxurious accommodations for their nanny, too. "Life is good, eh?"

"For me, this is the best it's ever been. I can't wait to watch my daughter grow up, to teach her to be a cowgirl and play music."

Brandon teased him, saying, "I think you'll be wearing frilly hats and having tea parties with her."

Tommy grinned. "If that's what she wants me to do, then I will. You can join us, bro. We can be frilly-hat dudes together."

"Sure. Why not?" Brandon wanted to be a fun-loving uncle. He wanted his niece to be able to count on him. "We should make Dad wear one, too."

His brother laughed. "His will have to be black."

"I'll bet he'd wear pink for Zoe."

Tommy nodded. "Yeah, he probably would." A second later, he sighed and said, "Did Dad tell you he wants to start dating again?"

"Yes, he told me. I encouraged him to give it a try."

"I guess it'll be okay, as long as he never hurts anyone again."

"I don't think he will." Brandon trusted their father to be a better man. "He's been trying so hard to change."

Tommy squinted in the sunlight. "Speaking of dating, I like your new lady. She seems sweet."

"She is." Totally sweet. Totally sexy. "I'm getting hooked on her."

"So I gathered. You wouldn't have brought her here otherwise. I know I probably shouldn't tell you this, but after Sophie and I got together, I was hoping that you'd find someone, too. Sophie warned me not to play matchmaker or try to set you up with anyone. She said that if it was meant to happen, you'd meet the right woman on your own." His brother squinted again. "Do you think that you and Mary might have a future?"

"I don't know. It's a bit complicated." Or a lot complicated, he thought, with how much he'd come to care about her. "She's been cautious since I met her, and after she read Dad's biography, it got worse. She's leery of him."

"Can't say as I blame her. Even he admitted in the book that he treated people like crap."

"He also said how sorry he was. With Mary, it seems as if there could be something more going on, something related to her family. Both of her parents are dead, and she refuses to talk about them. I'm starting to wonder if maybe her father was a womanizer. If he could've been like our dad, and that type of guy leaves her cold. He might've even been abusive to her mother."

"That could account for why she's so sensitive about her parents. And why it's difficult for her to discuss them."

"Yeah, but I can't be sure." Brandon was at a loss to know what Mary's issues were. "I invited her to Matt's wedding, but she's uncomfortable about going."

"She might come around by then."

"She has a younger sister, and I'm going to meet her this weekend. But Mary already warned me that her sister is jealous of our relationship."

"Sounds like you have your work cut out for you."

"I definitely do." Yet even as difficult as it was, his fascination with Mary grew stronger each day.

When he and Tommy returned to the nursery, Mary was holding the baby, rocking the infant as if it was the most natural thing in the world. Zoe kicked her little feet and cooed.

Brandon moved closer, his attraction to Mary spiking even higher. He couldn't force her to talk about her parents, but he wasn't giving up on her, either. He was going to be there, for as long as she wanted him.

On Saturday evening Mary and Alice fixed chicken and dumplings, something Mary had always thought of as comfort food. They also prepared green beans with bacon, sweet peas, mashed potatoes and fried okra. Mary baked corn bread, too. For dessert, she had double-chocolate brownies and strawberry-lemon bars ready to go. She'd made a frozen mint chip pie, as well. All she had to do was take it out of the freezer when it was time to serve it.

Brandon arrived bearing gifts. The wine he'd brought wasn't the problem. But the other things? Holy cow. Apparently it didn't matter that she'd told him not to bring

Alice anything. He'd done it anyway. But he'd brought Mary something special, too.

He gave her the fairy painting he'd wanted to buy her from before. Alice's gift was artwork, too: a beautifully framed acrylic that depicted fashion throughout the ages. She seemed impressed by it, even if she was treating Brandon with a cool and critical eye.

"Was it expensive?" Alice asked him, about her painting.

Mary wanted to kick her sister for being so rude. She'd been taught better than that. But Alice obviously didn't care about being well mannered in this situation. Thank goodness Mary had already warned Brandon what to expect.

Either way, he handled Alice just fine. He politely replied, "I'm an art collector, so I always give people the most valuable work I can find. I enjoy buying select pieces for family and friends."

"I'm not your friend," she said. "And we're certainly not family."

"Your sister is my friend, and you two are family. That's reason enough for me."

Alice shifted her booted feet. She was dressed in her fanciest cowpunk attire. "I'm going to look it up online later and see how much it cost."

He laughed a little. "Go right ahead. I won't be offended."

Alice glared at him. "You don't seem like the type who offends easily."

"Neither do you." He gestured to her outfit. "You have an interesting sense of style. My dad wears black all the time, too."

Alice stiffened before she said, "I don't like his music."

"I wasn't implying that you did. But you have the sort of attitude depicted in his songs. Even though he's drawn to gentle-spirited women, he writes about the sassy ones."

Alice narrowed her gaze. "My sister has a gentle spirit. Our mother did, too."

Mary nearly gasped. Was she going to tell Brandon who they were? She'd sworn that she wouldn't. Yet she'd just mentioned their mother.

"I'd love to see a picture of your mom," he said. "I didn't see any photographs last time I was here."

Mary held her breath, praying that her sister didn't betray her and dig out an old snapshot. She felt faint just thinking about it. Did Brandon know what their mom looked like? Would he recognize her?

"We keep her pictures private," Alice replied. "She's gone now. But she was a good person."

He spoke softly. "I'm sorry you and Mary lost her. I haven't lost anyone I'm close to. I don't know what that feels like. But I can see how painful it is for you."

Alice stepped back, putting distance between her and Brandon. Clearly, she didn't want his sympathy. Mary did, though. She wanted to cuddle in his arms and take refuge in his strength. But she wouldn't dare do that in front of Alice.

"We better sit down and eat before everything gets cold," Mary said.

"Thanks for inviting me," Brandon said. "Both of you." He gazed at Alice. "Mary told me it was your idea."

"I just wanted to know who my sister is sleeping with," she responded, in her usual snide tone.

He replied, "I'm not going to hurt her, if that's what you're worried about."

"Someone always gets hurt," Alice retorted, before she darted into the kitchen to put the food on the table.

Brandon turned to look at Mary, and she mouthed the words, *"I'm sorry."* But she wasn't just apologizing for her sister's behavior. She was sorry for her part in everything, too.

The meal went fairly well, considering the tension Alice had caused. Brandon certainly seemed to enjoy the food. He complimented them on their cooking, eating his fair share. He had two helpings of the chicken and dumplings and slathered loads of honey butter on his corn bread.

Afterward, he tried to help with the dishes, but Mary declined his offer, telling him to relax instead. Brandon wandered onto the patio while the women cleaned up. Mary figured he needed a break from Alice. The patio was just a tiny slab of concrete with a café table, but at least it would give him a place to breathe.

Since Brandon was outdoors and out of earshot, Mary waited for Alice to complain about him. And she did, of course, right on cue. "He's so rich and spoiled," she said. "Bringing us expensive gifts and talking about his celebrity dad. It was all I could do not to tell him that you've been playing him, like his dad played our mom."

Mary rinsed the empty potato bowl. "I was scared that you might say something."

"Well, I didn't. But now I'm thinking that you should try to marry this guy and take him for all he's worth."

"What?" Mary lifted her head.

"He's totally falling for you. Any fool can see it. And if you lured him into marrying you, you could get all sorts of expensive things from him. He would go to the ends of the earth to kiss my butt, too, just because I'm your sister."

"I can't believe you're suggesting that." Just the thought of it was making her hands shake.

"So what's the big deal? If you married him, you'd be getting the guy you want."

"I never said I wanted to be his wife."

"But now that I planted the seed, I'll bet you're going to start obsessing about it. Besides, if you married him and let him support us, we'd still be getting justice for Mama. He owes us that much, him and his bastard of a dad. If Kirby had bought Mama's songs like he was supposed to, you wouldn't be working your tail off, and I wouldn't be stuck having to take student loans."

"I would never try to con Brandon into marrying me." To her, that would be the ultimate betrayal, the worst thing she could possibly do. "I need to end it when I can."

"When you can? Seriously, what's stopping you?"

"I'm just not ready."

Alice rolled her eyes. "Why? Because he's such a great lay? I think it's because you're falling in love with him."

"I am not." Mary protested. By now, she was shaking so badly she nearly dropped the plate she was loading into the dishwasher. She couldn't let herself love Brandon. She absolutely, positively couldn't.

After the kitchen was clean, it was time to serve dessert. Mary brought the treats outside to where Brandon was waiting.

He turned and smiled at her, and she nearly melted on the spot. For a woman refusing to fall in love, she was headed for trouble—in the worst kind of way.

Later that evening, Mary went to Brandon's loft with him to spend the night. As they lay in bed, facing each other with moonlight streaming in through the windows, she wondered what it would be like to be his bride.

A shiver traveled down her spine. She had no business imagining herself as his wife. But even as she fought her feelings, she knew that she loved him. God help her, but Alice was right—and it was pointless to pretend otherwise.

He was being quiet, not saying a word. But he was staring at her, as if he had something on his mind. She took a chance and asked, "What are you thinking about?"

"I was just pondering how much I like you."

Her breath rushed out. "You already know how much I like you." They'd discussed it before. But she couldn't tell him that she loved him. She could barely say it to herself. Everything inside her was spinning a mile a minute. But no matter how she felt about him, it would never work. They could never stay together, not for real.

"Alice was pretty much what I expected," he said.

"You were being really nice to her, even when she wasn't very nice to you."

He shrugged. "She has a lot of growing up to do, but she's only nineteen. A lot of people are troubled at that age. She's just a screwed-up kid, looking for attention."

And Mary was a tortured adult who'd gotten herself into a horrible mess. "I should have been a better influence on her."

He frowned. "You can't take responsibility for her actions."

That wasn't true. If she hadn't promised Alice that she would help her get back at Brandon and his dad, none of this would be happening. "In the beginning I tried to teach her right from wrong, but as time went on, I just gave up."

"You're not her parent. You're her sister." He angled his head. "You're being too hard on yourself."

He didn't know the whole story. But she'd blinded him with her nice girl persona. "When we were young and she got upset about something, I didn't stop her from letting it fester. Sometimes I let things fester, too."

He smoothed a strand of hair away from her cheek. "That just makes you human."

A bad human, she thought. Mary still had ill feelings toward Kirby. She still hated him for what he'd done and the domino effect it had on her and Alice.

"I wish you'd confide in me about the rest of your family," Brandon said. "I can tell that something wasn't right with your parents. Things might have been off with your grandma, too."

"Our grandmother was a practical woman, conservative in her beliefs." That much she could tell him. That much she was willing to say. "But she treated us kindly. She was the one who first taught me to bake."

"Whose side of the family was she from?"

"She was our maternal grandmother. She didn't live near us. She only visited now and then." She'd died a few years before Mama. But she'd never known about Kirby. No one in the family had ever told her. Grandma wouldn't have approved of Mama's affair with him. Nor had she been aware of how truly depressed her daughter had been, either. Mama was good at faking it when she had to.

"Alice said something earlier about what a nice lady your mom was." He touched Mary's hair again. "But then she clammed up after she said it."

Her chest went tight. This wasn't a conversation she

wanted to have. "It's difficult for us to express our feelings about our mother."

"Did your father hurt her?"

Oh my God. He thought it was *her* dad who'd destroyed Mama. But in reality, it was *his*. She gazed into his eyes, the tightness in her chest working its way to her soul. "I'm sorry, but I just can't talk about this."

"Okay." He blew out a soft sigh. "But if you ever feel the need to talk about it, you can come to me. I'll be here."

"Thank you, but I'd rather keep it to myself."

They both went silent. Far too silent, she thought. She felt as if the room was going to crash in on her, right along with her heart.

A few painful seconds later, she said, "I didn't want you to buy me the fairy painting, but now I'm glad that you did." When their affair was over, it would be something warm and soft and magical to remember him by.

"That picture is meant for you."

"It definitely is." But loving him wasn't a cure for her deception. It wasn't lessening the shame or the guilt. If anything, it magnified it.

He lowered the strap on her nightgown. She'd worn a baby doll nightie to bed. Something far too innocent for the person she'd become. Far too sweet. Mary closed her eyes. She felt like such a fraud.

"What do you have on under this cute little thing?" he asked.

She opened her eyes. "Matching panties." She'd bought the ensemble to entice him. But now she wondered what she'd been trying to prove by resorting to girlish lingerie.

"Mmm." He reached down and slipped his hand into her panties. "It suits you."

No, it didn't, she thought. But he was making her wet just the same. She rocked her hips, rubbing against his seductive touch. He was already naked; that was how he slept every night.

They kissed, and the foreplay continued. She went after him, stroking him between his legs, giving him pleasure, too.

Soon he was peeling off her panties and tossing them onto the side of the bed. He did away with her nightie, as well.

He removed a condom from the drawer next to him and said, "You can put this on me tonight. There's no hurry. You can take your time. We can both enjoy it."

As familiar as she'd become with his body, this was just another layer of excitement. She opened the packet, and he guided her through it. She loved touching him.

Once he was sheathed, he braced himself above her. She opened her legs, inviting him inside.

He thrust deep, and they made long, warm, luxurious love, with breathless whispers between them.

Mary awakened in the middle of the night. No matter how hard she tried, she wasn't able to go back to sleep. So she finally crept out of bed and got dressed in the bathroom, careful not to disturb Brandon.

After leaving him a note, in case he woke up and noticed she was gone, she went to a twenty-four-hour market and bought the ingredients she needed to bake a special batch of cupcakes. Thanks to Brandon's chef, his kitchen was stocked with the cookware, utensils and appliances she required.

Hours later, while she was putting the finishing touches on the cupcakes, Brandon entered the kitchen. He was wrapped in a robe and handsomely tousled from sleep. She wasn't surprised to see him this early. It was Sunday, and he would be taking Cline to the park. For now, she assumed the dog was still crashed out in his own room.

"What are you doing, pretty lady?" Brandon asked.

"Making goodies for Tommy and Sophie." She showed him her handiwork. The pink cupcakes were artfully decorated with Zoe's name on them.

He studied them. "Oh, those are cute."

"I also made banana nut bread for you." She gestured to where it was cooling on a counter.

"Wow. I slept through all of this?" He cut a piece of the bread and munched on it. "As always, your treats are amazing." He brewed a pot of coffee while she packed up the cupcakes.

"Will you take these to Tommy and Sophie the next time you see them?" she asked. "If it's not within the next day or so, I can freeze them, and you can bring them whenever it's convenient for you."

"I can pay them a quick visit today. But you should come with me. You should give them the cupcakes yourself. We can go after we take Cline for his walk."

"Oh, I'm sorry. But I promised a coworker that I would work for her today. It's just for a few hours this afternoon, but I'll need to go home soon."

He poured the coffee and handed her a cup. He added cream to his, and she used sugar.

"I'm going to miss you," he said.

"I'll miss you, too." She looked into his eyes, battling her heart, struggling to cope with her feelings. Yesterday Alice had asked her why she was taking so long to end things with Brandon. And now Mary had no recourse but to ask herself the same question. How long was she going to keep this affair going? How long was she going to cling to him, falling deeper and deeper in love? "Do you still want me to go to Matt's wedding with you?" she asked.

He glanced up, gazing at her over the rim of his cup. "Of course I do." He put the coffee down. "Does this mean you decided you're going to take the trip with me? Or are you still just batting the idea around?"

"I'm still batting it around." But at this point, maybe it would behoove her to attend a Talbot family function. To come face-to-face with Kirby. To meet the man who'd destroyed her mother, and remind herself once and for all why she couldn't keep seeing Brandon.

She ached inside, just thinking about it. But it would give her a timeline, a schedule to follow. Otherwise, she might never summon the courage to end the relationship.

"You know what?" she said. "I think I should go with you." She moved closer to him. "But I don't know what's going to happen afterward."

The muscles in his face tightened. "What's that supposed to mean? That you're going to stop seeing me after the wedding?"

"We both know that we can't stay together forever. Sooner or later we'll have to go back to our regular lives." She tried to sound rational, to force herself to seem strong. Yet all she really wanted to do was cry. "No matter how hard we try, we're never going to fit into each other's worlds."

He quickly argued, "I'm completely willing to bring you into mine."

"By me wearing ball gowns and learning to waltz? It's not that simple, Brandon. I can't be around socialites who are going to look down their noses at me. I don't want them misinterpreting my feelings for you or calling me a gold digger." Even Alice had tried to get Mary to lure him into marriage for his money. "It's just not feasible." At least this way she could pretend that their affair had been based on something pure, instead of deception and lies.

"I don't care what other people think. Besides, I already told you that my friends have been encouraging me to find a nice girl." He pulled her into his arms. "When we get back from Texas, we're going to figure this out."

"There's nothing to figure out." She already loved him; she was already doomed. "I'm not the right woman for you."

"You're exasperating, that's what you are." He held her tighter. "And I'll be damned if I'm going to let you break it off before I'm ready."

"So when are you going to be ready?" How long was it going to be before he stopped wanting her? Before he didn't care anymore and moved on?

"Hell if I know." His voice went ragged. "I've never needed anyone the way I need you."

Mary squeezed her eyes shut. Had he fallen for her as deeply as she'd fallen for him? Alice certainly seemed to think so. "It's all so confusing."

"Tell me about it." He tugged on her braid, nudging her head back and kissing her hard and quick.

Her knees turned to jelly. If there was one thing Brandon knew how to do, it was to seduce her. After he lifted his mouth from hers, she said, "You make me weak."

"And you make me frustrated. You're the most challenging woman I've ever been with. And you're so damned mysterious, too. Nothing about you comes easy."

She could scarcely breathe. "Except for when you make me come."

He smiled a wicked smile. "There is that. The sex has definitely been good."

Too good, she thought, as he hauled her into the bedroom and stripped her bare. Not just her body, but her heart and her soul, too. Mary was never, ever going to be the same, not after falling in love with a man she couldn't keep.

Ten

Brandon took Cline to the park, then brought the cupcakes to Tommy's house. His brother seemed impressed with Mary's work.

He even took some pictures for his Instagram page to show them off. He was particularly pleased that they had Zoe's name on them. By now, he and Sophie had introduced their daughter to the world, by way of social media and the press.

"Mary agreed to attend Matt's wedding with me," Brandon said, as he and his brother sat outside in the sunshine, occupying a bench in front of an enormous jeweled tiger statue Tommy had bought for his garden. Sophie and the baby were inside, napping.

"That's good news." Tommy sipped from a recyclable water bottle.

"Yes, it is. But not completely. She's talking about ending it after we get back from Texas. She's always saying things like that. She's never been secure about dating me."

"I'm sorry she keeps pulling away from you. But I can see where she feels insecure. She's just a regular girl, and you're a big society guy from a celebrity family."

"That's the reason she keeps giving." Brandon heaved a sigh. "But I still think there's more to her story."

"The last time we talked, you mentioned her family and that you thought that her dad might have been hurtful or abusive to her mom. Do you still think that's what happened?"

"I don't know. I questioned her about it, but she said that she didn't want to discuss it." Yet the more she remained silent, the more concerned Brandon became. "I think that whatever occurred with her parents is affecting her relationship with me. I think that's the main issue." Sometimes when he looked into Mary's eyes, he saw how fragile she was. Like this morning, he thought. She'd seemed especially vulnerable.

Tommy swigged his water. "How'd the dinner go with her sister?"

"It was weird, but Mary warned me that Alice wasn't going to like me. She liked the artwork I gave her, though. She definitely seems like a materialistic girl. Mary isn't that way. Possessions aren't important to her." But he was glad that she'd accepted the fairy painting from him.

"You brought the sister a gift?"

"It seemed like the thing to do."

Tommy laughed a little. "You better be careful or you'll turn into Dad."

"That's not funny." Ever since Kirby got clean and

sober and was trying to become a better father, he'd been showering them and Matt with overly sentimental presents. Mostly to make up for the years he'd spent on the road. They'd barely seen him when they were growing up, and Matt had seen him even less. "Speaking of gifts, I shopped online before I came over here today and ordered a big stuffed husky dog for Zoe. But it's not from me, it's from Cline."

His brother smiled. "Is it a girl husky with a pink bow?"

"Yep." Brandon smiled, too. "I showed Cline its picture, and he gave me his approval."

"Yeah. I'm sure he did." Tommy shifted on the bench. "You're already turning into an incredible uncle. I think you'll make a great dad someday, too, if you ever decide to have kids."

Brandon's thoughts turned to his lover, to the woman driving him mad. "I just wish I wasn't so consumed with Mary." He frowned, troubled by her effect on him. "Maybe I should just let her break it off after the wedding and be done with it."

"That's totally up to you, bro. But you already seem miserable about losing her."

"I don't know how to reason with her." He'd never been so flustered by anyone. "She just keeps stating the same case, insisting that we don't belong together. But if I knew where her head was really at, if I knew what the deal with her parents was, maybe I could understand her better."

"You could do a security check and look into her past. You've got lots of resources for that."

"Yes, but in a situation like this, poking around in her family history seems pretty damn invasive." He'd never investigated anyone he'd ever dated. Of course, he'd never dated anyone as secretive as Mary. Still, could he take his curiosity that far? "It's not as if she's posing a security threat."

Tommy shrugged. "It was just a thought."

"I need to give myself some time to think about it."

"If things are still rocky with her after the wedding, maybe you could look into it then."

"I guess we'll see." The Texas trip was still three weeks away. "I'd rather not do it if I don't have to. But it's been tough trying to figure her out."

"I knew Sophie all my life, better than anyone. Of course we went through a rough patch when we were falling in love. Those are some scary feelings at first. But you know how tough it was for me. You and Matt helped me through it."

That was true; they had. But that didn't make Brandon an expert. He didn't want to think about how frightening it would be to fall in love with Mary. He had his hands full with how badly he needed her. Loving her would only make it harder.

Tommy's phone dinged, signaling a text. "Dad is here."

Brandon struggled to focus. "What?"

"Dad just stopped by to see the baby. But she's still asleep, so Dottie is sending him out here to hang out with us."

In no time, they spotted Kirby cutting across the lawn. As always, he looked like an outlaw, decked in black.

"Hey, boys," he said, by way of a greeting.

They both responded, and he sat on the base of the tiger statue, placing himself across from them. Kirby's graying beard was neatly trimmed and his eyes were deep and dark beneath a straw Stetson.

Brandon considered his father's past and the women in it. His former mistresses, including Matt's mom, had been regular girls, not starlets or groupies. Brandon and Tommy's mother was the most glamorous woman Dad had ever been with, but she still had the gentle nature he was drawn to. Mom had certainly deserved a better husband, but at least they were friends now.

"Are you seeing anyone yet?" Brandon asked him, curious if he'd followed through on his plans to start dating again.

"No. But I put the word out there with friends. No one seems to want to set me up with anyone, though."

"You don't exactly have the best track record," Tommy interjected. "So they're probably just being cautious."

Kirby nodded. "I might have to use a professional matchmaker. Or a dating site for rich old farts." He chuckled. "There's got to be an app for that, right?"

Tommy chuckled, too. "If there isn't, then we should create one just for you."

Brandon smiled, going along with their goofy joke. But overall, he couldn't stop thinking about Mary. He went ahead and told his dad, "I'm dating someone special. I don't know how long it's going to last, but she's a sweet girl."

"If she's that sweet, you ought to try to keep her."

"I'm working on it." Or he was trying to, anyway. "She'll be coming to Matt's wedding with me. So you'll get to meet her then."

"Sounds like a plan." Kirby arched his back. "So when did you start seeing nice girls? Weren't the diva types more your style?"

"She inspired me to change my pattern." She was

inspiring him to feel more than he might be able to handle, too.

Like the possibility of falling in love, he thought. And the big, shaky fear that went with it.

As the weeks passed, the wedding crept nearer and nearer. And finally, the time arrived. In fact, Mary would be boarding a private plane this very day, en route to Texas. At this point, she was in so deep she couldn't escape if she tried.

Every moment she spent with Brandon was more powerful than the last. She was starting to feel as if she'd known him her entire life. But she doubted that he could say the same thing about her. Was she going to end the relationship when their trip was over? Would meeting Kirby give her the strength to do it? Or would she keep putting off the inevitable?

When she finished packing, she brought her luggage into the entryway and set it beside the front door. Brandon was sending a limo to pick her up. He had some loose ends to tie up in his office this morning, so he would be meeting her at the airport.

Mary glanced into the living room, where Alice brooded on the couch. Her sister turned and said, "Well, look at you, preparing to go to Texas and make friends with Kirby."

She blew out a sigh. "I'm not going to become friends with him. I still hate him as much as you do."

"What if you stop hating him? What if he cons you into trusting him like he did with Mama, and you fall into the Talbot trap?"

Mary was already falling into it with Brandon, but he wasn't phony like his dad. He was the real deal. "I'm not going to let Kirby con me."

Tears rushed to her sister's eyes, but she quickly wiped them away. She looked oddly innocent today, with a pair of fuzzy skull-and-crossbones slippers on her feet.

"It was all a mistake," Alice said.

Mary sat beside her on the sofa. "What was?"

"The stupid revenge plot I came up with. I should have known better than to expect you to follow through on it the way it was intended."

"Please stop blaming me for caring about Brandon. I can't help it if I developed feelings for him. Besides, do you know how painful it is for me to be deceiving him? To look into his eyes and pretend to be someone I'm not? This hasn't been a picnic for me, and now I have to figure out when and how to end it without hurting him more than I already have."

"I still think you should try to charm him into marrying you. At least then we'd be getting something out of this. But instead, you're going to walk away with nothing. And leave me with nothing."

"I can't make this about money." Mary couldn't do that to Brandon. "And how long do you think we'd be able to stand being related to Kirby? Just think of what a nightmare that would be."

"I wouldn't care if it made us rich, and I don't think Mama would've cared, either. You know how badly she wanted to give us a better life."

Mary shook her head. "Yes, she wanted good things for us. But I doubt she would've approved of me marrying Brandon and using him as a sugar daddy." She studied Alice's expression. Her baby sister was pouting something awful. "That isn't who I am."

"I know you love him. And don't deny it this time. I can tell you do."

"You're right. I am in love with him. And that's exactly why I have to break it off."

"And you're hoping that meeting Kirby will motivate you to let Brandon go? That your disdain for his dad will be the catalyst that frees you? Well, good luck with that, Miss Goody Two Shoes."

"Don't poke fun at me. I'm just trying to do what I think is right for Brandon."

"But not what's right for me?" Alice got up and stormed into her room, slamming the door behind her.

Mary heaved a sigh. Between deceiving Brandon and fighting with her sister, things were a mess. But instead of chasing after Alice, she let her stew. She loved her sister, but she couldn't keep coddling her. It might do Alice some good to be left alone. For now, Mary had her own problems.

She checked the time. The limo would be here soon, and later today she would be in the Texas Hill Country, surrounded by Brandon and his family.

The Flying Creek Ranch was a remarkable place, steeped in nature. Mary and Brandon's cabin presented a spectacular view of the hills, and the decor was rife with Western memorabilia and Indian artifacts.

Mary hadn't met Matt or Libby yet. One of Matt's employees had gotten her and Brandon settled into their cabin. Of course, the bride and groom weren't causing her distress. She wasn't worried about making their acquaintance. It was Kirby who consumed her.

The rehearsal dinner was tonight, and she and Brandon were getting ready to go. This was it, she thought, the moment where she would come face-to-face with his father. She was so nervous, she felt as if her heart was sinking in her chest.

"You look pretty," Brandon said to her.

"Thank you." She was attired in a yellow eyelet dress and tan cowboy boots. She'd bought several Western-style outfits for the trip, using money from the overtime she'd put in at work. If Alice hadn't been so mad at her over the past few weeks, she would have engaged her help. But as it was, Mary had chosen her clothes on her own. "You look handsome, too."

"Wait until you see me in my tux tomorrow. This is the second wedding I've been part of this year. First it was Tommy's, and now this one."

"Always the groomsman and never the groom?" Without thinking about how it sounded, she teased him, regretting the words right after they passed her lips.

"I was Tommy's best man, but that premise still works, I guess." He came to stand beside her in the mirror. "Maybe I'll get married someday. Maybe I'll see it as something I'm capable of doing."

The sinking feeling in her heart turned darker, lonelier. "I think you'd make a great husband someday." For someone else, she thought. Not for her.

He turned toward her. "I know I shouldn't be starting a conversation like this when we're so close to heading out the door. But I have feelings for you that scare me. You've really done a number on me, Mary."

She'd done a number on both of them. "What I feel for you scares me, too."

"You've been uncertain around me ever since the day we met." He touched a strand of her unbound hair. "But I'm glad you came on this trip with me. I'm happy you're here."

He didn't look happy. He looked like a man who was on the verge of falling in love. Did he know that was why he was scared? Or hadn't he realized it yet? She certainly knew that she loved him, for whatever that was worth.

"We better go before we're late." She still had to deal with the anguish of meeting his father.

"Yeah, we'd better." He stepped back. "But after we come back here tonight, I'm going to put my hands all over you."

"I'd be disappointed if you didn't." She wanted to make love with him, as many times as she could.

Before it all came to an end.

The rehearsal dinner was in the dining room at the lodge, with knotty pine walls, limestone floors and big, bright chandeliers. Mary sat with the Talbots at their linen-draped table. Somehow, Kirby ended up next to her, with Brandon on her other side. Was the seating arrangement a joke from the universe? A punishment? She'd expected to meet Kirby, but she hadn't expected to be sandwiched between him and Brandon.

Mary could barely eat. She picked at her pasta, moving it around on her plate.

No doubt about it, Kirby was a charming man. He smiled; he made lighthearted jokes; he spoke with pride about his children and raved about his new granddaughter. He also bragged about Chance and how the boy had been named after one of his songs.

As overwhelming as this was, she could see where her mother had found him appealing. There was no denying his star power. Every time he looked at Mary, his eyes sparkled. He even patted her hand a few times. Clearly, he sensed her shyness and was trying to make her comfortable. He was being ridiculously nice. Painfully nice. And it made her want to scream, to yell, to shout at him, to defend her mother. But she kept quiet, the lump in her throat getting bigger with each breath she took.

Brandon's mother was kind and friendly, too. And beautiful. Mary had never seen a more gorgeous woman, with her long lean figure and silky blond hair. Everyone was treating Mary with care, doing their best to help her fit in. She'd already met Tommy and Sophie, so being around them helped a little.

But still, no one knew why she was so nervous. No one knew the truth. When people began to mingle, visiting guests at other tables, Brandon was called away for a quick meeting with the other groomsmen. He promised that he would be right back.

For Mary, being alone with his father was torture. The worst thing she could've imagined.

He leaned over and said to her, "My son is really smitten with you. You're the first woman I've ever seen him care so much about."

"I care about him, too." Her voice quavered. "Brandon is a good person."

"He's a lot better than I am. My family has put up with a lot of terrible things from me."

"I read something about that in your biography." It was the only response she could think to say.

"Well, then you know of what I speak." He sipped his ginger ale. "I'm lucky that Matt allowed me back into his life, let alone let me be part of his wedding."

Mary glanced at the groom, who stood at the bar, chatting with the bride's family. Tomorrow Matt would be exchanging vows with the love of his life. "He and Libby make a beautiful couple." She'd seen how tenderly they'd interacted with each other over dinner. "Libby is a doll." A bright and shimmering girl, Mary thought, who seemed as happy and content as a bride should be.

Kirby nodded. "Yes, she most certainly is. Without Libby, I don't think Matt would have ever forgiven me. She influenced him to make amends with me."

If Mary stayed with Brandon could they influence each other to make things right? Could he forgive her for deceiving him, and could she stop hating Kirby for what he'd done to her mother?

With that thought spiraling in her head, she stared at Brandon's father. Could she make things work with Brandon or was she dreaming of a fantasy that could never be?

"You seem sort of familiar," Kirby said suddenly.

Her heart nearly blasted its way out of her chest. "I don't know what you mean." Did he sense a likeness between her and her mother? That would seem odd. Mary didn't resemble Mama.

"It's just something about you. Maybe it's your girl-next-door quality. Matt's mother was like that when I met her." He gestured to his former mistress, a lovely fiftysomething brunette who sat at another table with her husband. "I made a mess out of her life, keeping her on the string the way I did. But she's happy now with someone else."

Mary relaxed a little. He was comparing her to Matt's mother, not her own. Then again, he'd branded Mama a stalker, so likening Mary to her wouldn't make much sense.

Kirby smiled at her. "You're easy to talk to. But that's obvious, I guess, with me doing most of the talking."

"I don't mind." It was easier for her to stay quiet.

"I hope you and Brandon can make a go of things.

It would be nice to keep seeing you at other family gatherings."

"Thank you," she replied, fretful about surviving this gathering, let alone more of them. She was actually starting to like Kirby, to view him as something other than a monster.

She could only imagine how upset Alice would be if she knew that Mary was bonding with Brandon's father.

She said, "You seem nicer than I assumed you'd be."

"Because of my arrogant reputation? As much as I hate to say it, I still have my pompous-ass moments." He lowered his voice. "But I'm genuinely sorry for the pain I caused the people in my life."

Would he admit fault for what he'd done to Mama? Would he take responsibility for it? Would he say he was sorry? Or would he insist that she was the stalker he'd made her out to be?

Mary was so confused she could barely see straight. Brandon returned to the table and leaned in to kiss her on the cheek. She loved him so much she ached from it.

Kirby said to his son, "I like your lady. She's sweet."

"I told you that she was," Brandon replied with a smile.

His father smiled, too, and got up to excuse himself. "I think I'll go hunt down my new grandbaby. As far as I know, the nanny hasn't put her to bed yet. Have you seen how excited Chance is about her? They're going to make great cousins." He tipped his hat to Mary. "You be good to my boy, okay?"

"I will," she said, even if that ship had sailed. How could she promise to be good to Brandon when she was lying about who she was?

He kissed her again, this time on the lips, and she closed her eyes, lost in the sensation of him.

* * *

Later that night, Mary and Brandon made love with vigor and passion. She couldn't get enough of him, and he couldn't seem to get enough of her, either. His hands were everywhere, touching, caressing, playing across her body and creating powerful ripples. Like waves, she thought. Like the sea at midnight, rising up in a storm.

Their mouths came together, tongues mating, teeth clashing. He growled in her ear, and she used her nails like weapons, digging into his skin.

She turned toward the window, where a three-quarter moon shone through the trees, casting a shadowy glow on their cabin.

She loved being here with him, deep in the Texas Hill Country. Even as painful as it was to be around his family, she felt as if she belonged with Brandon.

It was a false sense of belonging, she reminded herself.

They rolled across the bed, twisting the top sheet and knocking soft, fluffy pillows onto the rugged hardwood floor. Their clothes were strewn on the floor, too, just where they'd left them. She could see her bra and panties, her dress, her boots, one of which had fallen on its side, its heel upended. Her heart was falling, too, spiraling down a rabbit hole and spinning out of control.

As her thoughts scattered, Brandon pushed deeper, moving inside her like a madman.

Soon, they switched positions so she could straddle him. She bounced up and down, holding on to his shoulders for support.

But she couldn't steady her feelings. She couldn't stop loving him. It was too late for that.

He watched her with a hot gleam in his eyes, hungry for her to take him all the way, to make him come.

She leaned forward to kiss him, but it was a biting kiss, rife with sexual chaos and friction. When she removed her mouth from his, she increased the tempo, giving them both the orgasm that they wanted, needed, had to have.

They climaxed together—all the way.

In the seconds that followed, she collapsed on top of him, and he skimmed a gentle hand down her spine.

"It just gets better and better with you," he said.

He meant the sex, obviously. She caught her breath and replied, "You're all I want. You're all I think about."

"Likewise." He met her gaze. "Shower with me?"

It was an invitation she couldn't refuse. She wanted to get wet and soapy with him. "Definitely."

They went into the bathroom, and he disposed of the condom. The tub doubled as a shower, but it was smaller than the other shower stalls they'd used at Brandon's homes. Mary didn't mind. She liked being ridiculously close to him.

They washed the sex off their bodies, but it didn't leave their thoughts. They were still looking at each other with satisfaction in their eyes.

Afterward, they dried off and returned to bed, naked and clean. By now, they'd righted the bed, smoothing the sheets and replacing the pillows they'd knocked onto the floor.

As they lay side by side, gazing up at the ceiling, he said, "You made a wonderful impression on my family. They all really like you."

She did her best to seem calm, even if her pulse had begun to skitter. "I like them, too."

"Even my dad?"

The skittering continued. "Yes. He was very kind and complimentary to me."

"So the stuff that was in his book doesn't bother you anymore?"

"No." But what he'd done to her mother still did. She turned to face Brandon. She couldn't stand lying to him anymore. God help her, but she was going to tell him the truth, every last painful detail. Only now wasn't the time to do it. She would wait until the wedding was over and they were back in Nashville. She would tell him that she loved him then, too. She would spill all her secrets.

She had no idea where the truth would lead. But at least her conscience would be clear. And maybe, just maybe, they could make their relationship work.

He skimmed her cheek with his fingers. "You never cease to baffle me, Mary. You and your mysterious ways."

The confusion would be over soon, she thought. Once she told him the truth, he would know everything about her.

As ashamed as she was about what she'd done to Brandon, she hoped and prayed that he would consider the pain his dad had cast upon her family. That alone should absolve her.

Shouldn't it?

Needing to hide her expression, to shield her emotions, she moved into his arms and buried her face against his shoulder.

He touched her still-damp hair and asked, "What's wrong?"

"Nothing." Her response was muffled against his skin. "I just want to be close to you."

"Are you certain that's all it is?"

"Yes." She had no choice but to lie. Her final lie, she thought, the last of the tall tales.

"That's okay. I don't mind keeping you close." He

nuzzled the top of her head with his chin. “I’ll hold you until you fall asleep.”

“Thank you.” Although sleep would probably elude her, she closed her eyes, letting Brandon be her hero. Her dream lover, she thought, wrapped up in the stars and the moon and the secrets that still shrouded them.

Eleven

The wedding was sweetly romantic, Brandon thought. Beautiful in a way that he'd never experienced before. Matt and Libby had a history with National S'mores Day, and that's the day they'd chosen to get married.

The happy couple exchanged vows at dusk, surrounded by trees and hills and people they loved. Libby made a stunning bride, draped in a long shimmery dress, her white-blond hair adorned with flowers. Matt stood tall and strong, attired in a black tuxedo and Western hat.

Security was tight. There was no press on the premises. The family had done an excellent job of keeping it private.

As Brandon watched the ceremony, he glanced over at Mary. She seemed mesmerized by it all. She still baffled him, of course. Nothing had changed in that regard. He still considered his lover a mystery. But now he was wondering how it would be to spend the rest of his life with her, to fall madly in love, to get married.

Maybe he was already in love with her. If he wasn't, he wouldn't be having those sorts of thoughts. But it wasn't a calm feeling. He was even more scared of his feelings for her than he'd been before.

Suddenly Brandon was anxious for Matt and Libby's vows to end and for the reception to begin. He needed to escape this setting and have a quick, stiff drink.

Finally, Brandon got his wish. The reception offered an open bar. He ordered his whiskey neat and downed the amber liquid in a few anxious gulps. Normally Brandon was more controlled. In fact, he never resorted to alcohol to relax his nerves. That just wasn't his style. But it wasn't every day a man found himself falling in love with a woman he barely knew.

He considered a second drink, but decided against it. He would be better off trying to keep a clear head, to remain true to his normally controlled nature.

"Are you okay?" Mary asked him, as she sipped champagne. "You seem distracted."

"I'm fine," he replied. "I'm hungry, though. Are you?"

"Yes." She smiled at him.

But even in the midst of her smile, he noticed a haunted look in her eyes. Was she still thinking of leaving him? When they returned from Texas, would she disappear into a soft gray mist?

They headed for the buffet, where a feast of down-home cooking and uptown delicacies made a marvelous presentation.

Brandon and Mary filled their plates and socialized with other guests. As the celebration continued, the house band played cover tunes. Dad and Tommy sat in with them for a number of songs, making it a star-studded event. Needless to say, the music was spectacular.

"At least I don't have to worry about not knowing how to waltz tonight," Mary said.

Brandon nodded. It was country dancing, through and through. "Do you want to take a spin?"

"Yes, please." Her gaze met his. "It'll be our first time dancing together."

He reached for her hand. "Yes, indeed." There were lots of firsts zipping through his mind: the first day they'd met, their first date, their first kiss. She'd bewitched him from the beginning, and she was still doing it.

The music was fast and fun. Brandon had grown up on country songs. He knew them inside out.

He spun Mary around, and she two-stepped with the best of them. She was wearing the same boots she'd worn to last night's rehearsal dinner, only now they were getting some miles on them.

After a while, the band switched gears, slowing the music down. They played a variety of emotional ballads, packed with romance.

Brandon held Mary close, and they swayed rhythmically to the dreamy riffs. He couldn't deny how compatible they were, locked in each other's arms. Their bodies just seemed to fit, motion to motion, breath to breath, similar to when they made love.

"It's nice that we're going to have two more days here," she said. "I've never imagined being on a vacation like this before."

He'd been on lots of holidays, all over the world. But this was the most compelling—the scariest, too, with how deep and shaky his notion about loving her was.

She nestled closer to him. "I'm excited about going horseback riding tomorrow. And hiking and fishing the day after that."

He was glad that she was having a good time. But it was almost as if she was trying too hard to make this trip memorable. He even got the feeling that she was trying to convince herself that everything was going to be all right.

Whatever "everything" was, he thought. Mary's past wasn't any clearer today than it had been two months ago. And Brandon didn't know if he could take much more of being left in the dark.

He wanted answers. He wanted to know exactly who Mary McKenzie was and why she refused to talk about her parents. No matter how hard he tried, he couldn't make heads or tails of her life. He could look forever and still not see past the clouds in her eyes.

After they stopped dancing, they separated, with Mary wandering over to the bar to try the s'mores martinis that were being handed out.

Brandon took the opportunity to approach Tommy, who was also alone for now.

He said to his brother, "I'm going to do it."

"Do what?" Tommy asked.

"Run a security check on Mary and find out more about her. I'll email them tonight so they can get started on it. Then hopefully, by the time we get back to Nashville, I'll have some answers."

"Maybe her past won't be as traumatic as you think it's going to be."

"There's no point in speculating until I get the report." But at least he was going to find out for himself. At least he would have some clarity amid the chaos of falling in love.

* * *

Brandon spent the next few days with Mary, engaging in ranch activities. But the security check he'd requested was never far from his mind.

Then, on the day they arrived back in Nashville, he got word that the report was ready.

He was still with Mary, dropping her off at her apartment, when the call came. Once he parked in front of her place, they sat in the car, saying their goodbyes.

"I'm sorry I can't take you home with me," he said. "I have to go to my office today."

"It's okay. I need to unpack and get settled back in. I need to see Alice, too. I haven't spoken to my sister since I've been gone. We got in a fight right before I left."

He didn't ask what the tiff had been about. He was already aware of how moody her sister was. "Then you need to patch things up."

"Yes, I do." She smiled softly at him. "I had a wonderful time in Texas with you."

"It did turn out nice." But that didn't stop him from stressing about the choice he'd made to investigate her. If she knew what he was up to, would she be hurt or angry? Would she feel betrayed by him?

"Is there something going on at your work?" she asked suddenly.

He frowned. "What?"

"You seem anxious about going to the office."

He answered the best he could. "There's a report I need to tend to." He frowned again. "I could have received it as an email, but I had them drop off a hard copy to my assistant instead. I didn't want this information in an electronic file." He wanted it waiting on his desk in a sealed envelope, where he could brace himself before he paged through it.

"Is it something bad?"

As evasive as Mary was about her past, he didn't see how the report was going to contain something good. It was obvious that her problems stemmed from her parents, but to what extent, he couldn't say. "I just need to read it."

"Then you better go do that," she said.

"Yeah, I guess I better." He cupped her chin in both hands. As guilty as he felt for investigating her, he was still doing it for the right reasons. He needed to know who she was and what made her tick. He needed to come to terms with loving her, too. For now, it was like loving a stranger. "I'll call you later, okay?"

"Okay." She leaned forward, and they kissed.

Her lips tasted fresh and minty beneath his. So soft, so enticing, so confusing.

He ended the kiss, overwhelmed with the knowledge that he loved her. But as soon as he got his hands on the report, the puzzle that was Mary would be solved. He was overwhelmed by that, too. He wanted to help her get past her pain and whatever had caused it. But was he capable of restoring the damage, of making it better?

"Let me help you with your luggage," he said, and popped the trunk.

They exited the car, and he lifted her bag and wheeled it to her door. They kissed one more time, on the stoop, holding each other unbearably close.

He released her, wishing that she'd been comfortable confiding in him. It would've been so much easier than having her investigated.

She tried the door, but it was locked. "I guess Alice isn't home. School started this week, so she might have a class today." Mary removed her keys from her purse.

He stood back and watched her go inside. She

glanced back and waved, and that was it. Their vacation together was officially over.

He returned to his BMW and zoomed off to his office. Traffic was heavy, making his drive longer than usual.

Finally, he arrived. He entered the building and went straight to his desk. He opened the envelope and settled into his chair to read.

Within minutes, his chest twisted in pain, as if someone had stuck a knife clean through it.

The woman he loved was a liar, a con, an emotional cheat. According to the document in his hand, she was the daughter of Catherine Lynn Birch, a woman he and his father had filed a restraining order against eight years prior. Hell and damnation. Her mom had harassed his dad.

He kept reading, getting the rest of Mary's history. Her parents had lived together but were never married and never owned a home. Her father, Joel David McKenzie, was a truck driver who'd died when Mary was seven and Alice was just a month shy of her first birthday. He was self-employed and didn't have life insurance. The family moved to a smaller rental after he was gone and struggled even more to make ends meet.

There was no domestic abuse that came up. Her dad wasn't the villain in this story. It was her mother who couldn't be trusted. Catherine, or Cathy as she preferred to be called, had died earlier this year, leaving two grieving daughters behind. Two young women, he thought, who were obviously plotting against his family. Why else would Mary have just happened to show up at the park on the day they'd met?

Brandon considered her motives. Was it money? Was she more materialistic than she'd led him to believe? Was that the end game? Or was it something more sinister?

He read further. Some of what Mary had told him about her past was true. Alice was a party girl who had lots of boyfriends, and Mary was a proper young woman who'd kept her nose to the grindstone and dated her coworker at the bakery in Oklahoma where she'd worked. But that wasn't enough to make Brandon trust her. With the way she'd lured him into loving her, she was far more dangerous than her wild little sister.

In the wake of finishing the report, he wanted to scream at himself for being stupid. He'd brought Mary to Tommy's mansion to see the baby. He'd taken her to Matt's wedding. He'd welcomed her into his family, giving her carte blanche in their carefully protected lives. He'd even allowed her access to his home, anytime she wanted it.

He picked up his phone and called security at his loft, instructing them to change the code and keys. He never should've given them to Mary to begin with.

Brandon shook his head. He'd stepped out of his social circle and look what happened. He'd gotten swindled by the daughter of one of his dad's old stalkers.

Never again, he thought. No more supposedly innocent women. He was so raging mad, so hurt, so frustrated, he wanted to take legal action. But at this point, Mary hadn't actually committed a crime. The judgment had been against her mother, not her. And since Cathy had never violated the terms of the restraining order, she'd more or less been forgotten.

Nonetheless, he was going to confront Mary in a big way. But he wasn't going to return to her apartment. A public place wouldn't do, either. He didn't need any distractions. He decided he would do it here, in the privacy of his office. He didn't want her to suspect that she was under scrutiny, though. He intended to blindside her, just as she'd done to him.

Mary received a text from Brandon, asking her if she would come to his office around two. He said that he had a surprise for her.

She couldn't imagine why he wanted to see her so soon after dropping her off at her apartment, or what his surprise entailed, but she was excited about seeing him again. He'd even included little hearts and flowers emoticons in his message, leading her to believe this was going to be a romantic encounter.

Had he lied about rushing off to read a report? Had he dashed over to his office to set up her surprise?

Since Alice wasn't home yet, Mary had the bathroom to herself. She freshened up, adding a bit more lipstick and fluffing her hair. She was still wearing her traveling clothes. But if things got sexy with Brandon, he would probably divest her of them, anyway.

A niggle of fear and guilt crept in. Now that their trip was over, she'd promised herself that she would tell him the truth. But she couldn't do it today, not in the middle of his surprise.

She took a deep breath and left the house. A short time later, she arrived at his office, which was located in a charming old building near the Country Music Hall of Fame Museum. His suite was on the top floor.

His assistant, a young man with a beard and a trendy haircut, greeted her in the lobby. She hadn't expected anyone else to be there except Brandon.

The assistant called Brandon and let him know that his two o' clock appointment had arrived. Butterflies rushed to her stomach. It all seemed so formal.

"Mr. Talbot will see you now," the assistant said, gesturing down the hallway. "His office is the second door on the left. You don't need to knock. You can go right in."

"Thank you." She made her way to the designated door and opened it.

Brandon sat at his shiny black desk, with a colorful view of downtown Nashville behind him. He wasn't looking particularly romantic. In fact, he looked cool and detached.

Something was wrong. Very, very wrong.

"Close the door and have a seat," he said.

She did as he asked, shutting them in together, then perched on the edge of a leather chair that was positioned across from his desk.

"How does it feel to be brought here under false pretenses?" he asked, his blue eyes narrowing in on hers.

The hearts and flowers in his text had been a ruse, she realized. But even more disturbing was the folder that was sitting on his desk with her name typed across the front of it.

He pushed it toward her, but she didn't open it. She didn't need to know what it said. She already knew. He'd uncovered her identity.

"I'm sorry," she said, wishing she could go back in time and erase everything she'd done. "I was going to tell you everything. Honestly, I was."

"Really? How convenient for you now that you got caught." He leaned back in his chair, with a dark and lawyerly air. "Do you know why I had you investigated? Because I cared about you and wanted to help you get past whatever was going on in your life. Hell, I was even fancying myself in love with you."

She nearly pitched forward. Now the room felt as

it were spinning. She'd begun to assume that he loved her, but she'd never expected to hear it like this. "I fell in love with you, too."

"And I'm supposed to believe that? You've been conning me from the start. Admit it, Mary. This was a scam from day one."

"I do love you. I swear I do." She needed to make that clear, whether he believed it or not. "And yes, you're right, I conned you. But let me explain."

"Fine. Be my guest." He swept his hand across the report. "Explain away."

She started at the beginning, telling him how her mother had come to Nashville to sell her songs. She also detailed how she'd gotten duped by his dad. "She wasn't a stalker. She was only trying to get him to make good on his promise. But he filed a restraining order against her instead, with you as his attorney." Mary paused, hoping for some empathy, but his expression remained hard and unyielding. "Mama fell apart after that. She was never the same. Her depression was so bad that she was barely parenting us anymore, and since Alice was so much younger than me, I tried to help raise her. But I was never able to influence my sister to stop hating Kirby for what he'd done to Mama. She was consumed with it. I got consumed, as well, with the pain he'd caused. I hated him, too."

Brandon lifted his eyebrows. "So you took your pain out on me?"

"At first we tried to cook up ways to get back at your dad, but none of them panned out. Then Alice devised a scheme for me to draw you in. She saw some posts on your social media pages that your friends were encouraging you to find a nice girl, so she suggested that I should present myself to you in that way. She kept saying that I was a good girl, anyway. That it wouldn't be much of a stretch for me."

"Christ," he muttered, tension in his voice. He wasn't softening at all.

"I was mixed up from the beginning and unsure of how far to take it. Mostly I just wanted to find out how responsible you were in what happened to Mama. And once I got close to you, I realized that you never would've hurt her purposely. But by then, I was already in too deep. I was already developing feelings for you."

"You never thought to contact me outright and discuss the stalking situation with your mom? To explain your side of it?"

"No. We never thought of that. But we didn't know if we could trust you. Alice is still convinced that you and your dad should pay for what he did to our mother. I know my sister is really messed up and I obviously was, too, for having done something like this. But I've been learning my lessons, and this is turning out to be the hardest one of all." Facing the fact she'd hurt someone she loved, she thought. That she'd damaged him.

He sat quietly for a moment, as if he was contemplating the whole ball of wax. Then he said, "If what you say is true and my father cheated your mother in a business deal and falsified the stalking charges, I'll make sure that he fixes it." He blew out a heavy sigh. "But I need to talk to him and get his side of the story. I can't just take you and Alice at your word. I mean, really, Mary, how am I supposed to trust anything you say?"

"You're not, I guess." She glanced down at her hands, twisting them on her lap. "But if I could take back what I did to you, I would." She lifted her gaze to meet his. "I was never comfortable with it. That's why I was always talking about breaking it off. At first I thought it would hurt you less for me to disappear and for you to never know the truth. But when we were in Texas and everything was going so beautifully with your family, I decided I was going to tell you the truth once we got back. I even thought that maybe we'd be able to stay together."

He looked at her as if she'd gone mad. "For all I know, this sorrowful act of yours is part of a new ploy to rein me in, to use me for my money or whatever it is you really want."

"It isn't." All she could do now was continue to tell him the truth and pray for him to understand. "Alice tried to convince me that I should marry you for your money. But I'm not interested in that. If I married you, it would be for love."

He scoffed at her response. "Sweet little Mary, ever the enchantress. Well, you know what? I was so bewitched by you I actually wondered what it would be like to make you my wife." He shook his head. "But it worried me, how I was falling in love with a stranger, a woman who wouldn't talk about her past."

"I'll tell you anything now, anything you want to know." Her heart hurt so badly, she feared it was going to shatter into a zillion pieces. Knowing that he'd considered marriage made it so much worse.

"I'm not interested in anything else you have to say." He stood and came around his desk, towering over her while she remained seated. "I'll talk to my dad and get back to you. But it'll be his version of the facts that I'll be relying on, not yours."

"I understand. But as far as I'm concerned, there's nothing you or your dad need to make up for. What I did to you was just as hurtful as what he did to my mom. And I'm so sorry, Brandon. So incredibly sorry."

"Stop with the apologies. It's not helping." He leaned against the edge of his desk. "It's too late for me to keep feeling something for you. It's too late for everything."

She wanted to curl up and cry, but she couldn't do that in front of him.

"You can go now," he said. "I trust you can see yourself out."

"Yes." She stood, remembering every warm and romantic moment she'd spent with him. But it was over now. There was nothing left, except the ache that came with losing the man she loved.

Mary cried for hours, until there were no tears left. Still, Alice kept watching her as if she might burst out bawling again.

They sat on their tiny patio with dusk blanketing the sky. Their apartment faced the street, and she could see cars going by.

Mary's breath hitched. Her face was swollen, and her eyes stung. But the real pain was in her heart. "If I would've told him sooner, if I would've come clean from the start, he wouldn't hate me the way he does."

Alice frowned. "He has no right to hate you, not after the way his father trashed Mama."

"He said that he's going to talk to Kirby and get his side of it. And if his dad confirms that it's true, he'll make sure that Kirby fixes it."

"*If* his dad confirms it? You know damned well that he's going to lie and say that Mama was a stalker."

Mary thought about how sincere Kirby seemed at the wedding and how he kept saying he was trying to turn over a new leaf. "Maybe he'll tell the truth. Maybe he'll admit to what he did."

Alice shook her head. "That would take a miracle,

and this isn't feeling like a miracle-type situation to me. And on top of that, Brandon should have forgiven you. Isn't that the way love is supposed to work?"

"I don't know enough about love to answer that question. But I was hoping and praying that he would forgive me." She'd already forgiven his father. After what she'd done to Brandon, she was in no position to judge Kirby.

Alice dragged a hand through her platinum hair. "So if by some unexpected chance Kirby does corroborate our story, what do you think Brandon meant by fixing it?"

"I have no idea."

"Do you think it would involve money?"

"I don't know." Money was the least of her concerns.

Her sister turned quiet. A fly buzzed by and she waved it away. Then she asked, "Do you still love him?"

"Yes." She couldn't deny the truth. "But I wish that I didn't, with how it's tearing me apart. You warned me that I was going to get hurt, and you were right."

"I didn't trust him any more than I trusted his dad, and now you're paying the ultimate price. It's not fair that you're suffering."

"Are you sure you care about how I feel?" Mary shooed away the same fly when it came near her. "Because with how mean you've been to me, I'm surprised you're not gloating over my pain."

Alice winced. "I'm sorry I acted like such a bitch. And I'm sorry that Brandon broke your heart." She leaned into the table. "Truly, I am. You've been a really good sister to me." Her voice quavered. "When I was a kid, I just wanted Mama to be well, to be there when I needed her. But you were the one who took care of me. I love you more than you know."

"Thank you." Even as messed up as Alice was, Mary

could tell that her sister meant it. “I love you, too. But I wish we hadn’t grown up hating Kirby.” That hadn’t done either of them any good. “Our lives shouldn’t have been about that.”

“I still think he owes us for what he did to Mama. If they offer us a financial settlement, I’m going to take every last dollar they’re willing to part with.”

“Money isn’t my objective.” For Mary, there were deeper issues at stake. “I’d like to see Mama’s name cleared. And I’d like for Kirby to say he’s sorry. That would be enough for me.”

Her sister sighed. “I shouldn’t have gotten you into this mess. I shouldn’t have dragged you into something that wasn’t right for you.”

“I appreciate you saying that, but I made my own decisions.”

Alice angled her head. “You don’t think it’s my fault? You’re not blaming me?”

“No.” Mary was responsible for what she’d done. “I kept lying to Brandon, even when I had feelings for him, even when I knew the destruction it could cause.”

She’d alienated him all by herself.

Twelve

Brandon paced his dad's home studio, the place where the magic happened, where Kirby had recorded a good number of his albums. But this wasn't a magical day. He'd just confronted his dad about Cathy Birch and received a stunned look in return.

"She was Mary's mother?"

"Yes, I'm afraid she was." He stopped pacing and stood near a mixing board. "Was she a stalker? Was she harassing you?" Brandon remembered filing the restraining order. But he'd filed quite a few of them over the years. Cathy wasn't Kirby's only stalker—if she was one at all. "Tell me, Dad. Tell me exactly what transpired between you and Cathy."

Kirby grimaced. "It happened the way Mary said it did. The story she told you is accurate."

"Oh, God." If Brandon hadn't been standing so rigidly, his knees might've buckled. "What did you do? What did you make me do?"

"I'm sorry if I dragged you into a lie. But I was at my lowest then. Nothing in my life was going right. The drink and drugs were eating me alive."

"So you preyed on an innocent woman and offered to buy her songs? For what? The sex? The feeling of power?"

"It was all of that, I guess." Kirby rubbed a hand across his beard, his mouth set in a grim line. His eyes were partially shielded by the brim of his hat, his shirt collar turned up. "I took advantage of a lot of women in those days, and Cathy was no exception." He paused, his breathing rattled. "I wasn't lying to her about her songs, not at first. They were good, and they captured my attention. I wasn't going to record them myself. I was going to find a female artist who was better suited to them."

"But you were going to produce the project?"

"Yes. Except after I lost interest in Cathy, I lost interest in her music, too."

Heavens, above. Could his father have been any more of a jackass? "So you made her out to be a stalker?"

"She kept calling me, trying to get me to sign a contract with her, and I just wanted to be rid of her. I'd already moved on to someone else by then, so I convinced myself that she was harassing me."

Brandon could barely stand to be in the same room with his dad right now. None of this was tolerable. "When you were collecting stories for *Kirbyville*, you didn't stop to think to include her? To contact her and apologize? She was alive when you first started working on the book. You could've reached out to her then."

"Honestly? I forgot about her until now."

Everything inside Brandon was twisting and turning, tying his guts into knots. "You forgot? That's a lame-ass excuse."

"I know. But there was so much material for the book, and I was focused on family when I wrote it. I'm so sorry that her daughters suffered because of it. And I'm sorry that Mary hurt you."

"I don't want to talk about what Mary did to me." Brandon couldn't bear the ache it caused. He couldn't get past the knowledge that he'd fallen for a woman who'd used him for revenge. All these years, all this time, he'd never been in love. Then along came Mary with her warm and gentle ways, with her mystery, with her deception.

"Tell me what you want me to do, and I'll do it," his dad said, cutting into his thoughts.

"I want you to offer to buy Cathy's songs from Mary and Alice and find a female artist to record them, like you first promised to do. It's imperative that you help make their mother's music a success. I also want you to make a public announcement and admit what you did to Cathy. Of course, I expect you to apologize to her daughters privately. You can't skip that."

"Do you think they'll forgive me?"

"I don't know." Brandon couldn't predict anyone's behavior anymore.

"Are you going to forgive Mary for lying to you about who she was?"

"That's none of your concern."

"Yes, it is. You're my son, and I want to see you happy. If you love her, you should forgive her."

Brandon shook his head. His father was the last person he wanted advice from. "Don't stick your nose into my affairs, not after the havoc you caused."

"But you're a peacemaker, and you need to make peace with this."

"I am making peace with it." He stood and moved about the studio again, feeling trapped by the familiarity of his surroundings. When he was a kid he used to marvel at being here, listening to his dad record. Even back then, Brandon had wanted to be part of it somehow. But not like this, never like this. "I'm going to draw up the paperwork with the terms of your offer and arrange a meeting with Mary and Alice at my office. I'll need for you to be there, too."

"Of course." Kirby sounded more than agreeable. "Whatever you require."

Brandon sighed. "I'll advise them to bring their own attorney. I'm sure they'll find someone reputable to represent them." He didn't doubt that Alice would seek out the best.

"That's good, but that's not what I meant about you making peace with Mary."

"It's the best I can do." It was all he could do, he thought, short of telling Mary that he still loved her. And he hurt too badly to do that. Brandon was keeping his bruised and battered heart to himself.

Mary and Alice arrived at Brandon's office with Christine Norseman, a hard-hitting lawyer Alice had procured. Only Mary wasn't thinking about the business deal that was coming their way. She was blinded by the sight of the man she loved.

Brandon looked tall and dark and professional in a gray suit and burgundy tie. When he reached out to shake everyone's hand, Mary felt weak. By the time his hand enveloped hers, she could barely breathe. For a moment, she felt the electrical charge running between them.

Their gazes met, but neither of them spoke. She couldn't think of a single thing to say that didn't involve missing him. He broke the handshake and glanced away, leaving her staring after him.

He offered them a seat and said, "My dad is on his way. He's running a few minutes late." He then asked, "Can I get anyone anything?" He motioned to the bar in his office. "Coffee, juice, water, soda?"

Christine went for an apple juice and Alice took a soda. Mary didn't want anything, except for Brandon to love her once again.

Soon Kirby dashed in, carrying two single red roses. He handed one to Mary and offered the other to Alice. Her sister refused to take it. Mary gathered it up with hers, placing both flowers on her lap.

He sat down and said to them, "I'm so sorry for the pain I caused your family. Your mother deserved better and so did you girls. I hope that someday you'll find it in your hearts to forgive me."

"I already do," Mary replied, and exchanged a gentle glance with him.

He thanked her with an appreciative nod of his head, and the room went quiet. Until Alice said to him, "Mary doesn't want me to keep hating you. But I still do." She turned toward Mary. "I'm not like you. I can't forgive that easily. I just can't."

Kirby nodded and said to Alice, "It's all right. I accept however you feel. But before we get to the business part of this meeting, I want to tell you what I remember about your mother." He addressed both sisters. "She was kind and trusting and far too good for someone like me. We didn't talk about our children. We kept our kids out of it. But I'll bet if we'd shared that information, she would've told me how spunky her youngest was." He chanced a smile at Alice. "I admire your grit." He gestured to her cowpunk garb. "I like your retro vibe, too."

"Oh, right." She scowled at him. "The snake oil salesman, trying to win me over. Our mother didn't stand a chance with you."

"No, she didn't. But you do. If I had a daughter, I'd want her to be like you, Alice." He said to Mary, "I'd be pleased to have you as part of my family, too."

Her eyes nearly flooded with tears. She could tell that he was giving her his blessing to be with Brandon, if his son were inclined to be with her.

She glanced over at her former lover, but he just cleared his throat and said, "I think we should discuss the offer now."

"Yes, let's do that," Christine replied. She was a fiftysomething blonde with a no-nonsense personality, ready to get this show on the road.

So was Alice, it seemed. She perked up, obviously anxious for the negotiations to begin. But even so, she kept shooting Kirby sideways glances. It made Mary wonder if she was secretly impressed with the way he'd praised her. With Alice, it was difficult to tell. But even so, Mary didn't see her sister forgiving him anytime soon.

The offer involved an astronomical amount of money to purchase Mama's songs and market them. Christine went over the fine print and suggested a few changes. Brandon and Kirby agreed. They seemed willing to do whatever they could to give Alice and Mary what Kirby should have given Mama all those years ago.

But Mary didn't want the money. She'd already made up her mind about that. "I'd like to sign my share over to Alice," she said. "But with the stipulation that she gives my portion to charity." She gazed at her sister. "I want you to choose a charity that will be meaningful to you." She thought it was important for Alice to learn to do some good in the world. "Are you willing to do that?"

"Of course," Alice replied. "But are you sure you don't want to keep some of it for yourself?"

"I'm positive." Mary wasn't interested in a payout, and she never would be. She shifted in her chair and asked Christine, "Can we add a clause to the contract about the charity?"

"Definitely." The attorney made a note of it.

Mary spoke to Kirby. "I'm glad that you're going to make a public announcement to clear Mama's name. We worked really hard to hide the harassment charges from everyone she knew. But it was still a stain on her psyche. It's important that you're going to let the world know that she didn't do anything wrong."

"The public announcement was Brandon's idea," Kirby said. "I can't take credit for that. But I'm more than willing to admit my wrongdoings to the press."

"Good," Christine said, chiming in to the conversation. "Now we can proceed and get all of this enforced."

Yes, Mary thought. They needed to proceed. She looked across the desk at Brandon. He was watching her with a tortured expression, a frown that appeared to be emerging straight from his soul.

An ache Mary could feel, too.

He called in his assistant to make the necessary changes, and the contract was revised. Once it was ready, the lawyers went over it again, making sure everything was correct.

And that was it. The parties involved signed it.

As the group prepared to part ways, Kirby reached

out to hug Mary. She buried her face against his shoulder and wished it was Brandon wrapping her in his embrace.

But he merely stood back in silence. Kirby released her, and she turned and spoke to Brandon.

"Take care of yourself," she said.

"You, too," he replied, his voice low and unbearably soft.

Steeped in her loss, Mary headed for the door. But she couldn't stop herself from glancing back at Brandon.

Just to fill her vision with him one last time.

Brandon spent as much time as he could with Zoe. Being with the baby gave him comfort. But being around her made him long for what he'd lost, too.

The possibility of a future, of a family. He couldn't imagine ever feeling about anyone the way he'd felt about Mary, but that was over now. Two weeks had passed since he'd seen her at the meeting and he still couldn't face the truth of what she'd done to him. He remained hurt and angry and confused, with a hole clawing its way through his heart.

Today he was at Tommy's place, in Zoe's pink and puffy nursery, rocking her while she made cute little baby sounds. His brother stood nearby, watching him.

Tommy said, "With the way you've been monopolizing my kid, I think you need to hurry up and have one of your own."

"Yeah, as if it's just that easy." Brandon gazed at his niece and the flowery headband she wore. Tommy had dressed her up for Brandon's visit.

"I'm sorry that it didn't work out between you and Mary. I know how tough it's been for you. But I'll bet she's really broken up over it, too."

Brandon didn't want to think about how badly she was hurting, not with how much he ached. "I've always been so careful, protecting myself and our family. I asked her when we first met if she knew who I was, but she lied to me, every damned step of the way."

"I know. But a lot has happened since then."

A lot of pain, Brandon thought, a lot of heartache, with what felt like no end in sight. "Dad is going to make the public announcement about Mary's mom next week. He's got a press conference lined up."

"That's good. By the way, I heard that Alice rented a luxurious new condo."

Brandon cocked his head. "Who told you that?"

"Dad found out from Mary. He's been keeping in touch with her. Alice is still leery of him, but he and Mary are becoming genuine friends. Dad didn't tell you because he's trying to keep you out of his relationship with Mary."

Brandon wasn't surprised that they'd gotten close. He'd seen their bond at their meeting. He'd watched his dad hug her and felt the sting of not being able to hold her himself. "So Mary is alone at their old apartment?"

"Yes, but she wants to be by herself. She wasn't interested in moving into the condo with Alice."

Brandon had been spending a lot of time alone, too, except for when he was here with Tommy and the baby. He got up and placed Zoe in her crib. She was drifting off to sleep. To keep her comfortable, he removed her headband.

He and Tommy walked onto the balcony, letting the baby settle into her dreams. It was nice outside, with a warm breeze.

"Maybe I should go see Mary," Brandon said. "Not to rekindle our romance, but to at least find a way to forgive her." He didn't want to keep wallowing in this. It was just too damned painful. "I think it's what we're both going to need to move on."

"Then do it, bro. Do whatever you have to do to get through this. I don't want to see you hurting. Or Mary, either. It's not a good way to live. I agree that you both need closure."

"Thanks." He sucked in his breath. "I'm going to head out now." Before he took the coward's way out and lost his nerve. Because deep down, he was still afraid of the effect she had on him.

He left Tommy's house and drove straight to her apartment. Once he got there and knocked on the door, he discovered that she wasn't home. But then he realized that she was probably still at work, and he'd showed up a little too early to see her. He sat on the stoop and waited, with a lump in his throat.

A short time later, her car pulled up. She got out, her footsteps stalling as she neared the front door. Clearly, she was shocked to see him. For a moment, she just stared.

Then she said, "Brandon?"

"Hey." He stood and dusted himself off. He felt like a bubble-brained boy, lacking the finesse he needed to pull this off. Even as a youth, he'd never been this awkward. "I was hoping we could talk."

She hesitated before she asked, "Do you want to come in?"

"Sure." He tried to seem more casual than he felt.

She unlocked the door, and he followed her inside. She was wearing her bakery uniform, a plain white smock and loose pants. Her hair was neatly braided. He thought about the countless times he'd played with her hair. He wanted to move closer, to put his hands on her, to inhale her sugary scent.

"Sweet tea?"

He jerked to attention. "I'm sorry. What?"

"Would you like some sweet tea?"

"No, thanks." He went ahead and moved closer. They were standing in her living room, with the blinds drawn. "I'm just here to make things right. To forgive you, Mary, and stop both of us from hurting. I can't go on, aching the way I am, and neither can you."

Her gaze searched his. "So this isn't about us getting back together?"

"No." He reached out to skim his fingertips along her cheek. "It's just about finding some peace in all of this."

Her breath hitched. "Is touching me making you feel peaceful, Brandon?"

He shook his head. His ache was actually getting stronger. "You have the softest skin, the most innocent face. It's still hard for me to believe that you tricked me."

"I'm so sorry I deceived you."

"I know you are." He didn't doubt her sincerity. The truth was in her eyes. "I owe you an apology, too. I shouldn't have brought you to my office that day under false pretenses. I shouldn't have blindsided you that way."

"I understand how hurt and angry you were."

"I'm not angry anymore." He still ached inside, but that might never go away. "I should leave now." He removed his hand from her cheek. "I did what I came to do." To forgive her, he thought. Unfortunately, it hadn't brought him the closure it should have. She didn't look as if she felt much better, either. He backed away from her.

Now what was he supposed to say? Tell her to have a good life without him? He didn't know what parting words to use.

"Maybe you can stay a little longer," she said, her voice coming out choppy.

"What for?" he asked. He sounded disjointed, too. This reunion definitely wasn't going well.

She shrugged, a little too heavily, like a butterfly trying to lift its damaged wings. "I made chocolate chip cookies last night. You can have some with me."

"Cookies won't solve this."

"What will?"

"I don't know." But suddenly he didn't want to go. He didn't want to walk away and leave her behind. But he couldn't seem to find the strength to stay, either.

Before he could head for the door, she said, "Alice moved out. I live here alone now."

He cleared his throat and replied, "Tommy told me that she rented a condo. He said you've been talking to my dad a lot, too."

She nodded. "We've become really close."

It was strange how his father managed to make peace with her, but Brandon couldn't seem to do it. He was still so lost, so confused.

She bit down on her bottom lip. "He let me cry to him every night on the phone."

His heart tightened in his chest. Clearly, she'd been crying because of him. "I'll bet you never envisioned becoming friends with my dad."

"It's nice that he's been there for me. But it's still been hard, dealing with all of this." She glanced down at the floor. "I never should have done what I did to you."

"You don't have to keep apologizing." He couldn't

bear to see more of her sorrow. She looked as lost as he felt.

She lifted her gaze, fractured as it was. "I told Kirby that I would try to help him find someone to date. I think he's ready for a new relationship. I believe that he's a changed man."

Brandon wanted to be a changed man, too, to be free of the pain. But he didn't know how to do it. "I should go." He couldn't stay. He was only making both of them suffer.

"I can walk you out."

"No. That's okay." He needed to make a clean break. "Thanks for letting me come in and say what I needed to say." Even if it hadn't helped, he thought.

She stepped back. "I'll see you." She spoke softly, sadly.

"I'll see you, too." He didn't know when or if he would ever see her again, but it seemed like the proper thing to say.

He left her condo and climbed into his car. He was parked in a nearby guest spot, with a view of her front door. He suspected she might be on the verge of crying now, with tears flooding her eyes. Had he made it worse by coming here?

So what was he waiting for? He should get on the road, escaping as fast as his luxury sedan would take him. But he just sat behind the wheel, mired in pain and torment.

He glanced at Mary's door. He couldn't deny that he loved her. That he needed her. That he wanted her.

So what was he going to do about it?

Be the guy who fixes it, he told himself, *with the woman he loves by his side.*

Brandon got out of his car and returned to her apartment. He rang the bell, his pulse pounding in his ears.

She answered the summons, and he sucked in his breath. She did look as if she'd been crying.

"Do you still love me, Mary?" he asked. He was certain that she did, but he needed to hear it.

"Yes." She shivered where she stood. "God, yes."

"I still love you, too." He couldn't stop the rush of emotion that poured through him, admitting how he felt, letting her know what was going on inside him.

"Are you sure?" she asked. "Because I couldn't take it if you..."

"I'm positive." He knew what was in his heart, and he knew that living without her wasn't an option. He reached out to her. "Let's start over. As friends, as lovers, as everything we should've been before, but without any lies or secrets between us."

"I can't imagine anything better." She stepped forward, into the circle of his arms. "I've missed you so badly."

"Me, too." He'd barely been surviving without her.

She cried a little, but he knew they were happy tears, not the sad ones from before.

They both went silent, steeped in the commitment they'd just made. He closed his eyes and rocked her in his arms, her sweet scent enveloping him.

She lifted her head and whispered, "Make love with me, Brandon. Be with me."

He accepted her invitation, and she led him to her room. He was never going to lose her again.

They undressed each other, slowly, wanting to make the moment last. They kissed and got into bed. He glanced up and saw the fairy painting he'd given her, intensifying the magic.

He caressed her, filling his hands with her body. She touched him, too, in the most intimate of ways.

She had protection readily available. “I bought it a while ago,” she said. “In case you ever spent the night here.”

He took the packet, but he didn’t open it right away. For now, he wanted to profess more of his feelings, more of what the future would entail. “I want you to move in with me.” He breathed her in, all the way to his soul. “I want to sleep beside you each night and wake up next to you every morning.”

“I’ll be there, whenever you need me.” She pressed closer to him. “I want all of those same things.”

He finally put on the condom and entered her, letting the sensation of being inside her engulf him. She moaned when he pushed deeper, and they made love. In the middle of the day.

Together at last.

As they lay naked, sated from the sex, Mary smiled at her man. *Her man.* Oh, how she loved the sound of that.

Finally, they got up and slipped on their clothes. She didn’t put her uniform back on. She chose a simple white sundress from her closet.

“I can’t wait to see you in a gown,” he said.

“At a charity ball?” She was prepared to learn to waltz and meet his friends, to be part of everything that was Brandon.

“Actually, I was talking about our wedding.” He sat on the edge of the bed and swept her onto his lap.

Her heartbeat skittered. “We’re getting married?”

“We are if you’ll have me. I want to do more than just live together. I want to take vows, too. But we can take our time and do it right. We don't have to rush." He looked into her eyes. "Will you become my wife? Will you do me the honor?"

"I absolutely will." She kissed him slowly, romantically. She could kiss him for a thousand years and never get enough. Afterward, she said, "I think taking our time is a good idea. We need to relax and get to know each other better. I was hiding who I was before, and now I'm going to be the real me."

He nodded. "I'm looking forward to knowing the real you." He nuzzled her cheek. "I'm already getting attached to her."

Mary sighed. This was the best day of her life. Their relationship had started off wrong, but it was perfect now. He was perfect, too, her future husband. No matter what obstacles they faced, they would always have each other.

"After we have kids, we can move into my country house," he said. He hesitated. "You want kids, don't you?"

She quickly replied, "Yes, of course." She wanted to create a family, especially with him. "But when I was growing up, I never really understood motherhood."

"Because of how depressed your mom was?"

"I know she was hurting. But I wish she would have sought help instead of shutting everyone out. I still worry about Alice, too, and how wild she is."

Brandon gazed at her with admiration, with depth and care. "You're a good sister. She's lucky she has you. But getting our families together is going to be tough, with how much Alice probably still hates my dad." He frowned a little. "Do you think she's ever going to accept him?"

"I don't know, but he's going to try to develop a

working relationship with her. He wants to get her input on what artist should record Mama's songs."

"I think that's a great idea."

"So do I." She hoped that it would help give her sister some direction. She knew how important those songs were to Alice. They still meant the world to Mary, too.

"Dad is going to be thrilled when we tell him that we're engaged."

"I'd love for him to walk me down the aisle, the way he did for Sophie. I'd also like for Alice to be my maid of honor and help me choose a dress. So one way or another, she's going to have to get used to the Talbots."

"Considering that you'll be one of us?" He smiled, lifted her hand. "You and I need to shop for a diamond."

"It doesn't have to be anything overly fancy, but do you think I could have a sapphire or something blue? I want a ring the color of your eyes."

"That makes me feel good. But maybe it could be just a little bit fancy. I'm excited about giving you sparkly things. Come to think of it, there are blue diamonds. So maybe we could look into that, along with sapphires or any other stone you want. We can design it together."

"Thank you. That sounds fun. We can choose whatever feels right and put it all together."

"Marrying you feels right. Being the father to your children feels right." He paused and asked, "Do you think I should use Cline as my best man?"

She sputtered into a jovial laugh. "That would be adorable."

He laughed, too. Then he said, "Sharing my life with you is all that matters. I can't wait for you to move in with me."

"I'll pack today." She wanted nothing more than to

be Brandon's partner. Her heart was glowing, from the inside out.

"Things are going to be interesting, with us figuring it out as we go."

She thought about the world in which he'd been raised. "Maybe I can become a pastry chef for the rich and famous. Maybe that can be my new career. I'm going to get a lot of experience dealing with that crowd."

"You can do anything you want, Mary. You're as talented as anyone I know."

In the sweet silence that followed, he slanted his mouth over hers, and they kissed once again. She settled in his arms. No matter what the future held, they were both willing to do their best to make it work.

Sealing their fate forever.

* * * * *